The We...

Reese, Cassie, Gina...
Un...

They haven't seen each other in years, but
now Reese is getting married and she
wants everyone there.

It will be a reunion to remember—and the wedding
of the year! But what these feisty women haven't
reckoned on are the sizzling, scandalous, and
very surprising consequences...

Don't miss this fabulous quartet from your
favourite Modern Tempted™ authors—
Aimee Carson, Amy Andrews, Heidi Rice
and Kimberly Lang.

The Unexpected Wedding Guest by Aimee Carson
Available July 2013

Girl Least Likely to Marry by Amy Andrews
Available August 2013

Maid of Dishonour by Heidi Rice
Available September 2013

Marnie's Story by Kimberly Lang
Available October 2013

MAID OF DISHONOUR

BY
HEIDI RICE

First published in Great Britain 2013
by Mills & Boon, an imprint of Harlequin (UK) Limited,
Harlequin (UK) Limited, Eton House, 18-24 Paradise Road,
Richmond, Surrey TW9 1SR

© Heidi Rice 2013

ISBN: 978 0 263 91067 4

Harlequin (UK) policy is to use papers that are natural, renewable and recyclable products and made from wood grown in sustainable forests. The logging and manufacturing processes conform to the legal environmental regulations of the country of origin.

Printed and bound in Spain
by Blackprint CPI, Barcelona

Heidi Rice was born and bred and still lives in London. She has two boys who love to bicker, a wonderful husband who, luckily for everyone, has loads of patience, and a supportive and ever-growing British/French/Irish/American family. As much as Heidi adores 'the Big Smoke', she also loves America, and every two years or so she and her best friend leave hubby and kids behind and *Thelma and Louise* it across the States for a couple of weeks (although they always leave out the driving off a cliff bit). She's been a film buff since her early teens, and a romance junkie for almost as long. She indulged her first love by being a film reviewer for ten years. Then a few years ago she decided to spice up her life by writing romance. Discovering the fantastic sisterhood of romance writers (both published and unpublished) in Britain and America made it a wild and wonderful journey to her first Mills & Boon® novel.

Heidi loves to hear from readers—you can e-mail her at heidi@heidi-rice.com, or visit her website: www.heidi-rice.com

This and other titles by Heidi Rice are available in eBook format—check out www.millsandboon.co.uk

To my partners in crime—
Aimee Carson, Kimberly Lang and Amy Andrews—
for being such fabulous authors, such an inspiration to
work with and such cool women to boot.
We rock, ladies!

PROLOGUE

Hillbrook College Campus, Upstate New York, ten years ago.

'IT SOUNDS AWESOME, Marnie, but Carter and Missy shouldn't get overwhelmed by all the glamour of their wedding and forget the important part—that they love each other.'

Reese's words of whimsy drifted into Gina Carrington's consciousness—through the cloying perfume of hyacinth blossoms that infused the back porch, and the haze of one too many glasses of vintage champagne—and didn't improve her melancholy mood one iota.

Can we get off this topic now, please?

Her cheeks heated as a heartening flash of temper pierced through the hollow feeling of loss that had dogged her for days. Ever since she'd made the biggest mistake of her life. And in a life filled to bursting with mistakes of one sort or another that was quite an achievement.

'That won't be a problem. They're devoted to each other and they have been for years. When Carter proposed, Missy and I stayed up all night talking about how wonderful it was that we'd be sisters for ever.' Marnie laughed at her own observation, the high musical lilt clearing the fog from Gina's head like a knife slicing through flesh.

Funny to think she'd once enjoyed the sound of Marnie's laugh. Marnie had been so anxious and serious and unassertive when she'd first arrived at Hillbrook. It had taken them all a while to realise her perfect Southern manners had actually been a disguise for extreme terror. Gina had loved hearing that smoky laugh in the months that followed because it had come to symbolise Marnie's emancipation from the people she herself had described as 'the family that feminism forgot'.

But Gina wasn't loving it much now.

'So what's Missy's dress like?' Reese asked, still humouring her.

'Just so perfect,' Marnie purred, her Southern accent thicker than molasses. 'It's ivory silk. She's going to be a traditional bride.' Marnie flashed a smile Gina's way. 'I know not everyone here approves, but I think it's so romantic that her and Carter have decided to stay pure until their wedding night.'

Wasn't it just.

Gina's stomach heaved up towards her breastbone as she plopped her champagne flute on the porch table. 'Is anyone getting another bottle? I'm not sure I can stand to hear any more about love's young dream without alcoholic fortification.'

Cassie jumped up from her seat on the rail. 'It's gotta be my turn,' she said in her broad Aussie accent. 'I'll go.' She sent Gina a bland look that only made Gina feel more miserable.

Cassie knew what had happened a week ago when Marnie's big brother Carter Price had come to visit. And in typical Cassie fashion had been completely pragmatic about it. *'I don't see why you should feel guilty—he's the one that's engaged to be married.'*

But as Cassie headed off to the kitchen, obviously keen to escape from the tension that had been building all night and only Marnie seemed oblivious to, Gina knew Cassie the super nerd felt uncomfortable. And while Cassie would never judge her, Gina knew it took a lot to make Cassie uncomfortable in a social situation, because normally, unless a discussion involved gamma-ray bursts or cosmic radiation or some other esoteric astronomy principle, Cassie tended to disengage from social situations.

Gina turned to find Marnie watching her from her deck chair, the light blush on her cheeks a symptom of her confusion. She was probably wondering why Gina was being such a cow about the wedding of the century. Her brother Carter's marriage to her best friend, Missy, had been Marnie's hot topic of discussion for months—and Gina had enjoyed teasing her about the impending nuptials, but always in a good-humoured way.

But that was before last Saturday night, before she'd met the Sainted Carter, and set out to flirt him into a puddle of unrequited lust. Only to discover that Marnie's big brother wasn't the overbearing, self-righteous and boringly judgmental Southern gentleman he'd pretended to be, but a sweet, sensitive, and seriously intense Southern hottie who was as screwed up about his place in the world as she was.

The evening had started out as a joke, played at Carter's expense, but in the end the joke had been on Gina. How could she have known the Sainted Carter would be the first man to show her that sex wasn't always about physical gratification? That sometimes your feelings could actually become involved? And how could she have known that, when he looked at her the next day, with the disgust at what they had done together plain in his face, he'd also be the first man to make her feel ashamed of taking what she wanted? And force her to admit that trust and judgment and honour and duty weren't just buzzwords for boring people?

Those had been harsh lessons to learn in the last week, ever since Carter had walked away, but as Marnie's face flushed pink and she murmured: 'Gina, admit it, even you think it's romantic—that Carter and Missy are going to be each other's first?' it wasn't a harsh lesson she had it in her to appreciate, especially after two glasses of Dom—and the knowledge that her period was now four days late.

'It's not romantic, Marnie, it's certifiable. What exactly would your best friend do, if she got Carter into bed on their wedding night and discovered he was rubbish in the sack?'

'I'd have to agree that good sex is important in a relationship, if it's going to last.' Reese flushed as she took a sip of her champagne—that enigmatic look of excitement and trepidation she'd been beaming out all night lighting her eyes.

Marnie let out a soft laugh, but the colour in her fair cheeks went from pink to a light rosé. 'You think too much about sex—Missy and me both believe it's not the most important thing.'

'And how would you two little virgins know anything about that? Seeing as you've never actually had any?' Gina felt her temperature rising, the twin tides of panic and anger going some way to stem the crushing feeling of rejection and inadequacy.

'You don't have to have sex with someone to know you love them,' Marnie said, but her teeth had begun to chew on her bottom lip. 'Missy's not worried about how Carter will...' she hesitated, obviously having difficulty talking about her brother and sex in the same sentence as the blush went from rosé to stoplight red '...perform at the marital act. They've talked about it.'

The marital act!

Gina's temper ignited. From the little Carter had said to her—and the vast swathe of things he hadn't said—Gina happened to know that Marnie's best friend, Missy Wainwright, was a simpering, self-righteous little prude who'd rather sew up her vagina than let Carter so much as mention sex, let alone actually touch her.

The man had been literally starved of any kind of physical contact with his fiancée—so desperate to be touched it had almost made Gina cry the way he'd responded with such enthusiasm to a simple kiss and actually thanked her in that slow Southern drawl when she'd pulled down his zipper and placed her palm against the firm, resilient flesh of his erection. She hadn't realised then that he'd been a virgin, but when he'd admitted the truth afterwards, as they'd been lying in the heady rush of afterglow, his voice embarrassed and reticent, it had made her heart squeeze tight in her chest.

To realise that a man so virile, so handsome and so sexually curious had denied himself the most basic of human connections because the woman who was supposed to be his soul mate had demanded it of him… What kind of woman could be that clueless about the man she was marrying? And how cold and judgmental and frigid did you have to be to even want to?

The harsh laugh that came out of her mouth didn't sound like her, but somehow it fitted with who she was now: the Evil Sex Queen sent to split up the happy couple and then slink back into the dark forest of regrets and recriminations.

'Actually your good friend Missy hasn't talked to Carter about the *marital act*, but tell her not to worry.' The two-hundred-dollar champagne soured in her belly. 'As it happens her groom has a natural aptitude for bringing a woman to orgasm. Not only is he hung like a stallion, but he's also exceptionally dexterous, remarkably flexible and really goal-orientated. I should know—I road-tested him myself.'

'What?' Marnie's choked sob of distress was accompanied by Reese's spurt of shocked laughter.

'Gina, will you quit teasing her? It's not funny.'

'If that's supposed to be a joke, it's in really poor taste,' Marnie said, sounding like a child having a temper tantrum—naïve and judgmental and impossibly young, the way Gina had never been. 'Missy would be heartbroken if Carter broke his vow,' Marnie finished and Gina could have sworn she heard the rest of the sentence reverberating in her head.

Especially with a tramp like you.

Gina suddenly felt painfully sober, the buzz of alcohol clearing to make her feel reckless and vindictive. Carter had walked away from her determined to throw himself on the mercy of the Virgin Queen—but she wasn't going to keep his secret. Because she wasn't ashamed of what they'd done. She wasn't ashamed of the pleasure they'd shared, and she refused to regret the connection they'd made. It had been real and valid, even if it was only ever meant to be for one night.

'Don't upset yourself, Marnie.' Reese patted Marnie's back, as her mother hen tendencies came charging to the fore. 'It's just Gina's British sense of humour.' Reese sent her a quelling look, that held a trace of censure, but a much bigger trace of confusion. 'Stop being so cynical, Gina, and tell her the truth. I don't know what's gotten into you tonight.'

Gina heard the exasperation in Reese's voice and knew exactly what had gotten into her friend, the Park Avenue Princess, because it was written all over Reese's face, and had been ever since she'd returned from her trip to New York for their final night together. Reese had fallen head over designer heels for that marine she'd met in some diner. She'd seen Reese caressing the dog-tags under her shirt, when she thought no one was looking. And she'd announced earlier in the evening that Mason was 'The One'... As if she were quoting a line from one of those fluffy chick flicks she often forced them to endure on movie nights.

Bitterness and something that felt uncomfortably like envy scoured Gina's throat, making her want to hurt Reese too.

Reese the hopeless romantic, who actually believed in love at first sight. Thank goodness she'd never be daft enough to believe such an idiotic concept. Any more than she'd be dumb enough to fall for Marnie's dictates on the 'proper way to conduct a committed relationship'.

'Actually, Reese, the only thing to have gotten into me is Carter Price's stallion-like—'

'Stop, don't say any more,' Marnie shouted, covering her ears like a child that didn't want to hear the truth. 'It's not true. It can't be.' But Gina could tell the truth had sunk in as tears leaked out of Marnie's eyes. 'You're lying. Carter wouldn't do something like that. He has integrity. And he loves Missy.'

'He may love Missy, but he made love to me.'

'Gina, you didn't,' Reese whispered, hugging Marnie now, her confusion replaced with sadness and concern. 'How could you do something like that? You knew he was engaged.'

Because I talked and he listened. And he talked and I listened. And we touched and kissed and held hands and it meant something. Because he was smart and funny and tender and when he looked at me I felt sexy and special, instead of sexy and shallow.

But she didn't say any of those things, because they weren't really true. It had just been an illusion conjured up by the sultry summer night and the heady pheromones that had intoxicated them both—and it had all disappeared by morning. So she said the thing that had been true all along—before she'd gotten tripped up by feelings that she now knew she should never have trusted.

'I did it because he was hot and he was begging for it. Why do you think?'

Reese swore softly. While Marnie jumped to her feet, her face contorted with anger and disgust. 'But he's engaged to be married. Don't you have any honour at all? How could you be such a…such a tramp?'

Gina forced herself not to flinch. She'd been called a tramp before; in fact, she'd been called a great deal worse than that by her own father. But it was the first time it had been said by someone who meant something to her.

'She's not the tramp,' Cassie announced as they all turned to see her with the newly opened bottle of champagne frothing over her fingers. 'She's not the one who was engaged to be married. He is. Blaming Gina for his infidelity is just another example of the double standard that—'

'You *knew*?' Marnie interrupted Cassie before she could get into full feminist lecture mode.

'Yes. She told me the morning after it happened.'

'Why didn't you tell me?' Marnie cried, the emotional outburst in sharp contrast to Cassie's calm, unblinking stare.

'Why would I tell you? It was between Carter and Gina.'

'Because Carter's my brother and his fiancée is my best friend? Because I'm going to be her maid of honour. Because this is a disaster.' Marnie collapsed back into her seat. 'I can't tell Missy. She'll be devastated. The wedding's in a week's time. And Missy's devoted herself to planning it for over a year.'

'Don't worry, he's not cancelling anything,' Gina supplied. 'He went back to her, didn't he?' She inspected her nails, battling the clutching pain in her chest as she maintained the charade that it didn't matter, that she didn't care. 'I don't know why you're getting so worked up, Marnie. It was nice while it lasted but I didn't want to keep him.'

'I can't believe I respected you. I liked you. I thought you were cool. When all you really are is a lying tramp who has no heart and no scruples.'

'You got it in one, Scarlett.' Gina stood up, taking the opened bottle from Cassie. 'I'm the tart with no heart.' A phrase she'd heard so many times from her father—and had always believed until a week ago, when her heart had put in a surprise appearance.

She inclined her head towards the now dark athletic track,

the buff male bodies they'd had so much fun admiring together over the months now gone for good. 'Looks like the show's over for tonight, so that's my cue to leave.' She sloshed a final slug of Reese's priceless champagne into her glass and toasted them all. 'It's been a ball, but I'm off. I've got an early start in the morning for the flight back to London.'

'Wait a minute, what about our road trip?' Cassie asked, her eyes as round with concern as Reese's now. 'We're booking it tomorrow, remember?'

'I'll take a rain check on that.' She nodded towards Marnie, who was staring at her as if she had snakes instead of hair sprouting out of her head. 'Right at the minute, I'm thinking I'd rather not spend three weeks in a car with Scarlett staring daggers at me.'

She strode back through the house, Marnie's harsh words and Reese's concerned buzzing fading as she concentrated on keeping her back ramrod straight and the self-pitying urge to cry on lockdown.

Cassie caught up with her on the stairs. 'Gina, I don't get it. You can still come on the road trip. Marnie will get over it. What her brother did with you really isn't any of her concern.'

But just as she finished saying it the high, angry shout of 'whore' echoed through the house, making them both stiffen.

Gina pressed her hand to Cassie's cheek. And wondered how her friend could be so scary smart and yet so clueless about the most basic of relationship dynamics?

'We'll see. I'll speak to you tomorrow. See how me and Marnie feel then.'

But she already knew, Marnie wasn't going to forget it. Gina had made absolutely sure of that. Once again, she'd burned her bridges. Pushed the people away who mattered so she wouldn't have to let them mean that much. She already regretted her outburst. The cruel, outrageous, provocative things she'd said. But it was too late to take them back now. And it was probably better that way.

She wasn't any good at friendships. And the three of them needed to know that.

Cassie nodded. 'All right. I'm really going to miss you, you know.'

I'll miss you too. And Reese and even Marnie.

But instead of admitting that much, Gina simply nodded and walked away.

She called a cab the next morning before anyone was up. Happy with the deliberately flippant parting note she'd spent several hours before dawn composing.

> *Sorry for screwing up our last night together so royally, Awesomes. But I think we all knew, me and my insatiable appetite for man candy were bound to mess things up at some point. I hope you can forgive me.*
> *G x*

CHAPTER ONE

New York City, August, the present.

> *Something's come up. U & M will have to pick fabulous venue for Cassie's do without me. C u tomorrow at Amber's Bridal. 11a.m. Don't B late. R xxxx*

'REESE MICHAEL, I am going to murder you.' Gina Carrington glared at the text that had popped up on her smartphone.

This was a set-up, pure and simple.

Now her old college roomie was in the throes of second-chance nirvana with her sexy ex- and soon-to-be new-husband Mason, Reese was so full of the joys of spring—and Gina suspected really spectacular sex—that she was starting to make Pollyanna look like a killjoy.

The something that had come up was Reese's cock-eyed optimism, and leaving her and Marnie to have this meeting without her was her unsubtle way of getting them to kiss and make up properly after that fun-filled night a decade ago when they'd hurled words such as 'Tramp' and 'Whore' and 'Virgin' at each other before busting up the Awesome Foursome.

Gina's fingers hovered over the keypad of her phone as she cursed her own stupidity.

She should have seen this coming, as soon as Reese had

suggested that the three of them organise a surprise wedding party for Cassie and Tuck, the hot jock she was scheduled to marry at the Manhattan Marriage Bureau on the Friday before Labor Day.

But the truth was, Gina hadn't given it a second thought. Reese was classy, committed to her friends and a champion organiser—the original Park Avenue Princess—it had made total sense that she would come up with an idea like this.

In typical Cassie fashion, their super-geek friend had agreed to marry Tuck and then left the arrangements up to him. No fanfare, no fuss, no debauched fun or inappropriate frolics had been either planned or discussed. So after speaking to Tuck, Reese had decreed the three of them should handle that part of the programme without telling Cassie. Because Cassie would go into a geek-induced coma if they made too much fuss, they had opted to celebrate in understated style— inviting the minimalist guest list that would be witnessing the wedding at City Hall to a great meal at a great restaurant right after the event.

Hence the decision to meet at this ungodly hour of the morning in Gina's favourite diner near Grand Central Station and debate possible venues, before booking one.

But Reese being Reese had seen a way to turn what should have been a polite and straightforward affair, with her as the official gooseberry, into a peace-keeping mission of UN proportions.

Gina and Marnie had remained civil to each other, meeting again for the first time a little over a month ago, during the fiasco that was Reese's Wedding-That-Wasn't to Dylan Brookes—the original Mr Too Perfect. That should have been enough, Gina thought resentfully. They had spoken to each other, they had even joked with each other in a strained way. No insults had been hurled, no punches thrown, no eyes gouged out, which in Gina's mind was a result. But clearly, that hadn't been good enough for Reese, who was now a fully loved-up member of the sweetness-and-light club. Reese wanted all the dirty laundry properly aired and then washed clean—so the four of them could go back to being the carefree college roomies who'd hit it off instantly at Hillbrook College.

But to Gina's way of thinking, that simply wasn't ever going to happen. You couldn't go back and undo the mistakes you made. You simply had to learn to live with them. And she didn't think that Marnie would ever forgive her. Because she hadn't yet forgiven herself.

Not only that, but kissing and making up with Marnie would involve talking about a man Gina had promised herself she wouldn't even think about again, because she'd thought about him far too often in the intervening years. Namely, Marnie's big brother, Carter Price. The man she'd had one wild night with just weeks before his wedding day. A wild night the consequences of which had not only nearly destroyed her but, from what Reese had told her, had managed to screw up his life rather comprehensively too.

Gina's newly manicured nails tapped out a tattoo on the side of her smartphone as she glanced at the ornate clock on the diner's far wall—and the urge to quickly text Marnie and make her excuses increased. She still had ten minutes to do a runner before Marnie arrived—because for the first time in recordable history she was actually early.

Sighing, she locked her phone and slung it back in her bag. Ten years ago she would have gone with the urge—and run out on Marnie and the unpleasant conversation that loomed large in her foreseeable future. Because when she was nineteen, doing whatever took her fancy and then running away from the fallout had been her speciality. She smoothed damp palms over the vintage dress she'd picked up in a thrift store in Brooklyn a week ago. How inconvenient that she wasn't that reckless, irresponsible tart any more.

'Can I get you something, miss?'

Gina pasted a smile on her face at the helpful enquiry from the college kid who was waiting tables.

'Something hot and strong would be good,' she said, checking him out from force of habit.

His fresh face flushed a dull red. 'Umm… What did you have in mind, miss?'

'Coffee,' she said, taking pity on him as the flush went from pink to vermillion. 'And this morning I'm going to need it neat.'

He nodded. 'Coming right up.'

She watched him stroll off and smiled.

While she might not be in the market for indiscriminate flings any more, it was satisfying to know she hadn't lost her touch.

In fact, as she took a long gulp of the watery diner coffee ten minutes later, she felt almost mellow. Until the revolving door at the front of the restaurant spun round and out popped Marnie Price looking cute and efficient in her power suit and kitten heels. Gina lifted a hand to wave, and watched Marnie's expression go from keen to wary when she spotted the empty seat next to her.

The hollow roll of regret flopped over in Gina's stomach. While it was certainly true that she and the Savannah Belle hadn't had a thing in common when they'd first met at Reese's house on campus—and Gina had spent most of that first month teasing Marnie mercilessly about everything from her views on love and marriage to her perfect Southern manners—their friendship had eventually developed into something strong and supportive and surprisingly genuine.

The truth was, Gina had felt superior to Marnie then. Gina had considered herself a sophisticated, cosmopolitan woman of the world who knew all she needed to know about men and sex and relationships—unlike the sheltered, self-confessed Southern virgin.

But Marnie had grown on Gina, despite their differences. Because beneath those pristine Southern manners had been an admirable devotion to doing the right thing, being accountable for your actions and always believing the best of people. And then Gina had gone and mucked everything up by jumping into bed with the brother Marnie idolised—and discovered in the process she was hardly the poster girl for mature relationships either.

But if there was something Gina regretted even more than giving in to temptation that night, it was taking that bright, trusting light out of Marnie's eyes. Something that now appeared to be gone for good.

'Hi, Gina.' Marnie sent her a polite smile as she slid into the booth. 'Are we early?' she asked, probably hoping Reese—who was never late—would magically materialise and get them out of this predicament.

If only. 'Reese can't make it. Something came up, apparently.' Gina took a judicious sip of her coffee, resisting the urge to say the something was probably a key part of the hot ex-husband's anatomy.

'And I'll bet I know what it is,' Marnie murmured, making Gina choke on her coffee. 'I swear, you'd think Mason had invented sex the way Reese gushes about the guy.'

Gina put down her cup, a grin forming despite the underlying tension. 'Gushes being the operative word.'

Marnie gave a small laugh. 'All I hope is that it's more than just sex this time around—because there is no way I am repackaging a billion truffles again in this lifetime.'

'Amen to that,' Gina said, toasting Marnie with her coffee mug and smiling at the memory of how the four of them had spent two solid hours taking table-top truffles out of engagement-ring-style boxes when Reese had decided to reinvent her aborted wedding to Dylan into a celebration of… Well, no one had ever really figured that out.

'To be frank,' Gina added, 'if I ever see another truffle before I die, it'll be too soon.'

Marnie's lips curved, but Gina could see the concern in her pure blue eyes—and had the sudden realisation that she hadn't given Marnie her due in the last month.

Seemed they'd both done quite a lot of growing up in the last decade.

After ordering herself an iced tea and some wheat toast from the blushing waiter, Marnie got right down to business, tugging a smartphone out of her briefcase. 'Okay, I've narrowed a couple of possible venues down that can accommodate a party of seven on the required date, can provide a wedding cake and meet our "classy but not too intimidating" requirements.' She pressed a few buttons, her gaze flicking to Gina. 'My personal favourite is the Tribeca Terrace. Do you know it?'

Gina nodded. 'Sure, chic and funky with sensational food and a dance floor—so Cassie and Tuck can get up close and pornographic for our benefit.'

Marnie's lips quirked again. 'It's pricey, but totally worth it.'

'Done.'

Marnie blinked. 'What do you mean, done? We haven't gone through the other options…. And don't you have any venues you want to put forward?'

'I had a couple.' Gina shrugged. 'But none of them are as perfect as the TriBee,' she said, giving it the nickname it had acquired in the foodie press. 'You nailed it in one. Why shop around?'

The waiter arrived with Marnie's toast and tea and made a bit of a production about asking Gina if she had everything she needed. As he left Gina noticed Marnie's gaze follow him, before she concentrated on buttering her toast. There was no censure in the look, just a simple acknowledgement. But Gina could still hear the words running through Marnie's head even if the well-mannered woman would rather bite off her own tongue than voice them.

There goes another of Gina's conquests.

Ten years ago, Gina would have played up to that assessment and enjoyed it—and quite probably taken full advantage of whatever the young waiter had to offer. But not any more.

Placing her coffee mug back on the table, she waited for Marnie to stop buttering. When the bright blue eyes finally met hers, she could see the tension around the edges of Marnie's mouth and realised that—while she still had a low-grade urge to throttle Reese—their mutual friend had been right. They needed to get this out in the open, if they were going to have any chance of getting past it and repairing the friendship between the four of them the rest of the way.

Marnie and her would never be best friends, Gina had already screwed that up for good, but surely they could be more than just civil to each other. A bit more warmth between the two of them would also take the pressure off the other two—and as both Reese and Cassie had weddings coming up, she couldn't think of a better gift to give them both.

'I'm sure we both know why Reese didn't show this morning,' she said evenly. 'And for once I'm not convinced it has anything to do with her inability to leave Mason's bed first thing in the morning while he's still in it.'

Marnie's eyes widened a fraction. She raised her napkin to her mouth to remove an invisible crumb. 'Reese has always been a peace-maker.'

She put the napkin down, folded it carefully.

'But I'm confident she'll stop trying to be Mother Teresa when we turn up at Amber's Bridal tomorrow having booked an awesome venue for Cassie's party without having gotten into a catfight in the Grand Central Diner.'

Gina's lips curved at the droll statement. 'True, but funnily enough…' She took a deep breath, fortified by the odd feeling of connection between them—because right about now it seemed they both had a low-grade urge to throttle Reese. 'I think I can probably go one better than that.'

Wariness crossed Marnie's face. 'How?'

'By apologising for all the crappy things I said to you on our last night together—which were cruel and juvenile and totally unnecessary.' She huffed out a steady breath when Marnie remained silent.

Now for the biggie.

'And more importantly by apologising for seducing your brother the week beforehand—which was equally cruel and juvenile and totally unnecessary.' Even if it had felt very necessary at the time.

'My only excuse is that I was in a bad place at the time.' A bad place that had got a whole lot worse in the months after that night. 'And I did bad things as a result—including being a heartless, reckless, selfish, philandering tart. And although I can't promise that I won't do bad things again—because if there's one thing I despise more than a heartless tart, it's a hypocrite—I'm trying a lot harder not to.'

Marnie's face remained unnervingly impassive, before she gave her head a little nod. 'Thanks for the apology. But if you were being cruel and juvenile, I was too. And…' She paused. 'While I could have done without such a graphic description of my brother's…' she coughed, clearly struggling to get the word out '…assets, you didn't say anything that wasn't true.' She looked down at her hands, which were mangling the carefully folded napkin. 'Carter was the one that cheated, Gina. Not you.' Her eyes met Gina's, disillusionment clouding the blue depths. 'And after seeing his marriage die a slow, painful

death and seeing what a player he's become since his divorce—
I don't think you should take all the blame.'

A player? Carter?

Gina's throat constricted as the memories she'd filed
carefully away in the 'biggest disaster of my life' box had a
coming-out party.

Yes, he'd been devastatingly handsome, and moody and
magnetic and sexy enough to make any woman salivate un-
controllably, even an accomplished flirt like her. But beneath
that potent machismo had been a man who, like Marnie, had
been determined to do the right thing—who had been honourable and sensitive and touchingly reserved, despite the
hunger burning in those cool blue eyes. How could that man
be a player?

Nobody could change that much. Even in ten years….

'Reese told me Carter had got a divorce,' she said. The
guilt she'd worked hard to mask ever since Reese had told
her the news throbbed in her belly like a lump of radioactive
waste—alongside an inappropriate rush of heat, which she
studiously ignored.

'I'm sorry about that too,' she said. It would be conceited
of her to think she was wholly responsible for the failure of
Carter's marriage, but she still had to shoulder her share of
the blame. She'd slept with an engaged man and then tried
to push the blame onto the only innocent party in the whole
thing, Carter's fiancée, Missy.

'You don't need to apologise,' Marnie remarked with sober
certainty. 'The divorce wasn't your fault—they had a lot of
other…' her voice trailed off '…issues.'

'It's nice of you to say that.' And nicer still to see that she
actually meant it. 'But I was there when it happened, and I
know how hard he tried to resist me.'

Marnie shot her hands out in the shape of a T. 'All right,

time out, because you are straying back into "things I will never need to know about my brother" territory, here.'

Gina huffed out a laugh at the look of horror on Marnie's face. Maybe the Southern Belle had grown up, but it seemed she still had the same demure sensibilities when it came to discussing her big brother's sex life.

'The point is…' Marnie put her hands down '…I'm ashamed of the things I said that night too.' She drew a circle on the table. 'I wanted to put all the blame on you, because blaming Carter would mean admitting he didn't belong on the pedestal I'd put him on.' She sighed. 'We're not close these days.'

Gina felt the renewed stab of regret. 'Oh, Marnie, I'm so sorry. Did I do that too?'

'I don't think so,' Marnie said, sounding adamant. 'It would have happened anyway once I got older and wiser and realised what he was really like.' The wry smile on Marnie's lips did nothing to dispel the thoughtful expression. 'You know, I don't remember you having such an overdeveloped guilt complex.'

Gina chuckled at the observation. 'Unfortunately, it's the end result of believing everything is about you.'

Marnie sent her a quick grin, the unguarded moment a reminder of the easy friendship they'd once shared.

'Look, I hope we're good now,' Marnie said. 'Because my relationship with my brother isn't as important to me as my friendship with y'all.'

'Yeah, we're good,' Gina said, but felt oddly deflated as Marnie excused herself to go to the restroom.

Maybe they hadn't had a catfight, and maybe she'd finally got out the apology that she should have given Marnie ten years ago… But somehow it didn't feel like enough.

Maybe her thoughtless seduction that night hadn't been the only reason Carter's marriage had ended, but it had definitely helped to screw up his relationship with his sister. And Gina couldn't quite shake the thought that Marnie had fallen back on her perfect Southern manners to smooth everything over, but didn't really mean it.

The buzzing of Marnie's phone jolted Gina out of her guilt trip, and made coffee slosh over the rim of her mug. She mopped up the spill and made a grab for the phone as it vibrated towards the edge of the table. Then nearly dropped it at the photo that flashed up in the viewfinder under the text message.

Arrive @ The Standard 7pm 2nite. In NYC til next Fri. Txt me. We need 2 discuss yr allowance. C

Her heart leapt up to bump against her larynx and the swell of heat that she'd been busy ignoring flared. She pressed her thumb to the screen and ran it over the darkly handsome face that had hardly changed in ten years. His hair was longer, the brutal buzz cut now a mass of thick waves that curled around his ears and touched his collar. Those hollow cheeks had filled out a bit, the electric blue of his eyes looked colder and even more intense, and there were a few distinguished laughter lines, but otherwise Carter Price looked even hotter than she remembered him. She touched the tempting little dent in his chin—biting the tip of her tongue as a blast of memory assailed her. The rasp of stubble and the nutty taste of pistachio as she licked a rivulet of ice cream off his full bottom lip.

Stop fondling Marnie's phone, you muppet.

The sharp rap of metal on wood rang out as she dropped the phone on the table. Carter Price's unsettling gaze continued to stare at her, so she flipped it over—moments before Marnie appeared at her shoulder.

'Your phone was buzzing,' she offered, as nonchalantly

as she could manage, while blood coursed up her neck and pulsed at her temples.

'Right, thanks.' Marnie picked up the phone and slid back into the booth.

A frown formed on Marnie's forehead as she read the text. And Gina wondered for one agonising moment if Marnie would mention the texter—and then wondered how she was going to conduct a conversation while having a hot flush. But Marnie didn't say anything, she simply frowned, keyed in a few characters, pressed send and then tucked the phone into the pocket of the briefcase.

'Shall I go ahead and book the Tribeca Terrace?' she asked, her voice clear and steady and businesslike, the frown gone.

Gina's shoulders knotted with tension and the sinking feeling in her stomach dropped to her toes.

So Marnie had lied—maybe she wanted to pretend that they were both past what had happened ten years ago, that it didn't matter any more. But how could it be true when she couldn't even bring herself to mention Carter's name?

Marnie didn't trust her. And frankly who could blame her?

They made arrangements to meet up the next day for the bridesmaids' fittings at Reese's friend Amber's bridal boutique in the Manhattan Bridge Overpass District before Marnie—who seemed more than a little preoccupied—rushed off to get to her office in Brooklyn.

Gina watched her leave, and realised that there was only one way to win Marnie's trust—and prove to herself that she deserved it. And that was to finally make amends for everything that had happened ten years ago, on the night she'd thrown herself at a virtually married man.

She gulped down her lukewarm coffee as goosebumps prickled up her spine. Unfortunately that meant apologising to more than just Marnie.

CHAPTER TWO

GINA CLIMBED OUT of the cab under the High Line in New York's Meatpacking District and mounted the metal steps to the linear park constructed along an old L-train track. The concrete pathway, edged with planters of wild ferns and flowers, bustled with joggers, canoodling couples and families enjoying the pleasantly warm but not overly muggy New York evening.

Sweat trickled down her back as she stepped out of the heat into the cool lobby area of The Standard Hotel. The retro chic decor—all white plastic sculptures, distressed stone walls and dark leather scooped seats—made her feel as if she'd stepped onto the set of a sixties sci-fi movie.

She lifted her arms, to deter the sweat from dampening the armpits of the vintage Dior mini-dress she'd spent half an hour selecting from her extensive wardrobe of couture originals and thrift-store finds. The plan was to look cool and sophisticated and in control while finally confronting the ghosts of her past, not like a bedraggled rag doll.

She lingered for a moment—feeling a bit like an alien from the planet Zod—before taking a deep, calming breath, and stepping up to the reception desk.

The expertly coiffured receptionist took down the message she'd spent most of the afternoon composing. The perfect combination of polite, impersonal and not too pushy—the single sentence gave Carter the option of contacting her, so she could give him her apology in person.

Whether he would or not was entirely up to him. The sense of relief as she left the desk was immense. She'd done what she had to do. It really didn't matter now if Carter called her or not. But somehow she doubted he would.

Because as well as spending far too much time that afternoon composing the perfect message—she'd also spent rather a lot of it Googling information about the CEO of the Price Paper Consortium of Savannah, Georgia. After wasting a good twenty minutes poring over the numerous pictures, gossip items and local news reports featuring Carter Price and the ever-changing kaleidoscope of model-perfect 'possible future brides' who'd accompanied him to an array of high-society functions and charity events in the last few years, she'd had to concede that Marnie hadn't lied.

The sensitive, conflicted Southern gentleman who had once been so susceptible to her charms wasn't just a major player now, he appeared to be attempting a world record for dating and dumping the entire debutante population south of the Mason-Dixon Line.

This Carter was not the man who had rushed back to his childhood sweetheart crippled by guilt and self-loathing at what they had done. So she very much doubted he'd want to revisit that time in his life. But exactly how much of the change in him was her fault?

The thought struck and stopped her in her tracks—right beside the entrance to the hotel's lobby bar.

Damn, her throat felt as if she'd been swallowing sand. She glanced at her watch. Ten to six. Still an hour before Carter was due to check in. She had time for a soft drink without risking bumping into him.

She shrugged off the thought of how much Carter appeared to have changed in the last ten years as she entered the brightly lit bar. Apportioning blame for that now was a little late.

Crowded with New York's young and lively in-crowd celebrating the start of the weekend and a few tired-looking tourists ready to call it a day, the pristine blonde wooded space was already throbbing with life. One small table right on the outskirts of the action was still vacant. She nabbed it and waylaid a member of the wait staff.

'A club soda, please.... No, scratch that,' she said as indecision struck. 'Make that a small dry martini, light on the vermouth.' One drink couldn't hurt and she'd earned it.

When the martini arrived, Gina took a single sip, then placed it on the table in front of her, savouring the flowery taste of the gin and resisting the urge to down it in three quick gulps. She never drank to excess any more. Mostly because she now knew that inebriation had a direct correlation to stupid behaviour.

She speared the olive at the bottom of her glass with a cocktail stick and swirled it around, savouring the light buzz from the alcohol as the guttural chatter of the Japanese tourists at the next table cocooned her in the blessedly anonymous corner. The muggy scent of body odour and expensive perfumes and colognes overwhelmed the blast of cold air from the bar's air-conditioning system, drawing her back in time to a sultry summer afternoon a lifetime ago.

The ripples in her martini glass shimmered out to the rim and dissipated as the hazy memory floated at the edges of her consciousness and invaded her senses.

The phantom scent of lime polish and hyacinths tickled her nostrils as she recalled the pleasantly cool hallway of the clapboard house on Hillbrook College Campus. The parquet cold beneath bare feet as she tiptoed down the compact house's corridor with her shoes clutched in her fist. Guilt tugged at the pit of her stomach—because she was creeping home at four in the afternoon after an all-night frat party when she had promised faithfully to spend the day revising at the college library with Reese. And then she heard again the sound of an unfamiliar male voice, low and brusque despite being infused with the lazy rhythms of the Deep South, echoing down the stairs from Marnie's room on the first landing.

CHAPTER THREE

'NO IS MY final answer, Marnie. Mama's not going to allow you to go on a road trip with your friends and neither am I. Once the wedding is over, you will be staying in Savannah for the summer.'

Gina's brows drew down in a sharp frown. So the famous older brother, the Sainted Carter, had finally showed up to transport Marnie's stuff back to Savannah. She slipped her shoes back on and decided to stay put in her hiding place— and get some vicarious pleasure from hearing Marnie give the guy the smack down he clearly deserved.

What a tool, ordering his sister about like that.

'I don't believe I need your permission, Carter,' Marnie replied, succinctly. 'You're not Daddy—and Mama will come around once I've spoken to her.'

Way to go, Marnie.

Pride swelled in Gina's chest at the knowledge that a year ago, when Marnie had first arrived at Reese's house on campus from deepest, darkest Georgia, she never would have had the guts to talk back to the Sainted Carter like that. A man Gina and Reese and Cassie had all suspected was a total douche, hence the nickname they'd given him together, despite the way Marnie gushed about him.

'Mama doesn't control the mill's finances, I do,' came the

low, irritatingly patient reply. 'So I'd like to know how you're gonna go on this road trip, if I refuse to pay for it.'

'Daddy left me a share in the mill, surely I can—'

'Daddy left your share in trust,' he interrupted with the same implacable calm. 'A trust which he left me to administer until you reach your majority—and I'm refusing your request for funds on this occasion.'

'That's not fair, Carter.'

Gina's fingers fisted into tight balls as the argument continued and slowly but surely all the confidence and assurance Marnie had gained in the past year leached away as her brother refused to budge. In fact, Gina was fairly sure from his uninterested replies that he wasn't even listening.

For that alone, Gina could have throttled him with her bare hands. Why did so many men have to be like her father, judgmental and superior and always, always right?

She pressed back into the alcove as Marnie's bedroom door closed upstairs and footsteps came down the stairs. She caught a glimpse of a tall figure dressed in a creased chambray shirt and suit trousers as he strolled into the kitchen.

She stayed in the alcove, hearing his heavy sigh, and debated the wisdom of getting involved: with her tendency to be provocative she was liable to make it worse, and it really wasn't any of her business. But as she walked to the kitchen doorway and spied on him helping himself to one of Reese's chilled diet colas from the fridge, anger and resentment flared.

He closed the fridge, his broad back to her as he twisted the cap off the bottle and flipped it into the bin, then took a long swallow of the cola. One large hand gripped the edge of the sink but the rigid line of his shoulder blades relaxed.

Why should she respect his privacy when he hadn't respected Marnie's—and how could she possibly make things worse?

Leaning insolently against the doorjamb, she gave her voice the soft smoky purr she knew made men putty in her hands. 'You know, you really ought to take that huge stick out from up your arse. It's going to ruin the very nice line of those designer trousers.'

He swung round and her lungs seized in astonishment.

It seemed Marnie had failed to mention one fairly crucial bit of information about her big brother during all the gushing this year. Carter Price was a total hottie.

At six foot two or three, with mile-wide shoulders and the tanned skin of a pirate, he was as big and dark as his sister was small and fair, but the relationship was confirmed by the striking eyes that narrowed on her face—and shared the exact same shade of cerulean blue as his sister's. On Marnie they looked cute and appealing. On her brother they looked cold and intense.

The unblinking gaze drifted down her frame as he took another swig of the stolen cola and Gina felt the prickle of response, everywhere.

She settled back against the doorjamb, but clamped down on the urge to stretch her back—thus displaying what she knew to be an exceptional pair of breasts to their best advantage.

Focus, Gina. You're not here to flirt with the guy. You're here to tell him a thing or two about women's emancipation—and his sister's emancipation in particular.

'You've got quite a mouth on you, miz.' The deep drawl was as slow and seductive as molasses but for the steely hint of censure beneath. 'My daddy would have taken a hickory switch to my backside if I'd used that sort of language in the presence of a lady.'

'I guess we're both very fortunate then that you're not in the presence of a lady,' she replied tartly.

Carter Price wasn't just a hottie, he was also a sexist control freak, but no way was he going to control her, with his cool Southern manners and his total contempt for a women's right to self-determination.

She let her gaze drift over him too. 'Because I'd really hate to see what I can imagine is an exceptionally cute backside being whipped with a hickory switch—unless I was the one doing it.'

Let's see how you like being objectified, Buster.

Two dark eyebrows arched, and she felt the wave of satisfaction at the knowledge that she'd shocked him. Gina Carrington was no simpering Southern miss prepared to bow down to the dictates of a man. And the sooner Carter Price got that message, the better. But then his irises darkened and his lips twitched at the edges. And she had the strangest feeling she might have underestimated him, a tad.

'Why do I get the feeling your daddy didn't take a hickory switch to...' he paused to direct his gaze pointedly at her mid-section and she had to resist the urge to tuck in her bottom '...what I can see is also an exceptionally cute butt, nearly often enough?'

She wanted to be outraged at the suggestion—and any mention of her father and/or the corporal punishment of a child would ordinarily do that—but unfortunately she wasn't outraged. Because she was far too distracted by the surge of heat making her nipples tighten against the confines of her bra and the way her cute *butt* was now sizzling alarmingly.

'You're very perceptive, Mr Price. My father never hit me,' she informed him with as much dignity as she could muster while her behind was still pulsing from the imagined thrashing. 'Because he knew he would lose an arm if he tried,' she finished, with the purr still firmly in place, even though it was starting to sound less and less like an affectation—and more and more like an invitation.

'Seems to me an arm is a small price to pay when it comes to instilling good manners in your child.'

The outrage came without a problem this time as the sizzle fizzled out. The man was serious.

'If you actually believe that hitting a child—or a woman— is less heinous than bad manners, then an arm isn't the only thing you deserve to lose.'

She could see she'd done a lot more than shock him this time, when he stiffened and the twitch on those firm sensual lips disappeared. 'You mistake me, miz?'

'Carrington. Gina Carrington.'

'Miz Carrington. I've never hit a child, or a woman, in my life, and I never would. I respect women. Absolutely.'

'Is that something else your daddy taught you with his hickory switch?' she said, the contempt dripping now.

But instead of the smug affirmative she had expected, something flickered across his face, and she had the feeling she'd crossed a line she hadn't intended to. He turned away, and braced one hand against the sink. Then fixed her with an unsettling stare. 'You seem to have a problem with me, Miz Carrington. And as this is the first time I've had the pleasure of your company, I'd like to know why!'

It occurred to her that he hadn't answered her question, but this was the opening she'd been waiting for, so she took it.

'I heard you upstairs, bullying Marnie into doing what you wanted. Not what she wanted. She's eighteen years old and perfectly capable of coming on a road trip with us this summer. And as I understand it, you'll be on your honeymoon anyway, so why is it so important to have her sitting in Savannah twiddling her thumbs instead of having fun with us?'

The grim line of his lips thinned out and a muscle in his jaw clenched. 'So your exemplary manners include eavesdropping?'

'It would seem so.' What did she care what some self-righteous Southern prig thought of her manners? 'And while we're on the subject, there happens to be several things in life that are a great deal more important than exemplary manners. And letting your sister follow her heart's desire happens to be one of them.'

'Going on a road trip with y'all hasn't got a damn thing to do with following her heart's desire.'

So much for his Southern manners, Gina thought, relishing the spurt of temper. At last, here was something she could work with; she happened to be very good at handling male tantrums.

'How would you know that?' she said coolly.

'Because she's my sister.'

'And that makes you her keeper, does it? Perhaps Marnie doesn't need a keeper any more.'

His brows furrowed into a deep frown and she could almost see the frustration pumping off him. She knew he wanted to say something derogatory about her, and Reese and possibly Cassie right about now.

Because what other reason could he have for wanting to keep his sister away from them?

She waited for him to accuse all three of them of being a bad influence, but to her surprise, after several deep breaths, his shoulders relaxed and she saw him visibly draw himself back from the brink.

She dismissed the moment of admiration—control after all wasn't one of her strong points.

'I don't consider myself to be Marnie's keeper, Miz Carrington,' he said, in a tight voice, the drawl no longer quite so pronounced. 'But I am her brother and I intend to do what's best for her—with or without your consent.'

Her lips curved in a wry smile. Talk about getting hoisted by your own petard. It seemed Carter's perfect manners were going to prevent him from saying what he actually thought about her and her friends. Well, she hoped swallowing that down gave him heartburn. 'And why is what's best for her your decision and not hers?'

The muscle in his jaw pulsed. 'Because she's eighteen,' he said. But she could see what he wasn't saying in that look of calm condescension. *And because she's a woman.*

'How old are you, Carter?' she asked.

The frown deepened, as if he were looking for the trap. 'I'm twenty-two.'

'And how old were you when you got engaged?' she asked, although she already knew the answer, because Marnie had talked about her big brother's insanely romantic engagement to her best friend, Missy, incessantly when she'd first arrived at the house.

'It's not the same thing,' he said, seeing the trap too late.

'Umm-hmm. And why ever not? You were the same age as Marnie is now and yet you were mature enough to decide you were going to love your childhood sweetheart for the rest of your life.' She said the words with conviction, but couldn't help feeling a little sick to her stomach.

When had she ever been that romantic? That naïve? To believe that anyone was worth that much of a commitment?

'It wasn't like that. Missy and I are well suited. And it was the right thing to do after my father died. My mother and Marnie needed stability and they were both in favour of the match.'

It was Gina's turn to frown. And not just because Carter's description of the engagement was in sharp contrast to the wildly romantic whirlwind of love and devotion Marnie had described. Who the hell proposed marriage because they were being sensible? And he'd made it sound as if the primary motivation had been the approval of his mother and his kid sister? She was by no means a hopeless romantic, but wasn't that taking filial duty a bit too far?

'But you do love Missy, right?' The question popped out before she could stop it.

He looked taken aback. As well he might, because this really was none of her business. But curiosity consumed her. He'd only been eighteen. What on earth had he been thinking settling for 'The One' so young? What about hormones? And exploring your options? And sowing wild oats?

'Of course I love Missy. She's going to be my wife in two weeks' time. We're friends, we understand each other and we both want the same things out of life.'

None of which sounded remotely like convincing reasons for proposing marriage when you were just out of high school. But what did she know? 'What things?'

He shrugged, the movement stiff and defensive. And she realised for the first time that he looked unsure of himself. 'Companionship, trust, compatibility, children. Eventually.' The affirmation came out in a monotone, as if he'd rehearsed it a hundred times.

'Why, Rhett,' Gina said, fluttering her eyelashes and affecting a simpering Southern drawl. 'I can see how you must have swept Missy off her feet with that proposal. How romantic of you to compile a checklist for the perfect marriage.'

'Missy knows she can trust me,' he said firmly, the look on his face delightfully annoyed and confused. Clearly the Sainted Carter wasn't used to being teased—or questioned about his carefully planned love life. 'That's what matters.'

'Really? What about love and passion and adventure and…' she groped for another quality that might get the message across to this indomitable and resolutely anti-romantic man '…and the promise of multi-orgasmic sex for the rest of your life?'

His gaze flicked to her cleavage, then shot back to her face and a dull shade of red rose up his neck and made his tan glow on chiselled cheekbones. He looked away, taking a large fortifying gulp of the cola. And suddenly she knew.

Oh. My. God.

Carter Price had been eighteen when he'd proposed to his very-appropriate fiancée. And if Missy was as much of a sanctimonious prude as her best friend, Marnie, had been when she'd first arrived from Savannah—wearing a little promise ring on her finger that signified her purity, and had needled Gina no end—then Missy had probably demanded she remain a virgin until her wedding night.

She searched the long tanned fingers of Carter's left hand wrapped around the cola bottle. Was it possible that Carter had made a similar promise? Hadn't Marnie said boys wore them too, when Gina had lit into her for being a disgrace to Women's Liberation. Gina held back the gasp as she spotted the silver band on Carter's pinkie, identical to the celibacy ring that Marnie no longer wore when she was at college.

Oh, no, surely not? A man who was as virile and handsome and overwhelmingly male as he was, and who looked at her with that dark sexual intensity he couldn't hide? That man hadn't had sex since he was eighteen? It was just too delicious. And too ridiculous. No wonder he looked so tense and uptight. And no wonder he was far too involved in Marnie's personal life, because he clearly didn't have one of his own.

An intervention was called for.

The surge of excitement and anticipation gripped Gina's chest—and some other interesting parts of her anatomy. Suddenly she had the perfect way to bring the Sainted Carter down a peg or two. Prove to him that he was as human and fallible and sinful as the rest of them.

She was after all an accomplished flirt. And there was no harm in simply flirting with the man. Especially a man as stuffy and controlling and undeniably hot as this one. And once she'd proved to Carter Price that bad girls were people too, once she'd reduced him to a puddle of overactive hormones and sexual desperation, she'd be able to get him to agree to anything…. Even letting his innocent kid sister go on a riotous road trip with three loose women.

The man was celibate. He hadn't had sex in four long years. The challenge was simply irresistible. She'd lost her virginity at sixteen with her thirty-five-year-old biology teacher at St Bude's boarding school, and she hadn't looked back since. Carter Price wouldn't know what hit him. And while she wouldn't do the dirty deed with him, because she never poached on another woman's territory, why shouldn't she take her flirtation far enough to get Saint Carter primed and ready for his wedding night? Missy would end up thanking her.

'Would you like another martini, miss?'

Gina blinked, staring absently at the harassed young waitress as the question brought her spinning back to the present. And the bar at The Standard where she'd gone for a quick fortifying libation. And been blind-sided by too many memories.

She looked down at her glass, surprised to find it empty, the olive on its cocktail stick lined up on the table. 'No, thanks, just the check, please.'

The waitress nodded, clearing away the empty glass.

Tension tightened Gina's stomach as the reality of exactly how reckless and manipulative she'd been that night slammed into her in all its grim glory.

Maybe Marnie was right, and Carter was the one who had been cheating.

But there was no getting away from the fact that she had seduced him. Not the other way around. And it wasn't until twelve hours after meeting him in the kitchen and making a conscious decision to bend him to her will that she'd finally been forced to admit the magnitude of her mistake. As she lay in the dew-drenched grass under a maple tree, the dawn light casting a redolent glow on the rebel wave in Carter's cropped hair, her heart beating a staccato rhythm of shock and guilt, her thighs spread and aching, his erection still huge inside her and his pinkie ring cutting into her cheek.

Heat washed through her at the visceral memory—and it occurred to Gina that maybe the decision to cab it over to the High Line this evening and deliver her carefully composed message in person, when she could just as easily have phoned or emailed it, might have a lot more significance than she wanted to admit.

Had she on some subconscious level hoped to bump into the man whose picture she'd glimpsed on Marnie's smartphone that morning—for reasons other than closure and accountability? Was her new leaf not as well turned over as she thought?

Crap! She needed to get out of here now.

The waitress returned with the check, and Gina threw several bills on the tray without counting them. The guilty flush made her breathing speed up as she shot across the lobby.

Gloria Gaynor singing 'I Will Survive' blasted from her bag at top volume, making her steps falter. It took her a moment to remember that Gloria's strident disco classic was her phone's ringtone.

She paused, fumbled for the phone and stared at a number she didn't recognise. Glancing at the clock above the lobby's exit doors, she felt a little of the panic retreat. She still had thirty minutes before Carter was due to arrive. She took a steadying breath and clicked the answer button. This might be a new client responding to her recent social media campaign for new business. She couldn't afford not to answer. She'd simply have to talk and run.

But as she pressed the phone to her ear the deep laconic Southern accent had the heels of her sandals sinking into the deep pile purple carpet and her heart pounding into her throat.

'Hello, Gina. It's Carter Price. I got your message.'

'Carter. Hi. How are you?' she said, the false brightness making her wince.

Good grief, was he at the reception desk? Right behind her? Maybe he'd phoned ahead? Please let him have phoned ahead. She couldn't risk turning around to check. So she kept walking. The exit doors were only a few feet away.

'I'm good,' came the husky reply. 'Although I'm wondering where you're off to in such a hurry.'

Crapola!

She spun round. The phone dropping away from her ear as she spotted the man standing less than ten feet away, with one elbow propped against the reception desk, a phone at his ear—and cool aquamarine eyes locked on her face.

Her breath got trapped somewhere around her solar plexus—as she debated the probability of teleportation actually existing.

Beam me up, Scottie. Right now.

'Don't move,' he said into his phone, before switching it off and tucking it into his back pocket.

Her thighs quivered alarmingly as he walked towards her. She locked her knees, determined not to collapse into a heap as the shot of adrenaline collided with the explosion of heat in the pit of her stomach—and it occurred to her that the paparazzi pictures had not done him justice. Savannah's most eligible bachelor wasn't just hot, he was positively combustible.

She forced air through her burning lungs, grateful for the fortifying buzz from her martini as he got close enough for her to pick up the smell of soap and man—and remember how much taller he was. At five foot seven, she wasn't used to men towering over her, but Carter Price had no trouble at all making her feel like a midget.

His steady gaze swept over her—then arrived back at her face. 'It's been a while, Miz Carrington.'

But not nearly long enough, if the sweat popping up on her top lip was anything to go by.

'You've improved with age,' he said, his tone low and amused. 'Like a fine wine.'

So had he, she thought. The few strands of grey at his temples, the new creases round his mouth, the crinkles at the corners of his eyes and the waves of thick dark hair that now touched the collar of his white shirt only adding to the confident, take-charge charisma that had been all too evident in the paparazzi pictures.

Say something, you silly cow!

'It's flattering of you to say so,' she murmured, struggling to maintain cool distance and not give in to the throaty purr.

His gaze strayed to her cleavage and her breathing quickened again, keeping a natural rhythm with the pounding beat of her pulse. But then the heavily lidded gaze met hers. The deep, lazy Southern accent reverberated across her nerve-endings. 'It's good to see you again. Marnie told me you were living in New York now,' he said, surprising her.

So he had asked Marnie about her. And Marnie had answered.

Then, to her utter astonishment, he took her hand in long, cool fingers and lifted it to his lips. The quick gallant buzz on her knuckles spun her back in time to the clean-cut young man he'd once been. But then his thick dark lashes caught the overhead light as he blinked slowly, and the inscrutable gaze had all thoughts of the boy disappearing—until all she could see was the man.

'How about we catch up in the bar? And you can tell me what's on your mind?'

'Okay, that would work,' she said, thinking no such thing. His hand settled on the small of her back as he directed her towards the bar.

Terrific! How the heck was she going to get her head round the perfectly simple apology she'd planned, while her mind was being fried to a crisp by all the zaps of electrical energy now radiating up her spine?

CHAPTER FOUR

CARTER PRICE BLINKED eyes gritty from jet lag after his flight from Russia that afternoon, the fog in his brain blown off course by the pulse of heat in his gut.

After ten years of denial, the two-line message the receptionist had handed him had confused him—and shaken him a little. More than a little if he was being entirely honest. He'd thought about Gina Carrington way too much over the years. So the sight of her dashing towards the exit doors had an effect on his senses somewhere in the region of a category five hurricane.

She looked hotter than he remembered her. And he remembered a lot. The beestung lips, the wide green, slightly slanting eyes, the mass of chestnut hair that had tumbled over her shoulders in riotous curls back then, but was now piled on top of her head, making his fingers itch to send it tumbling again. Her tall, slender figure had filled out some since her college days—her high breasts were fuller, her hips more generous, and her legs looked never-ending in the ice-pick heels. The overall effect made all those lush curves even more mouth-watering.

He'd dated a lot of women since popping his cherry with Gina Carrington, and divorcing his wife, most of them a lot more conventionally beautiful—but not one of them oozed pure, unadulterated sex the way Gina did. Or sent a right hook to his senses with a single whiff of their spicy, sultry scent.

He shook off the thought as she perched on a bar stool.

Get your mind out of your pants.

Boy, did he need ten hours straight—he really had to be losing it if he was fantasising about the woman who had once blown his life to smithereens.

Not that he blamed her for that. He'd been like a fire-cracker, waiting to explode. All she'd done was light the fuse.

He caught the barman's attention. 'What'll it be?' he asked Gina.

'Club soda.'

'Make mine a Sam Adams,' he added, propping himself on the stool beside her.

He watched her throat bob as she swallowed heavily—and felt the surge of satisfaction. She seemed a little jumpy—and she'd definitely been planning to run out on him. Which gave him the upper hand. He made a habit now of never being at a disadvantage with women—and that went double for this woman, because she'd once had him at the biggest disadvantage of all.

But there had been a whole lot of water under the bridge, not to mention ladies in his bed, since that night. And he wasn't that lust-driven sex-deprived delusional kid any more. His pulse spiked as she pursed her full lips around the straw in her club soda and sucked.

He took a sip of the yeasty micro-beer.

Relax.

So what if he had some lingering lust issues where Gina Carrington was concerned? He had the control not to act on them now. Or at least not straight away. Not until he knew the score. His gaze skimmed over the silky dress and noticed how her magnificent rack rose and fell in staggered rhythm against the snug bodice.

Yeah, definitely edgy. A gratifying change from their first meeting, when she'd had all the moves and he'd been the one playing catch-up.

He took a long draft of his beer and waited for her to speak. She'd been the one to contact him, after all.

She glugged down a good portion of the soda, getting more jumpy by the second, but didn't elaborate, so he decided to push it. Her note hadn't exactly given much away. 'So I hear you've got your own business—website development and social-media strategy, right?'

Her eyes darted to his, the wary look gratifying. 'How do you know that?'

He shrugged. 'I've been thinking of investing in a social-media strategist for the mill. Your name came up in the research we did.'

And after the shock of seeing her name on the report, he'd looked her up on the Internet and discovered she was now living in the U.S. Not that he planned to tell her that.

Once he and Missy had called it quits, he'd been able to let go of the guilt over his night with Gina, and how much it had snuck into his dreams during the years of his marriage.

Given his current reaction to Gina, it was clear guilt wasn't the problem any more.

'Nice site, by the way,' he added. 'Clean and clear, and you've got some great testimonials there.'

'Thank you.' She watched him intently and he noticed the beguiling flecks of gold in the green of her irises.

'Is that why you contacted me?' He pushed some more.

Her eyebrows launched up her forehead. 'God, no! I'm not that desperate for new business.'

He grinned at her outraged denial, surprised to realise he was glad she hadn't gotten in touch just to tout for business. She took another long sip of the soda, but didn't say anything else. 'Then you're gonna have to give me a hint—because your message was kind of cryptic.'

She let out a puff of breath. 'Right.' She faced him, her long legs crossed at the knees and her short dress riding up to display a distracting amount of toned, lightly tanned thigh.

'I was having coffee with Marnie this morning and saw your text message,' she began. 'When I discovered you were going to be in town for the week, I decided to take the opportunity to…' She hesitated. 'To come here and apologise for what I did to you ten years ago.' The last bit came out in a rush as if she'd had to push the words out.

The heat kicked harder in his gut. She looked totally sincere. Was she actually serious? And what the hell had brought this on, ten years after the event?

'You're gonna have to be a lot more specific,' he said, exhilarated when her eyes flashed with annoyance. It felt good to have this particular woman at this much of a disadvantage. 'Because as I recall we did a lot of things that night.'

Gina's temper simmered at the wry comment. Was he making fun of her? And if so why? The failure of his marriage was hardly a joking matter, surely?

'I'm apologising for all of it,' she said, more sharply than she had intended when his lips twisted with amusement. 'For seducing you, and taking your virginity and ruining your marriage.'

The glass he'd been lifting to his lips hit the bar with a snap as his brows shot towards his hairline. 'You have got to be kidding me?' A choked chuckle burst out.

'Actually I'm not.' The retort did nothing to cut through the rumble of incredulous laughter. 'I'm sincerely sorry for what I did to you.'

Heat spread across her chest as he continued to chuckle. She lifted her purse off the bar, slid off her stool, the sincerity of her apology drowning in a puddle of humiliation. She'd made a twit of herself; time to make a dignified exit. 'I should go. Thanks for the drink, Carter.'

But as she went to walk past him strong fingers snagged her wrist. 'Where are you off to in such a hurry?'

'I'm leaving. Obviously this was a mistake.' She twisted her arm; his fingers tightened.

'Not a chance, sugar.' The casual endearment became *shoo-gah* in his low Southern drawl—and sounded so ridiculously sensuous she lost the will to resist for a moment.

He took the opportunity to place both palms on her waist and drew her towards him. She tensed, her will returning in a rush when she found herself positioned between his spread thighs. 'What are you doing?'

'Settle down, Gina. You wanted to talk, now it's my turn.'

She lifted her arms, in an attempt to step free without making too much of a scene, but his grip remained firm, anchoring her to the spot.

'Relax,' he said, still sounding amused. 'You're not going anywhere until I get to say what I wanna say.'

'Fine.' She folded her arms across her chest, disturbed by the long slow pull of arousal as his large hands drifted down to bracket her hips. 'You have my undivided attention. But I'm not sure what else there is to say.'

'That's because you've had your say.' He had the cheek to chuckle again. 'Now you get to listen.'

'Okay then, speak,' she snapped. They did not need to be standing this close, but short of putting on a show for the rest of the bar's inhabitants, who were already taking more of an interest in their conversation than she would have liked, she didn't appear to have much of a choice.

'I can see you're as quick-tempered as you ever were.'

She sent him a bland look. 'Is that what you wanted to say?'

He barked out another laugh. 'Point taken. I'll get on with it. I sure wouldn't want to bore you.'

One muscled thigh touched her hip and she shifted away from it, only to get trapped against the other one. Bored wasn't the word that was first and foremost in her mind at the minute.

'First off, you can shove your apology in one of those sweet places where the sun doesn't shine.'

She sucked in a breath, shocked by his crudity. 'That's nice, I must—'

'Hush, I'm still talking here.'

She shut her mouth.

Well, really. What had happened to those genteel manners?

'Second of all. You might have been my first, but I wasn't *that* much of a sap. You didn't take me, I took you.'

Heat cascaded through her at the seductive growl, which made her even more aware of the muscled thigh pressing against her hip.

'And thirdly, I screwed up my marriage all on my own, with no help from you.'

'I fail to see how you can say that, when I seduced you two weeks before your wedding day,' she argued, getting a little miffed at the lecturing tone. Where did he get off talking to her as if she were a two-year-old? 'I knew you were engaged and yet I set out to seduce you, deliberately, without a thought to your fiancée or anything else.'

'I believe I already covered that in point two,' he remarked, his eyes brightening with amusement—which only caused her temper to sizzle alongside the heat. 'You didn't force me to do a damn thing I didn't want to do. So you can quit getting your panties in a twist ten years after the fact.'

'Oh, pur-lease,' she hissed, struggling to keep the decibel level down in the face of his stubbornness. 'Just because you now want to look at that night through testosterone-tinted glasses it doesn't alter the fact that I put the moves on you, not the other way around. For goodness' sake, I had to practically throw myself at you before you'd even so much as kiss me.'

'So I was a slow starter. So what? I got the message eventually.'

'I know you did, that's not what I was trying to—'

His hands rode up to her waist, cutting off her protest in mid-sentence.

'Excuse me? Do you mind?' she yelped as those piercing blue eyes went from dark to dangerous and he leant forward to sniff at her hair.

'Not at all.'

She shifted back, but he only grinned, obviously enjoying her skittishness.

'You smell different,' he murmured. 'Did you change your shampoo?'

'In ten years?' she said, disarmed by the perceptive enquiry. 'Yes, of course.'

'I like it. More sophisticated but still sexy as sin.'

'Right.' She eased back, the pulse of arousal getting out of control. 'I really have to go.'

His hands dropped, but then he reached up to tuck a strand of hair behind her ear. 'No, you don't.' He patted the stool she had vacated. 'Stick around. One more drink. Let's talk. We never did get much of a chance to do that ten years ago.'

She should say no. Sitting next to him and sharing a companionable drink was a dangerous game to play while her erogenous zones were in meltdown. But when he shifted, his hand pressing into her waist to direct her to the stool next to him, and whispered: 'What's the matter, sugar? Scared you won't be able to resist seducing me again?' the tension snapped inside her and she laughed.

The statement should have sounded impossibly arrogant, but with that wicked light dancing in his eyes it sounded more like a challenge. And she'd never been able to resist one of those.

She gave him a deliberate once over, allowing her gaze to linger on the broad muscles of his chest and the sprinkle of chest hair revealed in the open neck of his shirt. 'I'm sure I can manage if I put my mind to it.'

He let out a rough chuckle. 'Touché.' He sat back on his stool. 'Take a seat. You know you want to.'

While she was sorely tempted to call him on the arrogant assumption, unfortunately she couldn't, quite. Because he was right. She did want to stay—and not just because of the potent arousal pulsing through every pore. She wanted to know why and how he'd changed so much—because the relaxed, charming, sexually confident hottie in front of her was nothing like the earnest and extremely uptight hottie she remembered.

'Okay, you've got me,' she said, conceding. 'One more club soda for the road.' She hopped back onto the stool beside him.

'Only a soda? It's Friday night? You didn't become a good girl when I wasn't looking, did you?'

'Hardly.' She snorted out another laugh at the wry comment. 'I've simply discovered that alcohol adds pounds where it's exceptionally hard to take them off again. And half an hour in the gym every morning is mind-numbingly boring enough.' And she had a feeling that keeping her wits about her in the next twenty minutes or so while they had their one drink for old times' sake was going to be fairly important.

His lips curved, shooting her blood pressure up a notch. *Make that very important.*

His gaze drifted down her figure, making her nipples tighten and her thigh muscles loosen. 'It sure appears to be time well spent.'

Make that completely imperative.

'I'll let my personal trainer know,' she quipped, fidgeting

with the straw of her dead soda—and ruthlessly stifling the wave of warmth. 'I'm sure she'll appreciate the compliment.'

'You do that,' he murmured before turning to signal the barman.

The sleeve of his shirt stretched across his biceps as he did so, drawing her gaze, and the wave of warmth crested. She tore her eyes away from the bulge of muscle flexing under the white linen and cleared her throat.

You can survive one more drink with the guy, surely.

She'd turned over a new leaf in the years since she'd jumped Carter Price at Hillbrook College and kick-started a chain of events that had changed both their lives irrevocably… But one drink was all she planned to risk.

If only she could have kept that resolve front and centre. And she probably would have, if he'd carried on flirting with her so openly—because she happened to be an expert at verbal foreplay. But it turned out the new Carter was a whole lot craftier than she'd given him credit for.

One drink turned into two and then three, until she stopped counting, as the man captivated her—not so much with those damn biceps, or the openly hungry looks, but with his knowledge and enthusiasm, when she steered the conversation to what she had thought would be the neutral topic of their working lives.

He talked with an infectious pride and dispassionate insight into the challenges he'd faced and overcome to drag the paper mill he'd inherited from his father when he was only seventeen into a thriving business. Then he'd listened with interest—and a surprising lack of criticism—to the string of careers she'd tried out before starting her web-design business last year.

They'd touched on a few personal topics—such as the hellish heat in Savannah in August, and her move from London to New York five years ago—but had neatly sidestepped anything too personal such as his marriage or his sister, or the apology that she'd originally come to deliver. Until, after two solid hours of non-stop conversation, Carter Price had managed to lull her into a sense of security.

Unfortunately, during their very grown-up, surprisingly comfortable conversation, she'd found herself becoming more and more aware of him on a purely physical level: the low appreciative rumble of his laughter that made the skin on her spine tingle; the flash of interest in his eyes that made her voice slip instinctively into the smoky purr of her youth; the intense expression when he was outlining the different funding options she might want to explore for her business, which reminded her of the expression he'd once worn when exploring her.

The hotel bar was emptying out, as New York's Friday night party people headed out to pastures new, and the sub-dued lighting, the intimate silences only made her more and more aware of the desire to make the conversation just a teensy weensy bit less comfortable. Now that he was an ur-bane, successful and well-travelled businessman instead of the sheltered boy he'd once been, what would be the harm in spicing things up a little?

After all, given the recent pressures of work, and the emotional stress of trying to repair the damage she'd done to the Awesome Foursome, she'd had a rather difficult summer so far. Flirting in particular had been off the agenda—especially flirting with someone as delicious as Carter Price.

'So, Carter, there is one thing I'd really love to know…' She stabbed her straw into the Cosmopolitan he'd insisted on ordering her after too many club sodas. 'For a man who's so dedicated to his business,' she continued, not quite able to resist a small purr when she took a sip of the Cosmo and his gaze dipped to her mouth, 'and has clearly spent a great deal of time and effort making it successful, I'd really love to know how you find enough spare time to date and dump so many different women.'

His brows winged up and then he chuckled—the easy sound triggering a new wave of tingles up her spine. 'Why, Gina, have you been checking up on me?'

She savoured another sip of the heady citrus-flavoured cocktail—not caring in the slightest that she'd been busted. 'I'll admit, I indulged in a quick Google this afternoon purely out of curiosity, you understand.'

'Oh, yeah,' he said, his voice lowering deliciously. 'I understand entirely.'

'And frankly I was quite staggered by the profligacy of your dating habits.'

'The profligacy, huh?' His lips curved, making her heart rate spike deliciously. 'I love when you use those longs words—they match that snooty English accent so well.'

'Flattery will get you nowhere. Answer the question.'

'There was a question in there?' he asked, the mock innocence making her grin back at him.

'You know very well there was—about your profligacy and your time-management skills,' she prompted. 'Which appear to be phenomenal if the evidence I found on the Internet is anything to go by. I did a little survey actually. And counted four different dates on your arm since you took Anjelique Montclair to the Georgia Governor's Ball on New Year's Eve.' She huffed to illustrate the point. 'I have major frock envy over that fabulous dress she had on, by the way. Very classy.' Not to mention a tiny bit of envy over how delicious Anjelique's date had looked in his tuxedo.

'She did look good, if I recall correctly,' he mused, still not answering the question, and not looking abashed in the slightest by her observation. Then again, she hadn't really expected him to.

'So?' she prompted again, actually more curious than she wanted to admit. 'Where *do* you find the time? Not to mention the stamina?'

He watched her, his gaze taking on a challenging glow, and the reckless thrill made her pulse leap.

Game on.

'The time and the stamina's easy to find, because while I'm socialising I'm usually working as well. Anjelique's father is a close friend of the governor's and I wanted an introduction to expedite a zoning request that the city council had been sitting on for months.' The smile he sent her was smug and completely unrepentant. 'In the South, mixing business with pleasure is the only way to get things done.'

'That sounds exhausting,' she said—and remarkably cynical. Had Anjelique realised he was dating her to expedite a zoning request?

'Not necessarily,' he murmured, his voice husky.

'How so?'

'Because I don't sleep with every woman I date.'

'Ah, I see.' She felt her cheeks heat. She hadn't expected him to be quite that blunt. Or for the admission to please her quite so much. But she quashed the burning desire to ask him directly if he'd slept with Anjelique. 'That's a relief.'

'It is?' he asked, lifting her hand from the bar to toy with her fingers. 'Why is that?'

The heat shot straight up her arm and joined the tingles migrating up her spine.

She tugged her fingers out of his. Damn, she'd walked right into that one. She certainly didn't want him thinking she was *that* interested in his love life. 'Because sleeping with someone to expedite a zoning request doesn't seem terribly romantic,' she remarked, struggling for flippant while her knickers were dampening with need.

'Uh-huh. When did you start thinking sex has anything to do with romance?'

When I slept with you.

She erased the foolish thought, and the silly spurt of vulnerability that came with it, and dipped her head to peer into her half-finished Cosmo.

Where had that come from? It wasn't even true—their night together had been hot and reckless and exhilarating, but ultimately wrong. Proving that even she had the capacity to confuse sex with romance. She pushed the drink away. Especially when she'd had too much to drink.

'I don't,' she replied, ignoring the blip in her heart rate at the intense watchfulness in his gaze. 'But maybe Anjelique does.'

'I wouldn't know,' he replied. 'Because I've never had sex with Anjelique.'

She tramped down on the idiotic surge of adrenaline. And decided she was definitely finished with her alcohol intake for the night.

But jolted, when he covered her hand, brushed his thumb across the knuckles. 'You, on the other hand...'

Her eyes met his and she felt a little dizzy—mesmerised by the cool blue of his irises.

'You wanna know the one thing I remember real clear from that night?' he murmured.

She shook her head, knowing she didn't want to know, especially not in that low seductive growl that was setting sparks off all over her sex-starved body.

'However wrong we were for doing it, it felt right while it lasted.'

Her pulse rate accelerated at the forceful tone. 'I don't think we should talk about that,' she whispered, her voice faltering along with her resistance. 'It's a really bad idea.'

He climbed off his stool, and pressed his hand to her

back—making the tingles hit meltdown as he rubbed the slinky silk over sensitised skin. He hooked her hair behind her ear and leaned in to whisper against her lobe. 'Bad ideas can lead to awesome sex.'

She shuddered, not caring any more that she was sitting in a public bar, or that she wanted to stretch against his palms like a contented cat.

'And it's not wrong any more,' he murmured, his breath hot and seductive against her ear.

She raised her head. 'Are you sure about that?' she said a little breathlessly, as it occurred to her just how far removed the Carter who stood before her now was from the innocent man she'd once seduced, if that cocksure look was anything to go by.

'I'm not dating right now—are you?' he said, deliberately misinterpreting the question.

'No, but.'

He pressed a thumb to her lips, silencing the feeble protest.

'Didn't you ever wonder what it would be like between us…without all the emotional garbage tripping us up?'

Emotional garbage.

She heard the words, and saw the harsh cynicism behind the hunger.

'Yes, I have,' she answered honestly, because there wasn't much point being coy when her desire had outstripped her caution a good half an hour ago.

Was she seriously considering this? And why couldn't she seem to consider anything else, such as running off screaming into the night, which had to be the smarter, safer, more sensible option?

He placed both his hands on her waist, and drew her off the stool, until she stood in his embrace, that spicy, musky scent intoxicating her. 'I have a whole hotel suite upstairs, if you want to find out the answer.'

'That would be insane,' she whispered. 'You're insane.' Why did he have to look so gorgeous and why couldn't she muster even a single iota of the guilt she should be feeling?

'And this would be relevant because…?' The quick feral grin sealed her fate.

Because suddenly she knew why she'd never been able to stop running from what had happened that night. It wasn't because of the mistakes they'd made, the bad things they'd done. She'd been punished a thousand times over for those and she'd changed enough to know she would never be that reckless, thoughtless girl again.

But she hadn't forgotten the glorious way he had made her feel either. He was the one that had got away. And she'd never been able to forget him. Not entirely.

And now he was back. And available. And this time, whatever they did together would just be about the sex. She could have him, enjoy him, get over the physical hunger that had burned inside her for years, and then let him and all the memories go, and walk away for good with no more nagging regrets.

Because if there was one thing she had learned in the years since that night—it was how to separate her sexual needs from her emotional ones.

'I guess it isn't relevant,' she murmured. 'Not any more.'

There was no Missy, no marriage in a fortnight, nothing to feel guilty about any more. And they both appeared to be two very different people now.

For whatever reason, Carter, the sensitive, conflicted, sex-deprived virgin had been replaced by Carter the cynical, commanding and sexually confident player. And, thanks to the devastation she'd had to face and overcome after their one night together—not to mention several thousand dollars' worth of therapy in the years since—she was no longer the screwed-up little flirt who thought having sex with any man who took her fancy could replace the love her father had denied her.

His thumbs pressed into the hollow of her hips as he brought his mouth close to hers. 'It was good then, but it'll be better now—because this time, we'll both know what the hell we're doing.'

She smiled, disarmed by the self-deprecating comment—even though she was sure it was disingenuous. 'Be careful, Carter,' she teased, the urge to flirt overwhelming her caution. 'You don't want to oversell yourself, because as I recall you were a remarkably precocious virgin....'

His answering chuckle arrowed through her. 'There's no doubting you were a powerful inspiration to me back then. But I've learned a few things since—about stamina and focus and technique.' He gave her bottom lip a playful nip, sending a delicious shiver down to her core. 'Which makes me confident I can do a lot better now.'

She let out a shaky breath, her arousal already long past the point of no return. 'Then I suppose the least I can do is let you prove it.'

'Amen to that.' He groaned, then clasped her cheeks in rough palms.

His mouth covered hers, his lips as hot and hungry as she remembered them. But this time he took control of the kiss. There was no tender, tentative, achingly sweet exploration, no moans of staggered arousal, just hot, insistent strokes as his tongue took possession of her mouth, and demanded her response.

She could vaguely hear the sounds of the bar around them—but the exhibitionist in her, that had never really gone away, had no problem wrapping her arms around Carter's waist, and letting her tongue duel with his, refusing to relinquish control and making her own demands in return.

Lust flowed on a heady wave down to her centre as he tried to force her surrender and she refused to submit.

'Hey, guys, you wanna get a room? We've got a whole hotel at your disposal here.'

They broke apart at the pained words from the bartender.

'Sure,' Carter replied as he threw several bills on the bar. 'You ready?' he asked as he grasped her hand.

She nodded. *As ready as I'll ever be.*

'Have a good evening, folks,' the bartender called after them, stuffing what Gina suspected was a hefty tip into his pocket.

She blew the guy a cheeky kiss, letting impulse take over as Carter led her out of the bar.

What harm could one night do, now? Carter Price was here and available—and hotter than ever. And they'd both changed so much from who they were then. But one thing had never changed. How easily he could send her senses reeling—until desire flowed through her veins like a heady drug. And if the only thing standing between her and complete closure was that lingering hunger—didn't she owe it to herself to give in to temptation one last time? And get a definitive answer to that question? Now she had the chance?

She'd waited ten years, for goodness' sake. Surely that was long enough?

She might have turned over a new leaf, but she wasn't a nun!

CHAPTER FIVE

ARE YOU OUT of your freaking mind?

Carter clasped Gina's hand, headed across the lobby towards the elevators and felt as if he were charging back in time.

Ten years. Ten long, life-altering years since that one dumb act of self-destruction. And he hadn't learned a damn thing, because all he could think about, all he could focus on, was the urge to get into Gina Carrington's panties all over again.

The hunger that had gripped him as soon as he'd seen her sweeping through the hotel lobby—convinced she had to be some kind of weird erotic apparition brought on by jet lag and frustration—had been gnawing at his gut all night. He'd managed to dial down the intensity for two solid hours, talking about his business to keep his mind out of his pants—but the insistent ache had snapped and snarled throughout like an angry dog.

Every time she swung her head and that up-do threatened to tumble down. Every time she puckered up round her straw and he felt the tug in his groin. Every time her voice lowered to make a point and the sultry purr prickled over his skin like a cat testing its claws.

As the night had drawn on he'd gotten fixated on the ache, and accepted the fact there was no way in hell he was going to be able to walk away tonight.

The elevator took an eternity to creep up to the fifteenth floor crowded with tourists and businessmen and the woman standing beside him, whose fingers remained cool and firm in his. His grip tightened as they finally escaped the crush and he strode down the corridor towards his suite.

He heard a muffled curse behind him. 'Carter, slow down, before I break an ankle.'

He stopped as she stumbled on those killer heels. The urge to pick her up and throw her over his shoulder was so strong—he went with it. No way was he risking a broken ankle putting this booty call in jeopardy.

'Carter, what are you doing?' she yelped as he dipped, scooped her up and swung round, her legs flailing as her lush butt pressed into the side of his head. 'Put me down, for goodness' sake.'

'Not a chance.'

'I can walk!' The protest came out in breathless pants as her stomach rode his shoulder blade.

'Not fast enough for my liking.'

'This is so undignified,' she announced, but the husky laugh spurred him on, reminding him of the bad girl she'd been. Good to know that girl was still there beneath all the poise and professionalism—and the dumb apology.

He balanced her on his shoulder as he slipped his keycard into the slot on the door of his suite—amazed his fingers were steady enough to get the thing to work the first time.

Kicking the door open, he marched into the room and dropped her on her feet. The night-time view of the Hudson River displayed by the suite's glass walls had taken his breath away the first time he'd stayed at The Standard. It barely even registered now as all his attention zeroed in on the woman framed by the panoramic cityscape. An errant curl cupped one flushed cheek while her uneven breathing tightened the silk across that amazing rack. Right now, he could have been staying in a Motel 6 and he would have felt like a king.

He grabbed her wrist, dragged her to him. 'Come here.'

'I am here,' she announced, the haughty tone calling to his inner caveman.

He plucked the pins out of her hair, let the mass of soft brown hair cascade into his hands. 'I want it down.'

She laughed, shaking her head until the riot of curls bounced over her shoulders. 'Do you now,' she murmured, draping her arms round his neck and twisting a finger in the hair at his nape.

'Yeah.' He held her head, nipped at her bottom lip, then feasted on that soft mouth, his tongue thrusting deep—his hunger intensifying when she thrust back.

He pulled away, his breathing harsh at the sight of her reddened lips, the dark dilated pupils.

'When did you become such a Neanderthal?' she asked, her tongue licking the spot where he'd nipped her.

'When I had to talk business for two hours to stop myself jumping you on a barstool.'

'How intriguing. I had no idea you were thinking about sex while discussing how to grow business opportunities in a hostile investment environment.' She purred the words like a phone-sex operator. 'You sounded very informative.'

'It's called multitasking.' He reached up to find the zip on her dress, yanked it down with a sibilant hum. 'The whole time I was imagining you naked.'

She gave a husky laugh as the bodice drooped to reveal the scarlet lace of her bra.

'Well, maybe it's time you stopped imagining.'

She stood back to wiggle out of the silky shift. It pooled around her feet as his gaze devoured the sight of firm, full breasts, the delicious curve of waist and hip and those mile-long legs, her nakedness barely covered by the skimpy swatches of lace.

Lust seared through his system as the last of the blood left his brain.

'Hell, you're like a Victoria's Secret catalogue come to life.'

'A man who reads lingerie catalogues.' She laughed. 'You may be my perfect date.'

He dragged her close, let his palms skim over lush flesh and struggled not to hold her too tightly. He wanted to be inside her, right this second. But more than that, he wanted to make this good, better even than their first time. He wanted to savour her, to seduce her, to make her beg, the way she'd once made him beg.

'I hate to ruin my perfect-date status. But not a lot of reading went on. That catalogue's the equivalent of *Playboy* when you're a twelve-year-old boy,' he whispered against her neck and felt the shudder of response. 'But Victoria and her secrets are dead to me now I have the real thing in my hands.' He unhooked the lacy bra, threw it away, and cupped the heaving flesh in rough palms. She let out a slow moan as he rolled her nipples between his fingers and watched them stiffen.

He fastened his mouth on one engorged tip, made it swell and elongate beneath his tongue, revelling in the choked whimpers of her surrender.

Her fingers fisted in his hair and she jerked his head back. 'I want you naked too, Carter.'

He grinned at the eagerness, all traces of subtlety, of subterfuge, of teasing gone. But he didn't plan to make it that easy—not for him, and certainly not for her—despite the fact that the pounding in his pants was now painful. 'Not yet,' he said. 'Take the panties off.'

A tiny crease crossed her brow and her chin firmed. 'I don't take orders,' she announced, the act of defiance somewhat undermined by the heaving breasts and the erect nipples, glistening from his attention.

'Take them off, or I rip them off.' He let his gaze drift to the delicate red lace. 'Your call, but they look pricey.'

Her eyes narrowed, but then she laughed. 'You want them off, *you* take them off. Knickers aren't that easy to rip...' she began.

He twisted the delicate lace in his fist and tore. 'You were saying?' he murmured as he flung away the tattered remains of her pricey underwear.

Her eyes went round, but he caught the flash of shocked arousal lurking in the deep green depths.

That's right, sugar. I'm the one on top now.

'Those were worth fifty dollars,' she gasped in a breathy whisper that sounded more surprised than outraged.

'Not any more, they're not.' He curled a hand round her waist, yanked her back.

Her palms flattened on the front of his shirt, and he saw the spark of excitement, a split second before she gripped his collar—and ripped.

'Two can play at that game, big boy,' she purred as the sound of tearing cotton, buttons popping, filled the air.

But when she let go of the torn fabric to touch his bare skin, he grasped both her wrists, swung her round, banded his arms around her midriff, and held her captive. 'But only one of us can win.'

'What the...?' She struggled as he brought her flush against him and her naked buttocks nestled against the stiff ridge in his pants.

'No touching,' he commanded, nipping her ear lobe. 'Until I say so, sugar. I'm in charge this time.'

And he didn't intend to relinquish control. Until they'd both been burned to a crisp.

* * *

What the heck?

Gina squirmed against the immobilising forearm, but her movements only increased the friction, making her more aware of his big body surrounding her—and what felt like a two-by-four nestled against her bottom. She stilled, sure she could feel the massive erection barely contained by his trousers swelling even more. And wondered how the hell she'd got into this position.

Trapped, vulnerable, overpowered and impossibly aroused.

'Look at yourself.' The low command whispered against her ear, the shiver of awareness skittering down her spine. Heat flushed through her as she lifted her head and saw the shocking reflection in the glass wall that looked out across the dark expanse of the Hudson River.

Moonlight illuminated her naked body—which glowed an unearthly white but for the stiff rosy nipples and the neatly trimmed raven curls at the apex of her thighs. Her pale shape contrasted sharply with the tall dark figure holding her captive—still fully clothed but for the glimpse of chest she'd exposed.

She gasped, shocked not just by the wanton view, but the fierce surge of desire. 'For goodness' sake, Carter, draw the blinds or something.' She fought his embrace. 'The whole of Manhattan can see us.'

She might be an exhibitionist, but she didn't want to get arrested.

'Settle down.' He chuckled, the sound thick with arrogance and amusement. 'The glass is treated. No one can see you but me.'

She stopped wriggling, far too aware of his forearm flexing under her breasts, the chest hairs prickling against her back and the rod of steel that pressed into her buttocks.

'And I intend to enjoy every single inch,' he murmured as

he lifted her limp arm and placed it around his neck, making her breasts thrust forward.

She swallowed, her throat parched as her eyes watched herself in the glass—mesmerised by the sensual image, and the harsh demand in his gaze as his eyes met hers. Suddenly this wasn't a game any more.

Shock and excitement burned away on a surge of lust so fierce, so all-consuming, she felt woozy.

He drew his thumb down the inside of her arm, making her whole body quiver as sensation arrowed to her centre. His forearm tightened around her waist, holding her upright for the delicate torment, as seeking fingers circled her breast, exploring in maddeningly slow circles.

She moaned, stretching into the teasing caress. 'You need to hurry up,' she demanded. 'Before I explode.'

He plucked at her nipple. The pinch was painless, but hard enough to send darts of sensation spiralling to her yearning sex. And make her cry out.

'Patience, grasshopper,' he whispered. 'Or you will be punished.'

A hoarse laugh popped out of her mouth—her mind dazed by the slow torture, and the unbearably erotic threat.

'Shh.' His lips nuzzled the soft skin of her neck. 'We've hardly even started.'

'Oh, God!' She jolted against the restraining forearm as his torturous touch left her breasts and trailed down. His fingertips caressed, stroked, seduced, but so slowly, she knew she'd probably die of anticipation before they got where she needed them to be.

'Please…' she sobbed as her belly shivered, each tormenting caress sending a new pulse of heat to her core.

'Please what, sugar?' he mocked, the thick molasses of his accent scraping at the last of her resistance. 'Please stop?'

'Don't you dare!' she demanded, her voice hoarse with

desperation as his fingers teased the curls that hid her sex, but stopped short of their goal.

Her eyelids fluttered open. She stared at their reflection, registering the dark hand so close to heaven and yet so far—and the feral arousal on his face.

Who was this guy?

'Tell me what you want,' he said, his voice strained but firm, 'and you just might get it. If you ask me real nice.'

'Touch me.'

'That's not nearly nice enough,' he mocked, still teasing her with his circling fingers.

'Touch me, please.'

She writhed as his fingers delved into the slick folds. At last. He swept across her swollen clitoris and the coil of desire tightened unbearably.

'That's not...' She protested, frustration rising and intensifying the need as he retreated again. Why wasn't he touching her *there*?

'That's not what?' She heard it then, the smug hint of amusement. 'Maybe you need to beg?' he teased.

'Oh for...' She bit off a curse, held back from that glorious oblivion by an invisible thread—that only he could cut. 'Will you just touch my...'

She cried out, the tirade interrupted as blunt fingers stroked over the burning nub.

'Touch you there, huh?'

She writhed, bucked, giving him his answer as he caressed the perfect spot—and she hurtled towards oblivion under the exquisite torture.

'Come for me, Gina.'

The wave crested, and broke in a shattering shower of bright white sensation, as if brought forth by his command. Then flowed over her in one glorious surge after the other as he stroked at the heart of her—in the perfect place, at the perfect pace—beckoning her up and over again.

His hand withdrew and she sagged against him, hollowed out, exhausted, by the staggering intensity of her orgasm, and the fight to maintain some control over her own body—and his effect on it.

A fight she was pretty sure she'd just lost. Completely.

Rousing herself, she swung round as his forearm loosened. And grabbed hold of his shirt, tearing the remains of it off his shoulders, determined to regain some of the lost ground.

She threw the tattered cotton over her shoulder. 'Oh, dear, look what I did to your shirt,' she mocked. 'I guess I won't charge you for the panties.'

'Damn straight you won't,' he replied, not looking cowed in the least. 'That shirt cost me over two hundred dollars. So I figure you owe me.'

She allowed herself a moment to absorb the breath-taking display of tanned skin and bulging muscles—before making quick work of his belt buckle. And drawing down the zip to reveal the huge bulge straining against his boxers. Her eyes met his and she cupped the firm package. 'Then it must be payback time.'

So what if he could seduce her into a coma? Didn't mean she couldn't seduce him right back.

'Yeah, I guess it is,' he said, the challenge in his cobalt eyes unmistakeable. 'Give it your best shot, sugar.' The low chuckle was as smug as ever as he kicked off the rest of his clothes, and stood before her gloriously naked.

She took a few extra moments to get her breath back.

Goodness.

His body had matured, the once lean, coltish physique gaining muscle bulk in all the right places—making his shoulders broader, the V of his hipbones more defined, his triceps and biceps a lot more prominent and the ridged six-pack quite simply awe-inspiring.

Someone had been working out. A lot.

She touched a nail to the new swirls of chest hair that now surrounded his flat brown nipples and then traced the happy trail down to the thicket where his erection jutted out.

Oh, my word.

Was it her imagination, or had that got even more magnificent too?

'Carter, you're beautiful,' she said, running her tongue over her lips as she dropped to her knees. She smiled up at him, adrenaline surging through her veins like a heady drug as she circled his girth, felt it twitch against her palm—and saw the fierce flash of need cross his face. 'Brace yourself, sugar,' she purred, mimicking his lazy, moonlit and magnolia tones. And then swept her tongue from the root to the tip and heard him moan.

Holy hell!

Carter ran his fingers into her hair, caressing her scalp, as his knees turned to Jell-O and the fire in his gut became an inferno.

Stay upright, damn it.

He dragged his gaze away from the sight of those soft, full lips surrounding him, and struggled to take the exquisite punishment like a man. But then he saw their reflection—and the decadent image of Gina on her knees, pleasuring him with her mouth, nearly had him collapsing in a heap.

She should have looked submissive as she knelt before him, but instead she looked bold and defiant, like an Amazon goddess, feeding into every schoolboy sex fantasy he'd ever had about her. And he'd had a heck of a lot of those over the years.

Hellfire and damnation.

That was where he was headed and he didn't care.

He tried to force his mind to engage in banalities to stem the tidal wave of his orgasm and keep from disgracing himself. Against shuttered lids, he conjured a picture of the Sunday service at Riverbend Church; the board of directors of the Mill discussing the end of year's report…but every single image crashed and burned to be replaced by the glorious sight he'd glimpsed in the dark glass as her tongue licked and swirled, her mouth suckled. An image he feared would now be lasered into his brain for ever more.

He groaned, the heat curling and twisting and then yanking hard in his groin as her hot, beautiful mouth feasted on the last few ounces of his self-control.

His fingers tightened in the mass of curls as he dragged himself away from her. 'Enough.' Hooking his hands under her arms, he hoisted her off her knees.

Her cheeks pinkened as those bright green eyes flickered with challenge. 'Why did you stop me? I was enjoying myself.' The pouting lips made the heat pulse and throb harder.

He grabbed her wrist as she reached for him. 'Uh-uh. I said enough.'

She cocked one perfectly plucked eyebrow. 'Why? From all that moaning you were doing, I got the definite impression you were enjoying it too.'

He grinned. Damned if she wasn't as wild and reckless and wanton as she'd ever been beneath that layer of chic sophistication—and didn't that make her perfect for him? In the only way that mattered now.

'I didn't say I wasn't enjoying it,' he said, his gaze steady and his voice firm, or as firm as it could be while he was clinging onto control by his fingertips. 'I just don't want to come that way. Not this time.'

'Spoilsport.'

He laughed, but tightened his hold on her wrist and brought her fingers to his lips. 'I want to be inside you, Gina. I want to watch you climax with me—you're even more gorgeous when you come.'

He kissed her knuckles and a wary look crossed her face, giving him another disarming glimpse of the girl he remembered, who had been so bold sexually, and yet so unsure at the slightest sign of tenderness.

She draped her arms over his shoulders, threaded her fingers into his hair to drag him close, the siren returning full force—and he dismissed the sentimental thought. After all, there was nothing tender about tonight, and what he planned to do to her.

'Well, all you had to do was say so, Rhett,' she purred.

Brushing the riotous hair back from her face, he kissed her long and hard, thrusting his tongue into her mouth and forcing her to submit this time.

Cupping her generous butt in his hands, he boosted her into his arms, dumped her onto the room's kingsize bed. 'Consider yourself told.'

Gina laughed, the desire coursing through her veins and the electric connection that snapped to life between them making her feel free and unencumbered for the first time in a long time. It felt so good to relinquish control, to be able to take what she wanted without fearing the consequences.

Carter wouldn't judge her, because he knew who and what she really was. When it came to sex—hot, hard, explosive sex—they had always been kindred spirits.

He bracketed her hips and pressed his lips to her pulse point, drawing her knees up and positioning himself above her—but as she took in a deep lungful of that tangy masculine scent the press of his erection registered. The intoxicating desire ripped away to be replaced by a jolt of panic. Slapping her hands against his shoulders, she forced him back.

'Wait, Carter. You have to use protection.'

He lifted his head, his eyes a little unfocused, a little dazed.

'Please tell me you have something with you, because I don't,' she continued, the panic making her voice hitch. She should have said something sooner, much sooner. Why hadn't she?

'Yeah, sure. Sorry.' He raked a hand through his hair. 'Wait right there.' He jumped off the bed and padded to the suite's bathroom, his naked butt gilded by the moonlight.

She stared at the ceiling, the sudden realisation of what they'd almost done—a second time—dousing the flames.

He reappeared in the doorway of the bathroom. Her pulse hammered at the imposing sight silhouetted in the doorway. But as he returned to her she was hurled back to a time in her life that had left her hollow and empty and devastated. A time she had forced herself never to acknowledge. She sat up, threw her legs over the bed.

'I have to go,' she said, struggling to keep her voice steady as the brutal memory hovered too close, threatening to engulf her.

'Why?' He caught her wrist, preventing her from moving as he sat beside her. 'I found what we needed.'

He threw a handful of foil packets on the bedside table.

'That's great. But we don't need them now. This was a mistake.'

She braced herself, ready for him to object, to call her names—it wouldn't be the first time she'd been branded a tease or worse. And given how his arousal didn't seem to have abated one bit he would probably have a point. But right now she was too busy protecting herself to worry about any injuries she might have caused him.

But to her surprise, instead of getting angry or annoyed, he lifted a palm and cupped her cheek. 'Why is it a mistake all of a sudden?'

She shook her head to dislodge the possessive touch—this

was fine when it was just sex, but she didn't want to risk getting her emotions involved. 'No reason.'

She tried to rise again, but he simply held her waist, making it impossible for her to move without getting into a wrestling match—something she definitely didn't intend to do, because, while her head was telling her clearly making love with Carter Price would be a very bad idea now, she couldn't rely on her body to play ball.

'There is a reason,' he replied in that CEO tone he'd been using all evening. She'd found it a major turn on during foreplay; she was finding it somewhat less so now. 'And you need to tell me what it is.'

'No, actually, I don't. I'm under no obligation to—'

'Think again, Gina,' he interrupted. 'Because you're not going anywhere until you do.'

She sucked in a breath, trying to remain patient and sensible, and stave off a hissy fit.

'I'm sorry,' she said, her voice tight with the effort to sound conciliatory. 'I realise you're still extremely aroused…' She flicked her gaze to his crotch and heat crept up her neck at the sight of the magnificent erection. 'And that's obviously partly my fault…'

'*Partly?*' he interrupted, giving an incredulous laugh.

She looked away as the heat hit her cheeks. For Pete's sake, was she actually blushing? She never blushed.

'Okay, fine, *mostly* my fault,' she added, in the interests of complete disclosure. Because she'd never been coy either. 'But that doesn't mean I have to sleep with you if I don't want to.'

He cursed. 'Give me some credit here. I'm not a kid, any more. I do have some control. And I would never expect any woman to sleep with me if she didn't want to—no matter how aroused she's gotten me. I may not be the gentleman my mama raised me to be, but I'm not that much of jerk.'

'Okay, good,' she said, relief flowing through her. He

sounded more affronted than angry. Not that she cared if he was angry, she told herself staunchly; she'd never had a problem dealing with male tantrums. But right now she felt too exposed to relish dealing with one from him. 'Then I'd like to leave.'

She waited, but, instead of releasing her, he began to stroke his thumbs back and forth over the skin beneath her ribs, in a light caress that sent darts of sensation places she really didn't want them.

'Carter, let go of my waist,' she said, breathlessly.

'Not until I get an explanation. What made you change your mind?'

She couldn't tell him that. Would never tell him that. Because it would mean revealing something she had decided a long time ago he had never really been a part of. The pregnancy had been an accident, a biological blip, that had ended almost as soon as it had begun—and forced her to re-evaluate who she was and what she was. But she'd come out the other side. She hadn't thought about it in years. And if she could get away from him, she wouldn't have to think about it now.

She sent him what she hoped was a bored look. 'It doesn't seem spontaneous any more. And I'm really not that turned on now.'

'You're really not, huh?' His mouth curled on one side and she saw the sceptical gleam in his eye. 'Why are you lying?'

'I'm not.'

She'd always been an exceptionally convincing liar—after all, she'd had a lot of practice in her teens—but unfortunately as she said the words her lungs seized as if all the oxygen had been sucked out of them at once—and the denial came out on an unconvincing hum.

'How about we test that theory?' His voice deepened as his hands stroked down her naked thighs and gripped her knees.

'If you were any kind of a gentleman, you'd take my word

for it,' she murmured, pushing the words out past the constriction in her throat as he parted her legs. A move she appeared powerless to resist as her centre throbbed in anticipation.

'That's true enough.' His thumbs blazed a trail of goosebumps, caressing the sensitive skin of her inner thigh as his hands headed back towards heaven. 'And if you were any kind of a lady, you wouldn't lie about it.'

'I'm not lying.' Those damn thumbs angled across the juncture of her legs, and caressed—back and forth, back and forth—making the protest compete with the telltale hitch in her breathing.

Kneeling in front of her, he pushed her thighs wider and let his thumbs touch the slick swollen folds. She braced her hands on the bed, let her head fall back and struggled to breathe as all thought, all feeling, all memory burned away in a blaze of lust.

'There now. You seem to like that well enough, sugar.'

She could hear the arrogance and the amusement and she would have objected, but all she cared about now was concentrating on the heat, and forgetting the rest. The orgasm fluttered towards her on soaring wings as he used his thumbs to hold her open and then licked at the heart of her.

She sobbed, the sound echoing back at her off the room's hard, designer surfaces. Then he fastened his lips on her swollen clitoris and sucked. She screamed. Soaring straight into the cosmos.

The orgasm slammed into her, radiating out through her belly, her breasts, her fingers and toes. She collapsed back on the bed as he stood above her. He grabbed the foil packet, ripped it with his teeth, rolled on the condom, then sat on the bed and hauled her up, to straddle his lap.

She held onto his shoulders as his hands cupped her buttocks and positioned her over the huge erection.

'I want to be inside you, Gina.' The naked need in his eyes

matched the strain in his voice, the tendons standing out on his neck, and sweat slicking his brow. But still he held her poised above him, and made no move to take her. 'Don't make us wait any longer.'

She impaled herself in one smooth stroke—the staggering fullness making her head snap back, her fingers clutch at his shoulders. And then she began to move. Rising up, sinking back, the intimate stroking touching that place deep inside that only he had ever reached.

'That feels so damn good,' he coaxed, urging her on, guiding her movements, the wild ride racing them both towards oblivion.

She cried out, her nails digging into muscle, her breathing ragged, the exquisite pleasure becoming too close to pain as she hurtled over—with him this time.

Gina let the blissful fatigue of afterglow wash over her as she collapsed on top of his big body.

Carter Price hadn't been boasting. He'd certainly perfected his technique since their first merry meeting, not to mention his stamina.

'Damn, woman. That was something else,' he murmured as he swept the curtain of her hair away from his face, and kissed her.

'Hmm,' she hummed in agreement, rolling off him.

She let out a weary laugh at his heartfelt moan as she crawled up the bed, her arms and legs more than a little shaky.

'Hey, come back here,' he declared, as he hauled himself up. 'Where are you going?'

'Nowhere at the moment,' she replied as she flopped back onto the pillows, her whole body pleasantly numb. 'You've rendered me senseless.'

'Then we're even.'

She lay back on the stack of plump pillows, gazed out of

the glass wall, and tracked the tiny lights of the tourist boats plying their trade across the bay. How foolish to think that this had ever been about anything other than sex.

Carter joined her, dragging the quilt folded over the foot of the bed up to cover them, then wrapped an arm around her shoulders to draw her to his side.

She would have objected to the possessive gesture. She generally didn't snuggle after sex. But she let it pass for now, because she wasn't entirely sure she was capable of coordinated movement. And he smelt delicious.

She rested her head on his shoulder as his arm tightened. And took in a lungful of that unique scent. Soap and pheromones and man, now layered with the tangy aroma of sex. She squeezed her thighs together, a little disturbed by the renewed pulse of arousal.

No way. She couldn't have another orgasm tonight. Or she'd pass out. Plus she needed to consider leaving soon.

His fingers delved into her hair, lifting and separating the strands and making her scalp tingle. 'So now we've got proof,' he murmured, the words low and intimate in the dark room.

'Proof of what?' she asked, around a huge yawn.

'Proof our first time was no fluke.'

She stiffened, not liking where this might be leading. Or the confidential tone of his voice. 'It wasn't my first time, remember,' she said. 'It was yours.'

His hand stilled on the back of her head. 'Why are you so hung up about that?'

She tapped her fingers on his chest. 'Hung up about what?'

'You know what. That you were my first.'

'That's ridiculous, of course I'm not,' she said, but could hear that telltale hitch in her breathing. Damn, why couldn't she lie around Carter with any conviction? It was as if he had injected her with truth serum.

He remained silent for a while, making her wonder if

maybe she'd got away with it, but then he said, 'It wasn't that big a deal back then, and it sure isn't any kind of deal now.'

She levered herself up, stared down into his handsome face. 'Then why were you getting all sentimental about "our first time" a minute ago?' She did air quotes.

His lips quirked, the sensual smile making her heart flip over in her chest. Damn it, why did he have to be so ludicrously sexy?

'You mistake me, Gina.' He bunched her hair at the back of her neck and gave it a tug, forcing her head back and making her breasts more accessible. He covered one with his palm. 'That wasn't sentiment.' His gaze drifted to her breast as he toyed with the nipple. 'That was purely an observation about our sexual compatibility.'

'I see…' The tension coiled in her abdomen as he rose up on his elbow, forcing her back into the pillows. She gasped as he captured the beaded nipple with his lips and drew it into his mouth. The hot flow of lust and endorphins charged into her sex, making her arch off the bed and the still tender spot between her thighs throb painfully. 'Carter, stop,' she hissed, her hands fisting on the bed sheets. 'I really can't do it again so soon…'

And how on earth could he?

'Sure you can,' he countered, before getting back to the business of proving her wrong.

CHAPTER SIX

GINA WINCED AT the blast of light on her retinas, before awareness of the big body wrapped around hers yanked her the rest of the way out of dreamland. Slow, steady breathing stirred the hair on the back of her head, a heavy forearm lay across her midriff, and something indisputably long and solid nestled against her backside.

Good grief, I'm spooning with Carter Price—and he's hard as a rock. Again!

The memory of the torrid hours they'd spent before dawn came tumbling back. The man had the stamina and fortitude of a prize stallion—and he'd learned a great deal, in the years since she'd popped his cherry. She dismissed the foolish punch of her pulse at the realisation that while she might have been Carter's first, she certainly hadn't been his last.

No wonder she felt limp and sated—she edged across the mattress, testing the tender spot between her thighs—and frankly rather sore.

The heavy forearm tightened as a large hand cupped her breast and gave it a friendly squeeze. 'Morning, sugar.'

The husky murmur, heavy with sleep, had her shifting round to glance over her shoulder.

'You're awake?' With his eyes closed, his wavy hair delightfully rumpled, what looked like a two-day shadow on his jaw and his mobile mouth sporting the hint of a smile, it was hard to tell.

One eyelid lifted, the cobalt-blue gleaming in the light from the bay. His lips twisted into the full megawatt smile. 'Can't you tell?' His erection nudged her bottom.

She laughed, a little nervously. 'Forget it, Rhett. After the night we had, I'm not going to be operational for at least a week.'

The warm palm strayed from her breast to curl over her hip and stroke. 'You sure about that?'

She wasn't, not in the slightest, if the heat surging through her was anything to go by, but she didn't plan to negotiate. Because where Carter was concerned, her will power came a very poor second to her libido. And unfortunately he knew it, from the wicked grin as the stroking hand migrated to her backside.

Swiping his hand away, she flung the quilt back and bolted off the bed. 'I have to get going.' She checked the clock on his bedside table. 'I'm meeting the Awesomes at a bridal boutique in Brooklyn at eleven for a bridesmaid's fitting and I can't be late.'

'Now who's the spoilsport?' He propped himself on the pillows.

She scooped her now hopelessly wrinkled dress off the floor and held it over her nakedness, a little too aware of his patient watchful gaze as she hunted up the rest of her clothing.

'Do you mind if I use your shower?' she asked, ignoring the sizzle in her breasts as he tucked a folded arm behind his head, apparently settling in to enjoy the show.

'Sure. You want company?'

'Better not,' she said quickly as the sizzle went into overdrive and she grabbed her bra from its resting place hooked onto the corner of the room's huge plasma TV. 'I can't imagine sharing a shower with you will be particularly time efficient.' She spotted the remains of her Indian lace knickers and picked them off the satellite console. Heat flushed through her at the memory of Carter ripping them off her the night before.

'Damn it.'

How on earth was she going to explain a complete absence of underwear to her pals in the changing room? It was already nine-fifty. She didn't have time to get all the way back to her apartment in Red Hook. Maybe she could stop off at a department store on the way to the Manhattan Bridge Overpass District, where Amber's boutique was situated? Or have a quiet word with Reese's friend when she arrived? Did bridal boutiques sell emergency underwear?

'Will my sister be there?'

She stared at Carter, momentarily confused by the question until he added, 'Could you get her to give me a call? We need to set up a meet while I'm in town.'

And then the stupidity of what she'd done hit her right between the eyes—like a cold hard slap, knocking the breath out of her lungs and making the back of her neck feel as if someone had yanked out all the small hairs.

The remains of her knickers dropped from her numbed fingers.

After six months of celibacy—and confining herself to the automative delights of Justin, her trusty vibrator—she'd come tumbling off the wagon with the one man guaranteed to screw up the friendship she'd spent most of the summer trying to repair.

Not that she hadn't considered this last night. Fleetingly, and through a haze of hormones…. But now, suddenly, it didn't feel nearly so defensible. Of course it wasn't any of Marnie's business who her brother slept with, especially now that Carter was a free man and no longer bound in matrimony to Marnie's best friend—and she very much doubted that even if Marnie knew about what they'd spent the night doing together she would make a fuss. She was far too mature and pragmatic and, well, polite for that.

But sleeping with Marnie's big brother again suddenly felt hopelessly tacky and immature.

It wasn't exactly a great way to restore Marnie's trust in her as a person and as a friend…. Nor would it do much for Marnie's already rocky relationship with her brother. Which Gina knew had been set on its current course as a result of their first indiscretion ten years ago.

'What's the matter? Is it the panties?' Carter asked, then reached for the hotel phone. 'Don't sweat it. I'll order you a new pair.'

'No, don't, it's not that, it's…' She blinked at the tattered lace now resting on her big toe. Her stomach began to feel tight and achy, the way it always had in the past when she'd gone too far. She put her hand up, to stop him dialling the concierge. 'Marnie *will* be there, at the boutique.'

'Yeah, I know.' He didn't look remotely surprised or concerned as he placed the handset back in its cradle. 'You said the Awesomes. That's what you guys used to call yourselves, right? You and Marnie and Reese and the mousy geek girl.'

'Cassie's not a geek, she's just brilliant, and, considering she's about to marry Sam "Tuck" Tucker, the football player, I'd say mousy is the new hot.'

And they'd called themselves the Awesome Foursome, because their friendship had been Awesome. Awesome for her at least. Until that year in college, she'd never had any close female friendships—her mother had died when she was so young she didn't remember her and she'd always seen the other girls at school as competition. But during her year at Hillbrook she'd come to realise how important female friendships could be. And then she'd gone and torpedoed it.

But she wanted it to be Awesome again. Truly awesome.

And that meant regaining Marnie's trust. But how could she do that, if Marnie found out about her and Carter?

'The NFL quarterback?' Carter gave a low whistle, sounding impressed. 'Still waters, huh?'

'Yes, precisely,' she muttered, gathering her clothes to her breasts again, when Carter's gaze dipped noticeably.

'Damn, are you sure you've got to run off? How about I text Marnie, tell her you're going to be late?'

'No!' she yelped, she actually yelped—as all the blood headed out of her brain and exploded into her heart. 'You can't do that.'

The crease on his brow became a furrow. 'Why not? I've gotta arrange to meet her some time this week anyhow.' The sexy smile returned as he reached for the hem of her dress, gave it a playful tug. 'And it'd give me time to order you up some new panties. And help you wash your hair.'

She yanked the dress out of his fingers. Was he completely insane? 'You're not telling Marnie about this. About us. About last night,' she clarified when he continued to look at her as if she'd just sprouted an extra head. 'You can't.'

'Why can't I?'

'Because I don't want her to know, obviously.'

'Obviously. my butt. Why don't you want her to know? It's not like she doesn't know I have sex,' he added, apropos to absolutely nothing.

'Yes, but she doesn't know you've just had sex with me, does she?'

'Not yet, she doesn't.' He grasped her hand, dragged her back towards the bed. 'But I don't plan to keep it a secret. Why would I?'

She tugged her hand free, cursing the heat shimmying up her spine. 'Because Marnie doesn't need to know.'

'That doesn't answer my question,' he said, an annoyingly astute look crossing his face.

'Please, as a favour to me, Carter,' she said, trying her best puppy-dog pout. 'Don't tell Marnie about us. I said some pretty hideous things to her when this happened the first time. And I really don't want to revisit that situation in any shape or form.'

He shrugged. 'Okay, I guess it's no skin off my—'

'Pinkie swear,' she begged, keen to get a commitment out of him. But when she demonstrated the technique by crossing her own pinkie over her heart and kissing the tip, his brows lowered ominously.

'Don't push it, Carrington. I don't do pinkie swears.'

'Why not?'

'Because it's girlie and I'm a guy.' His lips lifted into a sly grin. 'You want me to prove it?'

'Absolutely not.' She stepped out of his reach, before he could kick off yet more sizzles and shimmies. 'I have to shower. Alone,' she added for good measure when he chuckled.

She needed to make a quick getaway now—no matter how much she might be tempted to stay. Sleeping with Carter again had been a mistake, on a lot of levels, however great it might have felt at the time. Not least of which was that he was a man she didn't seem to be able to wrap around her finger as easily as every other man she'd ever dated. Getting him to say he wouldn't mention this to Marnie was the best she could hope for. They wouldn't be doing this again. As he would be safely back in Savannah by the end of the week, and she would be steering well clear of him—and his addictive pheromones—until then.

'Aren't you forgetting something, sugar?'

She swung round at the laconic question. 'No, I don't think so.'

'My little sister's not as clueless about carnal relations as she used to be.' His gaze dipped pointedly to her bare bottom. 'I'm guessing she may well figure out something's up when you show up with no panties on.'

He laughed, obviously enjoying her distress immensely.

'Oh, go to hell…' she huffed, waltzing back towards the bathroom.

'Your butt looks real cute when you're mad.'

She shot him the finger and slammed the bathroom door to cut off the sound of his full-bodied laughter. But as she dropped the dress and stepped into the enormous power shower her whole body started to shake.

Last night's activities had the potential to be a disaster…. Not just because Marnie might find out—but because she was going to have to keep well away from Carter for the next seven days. And after the night they'd just shared, that was going to be a very tall order.

'What were you thinking?' she snapped at herself as the hot water hit her full in the face.

This didn't just have the potential to be a disaster, it already was one. And like every other disaster in her life so far, it was entirely of her own making.

Carter's laughter subsided as he picked up the hotel phone. 'Give me the concierge.'

Damn, but she fascinated him. She got worked up about the weirdest things. Marnie wouldn't care about them now. His sister was hardly the starry-eyed little romantic she'd once been, any more than he was the big brother she'd once looked up to. And while he'd always regretted her finding out he wasn't the man she thought he was the way she had— he didn't see why he, or Gina, should have to tiptoe around Marnie's sensibilities now.

His kid sister had been living in New York for five years— making her own way in the big bad Yankee city and steadfastly refusing to let him have any kind of foothold in her life. He was proud of Marnie and what she'd achieved—even though he'd never tell her, because she'd only accuse him of patronising her. But the point was, she'd moved on, made a life for herself away from Savannah, and she sure as hell didn't care about his love life any more. So why was Gina so hung up on Marnie finding out about them?

He shrugged off the thought as he got patched through to the concierge. Women. Who knew why they got hung up on half the stuff they got hung up on?

He made the request to the concierge and included a powerful incentive if it could be fulfilled in the next twenty minutes. He figured if Gina was like all the other women he'd ever dated, it would be a miracle if she was out of the bathroom before then.

Listening to the sound of running water, he imagined that lush body slick with soap suds. Heat pooled in his groin, and his morning erection perked right up.

He had to head off to The Waldorf for a lunch meeting with some Chinese investors, so it was probably a good thing he hadn't been able to persuade Gina to blow off her friends.

Resigned to the fact that he'd have to take a rain check for their next booty call at least until tonight, he hunted up a pair of sweat pants and a T-shirt from his suitcase. Dialling room service, he ordered breakfast and coffee and then stood by the glass wall to contemplate the awesome view—and the low-level hum of endorphins still cruising through his system.

He rubbed his palm across his midriff. He hadn't felt this sated and well rested and energised in years. Despite the fact that at a rough estimate he'd totalled about three hours' sleep in the last twenty-four.

And he gave Gina credit for that.

She really was his ideal sexual partner. He'd thought he'd been imagining how good they'd been together that night. But that night had only been a taster.

She was as wild and insatiable in the sack as he was, and even more wary of commitment out of it. He'd heard the caution in her voice when he'd asked any personal questions, felt her discomfort when he hugged her after sex, could tell she'd been reluctant to fall asleep in his arms, until he'd exhausted her—and himself. And he had a feeling this dumb notion about Marnie finding out was just another of her tactics for keeping a safe distance. She might even have persuaded herself her friendship with Marnie was a good excuse to call a halt to things.

Not gonna happen, sugar.

It was just plain dumb to throw a physical connection this perfect away over something so insubstantial.

The two of them were the perfect match. Last night had proved it beyond any reasonable and several unreasonable doubts. Having spent five torturous years suppressing his more basic sexual urges so his wife wouldn't freak out on him—and then five more trying to find someone who was happy to satisfy those needs without demanding more—he knew how rare Gina was.

He'd found her once and lost her, because of some dumb notion that he was a better man than his daddy. That he could be the marrying kind if he put his mind to it. Well, he'd been there, done that, and now had the decree absolute and a few thousand dollars a month in alimony payments to show for it.

He didn't plan to make the same mistake twice. He wasn't the marrying kind. But he did have a healthy sex drive—which he now had the chance to indulge in for a whole week with a woman who enjoyed sex as down and dirty as he did.

So he didn't plan to let Gina go so easily a second time. Not until they'd gotten their fill of each other while he was in New York. And whatever weird notions Gina had about Marnie—she could forget trying to persuade him they'd got their fill of each other in one night.

Something he would have to make clear to her, when she finally stopped hiding out in his shower.

Of course, he should probably ask her nicely instead of telling her. That would be the polite Southern thing to do. Especially as he knew how ornery she could be.

He saw the slow smile forming on his lips reflected in the glass.

Forget it.

He wasn't a gentleman. And he'd stopped asking nicely when he'd figured out that nice wasn't part of his nature.

And anyhow, taming Gina and that quick-fire temper of hers was all part of the attraction. She might have a history of wrapping men round her perfectly manicured pinkie—him included, once upon a time—but he was more than man enough to take her on today.

And harnessing all that fire and passion would make this wild ride even wilder.

Gina dashed into the bedroom of Carter's suite almost an hour later to find him flicking through *The Wall Street Journal* with the remains of his breakfast in front of him.

It had taken her longer than she'd planned to shower, wash and dry her hair, put on a semblance of decent make-up from the inadequate emergency supply in her purse and steam out the wrinkles in her dress—not to mention formulate exactly what she was going to say and how she was going to say it so that she could end her night of madness as quickly and cleanly and with as little fuss as possible. She had to pitch the brush-off just right. Most of all, she didn't want Carter getting any ideas that her refusal to see him again was in any way a challenge. Because if there was one thing she'd learned during their epic sex session last night, the new Carter, not unlike the old Carter, was a man with a sizeable ego and a well-honed competitive spirit—who was not a good loser.

Unfortunately, the fact that she'd spent an extra twenty minutes in the bathroom than she'd bargained for meant she was going to have to do all that in ten minutes flat—if she didn't want to turn up for her fitting more than half an hour late, and encourage even more probing questions from her friends.

'There you are.' He folded the paper on his plate. 'I ordered you up some breakfast, but it arrived a while back. It may be a mite cold now.'

He lifted the silver dome on the plate opposite to reveal a splendid assortment of freshly cut fruit, waffles and syrup. Saliva pooled under her tongue. 'I'm sorry, I really don't have time to do that justice. Maybe just a quick cup of coffee?'

'Sure thing.' He plopped the dome back over her breakfast, apparently unconcerned by her refusal, and picked up the silver pot next to his plate.

Maybe this was going to be easier than she had assumed. The heady aroma of fresh coffee filled the air as he poured her a cup. 'Cream and sugar, sugar?' he teased.

'Black's fine.' She took the cup, gulped the bitter liquid down, not quite as pleased with his nonchalant tone as she probably should be.

After fortifying herself. She popped the cup back on the table and toed on her stilettos. 'Well, I guess this is goodbye, then?' she said, feeling stupidly nervous all of a sudden. 'It was quite a night.'

'It sure was,' he said, his gaze roaming over her and making all the sizzles and shimmers buzz like alarm bells.

'Right, I'll just…' She shot a thumb over her shoulder. 'Leave.'

She headed for the door. She hadn't given him a single word of her carefully planned speech. Because she obviously hadn't needed to. Clearly she was just another of the many, many notches on his bedpost.

'Hold up, Gina.'

She swung round, the odd leap in her heart completely counterproductive, but there nonetheless. 'Yes?'

'I got you something.' He lifted a pale blue paper bag off the bed with the logo of an exclusive designer boutique on the front and handed it to her.

She took the package, somewhat dazed by the intensity of his gaze. Why had he bought her a gift? And why was her heart practically beating its way through her chest wall?

Opening the bag, she lifted out a pair of exquisite red lace panties—and laughed. 'Oh…' She didn't know what to say—at once touched that he would have thought of it, and turned on, as she suddenly became one hundred per cent more conscious of her current lack of underwear. 'Thank you. That was very thoughtful of you.'

'Not really.' His lips curved into a tempting grin. 'More like a necessity. That's a mighty short dress. I don't want anyone else getting a load of your naked butt but me.'

The blush fired up her neck. As heat swelled in her sex. Dropping the bag, she slipped her shoes off, and shimmied the red lace up her legs to cover her naked butt before she got any ideas about that teasing grin and the husky tone of his voice.

Not gonna happen, Gina. You're wearing your big girl panties now.

Grabbing her purse, she pressed her palm to his cheek, rubbed it over the rough stubble and gave him a quick kiss on the lips—keeping it short, but sweet.

She fluttered her eyelashes as she drew back. 'Why thank you, Rhett. My naked bum is now safe from unwanted attention.'

But as her hand dropped from his face, he snagged her wrist, and the light in his eyes darkened. 'How about I give it some wanted attention? Back here. Tonight?'

Even though she'd prepared herself for the request, her

breathing slowed, her heart thumping harder against her ribs as his thumb stroked her wrist. 'We can't, Carter. This isn't going to happen again.'

'That's a shame. When we both enjoy it so much.'

She could hardly argue with that, given that her pulse was currently doing the foxtrot under his stroking thumb.

His eyebrow lifted. 'Do you have a reason, or am I gonna have to guess what it is?'

She pulled her wrist free, and gripped the strap of her bag. 'I just don't want this turning into a…a…' *What?* 'A thing.'

'A thing, huh?' He ducked his head, and ran a finger across his bottom lip, as if considering her response, but she could see he was struggling to suppress a grin. 'You're gonna have to tell me why a *thing* would be a problem.' His eyes lit with amusement. 'Because I've gotta tell you, I think we've already got a thing going here. It certainly felt like a hell of a thing last night.'

She clamped down on her temper, because with temper came heat, and she knew he'd exploit that straight away. 'A *thing* would be a problem,' she said patiently, 'because a thing can so easily turn into a fling.'

'O-kay.' He nodded sagely. 'And a fling is bad because…?' He gestured with his hand as if encouraging her to continue.

'You're not taking this seriously.' There was a limit to how patient she could be when he was deliberately taking the Mickey.

'Ya think?' He took her hand, linked his fingers through hers—that aggravating grin still firmly in place. 'That's because you're taking it way *too* seriously, Gina. All we're talking about here is great sex.' His thumb did that sizzling thing again, pressing into the palm of her hand. He gave her a little tug and kissed her. The touch of his lips oddly tender, behind the usual heat. 'There's no need to get your new panties in a twist. Okay, sugar?'

'Carter! You…' She huffed out a laugh. The cheeky comment and the tempting kiss making her temper dissolve into something liquid and warm.

Good heavens, the man really was dangerous. If she couldn't even stay mad at him when she needed to.

She slapped a hand on his chest, to wrench herself away from that handsome face, those tempting lips, and the wicked promise in his eyes. 'I have to shoot. Thanks for the panties.'

He let her go, and remained silent as she rushed to the door, far too aware of the soft lace stretching over her moist sex. But as she left the room without risking a backward glance she knew she hadn't finished their fling—or thing, or whatever the heck it was—quite as quickly or cleanly or concisely as she had intended.

And that was a definite worry.

Much more of a worry, though, was the intoxicating spurt of endorphins that accompanied the thought.

CHAPTER SEVEN

GINA STEPPED OFF the cobblestone street into the exclusive bridal boutique nestled under the Manhattan Bridge Overpass. Rails full of fanciful white and ivory dresses crowded the front of the shop, but she could already hear the musical lilt of female laughter from the back of the store. Reese appeared in her usual pristine combo of skinny designer jeans and a chic fitted blouse, her hair pinned up in an unfussy chignon and with a champagne flute full of what Gina hoped was something alcoholic in her hand.

'Late as usual. Where have you been? The start time was eleven a.m. prompt, not—' she shot a look at the gold watch on her wrist '—quarter to twelve.'

Gina opened her mouth to deliver the white lie she'd been working on during the cab ride to the hip-and-happening Brooklyn neighbourhood when Reese simply waved her hand and passed her the flute. 'Don't bother, I can take a wild guess. I just hope he was worth it.'

'Good to know I'm that transparent,' Gina remarked dryly, taking a healthy sip of the fruity mimosa to cover the tremor in her fingers and project her usual cool. Reese didn't know about her new leaf, so she'd probably just assume last night had been another of her casual hook-ups. Which of course it was, she corrected herself smoothly. Completely casual.

Reese grinned and looped her arm through Gina's to lead

her to the back of the shop. 'I know a well-screwed look when I see one.'

Gina spluttered, the second sip hitting her larynx. Was it *that* obvious?

'Why, Gina?' Reese stopped to study her.

Heat leached into Gina's cheeks.

'That's not a blush, is it? Have we slipped into an alternative reality?'

'Hardly. I just didn't get a lot of sleep last night—as you so correctly assumed.' Gina pressed the cool glass to her cheeks to get the stupid blush under control as they entered a small, intimate salon.

The remains of bagels, take-out coffee mugs and a fruit plate littered the low table in the centre of the room beside a half-full bottle of champagne and a large jug of iced orange juice.

'Gina, you're here!' Cassie sent a slightly desperate smile from her seat on one of the soft leather sofas that framed the table. 'Nearly an hour late, as usual.' She frowned. 'I wonder if you can have a genetic compulsion to inefficient time-keeping?' Dressed in her geek's uniform of battered jeans and a shapeless T with the proclamation 'Soil Scientists Know All the Dirt' printed on it in bold pink lettering, she had that rabbit-in-the-headlights look she always got when forced to make fashion choices.

'There you go, Reese,' Gina chimed in, grateful for the change of subject. 'It's a genetic compulsion. I can't help being late.'

'Given what you were up to last night,' Reese chirped in, dragging the subject back to where Gina didn't want it, 'inefficient time-keeping's not your only genetic compulsion.'

'Hey, Gina.' Marnie caught her gaze in one of the salon's mirrored walls as she modelled a stunning off-the-shoulder chiffon gown for Reese's petite friend Amber—who looked

like an industrious pixie buzzing around Marnie with a row
of pins held between pursed lips. Amber threw a quick wave
of greeting, which Gina returned, before getting back to the
business of popping the pins into the gown's hem. The deep
aquamarine of the material intensified the blue of Marnie's
eyes—and gave Gina an uncomfortable memory flash of another penetrating gaze. She broke eye contact and shrugged
off the guilt.

None of her friends would ever know who she'd been with
last night. Least of all Marnie. It had been a one-off. A steamy
swansong to that night ten years ago brought on by chemistry
and curiosity. Well, they'd both satisfied that curiosity now.
Maybe not completely satisfied it, because the chemistry was
still super hot, but satisfied it enough. So there would be no
need for a replay and nothing to feel guilty about.

Reese leaned in and whispered theatrically, 'I'll want the
full story on your coffee morning later. But Marnie says you
booked an awesome venue for you know what.'

Gina gulped down the last of the mimosa and sent Reese a
bland stare. 'Be aware, I still haven't forgiven you for setting
me and Marnie up with your little disappearing act.'

Reese's grin only widened. 'What are you talking about?'
she said, not even attempting to look innocent. 'I was un-
avoidably detained.'

'Where exactly? In Mason's boudoir?'

'Possibly.' Reese wiggled her eyebrows, the grin taking
on a cheeky quality.

'What are you two whispering about?' Cassie came over
to join them, popping a piece of melon in her mouth.

'Mason's bondage techniques,' Gina said dryly. 'What
else?'

Cassie rolled her eyes, comically. 'What? *Again?*'

Reese laughed. 'Excuse me, but who was it who was just
regaling us with Tuck's amazing powers of recuperation?'

Cassie frowned, nonplussed. 'I was simply trying to con-tribute to the apocryphal data being accrued. I never men-tioned Tuck's name.'

Reese patted Cassie's cheek with loving condescension. 'Let's just say we all made an informed decision about who your subject matter was based on the factual data you logged in the discussion. And the fact that my cousin is the only guy you're sleeping with now and for ever. Unlike our friend Gina.' She sent a sly glance Gina's way. 'Maybe you'd like to contribute to Cassie's research on the performance capacity of the adult American male with a contribution of recorded data from last night's mystery man? Assuming of course he was another Yank.'

'Actually, he's not a...' Gina cut off the wry quip—before she blurted out far too much recordable data about her mys-tery man, who'd once explained to her on a moonlit night in Hillbrook that calling a Southerner a Yankee ranked right up in the league table of unforgivable national slurs with calling an Irishman English.

'So not a Yank?' Reese's brows rose with interest. 'How very cosmopolitan of you.'

'Why don't those who are getting regular sex stop boast-ing about it?' Marnie cut in from across the room. 'So Amber can get the rest of these glorious bridesmaids' gowns fitted and we can get down to the important business of finishing the mimosas.'

'I'll second that.' Gina rushed to re-direct the conversation, again, and avoid any more out-of-character blushes. 'Amber, you've outdone yourself. That design is absolutely stunning. And the colour looks fabulous on you, Marnie.'

'Thanks, that's real sweet of you.' Marnie nodded, ac-knowledging the compliment, the smile on her face less re-served than their last meeting. 'It's like wearing a work of art.'

Amber smiled brightly as she stood to stretch her back and

admire her own handiwork. 'Reese and I wanted a design that would flatter you all without being too overblown. I've done yours in emerald. You want to strip off and I'll go get it?'

'Absolutely,' Gina replied, sending up a silent prayer of thanks for Carter's knicker gift as she stripped down to her underwear—and the conversation lapsed into a debate about styles and fabrics and colours, and the brilliance of Amber's designs, and sashayed comfortably away from the subject of her mystery man.

She didn't miss the irony though as the morning wore on in companionable girl talk, the five women enjoying some serious bonding time together in preparation for Reese's big day at the end of next month, and—while Cassie was firmly out-of-earshot in the dressing room forced to try on some push-up bras—in the whispered preparations for Cassie's impromptu wedding to Tuck. Who would have predicted ten years ago the once hopelessly romantic Marnie would be the only one of the Awesome Foursome—apart from her—not to find the man of her dreams?

Gina wondered if Marnie still harboured any of those fanciful hopes about finding Mr Right—that she had once sneered at.

It was pretty ironic that the only wobble she'd ever had in that regard had been Marnie's big brother. After ten years and the roller coaster she'd been forced to ride after that long ago summer, she doubted she would make that mistake again—but given her history with Carter, steering clear of him for the rest of the week until he was safely back in Savannah made sense. What made it imperative though was a morning spent observing Amber and Reese and Cassie. Because the evidence of how far gone the three of them were over the men in their lives was both irrefutable, and pretty damn scary.

Take Amber and her insane decision to sublet her apartment above the shop and move into Parker's place located near his job in the fifty-seventh precinct—thus giving herself an hour-long commute into work every day—just because her taciturn cop had said he'd rather be shot in the head than live above a bridal boutique. Or Reese and her equally insane decision to set up a non-profit organisation with Mason to utilise the skills of military veterans in disaster zones. Second Chance, First Response sounded like a worthwhile concept, but also like a lot of hard work, something she wasn't convinced Reese had considered before she'd committed to the project. Because it was pretty obvious when Reese had explained how tough it was for veterans to adjust to civilian life, using Mason's ongoing struggle since his honourable discharge as an example, that Reese had made the decision to commit to the non-profit with her heart first and her head a distant second.

But by far the biggest shock of the morning had been the change in Cassie—grounded, academically brilliant, IQ-off-the-charts Cassie—the person Gina had always relied upon to give her a no-nonsense, pragmatic perspective on her own sometimes volatile emotions. Cassie had actually emitted something that sounded suspiciously like a giggle when talking about her upcoming wedding. Since when had her friend become a giggler? What else could have caused that but the Tuck Effect?

So now she had conclusive proof. Great sex could lead to dementia. And while she found it unbearably sweet that Reese, and Amber, and Cassie had found men who they were prepared to change their lives for, risking getting a dose of that dementia wasn't for Gina. She was a single girl, who loved living her life solo. Men were great in small doses, especially when you needed that special flesh-on-flesh endorphin fix, but they were not an option for the long haul. Not for her.

She didn't want to compromise her life, to adjust her dreams, to shrink her own ambitions to fit somebody else's.

And while Carter had certainly proved he could hit her happy buttons with a great deal more style and panache than any other guy she'd ever dated, he had also been the only man ever to come close to making her want more than great sex and stimulating small talk. And while that had happened a long time ago, in a galaxy far, far away—she wasn't interested in a return journey.

'Hey, earth to Gina?' Cassie waved a hand in front of her face.

Gina's head jerked, making her bobble the mimosa she'd forgotten she had in her hand. She saved it in the nick of time from splattering her dress.

'Sorry, I didn't mean to startle you, but Amber was asking if you had a preference for gold or silver trim on your gown.'

'Oh, right, yes, I think silver,' she said off the top of her head, trying to remember what colour her gown was, while four pairs of eyes looked at her quizzically.

'Where were you?' Cassie asked, a small frown on her brow. 'You looked several light years away.'

'Nowhere in particular.'

'I think I can take a wild guess.' Reese refilled her glass. 'You weren't somewhere in the vicinity of the Mystery Studmuffin, were you?'

'The mystery what?' Marnie asked.

Damn. She should have been paying attention to the conversation instead of wasting time thinking about the mystery studmuffin she was never going to see again.

Heat seared Gina's neck as Reese toasted her with her flute.

'Bingo.' Reese winked at Marnie. 'The Mystery Studmuffin is the hot guy Gina was with last night—and this morning while she was supposed to be with us. All we know about him so far is that he isn't an American, he's a hot enough date to give Gina a genetic compulsion to terrible time-keeping...'

'Her date can't have caused it if it's a genetic compulsion no matter how hot he is,' Cassie corrected her.

'Point taken…' Reese continued, undaunted. 'But he is hot enough to make the Unflappable Miss Carrington blush. So on a hotness scale of one to ten, I'm guessing the Mystery Studmuffin goes all the way to eleven.'

Marnie and Amber both laughed, while the blush climbed into Gina's cheeks.

'So who is he?' Reese teased. 'Enquiring minds want to know every intimate detail.'

'Well, enquiring minds can mind their own business,' Gina replied, pretty sure the blush was about to reach her hairline. 'Unlike you lot, I'm not into shag and share.'

'Since when?' Reese looked genuinely surprised.

'Since I became a grown-up.' She slapped her glass down on the table, the hot ball of resentment in her stomach only intensifying the guilty heat now scalding her scalp. 'And stopped banging every guy that took my fancy. Not that anyone here would believe that of Gina the Unflappable Whore.'

Reese's teasing smile disappeared as her jaw went slack, while the other women's eyes popped to the size of dinner plates.

'Gina, I'm sorry, I was only messing with you,' Reese murmured, looking thoroughly crestfallen.

Gina hoisted her purse off the floor and stood. 'I should go,' she said stiffly, wanting to apologise for the petulant outburst, but not sure how to do it without making things worse. 'I'm tired and it's making me more of a bitch than usual.'

Reese jumped up to press a hand to her arm. 'Please, Gina, don't go. I feel awful. No one thinks you're a whore.'

Gina caught Marnie's eye, and the other woman blinked, her face ashen, clearly shaken by the mention of the word that had once torn them all apart.

You would though, if you knew who I was really with last night.

She patted Reese's fingers, then gently disengaged them from her arm. 'Really it's okay. I was being ridiculously over-sensitive. And I really do need to crash. I'll speak to you in the week about…' she lowered her voice to a whisper so only Reese could hear '…you know whose surprise party.'

'All right, if you're sure.'

'Sure, I'm sure.' She bade goodbye to the others and left, escaping before their gestures of support and concern could make her do something dopey, like bursting into tears.

It wasn't until she was in the cab home, bouncing across the cobblestoned street past Brooklyn Park, and she'd got the foolish urge to cry under lockdown, that she began to wonder where exactly the hot ball of resentment had come from that had caused her to end an immensely enjoyable morning of BFF bonding on such a sour note. And once she'd digested the only possible answer to that question, she then had to ask herself why she should resent what Reese and Cassie and Amber had—when she'd decided years ago that she would never want the same thing for herself.

Once back at the minute loft apartment she was struggling to pay the rent on in Brooklyn's funky Red Hook district, Gina stripped off her clothes, took another hot shower and crashed straight into the fanciful iron-framed double bed she'd crammed into the loft's bedroom. Given that she was now at the grand old age of twenty-nine and somewhat out of practice, clearly her all-nighter with Carter had taken a physical toll that had had emotional repercussions. But once she'd caught up on her sleep, she'd be herself again—and everything would snap back into sharp, vivid focus.

Several hours later, after a fitful nap that had been filled with far too many erotic dreams featuring the Mystery Stud-

muffin who should not be named, the door buzzer sounded.
She crawled out of bed, her pulse pounding into her throat
and a few other more intimate parts of her anatomy—until
she spied Cassie's face through the peephole. The dip in her
stomach had nothing whatsoever to do with disappointment,
she decided as she yanked open the heavy security door.

'Gina, you look wasted,' Cassie announced as she stepped
into the flat with a garment bag hooked over her shoulder.
'Maybe you're coming down with flu.'

If only.

'No, I have the constitution of an ox. I'm just exhausted.'

Cassie sent her a bland look, but fortunately didn't probe.
'Amber asked me to drop this off for you.' She handed her
the garment bag, which had the white logo of Amber's Bridal
emblazoned across it. 'She told me to tell you she's done the
necessary adjustments, but she needs you to try it on and send
it back, just to make sure the fit's good before she starts adding the other bits.'

'Thanks for bringing it over.' Gina laid the bag over the
back of her sofa. 'I'm sorry you had to come all this way. I
should have stuck around, shouldn't I?'

Cassie simply said, 'Are you asking me a question? Because I know absolutely nothing about the etiquette of bridal
fittings.'

Gina smiled at the clueless comment. 'How about a coffee for your trouble?'

'Only if you're sure you don't want to get back to your
nap?'

'Positive,' Gina replied, keen to avoid returning to her nap,
which was causing more problems than it solved.

To her great relief Cassie agreed to stay and Gina set about
making the coffee.

'Is everything okay? You seem a little shaky.' The cautious
comment had Gina's hand halting as it ladled coffee into the

French press. Cassie wasn't the most intuitive person in the world, so it had to be really obvious.

'Yes, of course,' she said, determined to make it so as she started ladling again. 'Why wouldn't it be?'

'You totally overreacted to Reese's teasing,' Cassie replied with her customary bluntness. 'Which made me wonder if something bad happened last night.'

Gina smoothed her palms down her robe, touched by Cassie's concern. She filled the French press with boiling water and faced her friend. 'And there I was thinking I had my poker face on.'

'I would strongly suggest you don't enter any poker tournaments, then—you wouldn't make much money.'

Gina sent Cassie a weak smile. 'Don't worry, Cass, nothing bad happened. It was all good.' *Way too good, really.*

'Was it Marnie's brother?' Cassie asked, her expression direct and totally non-judgmental. 'The guy you were with last night?'

The blush fired up Gina's neck as she opened her mouth to deny it—but her mind went completely blank, and the manufactured outrage, the clever evasions, the bald-faced lie she wanted to tell got trapped in her throat somewhere in the region of her Adam's apple. Until all she could manage to choke out on a panicked whisper was: 'How did you know?'

'It was obvious once I'd analysed the available data.' Cassie stirred sugar into her coffee, apparently unfazed by the admission of guilt.

'Which was?'

Cassie shrugged and sipped. 'Marnie took a call from him just before you arrived, and arranged to meet him at The Standard Hotel for lunch on Tuesday, so I knew he was in town.' Cassie placed her mug on the counter with calm deliberation. 'And the only other time I've seen you blush like that is the morning after you slept with him the first time. Well, until right this minute, that is.'

'Terrific.' Gina's teeth ground together as the heat scalded her ears. 'Did you share your brilliant powers of deduction with anyone else?'

'No.' A tiny frown bisected Cassie's brow as Gina's breath gushed out and the knots in her shoulders loosened a little. 'But why would that be bad?' Cassie asked, giving a slow owlish blink—which Gina knew meant she was trying to process something particularly complex.

'Because I don't want Reese and Marnie to know.' She ruthlessly resisted the urge to say 'Duh'. It wasn't Cassie's fault she'd figured out the truth, or that she was so clueless about the dynamics of female friendships.

'Why don't you want them to know?'

Oh, for Pete's sake.

'Because I screwed up this friendship once before by screwing Marnie's brother—and I don't want to do it again.'

'But you did screw him again, so whether they know or not is sort of academic, isn't it?'

'Yes, but...' Gina stammered to a halt, totally lost for words in the face of Cassie's objective reasoning. 'I can't believe I've done this again. It's like I've got a genetic compulsion to screw up this friendship.'

'Not necessarily,' Cassie said, taking the statement literally as always. 'To determine that you'd have to examine the cause and effect.'

'The.... Well, it wasn't planned, if that's what you're asking.' Because who knew what the heck Cassie was on about now? 'I went to his hotel to apologise to him.'

'What for?' Cassie cut in, looking shocked for the first time.

'For the failure of his marriage.'

'How was that your fault?'

'Apparently it wasn't,' Gina added, suddenly keen to end this topic of conversation. Because the apology excuse for seeing Carter again was sounding less and less valid, even to her. 'Do you want to hear the rest or not?'

Cassie's eyebrows rose fractionally at the tone. 'Yes.'

'Fine, well, then, after he'd told me his divorce was none of my concern, we had a few drinks, one thing led to another and before I knew it we were tearing each other's clothes off in his very nice corner suite overlooking the Hudson.' She sighed. 'The views really are spectacular from that hotel, by the way.'

'What view are we talking about?' Cassie said, so dryly Gina choked out a laugh, the burden of guilt lifting for the first time since her meltdown at the salon.

'It's not funny,' she replied. 'It's disastrous. I know that. But the good news is, it won't happen again. I told him in no uncertain terms this morning that we'd made a mistake.' Well, the terms hadn't been that uncertain, but still.

'How was it?' Cassie asked.

'How was what?'

'The mistake?'

'You mean the sex?'

Cassie nodded.

'Honestly?'

Another nod.

'Fabulous.' Why lie about it? 'As I believe I mentioned ten years ago, the man was a gifted amateur. He's more than lived up to that early promise.' Which she was beginning to realise only made the mistake of sleeping with him all the more enormous—because her ability to conjure up an image of him naked and ready with complete clarity was not helping.

'Maybe that explains it, then,' Cassie mused.

'Explains what?'

'Why you slept with him, despite your misgivings. Studies

have shown the release of endorphins triggered by orgasm—which for the purposes of this discussion we'll call fabulous sex—can impair your cognitive skills. They certainly impaired mine when I had sex with Tuck the first time. And the second. And the…'

'I get the picture,' Gina muttered. Trust Cassie to come up with a scientific solution—that made perfect sense to her and no sense in the real world. 'Cass, what you and Tuck have is not the same as what Carter and I have. Frankly, having sex with Carter could turn me into Dumbo, but all it would ultimately prove is that Marnie was right about me all along.'

Cassie gave a pensive hum. 'Are you sure you're giving Marnie enough credit? Why don't you ask her whether she cares about you and Carter getting back together.'

Gina choked on her coffee. 'Are you on crack or something?' she whispered furiously. 'Carter and I are *not* back together, because we never were together. This isn't a relationship. It's one night of madness.'

'Two now, actually.'

'All right, two,' Gina conceded. Trust Cassie to be pedantic about the maths. 'But now it's over.' Of that much she was certain.

'Did you tell him about the baby?'

The blood drained out of Gina's face and slammed into her heart. 'No, of course not. Why would I?'

'I just thought…' Cassie began. 'He's not married any more—so why would you need to keep it a secret still?'

'Because it's ancient history. Because there would be no point in telling him all these years after the fact.' She coughed, trying to lower her voice, which had become a little shrill in the face of Cassie's passive-aggressive interrogation techniques. 'And anyway it was never a baby. It was a miscarriage.' And she'd spent a great deal of time, not to mention money, making herself believe that.

It had taken her years to repair the damage she'd done to her sense of self-worth and self-esteem. And even longer to become a more stable, sorted person—a person who could actually look at herself in the mirror every morning and like what she saw. She'd had to get over the insecurities of her childhood, the recklessness of her adolescence and the horror of what had happened when she'd returned to England with Carter's child growing inside her womb, harbouring some idiotic notion that she'd fallen in love with a man who was totally unattainable.

But none of that had really had anything to do with Carter. She'd latched onto him, because he'd listened to her that night, he'd been sensitive and sweet and the few things he'd told her about his father had made her think they might be kindred spirits. But the truth was, he'd just been the catalyst.

Unfortunately, last night proved that she still had a ways to go before she could rely on herself to resist all temptations. But last night had no real bearing on her past. It had been nothing more than a biological urge. An irresistible biological urge. Which meant the decision not to see Carter again, and stir up any more irresistible biological urges, was the mature choice. And if Cassie would just back off, and stop making ridiculous suggestions, she might actually be able to embrace it.

'Okay, if you say so,' Cassie interrupted her panicked revelry, her calm grey eyes fixed on Gina's face.

'I do say so, because it's the truth.'

Cassie looked doubtful—what she wasn't saying hanging in the air between them, like a huge pulsing neon sign. And Gina knew exactly what the sign said.

You're in denial.

She could see Cassie believed it wasn't panic over screwing up her relationship with her friends that had Gina steering clear of Carter now. It was all the messy, unfinished business between the two of them that she didn't want to confront.

And it was hardly surprising Cassie had that misconception.

Because during those months after Gina had left Hillbrook—when she'd discovered the pregnancy and a few crucial months later lost the baby—Reese and Cassie had been there to help her pick up the pieces, at the end of a transatlantic phone line. They'd let Gina rant and rave, and cry and carry on and finally come to terms with her loss and her grief, but there had been one thing her two best friends had disagreed with her about. They both felt Gina should have contacted Carter. That he should have been forced to share some of the emotional burden, because he had been as responsible as Gina for that short, helpless little life.

Gina placed her fingers on Cassie's arm and squeezed. 'It's not what you think, Cass. Honestly. I'm not a basketcase any more. I'm all grown up. I got over it. I couldn't be more different from that girl. And Carter's a completely different guy too. Give or take the odd super power in the sack,' she added wryly.

Cassie sent her a tentative smile. 'Maybe you're right.'

'I know I am.'

'But if that's the case, it does pose another question.'

'Which is?'

'If all the variables have changed, and Reese and Marnie never need to know about this—what's preventing you from availing yourself of Carter's super powers again?'

CHAPTER EIGHT

Cassiopeia Barclay, I want to throttle you.

Gina took her eyes off the phone, punched her computer's start-up button and lobbed Carter Price's card into the wastepaper basket—for the fiftieth time in the last seven days.

The big digital clock above her kitchen counter clicked from 10:59 to 11:00 as she struggled to focus on the screen and ignore the residual hum of heat pulsing in her abdomen.

Ignore it. He's probably already on his plane to Savannah. You did it.

Why she didn't feel particularly thrilled with her powers of resistance was neither here nor there.

She dragged her gaze back to the blog she was designing for an organic farmer's community up in Westchester. It was a new commission and she'd been toying with different basic designs for two days. She punched keys, finally picking a beautiful leaf green for the background to complement the community's logo.

At last, progress.

Business had been painfully slow recently—people generally didn't think too much about social-media marketing campaigns when they were struggling to pay their bills—and she needed to make an impact with this commission. She'd promised the co-operative at least fifty thousand unique visitors in their first three months, which meant putting together a blog package with the wow factor.... And achieving that when the majority of your subject matter was organically grown potatoes was no mean feat.

Once she'd finished the preliminary designs, she began to rough in some of the copy they'd sent her for the launch. And pretended not to notice the insistent punch of her heartbeat every time she glanced at the clock—and another minute had crawled by.

Carter leapt up the steps to the loft apartment two at a time. He had exactly an hour till check-in closed on his flight to Savannah. With a major board meeting scheduled for five this afternoon in Georgia he couldn't miss his plane. So what the hell was he doing getting his cab driver to detour to Brooklyn?

He guessed he was about to find out as he reached the second floor landing and pressed the door buzzer marked Carrington Web Designs.

If she was out, that would be all the answer he needed. He'd left it up to her to call and she hadn't—but he figured she owed him an explanation. She'd approached him, she'd made the first contact, and then she'd blown his mind in that damn hotel suite, leaving him tense and edgy and unfocused for the rest of his trip when he should have been concentrating on business.

He'd drifted off during more than one important negotiation in the last week—eventually making the trip a wash with the Chinese clients he'd been pursuing for months, who now thought he was the next best thing to a narcoleptic.

He could have happily lived the rest of his life never having stirred up this hornet's nest again. But she'd insisted on stirring it up, and then figured she could just unstir it again at her own convenience. Well, to hell with that.

He thumped on the security door, drew back his fist to

thump again, when the door swung open. And the muscles in his gut cinched into a tight knot.

It was eleven ten on a Friday morning but she looked as if she'd just rolled out of bed. Her hair fell around her shoulders in big, fluffy, unkempt waves that made him want to plunge his fingers in and ruffle it up some more. Her clear, pale skin glowed, scrubbed clean without the benefit of the carefully applied make-up she usually wore, while the loose robe gave him a painful glimpse of a lacy camisole barely covering firm breasts.

'Carter, what the…? You're supposed to be in Savannah!'

She tightened the tie on her robe, and her breasts plumped up, threatening to spill out of the lace altogether. The knot in his gut sank lower, loosening muscles that had been too tight for days.

He dragged his gaze away from her cleavage—and suddenly knew the answer.

This wasn't over, not till he said so. Not this time. But from now on he was playing the game on his terms. Not hers. And that meant getting the upper hand right from the get-go.

'I'm on my way to La Guardia now, but I've got a proposition for you that I wanted to deliver in person.'

'What proposition?'

He stroked a finger down her cheek, enjoying the way her lips parted and a sob of breath came out.

She was no more immune than he was to this *thing*. And it was a *thing*, however you wanted to call it.

'I want you to come to Savannah for a couple of weeks.'

She blinked, the movement slow and tremulous, as if she were trying to process the invitation. 'I can't do that, Carter. We're not kids any more and I don't think…'

He pressed his finger to her lips, silencing the protest. 'Now don't go getting your panties in a twist again—that's not the kind of proposition I'm talking about.'

'Oh?'

He felt the surge of satisfaction at the catch of disappointment in her voice and the pucker of confusion on her brow.

You're not the only one who can play hard ball, sugar.

'As great as it was on Friday night, this is a business proposition.' *Mostly.*

'What kind of business proposition?'

The pucker got more pronounced, but he could see the spark of interest lurking behind the caution.

'I've been giving it some thought.' At least ten seconds anyway. 'And I'd like to commission you to work on a social-media campaign for the mill. We're expanding into a number of new markets and we need to up our profile—social media is a way to do that without breaking the bank.'

'That's... Really?'

'Yeah, really, at the moment we only have a website— which we'll need you to redesign—but we're also looking to build a more comprehensive strategy across all the appropriate social-media platforms.'

'That's an excellent idea—over two billion people use the web. But I should warn you that it doesn't necessarily translate into sales straight away. The idea is to...' She stopped suddenly, pushed the door open, the enthusiasm sparking in her eyes almost making him feel guilty. But then he remembered it was a real job, he'd got the funding approved by the board months ago—and he got the final say on who to hire, so he could hire her if he wanted. 'Why don't you come in? We can discuss it further.' She glanced at her clothing. 'I'll get dressed and we can...'

'No need to get dressed on my account.' He let his gaze drift down the shorty robe past long, toned legs to bare feet, and toes painted cotton-candy pink. And imagined himself nibbling on that cute little pinkie. He let the innuendo heat the air, before returning his gaze to her face. Her breathing had speeded up, making her cleavage rise and fall against the confining lace. 'I can't stop to discuss it now. I've got a plane to catch. That's why I need you to come to Savannah.'

'But I don't have to be in Georgia. Everything can be done online and we can correspond via email.'

He smiled—he'd definitely heard the disappointment that time. And the way her voice had lowered to the throaty purr that signalled her arousal.

'I want you to see the mill, talk to the folks that work there, get a clear picture of who we are and what we do.' Damned if he hadn't almost convinced himself by the time he'd finished outlining all the elements of the operation he wanted her to get acquainted with.

'Well, I suppose…'

He leant in and pressed a quick perfunctory kiss to her lips, heard her sharp intake of breath. 'Great, that's all settled. I'll get my PA to negotiate a contract and email flight details. Can you make it down early next week?'

'If you're sure you need me to be there.'

'I'm sure.'

'Then I guess that settles it.'

He stepped back, cursing the fact that he'd be riding an erection all the way to the airport as his lungs filled with the sunny scent of her hair. He let his gaze wander over her figure. 'As much as I like that get-up, you might want to pack a few more clothes. But keep them light—it's hot and sticky in Savannah at this time of year.' And even though his house in the city's Victorian Historic District was well air-conditioned, he had a feeling it was going to be even hotter and stickier there once she was sleeping down the hall.

The smile she sent him made him suspect she wasn't going to play all that hard to get. But then neither was he. 'Okay.'

'See you later.' He nodded, the words more than a little husky.

But as he turned to go she touched his arm. 'Just a second, Carter. Did you speak to Marnie this week?'

'Sure, we had lunch on Tuesday.' The usual strained, stilted affair.

'And you didn't tell her about us? About Friday night?'

'I said I wouldn't,' he replied, not sure where the irritation came from. It wasn't as if he and Marnie were bosom buddies. Even though their mama had raised her never to say it, he knew Marnie thought he was a womanising jerk. He knew that and he accepted it—it was part of the penance he paid for that night—and frankly Marnie's bad opinion had been the least of his worries as he watched his marriage disintegrate.

Since the divorce and their mother's death, Marnie had kept her distance, pursuing a career in New York that he knew very little about—and making caustic comments on the few occasions they met about his being the playboy of the western world. He didn't bother to deny it, because he didn't need her approval—and he hadn't exactly been a monk. But he also didn't plan to give Marnie more ammunition, so the last thing he'd be likely to do was mention to his sister that he'd had an all-nighter with Gina again. But the spurt of annoyance was there none the less. Not just because Gina had doubted his word, but because she seemed so damned determined to keep their *thing* a secret. He didn't like secrets, because they could come back and bite you on the butt.

'Could I ask you to keep quiet about this arrangement too?' she said.

'Sure, if that's the way you want it.' He shrugged, trying not to care. 'Marnie doesn't get involved in mill business, she just helps herself to the company's equity,' he said, the statement coming out with more bitterness than he'd intended when he saw Gina frown.

'If you say so,' she murmured and the prickle of irritation became a definite stab. 'I'll see you in a few days.'

'Yeah.' He waved her goodbye and jogged down the stairs, conceding that a few days seemed like a mighty long time.

Gina slammed the door and leaned against it, her diamond-hard nipples making the silk of her camisole feel like sandpaper.

Way to go, Gina. After going cold turkey for a whole week, your drug of choice appears and you resist temptation for precisely ten seconds.

She rolled her eyes and squeezed her thighs together to stop the insistent ache that had settled there as soon as she'd encountered Carter Price standing on her doorstop. His dark hair furrowed into rows and those cobalt eyes even bluer than usual.

She pursed her lips.

Carter wouldn't have offered her this commission unless he thought she would do a competent job—his business was far too important to him for that—but the lingering sizzle where his mouth had touched hers in that casual but proprietary kiss told a slightly different story. That the decision to offer her this opportunity might not be entirely based on the glowing testimonials on her website.

As an independent working woman with a fledgling business she was proud of, she should be outraged.

She padded across the apartment to the bathroom and shrugged out of her robe. Tossing the camisole over her head, she stepped into the enamel bath and switched the dial on the shower unit to scalding.

Unfortunately, though, she couldn't quite muster the required indignation because her decision to accept Carter's offer had had more to do with the intoxicating pheromones he released without even trying—which had caused every one of the synapses in her brain to fuse in unison the second she saw him—than it did with the fabulous opportunity this commission would offer her struggling business.

As the water pounded down, and she soaped her over-sensitive breasts with rather more vigour than was entirely necessary, she could almost hear Cassie's dry Aussie accent saying: 'I told you endorphins are addictive.'

CHAPTER NINE

GINA DABBED AT the sheen of sweat on her brow as she sat in the airy outer office of the Price Paper Mill. A large picture window looked down on the factory floor, where the mill's mostly recycled paper products were manufactured, giving her a slight flutter of vertigo to go with her nerves.

She gripped her laptop bag as Carter's young but efficient PA Bella Delmarr smiled benignly at her from behind a neat white desk.

'Mr Price will be along shortly, Miz Carrington. Would you like some iced tea or a soda while you wait?'

'No, I'm fine,' she replied, not sure she'd be able to swallow without choking, given her jumpy stomach. Which was ridiculous. Why was she so apprehensive about seeing him?

She'd done her homework in the last three days, putting together a preliminary package for him to review—which included projections for the different social media platforms, what they could hope to achieve, some blog designs, website analytics and ideas for possible marketing campaigns to enhance the company's profile. Unfortunately, while doing all that, she'd discovered that the Price family's paper mill had grown from a virtually bankrupt business when Carter had stepped into the CEO's shoes after his father's death into a huge multinational enterprise cleverly cornering the market in the South in recycled products. All of which made Carter's offer of a commission not just a great opportunity, but easily the best she'd ever had.

She could not afford to mess this up—which meant she could not afford to mess with Carter. And while that was extremely disappointing on a number of levels, by far her biggest concern was getting her libido—and Carter—to co-operate. Because she had a feeling his agenda might not be quite so professional—and saying no to him had never been one of her strong suits.

She smoothed damp palms down the linen trousers she'd worn to ward off the intense humidity—only to have the sweat pop back out onto her top lip as the man himself walked through the adjoining door from his office.

'Gina, you made it.'

She got out of her chair and shook the hand he offered. The familiar shot of adrenaline raced up her arm at the touch of his cool dry fingers. 'Yes, I have some projections for you to look at.' She lifted her laptop.

'Great, why don't you leave that with Bella?' He nodded to his PA. 'I'll give you the tour first and then we can take a look.'

She passed the laptop over, disconcerted by the intense cobalt gaze that wandered over her outfit, contradicting the businesslike tone.

'I hope you're not too hot.' He placed a wide palm on the base of her spine, steering her to the stairwell that led to the factory floor. 'Humidity hit ninety per cent today—which is manageable for a native, but let me know if you're gonna wilt and we'll take a break.'

It wasn't the humidity that was likely to make her wilt, she thought, as his palm rubbed before it dropped away, sending tendrils of heat shooting up her spine through the silk of her blouse.

'Ninety per cent is more than I'd bargained for,' she replied as they left the air-conditioned stairwell and hit a wall of heat. It was like walking into a steam room, the wet, humid warmth slapping into them with the force of a wave. 'When you said hot and sticky, I wasn't expecting the Seventh Circle of Hell,' she added, deciding that talking about the weather was probably the safest bet.

He rolled up his shirt sleeves, and she could see the glow of sweat on his brow beneath his hairline. Her mouth dried as she registered the sudden urge to run her tongue across his forehead and lick off the salty beads of moisture. The way she'd done on that hot summer night in Hillbrook.

Down, girl. Remember: businesslike, professional, focused, at all times. You're not going to screw up your big break for an endorphin fix. This is your new leaf talking.

His sensual lips curved into an easy smile that had 'focused' falling by the wayside straight away. 'Ninety per cent is nothing,' he said in that lazy Southern drawl that never failed to reverberate in her abdomen. 'Forecast is for it to get a whole lot hotter over the next couple of weeks.' The wicked glint in those heavy-lidded eyes made it fairly obvious this was not a conversation about the weather any more. 'You think you can handle the heat?'

'Absolutely,' she lied.

The rest of the afternoon passed in a haze of information as he showed her round the whole operation, displaying a hands-on knowledge of the production process—and his employees— that surprised and intrigued her.

From the little Marnie had let slip about her brother and what Gina had discovered on the Internet, she'd assumed Carter Price CEO would be as dominant and cynical as Carter Price Lover Man.

But after taking the tour of his factory, she'd discovered the sheep in wolf's clothing.

She'd thought he would focus on the big picture, the business side of his business—and leave the nitty-gritty of production and supply to his minions. And she hadn't expected him to know every one of his employees by their first names—right down to the pimply faced teenager who swept the loading bay. Or to know enough about their lives to ask after new babies, or recent marriages, or Great-Aunt Merilou's bursitis. But Carter Price had known about all of those things, chatting in a relaxed, comfortable way that suggested these people weren't his minions, they were his friends. And it was also obvious they all felt the same way about Carter—talking to him with easy smiles on their faces and affection as well as admiration in their eyes.

Of course, the mill was an essential part of the local economy and Carter had saved it from going under, so it was no surprise his employees were grateful to him. But she sensed something more going on, a sort of proprietary interest, almost as if these people had the status of family as well as friends, which explained the reserved Southern manners and considered glances she'd received when he introduced her—as if they were sizing her up. She dismissed the prickle of unease, remembering that she was a professional, here on professional business, even if he did insist on touching her arm and smiling confidentially at her, in front of his 'people'.

But despite her best intentions, by the time they had settled into Carter's low-riding convertible and were bombing along a country road flanked by the ubiquitous kudzu vines that swallowed most of the landscape en route to Savannah, Gina had to admit she was feeling more than a little dazed trying to assimilate everything she'd learned.

She stole a glance at the man beside her and her pulse slowed, taking in the play of muscles as he shifted gears, the sculpted angle of his cheekbone in profile, and the way the wind whipped at his hair—making her fingers itch to sweep it back off that high forehead.

Rats. Seeing Carter Price in his natural habitat wasn't going to make him one single bit easier to resist.

'So what do you think?' He shouted the question across the console.

You're gorgeous.

The words echoed in her head, as they had been doing most of the afternoon. And it occurred to her she wasn't just admiring his looks any more, or his super powers in the sack, or even the sharp intelligence he'd shown during their chat in the Standard bar a week ago. While walking through his business with him, she'd got a glimpse of the boy she'd met a decade ago. The cynical player slipping away to reveal a man with warmth and intelligence—and an almost boyish pride in what he'd achieved, not just for himself and his company, but for his community. She wondered if Marnie had ever seen this side of him. Surely she couldn't have and still think so little of him?

But then families were often unpredictable. Growing up in close proximity to someone didn't automatically make you able to understand them—or even like them.

Take her own father—and her impossible relationship with him. Arthur Carrington had been a low-ranking member of the British aristocracy who'd inherited a venture capitalist firm from his own father—her father's ruthlessness in business had been legendary. He'd grabbed all he could with the arrogance of a man born into status and given very little back, not just in his professional life, but in his personal life as well. And although he'd been dead for over six years, Gina still shuddered when she thought of him and the cold, hard glint in his eyes as he'd kicked her out of his house ten years ago.

From what Marnie had said about Carter's chequered love life since his divorce, and from what she had discovered during the last few days about the phenomenal success of his business, Gina would have expected him to be cut from the same cloth, albeit with a layer of Southern charm added. But it seemed nothing could have been further from the truth. Was it possible he really wasn't that far removed from the idealistic and sincere young man she remembered at Hillbrook? Who had been striving to pull his family's business back from the brink but had been determined to do so in an ethical way?

And why did that concept only make her visit to Savannah seem that much more perilous?

'I'm impressed,' she said. 'You've built something amazing here—just like you hoped you would,' she added, the memory of the starry-eyed enthusiasm with which he'd once outlined his dreams for the mill all those years ago making her forget to be cautious. 'And you didn't have to become your father to do it.'

A small crinkle formed on his brow. 'What do you know about my father?'

'Only what you said about him that night.'

He slowed the car, shifted down a gear to observe her for several long moments. 'What did I say about him? I don't recall.'

Her heart bobbed into her throat and it occurred to her she had just strayed into forbidden territory. Why had she mentioned that night? They were so far past it now. And she would do better not to equate the man Carter was now with the boy he'd been, because that boy had had a very unpredictable effect on her. And if she wanted to maintain a professional distance, sharing intimate recollections probably wasn't the smartest way to go about it.

'I can't remember, not a lot.'

'You remember, or you wouldn't have made that comment.'

He didn't sound annoyed, but his expression was far too intense for merely curious—forcing her to give him an answer.

'I got the impression you didn't like him much....' A confidence that had instantly made them connect, because it was exactly how she had always felt about her own father.

'Did I tell you why?'

She shook her head. 'Not really.' He hadn't elaborated, even when she'd pushed and she couldn't deny the spark of curiosity even now. 'Marnie always described him as being larger than life—a force to be reckoned with. You seemed less impressed with him. That's all I remember.'

But she'd always wondered where that disillusionment had come from. Especially the next morning, when he'd woken up in her arms in her tiny bedroom in Reese's house and then shot out of her bed, the horror and regret plain on his stricken face. And all her stupid notions about some cosmic connection between them had shrivelled up inside her as he'd apologised with the stiff politeness of a puritan minister while rushing to get his clothes on—so he could escape out of the window and pretend he'd never been there when he returned to collect Marnie's stuff. Before racing back to Savannah to throw himself on the mercy of the woman he was due to marry. The woman he loved.

'I sure must have shot my mouth off that night.' He sent her a quick grin. 'You must have thought I was one hell of a sap.'

She hadn't thought he was a sap—not after she'd cut through the macho posturing and discovered a young man who'd seemed as lost and alone and confused as she was. She flinched at the stupidly romantic thought. 'You were certainly rather full of yourself,' she replied—because he had been, at first. 'And hopelessly sexist.'

He sent her a quick grin. 'Yeah, and as I recall you weren't shy about telling me. I still remember that comment about exactly how I was ruining the line of my designer points.'

He gave a rueful chuckle, but she cringed inside—knowing even then she'd been flirting with him.

'But I realise now you were simply looking out for you sister in the only way you knew how to.'

'That bad, huh?' he teased, but she couldn't bring herself to share the joke, the memory of that intense, conflicted young man and the way she'd mocked him far too vivid.

'And in complete denial about your sexual needs—which made you an irresistible challenge for a tramp like me.'

He flicked up the indicator to turn off the country lane onto a two-lane highway. 'Gina, honey, you weren't a tramp,' he said, with surprising conviction. 'You had a healthy libido and you weren't ashamed to enjoy it. Unlike me. I sincerely hope you are not still blaming yourself for what happened?' he asked, the question a little too astute for comfort.

She forced out a husky laugh. 'I've never been ashamed of enjoying sex. I think I gave you conclusive proof of that last week.'

'True enough,' he purred, the heavy-lidded look far too suggestive.

'But I certainly had a quality-control problem in my teens,' she added, steering them away from yet more forbidden territory. 'These days I make a point of not giving in to every passing fancy. Despite all evidence to the contrary last Friday night.'

He sent her a curious smile. 'I sure hope you're not suggesting I'm only a passing fancy, sugar?'

She drew in a breath. He'd given her the opening she needed. 'Actually, you're going to have to be,' she murmured, surprised at how depressed the thought made her feel. 'As your newly appointed web designer and social media strategist, I don't think we can afford a replay of Friday night. I will be too distracting.'

'Uh-huh?' he said, the curious smile twitching. He didn't seem annoyed by her comment, which was a good thing. Not so good was the fact that he seemed to find it fairly amusing.

You ever try multitasking?' he asked, the glint in his eye deliberately provocative.

'I'm afraid so. And unfortunately I'm exceptionally bad at it.'

Damn, how could he have forgotten how forthright she was? She talked about sex without an ounce of calculation or suberfuge or fake modesty, in that clean crisp smoky British accent that arrowed straight into his crotch. After years spent handling women who figured sex could be bartered for love and marriage and happy ever after, Gina Carrington's attitude was refreshingly straightforward—and one heck of a turn-on.

Not so much of a turn-on, though, was what she was saying through those luscious lips of hers. Lips he'd wanted to feast on as soon as he'd seen her sitting in the mill's reception area looking hot and determined and aloof.

Swallowing down the groan that was threatening to rumble out of his throat, he kept his hands on the steering wheel and his gaze on the road ahead—and mulled over the problem.

What had seemed like a fairly simply seduction at the mill had become a mite more complicated. Gina's professional scruples weren't something he'd given a whole heck of a lot of thought to before offering her the commission. And now he'd seen her work, he probably should have. She was good, even better than he'd expected—the strategies she'd roughed together already exactly what they'd been looking for. Economical, well-directed and expertly designed with an originality that would make people sit up and take notice.

'I'm not gonna pretend that isn't a disappointment,' he said, keeping the lazy drawl in place as he played for time. 'But that's your prerogative.'

Just as it would be his prerogative to change her mind.

He rolled his shoulders, edging his foot off the gas pedal as the car bumped over a set of railroad tracks, and drifted into the urban sprawl of strip malls and tree-lined neighbourhoods that marked the edge of town.

Scruples or no scruples, Gina was dead right about one thing: good sex was distracting—it was supposed to be. And when they had sex it had the potential to be nothing short of combustible.

He watched her out of the corner of his eye, the determined tilt of her chin almost as beguiling as the tremble in her plump bottom lip.

Well, hell.

Gina might not be as wild and untamed as she had been as a teenager, but she still had the same volatile libido. That tiny lip tremor told him louder than words she didn't want to say no any more than he wanted to hear it. Adrenaline charged into his system, making heat pool in his lap.

While Gina might not be much good at multitasking, he happened to be a master at it. The heat surged and crested. Once upon a time, Gina had done him the favour of showing him that he couldn't deny his own libido. Why not use the skills he'd acquired in the years since to teach her a valuable lesson in return—that great sex, while distracting, didn't have to be a disaster if you knew how to handle the fall-out?

He pressed his foot onto the gas, to surge past an old truck, and felt his confidence soar at the thought of the game of cat and mouse that awaited them. There would be time enough over the next few days to enjoy Gina's company, work closely together on her marketing plans—and lead her slowly but surely into temptation.

Once upon a time, she'd broken down all his inhibitions by being bold and sexy—and flirting outrageously with him—and in so doing had set him on the road to where he was now. And okay, he wasn't gonna lie, it had been a tough road during the difficult years of his marriage, rocky and painful and far far too long, but the journey had been worth it, and the des-

ination liberating. Discovering that while he might well be
his father's son, driven by the same weaknesses of the flesh,
he didn't have to make the same mistakes.

So why not show Gina that she could have her cake and
eat it too?

Because he had a feeling Gina's objections now had as
much to do with the girl she'd been back then—who had sat
in her tiny bed and accepted all the blame for his infidelity
with agonising flippancy—as it did to do with the career
woman she was now and her professional scruples.

Why not show Gina that them enjoying themselves together
didn't have to screw up their professional relationship—
because in the end, however distracting, however combustible they were together, it would only be sex. And that there
really wasn't any blame to be apportioned for what had happened ten years ago any more—because as he had eventually discovered when he'd come to accept his true nature, it
had been inevitable.

He took the exit off I-16 and headed into the city, towards
the Historic District and home.

'With that in mind,' Gina piped up — the proprietary tone
telling him she thought his silence had signalled acquiescence to her plans, 'I should probably check into a hotel during my stay.'

I don't think so, sugar.

He erased the itch of frustration and pasted on an easy
smile. 'Now why would you do that?'

'Well, I…' she began, her tone not quite so sure.

'My home has a study with all the computer equipment
you'll need to work on your plans for the mill while you're
here,' he said, moving in his king to threaten her queen. 'And
it'll save me having to drive to a hotel every time we want to
work on them together. It's a whole lot more efficient if you
stay at my place.'

'I'm still not sure…'

'Of course, if you're scared you won't be able to keep your hands to yourself?'

The prickle of irritation made it clear she hadn't spotted the trap. 'I'm perfectly capable of—'

'Then we don't have a problem, do we?' he cut in and rolled through the four-way stop sign that stood at the corner of Peachtree and Divine.

Checkmate, sugar.

Gina pushed the flicker of panic to the back of her mind at the knowledge that she'd just been rather neatly outmanoeuvred.

Don't be ridiculous.

They were both adults. He hadn't objected to her stipulation about no sex. In fact, he'd been remarkably unconcerned and accommodating—to the point of being a little ego-deflating, really. Seemed she might have overestimated her charms—and his intentions.

The car glided into a tree-lined square with a decorative stone fountain as its centrepiece.

'This is pretty. Where are we?' she asked, determined to soak up Savannah's elegant architecture and stop obsessing about the distracting man next to her.

'We're in the Southern Historic District and this is Divine Square. My place is on the far side.' He pointed past the fountain.

'It's beautiful.'

The imposing three-and four-storey Victorian houses stood back from the road on all four sides of the square behind high fences or fancy iron railings, their ornate balconies and colourful gingerbread trim vaguely reminiscent of New Orleans' French Quarter. But with the houses' imposing wooden shutters closed tight against the muggy heat and the peaceful patch of flower beds and scrubs surrounding the fountain devoid of tourists, the historic square projected a well-bred gentility in direct counterpoint to the loud, louche ambience of the Big Easy.

'Here we go.' He stopped in front of a Civil War-era mansion that took up one whole side of the square. He leaned across to pull a small black device out of the glove compartment, giving her an enticing whiff of sweat and soap, before he pressed the button and the gates swished open.

'How long have you lived here?' she asked, oddly depressed at the thought he might have shared this home with his ex-wife.

'My family have owned the house for generations. I moved in a few years back,' he replied, inadvertently answering her question and making the knot in her stomach release a little. 'After my mother passed it was either move back in, sell it or watch the place fall into disrepair. Option one seemed the easiest for now.'

After parking in the house's driveway, he clicked the button to close the gates, slung the device back in the glove box and switched off the ignition. He swivelled round in his seat, a wry smile curving those firm sensual lips. 'The place has eight bedrooms, but I can get my housekeeper to open up the pool house, if you'd prefer more privacy.'

'Right,' she said, biting down on her bottom lip and the idiotic urge to pout at just how accommodating he was being to her no-sex suggestion. 'That would be ideal.'

Her breathing accelerated as he climbed out of the car and skirted the bonnet to open the passenger door. Standing back, he swept his hand out to encompass a front garden planted with flowering scrubs and a giant weeping willow that cast the stairs leading up to the mansion's front entrance in glorious shade. 'Welcome to the Price family's humble home, Gina.'

There was nothing humble about it or the wickedly tempting gleam in those devastating blue eyes.

Accepting his offer of the pool house hadn't been cowardice—it had been insurance. Resisting him wouldn't be that hard.... If she set her mind to it.

But she drew her fingers out of his as he took her hand to help her out of the car—and mounted the steps alone.

CHAPTER TEN

IN THE DAYS that followed, Gina surprised herself—sticking religiously to her decision to keep her association with Carter professional while working out a killer media strategy for the mill.

That said, the only way to stick to her plan had been to keep Carter at arm's length. Luckily for her, he'd helped to facilitate her avoidance by providing her with a sporty little Mustang to use as a runaround. After mornings spent at the mill getting acquainted with Carter's staff and the factory's production processes, and studiously avoiding too much consultation time with the man himself, she could escape in the afternoon to do 'important research' in Savannah.

Which turned out to be a surprisingly fascinating endeavour. She'd never been to the South before, having always dismissed it based on popular stereotypes and one too many viewings of *Gone with the Wind*. But instead of discovering a city marred by the legacy of slavery and the civil war, Gina discovered a thriving metropolis founded on commerce that had since become a cultural melting pot. Speciality bookshops, retro ice-cream parlours, rehabbed movie theatres showing old classics and Internet cafés filled with students and tourists alike vied for space with the grand mansions and garden squares of the Historic District. Despite its stately grandeur Savannah was a vibrant hub of activity filled with the curious and the ambitious.

Carter himself seemed to fall comfortably between the two—his easy-going manner matched by a sharp intelligence and a killer business instinct. It was hard not to admire his single-mindedness—even when that single-mindedness was aimed squarely at her. Because while she had made the commitment to keep their relationship professional, she wasn't convinced Carter was entirely on board with it. Her suspicions were aroused her first morning at the pool house, when she'd woken up to the sound of rhythmic splashing coming from right outside the front door.

She'd flipped up the curtain while making her morning coffee to see who was using the pool and got an eyeful of bronzed male muscle soaking wet. An eyeful she had not been able to erase from her brain no matter how hard she'd tried.

On day three of her self-imposed exile, she heard the sound of Carter doing his morning laps in the pool and resisted the urge to flip the curtain up again. For about fifteen seconds.

She caught him as he levered himself out of the water and stood on the tiles drying himself—her throat dried to parchment as heat pounded into every one of her pulsepoints.

'Carter Price, you wicked tease,' she whispered on an exasperated hiss, her fingers trembling on the curtain.

Was it her imagination or were those skin-tight trunks doing even less to cover his package this morning?

She blew out a breath of frustration. No wonder the blasted man had offered her a chance to stay in the pool house. 'A more private place to stay, my butt. More like a ringside seat to temptation.'

His ridged six-pack tensed as he lifted his arms to dry his hair—making his abdomen resemble that of a Greek statue. Sunlight peeked through the willow trees that separated the pool enclosure from the rest of the mansion's walled garden and rippled over firm, tanned flesh. Gina's tongue darted out to lick dry lips as he looped the towel round his shoulders and glanced towards the pool house.

She dropped the curtain as if it had been electrified with a two-thousand-volt current.

Had he spotted her peeking?

She poured herself a cool glass of lemonade from the pitcher in the house's tiny fridge and ignored the weight sinking in her belly.

After three quick swallows, she marched into the house's small bathroom—to complete her own morning ritual.

Who cared if he had spotted her looking at his nearly naked body in those ludicrously revealing swimming trunks? Peeking didn't count.

As long as she didn't go out there and rugby tackle him to the ground—she was still sticking to her curfew. With no help from him.

The man was being deliberately provocative. And she hadn't risen to the bait. She'd been mature and sensible and disgustingly celibate for three whole days now, while living in his home and being subjected to his buff body less than three yards from her bedroom door every morning.

And managing not to make any reference to his exhibitionism during the hours they spent together gave her a free pass to sainthood.

That said, her abstinence had cost her. It had taken her several hours to fall into a fitful sleep each night, the evenings she spent with Carter at the big house only adding to her torment.

Because while she'd managed to keep the conversation entirely innuendo free, sticking to topics such as her work on the new website design, blogging strategies, the history of Savannah and even the American Civil War—which Carter referred to with a wry smile as 'The War of Northern Aggression'—

and she hadn't salivated once, or not in his presence anyway, the pressure had built each night anyway.

All those long lazy looks, all those wide easy smiles when she said something sharp or witty, all those considering hums of approval that rumbled up his chest when he listened with alarming intensity—were not remotely innocent. And the swimming, right outside her bedroom window.… That was the biggest tease of all.

But she was holding up.

She swallowed down the lump of lust and risked another peek. An odd mixture of regret and relief swooped into her stomach at the sight of the empty pool patio, the wet footprints on the sun-soaked tiles leading out of the walled garden back towards the house. The still surface of the water glinted, a visible echo of the shimmer of sensation rising up her spine.

While her behaviour so far had been exemplary, she had over a week to go. And as each day passed—she could feel her resistance crumbling.

She let the curtain drop, stripped off the T-shirt she wore to sleep in and stepped into the shower. Ten days wasn't that long. She'd gone nearly six months before that thoughtless night a week ago with Carter. She could handle ten days. Surely.

And then she'd be free and clear and have conclusive proof that she could do denial. When she had to.

But then she pressed the palm of her hand to the mound of her sex, felt the insistent throb of arousal as she pictured his torso—and that damn package defined to perfection behind black Lycra—and flicked on the cold tap. She shuddered as she stood under the frigid spray, and had to admit that cold showers were getting seriously old.

So old, in fact, that tonight she might have to confront Carter when he returned from the mill for their regular dinner date at the mansion and let him know she was wise to his little game—and she wasn't playing.

'So did you enjoy yourself in Savannah today?'

Gina placed her fork beside her plate with deliberate precision and eyed Carter, who was sitting across from her at the large walnut dining-room table with a typically assured smile on his face.

'Yes, thank you. I took some nice shots down by the river and along Decatur to illustrate the weblog I'm planning. But I don't think I need to stay any longer. I thought I'd catch a flight home tomorrow.' And if the thought made her feel a little down, it had no bearing on anything.

'I thought we agreed you'd stay a couple of weeks? You've only been here three days.'

'I thought we agreed to keeping this relationship professional,' she countered. 'But that was before I discovered you were an exhibitionist.'

The crinkle of a frown cleared from his brow to be followed by the knowing curve of his lips. 'So now it's my fault you can't multitask?'

She tapped a fingernail against the shiny walnut veneer and glared at him. 'I didn't say I couldn't multitask, I said I didn't want to—because it'll distract me.'

'No, actually, you said you weren't good at multitasking.' The curve widened into a grin. 'So what you need is more practice.'

'Your morning swim is unnecessarily provocative. And you know it,' she snapped, determined to refocus the argument where it belonged—with the blame for her frustration firmly on his shoulders.

'Provocative or proactive?' The wry tone thickened with innuendo. 'I'm real good at multitasking, sugar, and I'm ready and willing to show you how it's done.'

She narrowed her eyes, and wished she had Superman's ability to sear lead with a single glance. 'Has it ever occurred to you and your gigantic ego that maybe I don't want to sleep with you again?'

He leant back in his chair, the nonchalant grin widening. 'As me and my gigantic ego have caught you peeking more than once,' he drawled, 'we know you want to, so I'm figuring it's not me, or the sex, you're scared of, it's yourself.'

'Scared of…' She scoffed, or tried to as the dart of shame she'd suppressed for so long closed her throat. 'Don't be ridiculous. Why would I be scared of myself? Scared of what exactly?'

'You tell me,' he replied, the smile fading as his gaze sharpened—and she had the uncomfortable feeling he could see into her soul. 'You're the one who apologised for something that didn't have a damn thing to do with you. You're the one who called herself a tramp…. You're the one who's putting business before pleasure when there's no reason why we can't enjoy both while you're here. We're both consenting adults, we're both unattached at the moment, we both enjoy sex—especially with each other—and we're both too good at what we do to let something as inconsequential as sex distract us. So why shouldn't we go for it?'

She placed her napkin on the table, then stood, bracing her palms on the polished wood to disguise trembling fingers.

'Thank you for the commission. I'm going to do an amazing job. And thank you for your Southern hospitality.' She forced servility into her voice, searching for the professional distance. 'Savannah is a beautiful city, and I've enjoyed my stay here.' Give or take the odd sleepless night. 'But I think I'll pass on the free psychoanalysis *and* your generous offer of anonymous sex on the side. And head home tomorrow.' Where she should have stayed all along.

He stood as she left the room, the gallant gesture in contrast to the open hunger in his gaze as it met hers. She made herself take brisk, sure, sensible steps, despite the pulse of longing making her limbs lethargic.

He didn't know her, and he didn't know what she'd been through ten years ago. And he never would, because telling him now would be painful and pointless—and far too personal. But she had to admit that he'd been right about one thing. Her desire to avoid more intimacy between them had nothing whatsoever to do with the commission or her multitasking skills and everything to do with the man.

Because she'd discovered a long time ago that sex with Carter Price was never inconsequential.

Carter whispered an expletive as the door clicked closed, and threw down the napkin clutched in his fist.

Cute, Price. Real cute.

After three days of keeping his cool, of keeping his distance, of letting her have the time she needed to get over her misguided professional ethics, and being real careful not to show his frustration—and parading around on that damn pool terrace every morning like a prize stud—he'd had his moment and he'd screwed it up. Because he'd pushed. And he never pushed...

Mercy, had he actually used the word inconsequential? No wonder she'd heard the word anonymous instead.

He might as well have hoisted her onto the table, flipped up her skirts and torn off her panties again for all the finesse he'd used.

He crossed to the drinks cabinet, pushed aside the imported single malt whiskey he usually favoured to clasp the bottle of his father's locally distilled liquor that lurked at the back. He downed a generous slug, then flinched as it shot down his throat like a burning bullet and exploded in his stomach.

He thumped a fist to his chest, to restart his heart, and let out a harsh cough.

Gina Carrington might be the most sexually liberated woman he'd ever met, but she was still a woman. Which meant she deserved to be wooed, not bullied, into his bed.

Carter, honey, have you ever thought your desires might be a little unnatural? Delfina tells me her Jim doesn't expect her to do her marital duty more than once a month and yet you are pestering me every other night.

The long-forgotten memory of his young wife's barbed enquiry pierced through his frustration—bringing with it the crushing echo of guilt and humiliation. He shoved the bottle back into the cabinet, raked not-quite-steady fingers through his hair.

Where the hell had that come from? He wasn't that green kid any more, trying and failing to satisfy a woman whose needs had never matched his own. Women enjoyed his company now, in bed as well as out of it. And his marriage to Missy hadn't failed ultimately because of their sexual problems, but for a whole host of other reasons.

When he was sixteen and they'd first started dating, Missy Wainwright's sweet, peaceful, non-confrontational company had been his sanctuary from a home where his father's bullying, overbearing presence and his mother's rigid insistence that keeping up appearances was all that mattered had made him feel sullen and tense and disillusioned.

But after his father's death, and that incendiary one-night encounter with Gina Carrington—a woman who couldn't be sweet and peaceful even if you gagged her—he'd begun to see that Missy's sweetness stemmed from a lack of intelligent conversation, and her refusal to argue about anything openly was actually more passive-aggressive than peaceful and non-confrontational.

Missy had said she'd forgiven him, when he'd returned to

Savannah and confessed the sin he'd committed with Gina. But the knowledge had been there festering between them, the wounded expression she wore every time they had a disagreement reminding him without words that he was the one in the wrong—he was the one who couldn't be trusted. And the fact that he'd never been able to forget Gina—and how much he'd enjoyed sinning with her—only increased his guilt.

During the increasingly bitter, barren years of his marriage, he'd got a little fixated on the exquisite pleasure of that one night. The surge of excitement, of exhilaration when Gina kissed him and caressed him with such fervour in places Missy had barely been willing to touch—and made love to him with a fierce, untamed determination that told him she wanted him, that she accepted him despite his faults.

Missy's deflating words, the wounded look she'd wielded so effectively, faded as two searingly erotic visions of Gina took their place and merged into one. Not quite two weeks ago riding him to climax—and a decade before that as she impaled herself on his thrusting erection for the first time: her unguarded expression full of the same wild hunger he'd glimpsed from behind the pool house curtain that morning.

His heart kicked so hard he could hear it above the ticks of his mother's antique carriage clock on the mantel. The heavy weight of his erection strained for release against the confinement of his suit pants.

Maybe it was time he stopped kidding himself that his desire to have Gina again had nothing whatsoever to do with that night a decade ago. Was that why he'd screwed up this seduction so royally? Because a part of him was still desperate to prove his desires weren't unnatural and they never had been? Because he needed to recapture that addictive feeling of euphoria, that heady feeling of connection they'd shared under a maple tree in the campus grounds and on her narrow bed in Reese's house—and just under two week ago in the cool lines of a New York hotel room.

Gina Carrington still had some weird hold over him. Or rather, she had some weird hold over his body. Probably because she'd been his first. A hold he intended to break over the next ten days. So he could sever for ever his ties to that green, needy boy.

But to do that he had to get Gina to play ball.

So instead of standing here, drinking his old man's bootleg liquor and beating himself up about her decision to leave, what he needed to do was get her to stay.

Yeah, Gina was a woman but she wasn't like any other woman he'd ever met.

You couldn't reason with Gina, or cajole her, or control her…. The only way to get what you wanted was to take it, and give her what she wanted in return.

He walked to the door of the dining room, headed down the corridor to the back of the house, purpose in every stride.

To hell with sense and caution and business scruples.

Raindrops splattered his face as he strode through the darkened gardens towards the pool house. The ominous grumble of distant thunder had a grim smile lifting his lips—and seemed mighty fortuitous in the circumstances.

Given that he was about to fight fire with fire… A monsoon might come in handy to ensure they didn't both get burned.

Then he walked silently through the gate that led to the pool patio and his erection hit critical mass. A dark figure stood at the far end of the pool beneath the overhanging branches of the willow tree. Her arms stretched skyward, beckoning the rain forth to drench the thin silk of her blouse and reveal the lacy bra beneath.

Seemed he wasn't the only one who needed relief from the heat.

She twirled under the deluge, the sinuous movement effortlessly sensuous, artlessly sexy—and demonstrating the extent of the need she'd tried so hard to hide.

She was magnificent—and for the next ten days, he was going to make sure she was all his.

He stepped forward as the heavens opened and the rain soaked through his shirt and trousers in seconds. The ripple of lightning glimmered off the water and lit her face as her gaze darted to his.

She dropped her arms. Shock and desire made a devastating combination on her face as she stood completely still, observing him, then swept the damp hair over her shoulders—the bold, provocative move part instinct, part invitation but mostly challenge. The dark outline of her nipples jutted through her transparent clothing as the rain continued to pound down.

'I told you we're not going to do this,' she shouted above the clap of thunder. 'I'm leaving tomorrow.'

He could see her staggered breathing, but she didn't retreat when he reached her, or shrink away when he gathered a fistful of her wet hair, and drew her head back. Water slicked down her face and made her eyelashes glitter above the defiant glare.

'You're not going anywhere,' he yelled back. 'We need to finish this once and for all.'

She shuddered and braced her palms against his chest, but instead of pushing him away her fingers gripped, her gaze full of the sexual knowledge that had always inflamed his senses. 'And how exactly do you propose we do that?'

He wrapped his arm round her waist, yanked her towards him, grinding the painful erection against the soft, yielding flesh of her belly. 'The only way we know how.'

Then he slanted his mouth across hers—and plundered.

CHAPTER ELEVEN

WE NEED TO finish this once and for all.

Carter's ultimatum echoed through Gina's mind as she plunged her fingers into his hair, and their tongues tangled.

This wasn't the fun, teasing, flirtatious exploration of their New York encounter. This was raw, basic, elemental need. She had thought she could resist him. She'd been wrong.

As her fingers clutched the short curls at his nape and the rain pummelled them both, the fire consumed her. Sense and reason deserted her. Why couldn't they do this? He was right. They were consenting adults, they both enjoyed sex, especially with each other, and no one need ever know.

And how was she ever going to be able to rely on her new leaf with this burning hunger for him lurking in the background?

Wide palms gripped her hips and ground her against the thick ridge in his trousers. He lifted his head, water dripping off his brows, and shouted above the rain. 'Let's take this inside before we drown.'

Grasping her hand, he jogged to the pool house and dragged her inside. Wet clothes stuck to hot, damp skin as they battled together to get naked as fast as possible.

He tore her blouse, she ripped his shirt, but after a furious battle they touched flesh. She shivered as he hauled her close and they feasted on each other. Her back bumped against the closed door as he lifted her, positioning her to take him. Then he reared back and swore softly, letting her go.

'Damn it!' He grappled for his discarded trousers, retrieved the foil package, and sheathed himself.

'Good thinking, Batman.' She kissed him, framing his face with shaking hands. 'Now hurry up.'

'Yes, ma'am.' He boosted her into his arms, thumping her back against the door, and took her in one solid thrust.

The shocking fullness turned to exquisite pain, mind-blowing pleasure. He withdrew, thrust back—the movements harsh, rough, and lacking his usual finesse, but so perfect, so right. Tears stung her eyes as she rode the glorious wave to completion.

He shuddered and with an incomprehensible grunt followed her over seconds later.

They stood together, his fingers digging into her thighs, her legs hooked around his waist, his erection still huge inside her. The patter of slowing rain hitting the door masked the jagged pants of their breathing. He dropped his forehead to hers, and whispered, 'I think I just died and went to heaven.' She tightened her arms around his neck as he buried his face in her wet hair, the sudden urge to stay for ever in the semiconsciousness of afterglow overwhelming. She didn't want to worry about consequences. About right, or wrong. Sense or insanity. She just wanted to feel him inside her.

Easing out of her, he let her down gently. A single tear slipped over her lid—the moment of connection, of acceptance, gone. She shook off the sentimental thought and scrubbed away the tear with an impatient fist.

Don't get mushy, you ninny. This is sex. Great sex. You don't want more.

Holding his head, she lifted his face, and grinned.

'Isn't that sacrilegious?'

'What?' he asked, clearly a little dazed.

'Mentioning heaven after what we just did?'

'The hell you say.'

He grinned back at her. 'Which is exactly why you love me.'

She forced a smile, the casual use of the *L* word a shock. And not a pleasant one. 'That would be your ego talking,' she replied dryly.

She stepped out of his arms—needing distance. But a muscled arm banded round her waist, halting her retreat. 'Hey, we're not through here.'

He nuzzled her neck and sensation raced down her spine, the thick ridge of renewed arousal nestling between her buttocks.

'My ego wants to try out the bed.'

'Oh, it does, does it?' She turned, and draped her arms over his shoulders, locking her knees against the foolish fragility—then glanced down, pointedly. 'I must say, your ego has remarkable powers of recuperation.'

He tucked a finger under her chin, and raised her face. 'Only where you're concerned.'

'Good to know.' She forced flippancy into her voice.

Just great sex. Remember.

Taking her hand, he crossed to the bed and in one smooth move swung her into his arms and then dumped her into the centre of the mattress. Laughter bubbled in her chest, forcing out the vulnerability. This could never be more for her, or for him, than a quick fling. So why stress about it? She didn't do ties, or commitments, because she hated regrets. And she had far too many of them already. Especially where Carter Price was concerned.

Lying down next to her, he combed his fingers through her hair and traced his thumb across her cheekbone. 'Damn, Gina, but you're irresistible.'

Her heart squeezed at the gleam of admiration in those

pure blue eyes. She held his wrist and lifted his hand away from her face. 'So are you. Which would probably explain why, despite my best intentions, this keeps happening.'

He toyed with a damp curl that hung over her shoulder, tantalisingly close to her breast, a slow smile forming. 'I'm hoping that means this isn't another one-off.' He lifted the curl to his lips and kissed it, the tenderness of the gesture causing the blood to thunder in her ears. 'And you're not still planning to run out on me tomorrow.'

'I think we both just proved neither of us are *that* good at denial.'

He dropped the curl, the smile widening. 'So is this a *thing*, or a *fling*?'

The mocking question eased the squeeze on her heart. 'A fling. But that's all it is. My flight back's in just over a week's time and that's when this will have to end.'

The broad smile didn't falter. 'Works for me.' His hand skimmed down her neck and cupped her breast, his thumb circling the rigid nipple. 'But no more dumb stuff about work.' His eyes met hers, the expression more determined than playful. 'What we do in bed together—and anywhere else we choose—hasn't got a damn thing to do with your commission. You got that?'

She stretched, trying to focus on the conversation while his absent caress sent sensation into her sex. 'Yes, boss.'

His eyebrows shot up and she laughed. Grabbing her wrists, he yanked her arms above her head and held her captive for a quick hard kiss. 'Damn, but I want you again, you little tease.'

'What's stopping you, Rhett?' She rubbed her leg against his, enjoying the feel of the soft hairs, the muscled flanks and the sight of his eyes dilating to black.

'Lord, give me strength,' he murmured, trapping her legs with one hard thigh. 'We're gonna have to take a rain check.'

He glanced out of the window at the dying storm. 'Literally. I need more condoms. A lot more.' His gaze roamed over her. 'I'm thinking a whole box wouldn't go amiss.'

'Not a problem, sugar. Like all smart, responsible, twenty-first-century women, I keep an emergency supply in my toiletry bag.' She reared up to kiss him on the nose, feeling ridiculously perky, and carefree and relieved. There was no need to read more into this fling than there actually was—they had a history, but one he need never know about, and one she had come to terms with a long time ago. 'I'll go get them.'

'Nuh-uh.' He snagged her round the waist as she launched off the bed. 'Right now I'm a big fan of female emancipation, but I'm still the guy. I'll get them.'

She laughed, the command delivered in a wry monotone that was both stupidly macho and surprisingly cute. 'My hero,' she purred, the endorphins shooting round her body overriding the last of her caution. She lounged against the pillows and watched him march into the bathroom, gloriously naked. A man on a mission.

She admired the tight buns as his bare butt disappeared from view and sent up her own silent prayer of thanks. They had just over a week to finally finish this. To satisfy the sexual hunger that had always burned so brightly, so insistently between them. And this time there could be no harm done—because she wasn't that wild, reckless, vulnerable girl any more, but a smart, sorted career woman who...

'What the *Sam Hell*...?'

The startled oath had her shooting upright—the smug contentment faltering as she recalled exactly what else she kept in her toiletry bag.

Carter emerged from the bathroom with a fistful of condoms in one hand, and the long column of moulded plastic held delicately between the thumb and forefinger of his other hand—as if it were an unexploded bomb. He cleared his throat dramatically and held it up for inspection. 'Well, now. What do you have here, Miss Gina?'

She flopped back on the pillows, and stared at the ceiling fan, struggling to quell the blush blossoming across her chest. 'You found Justin.'

'You gave it a *name*?' The question came out on a choke of outrage.

She inched up on her elbows, the blush subsiding as her lips quirked. 'Well, of course I did. I don't want to be getting it on with a stranger.' What was there to be embarrassed about? If a smart, responsible, twenty-first-century woman was single and intended to stay that way, a vibrator was essential equipment.

He made a sound in his throat as if he were choking. 'I think I just died and went to hell! What did you call it, again?'

She covered her mouth to suppress the unladylike snort of amusement. 'Justin.'

'Hell, I thought so.' He peered at it. 'Not only did you give it a name, you gave it a sissy name.'

The snort popped out, tinged with mock outrage. 'Justin is not a sissy name. I happened to have a major crush on Justin Timberlake once upon a time. So it seemed appropriate.'

'Sugar, I don't know what kind of guys you've been dating. But nothing about this *tool* is appropriate. It isn't even anatomically correct. No guy's got that much heft this side of an elephant.'

She giggled, crawling across the bed to perch on the edge and cup him. She stroked, and hummed deep in her throat, her gaze sweeping down to assess the firm flesh as it swelled and hardened. Her gaze swept back up to peer at him through lashes that fluttered demurely. 'I don't know... You seem to be giving Justin a fairly good run for his money.'

'Right, that does it.' Flipping the vibrator over his shoulder, he gave her shoulders a shove, tumbling her onto the bed. He climbed on top, caging her in, his rough chuckles mingling with her giggles.

'Hey, be careful with Justin!' she said, still channelling the mock outrage. 'He wasn't exactly cheap.'

'Sweetheart, in case you haven't figured this out yet...' He rubbed the heel of his palm against her mound, the dire warning in his voice promising all sorts of delicious retribution '...from here on in, you are dumping *Justeen* in favour of a real man.'

She laughed out loud, sucking in a breath when he licked one thrusting nipple and drew it into his mouth. The areola tightened and throbbed. 'Yes, but do you have seven different settings?' she demanded on a breathless sigh.

He blew softly on her aching nipple, lifting his head when she groaned. The confidence in his gaze was as arousing as the expert stroke of his fingertips on the slick wet flesh between her thighs. 'Sugar, when you're as good as I am, you only need the one.'

She was still laughing as he stroked her over the edge.

CHAPTER TWELVE

IN THE BLISSFUL days that followed, Gina worked hard to create a magnificent new website and excellent media strategy for the Price Paper Consortium. She worked even harder at fulfilling every prurient sexual fantasy she had ever had about the consortium's CEO. And harder still at ensuring her emotions didn't get in the way of the good time she was having, and the even better sex.

But as the days passed a hitch appeared in her plan that involved an unfortunate discovery. Carter Price was as irresistible out of bed as he was in it.

And if she didn't know better, she could have sworn he had orchestrated that giddy glide into romance, almost as carefully as he had orchestrated their red-hot ride into lust.

Why else would he have organised an evening watching classic Hollywood movies at the retro cinema a ten-minute walk from his home—and then made her heart flip-flop by necking with her in the back row? Why else would he have insisted on holding her hand during their lazy afternoon stroll through the redevelopment of trinket shops and parkland on River Street? Or whispered wicked suggestions in her ear to make her laugh as they browsed the antiquarian delights in a dusty basement bookshop?

Even at the mill, where she insisted on them maintaining a respectable distance in front of his employees, his sharp, insightful and always enthusiastic comments about her ideas had become as seductive as all those casually possessive gestures and throwaway displays of affection. She felt as if she'd been caught in the silken web of his friendship—become a prisoner to all that charm and charisma and affability, powerless to resist the steely determination that lurked beneath.

Dating Carter Price was certainly unlike any of her other dating experiences—which, although not nearly as prolific as most people believed, fell into two distinct categories: the standard 'hot, short and sweet', or, on those rare occasions when she didn't end the affair soon enough, 'hot, short and not-so-sweet'. Carter should have fallen easily into the first category. That had been the plan. But he wasn't hot, he was scorching, and as the day approached when she would have to leave Savannah and return to her single life 'short and sweet' was becoming 'short and potentially sticky'. Sticky in a way that confused and disturbed her, because the single life she loved was starting to seem boring and even a little lonely simply because it wouldn't have Carter in it.

Gina stretched limbs pleasantly sore from the night-time's activities and rolled onto her side to contemplate the man lying next to her in the generous tester bed—and all the reasons why their fling was starting to bother her.

She frowned. And that was another thing. They'd relocated to his palatial bedroom in the main house after their first night at the pool house, Carter insisting that the queen bed was way too cramped for them to explore each other properly. Given the scope of exploration he'd had in mind—which even she, with her suitably filthy mind, hadn't anticipated—she had to concede he'd had a point. And staying in his room, with its solid, intricately carved mahogany furniture and the wide French doors that opened onto a charming balcony overlooking the square, hadn't exactly been a chore.

But as the morning sun streamed in, illuminating the handsome face that had captivated her a decade ago, she also had to concede that moving into the main house was just another in a long line of concessions she'd agreed to without putting up much of a fight. Right from the moment he'd looked at her across the bar in The Standard Hotel with that dangerous allure in his eyes, she'd been giving in to him over and over again—and that was bothering her too, almost as much as her reluctance to walk away from him in a few days time.

She searched his face for clues as to how he'd managed to slip under her guard—and make her crave his attention. She studied the dark brows, that tempting dent in his chin and the small creases of amusement at the edge of his mouth that he wore even in sleep. She blew out an unsteady breath. No wonder she was captivated—and behaving like a rabbit caught in the headlights of an oncoming freight train. The man was a total studmuffin, just as Reese had described him—and that was without even factoring in the effect of those killer blue eyes that could tempt a saint into fornication when he was awake.

He shifted in his sleep, mumbling something before a heavy hand came to rest on her hip. An errant curl of dark hair fell across his forehead. She smoothed it off again with a fingernail and his eyelids snapped opened. She snatched her hand back. Too late. She was already trapped in that penetrating blue gaze.

'Hey there,' he growled. His fingers tightened on her hip and he eased her closer, the familiar morning cuddle something she'd got too accustomed to as well. 'How you feeling, this bright and beautiful morning, Miss Gina?'

Not as safe as I'd hoped. Why do you have to be so irresistible, Carter Price?

Swallowing down the solid object lodged in her throat, she lifted the sheet to inspect the equally solid object nudging her belly. 'Not as perky as you, obviously.'

He yawned, and stretched through a rumble of self-satisfied laughter. 'Well now, sugar. That's just a natural male reaction to waking up beside a beautiful...' The suggestive comment drifted to a halt as he squinted into the sunlight, then jerked into a sitting position and thrust a hand through his hair. 'Damn it, what time is it?'

'About ten, at a conservative estimate.'

He swore, whipped back the sheet and jumped out of bed, protective hands cupping his morning erection as he raced to the dresser.

'What's the matter?' She sat up, hugging the sheet to her bosom, and smiled, his panicked antics dissolving the tightness in her throat.

Honestly, what on earth was she worrying about? She'd be leaving soon and, while it might be a bit more of a wrench than she'd anticipated, nothing would make her change that. Of course she felt drawn to him, in a way she hadn't with other men, because they had a past. But that didn't mean they had a future.

'It's the weekend today,' she supplied.

'It's Sunday,' he declared, as if that explained everything. He dug out a pair of boxers and hopped across the room while shoving a foot into them—nearly falling over en route to the wardrobe. The resultant muttered curse elicited a chuckle from her ringside seat on the bed.

'As much as I'm enjoying the show,' she said, the now familiar giggles floating out as he yanked a perfectly pressed white linen shirt out of the wardrobe, 'isn't it bad karma to be swearing like that on a Sunday?'

He swung round, buttoning the shirt. 'Very funny.' Strolling back to the bed, he tugged the sheet out of her hands, his eyes glittering with retribution.

'Hey,' she protested, only to have the sheet flipped off entirely.

'No need to look so smug, Miss Gina. Because you're coming with me.'

She scrambled to retrieve the sheet. 'Says who? And where exactly do you think you're taking me?'

'To church. Where else?' He wrestled the sheet away with ease when her fingers went numb.

'I haven't been inside a church since I was sixteen and I got kicked out of St Bude's.'

'Why did they kick you out?'

She sent him a glare while trying to grab back the sheet. 'I seduced the biology teacher,' she replied, hoping to shock him with the truth—and get her hands on the stupid sheet.

Instead of looking shocked, though, he only laughed, balling up the sheet and tossing it across the room. 'Lucky guy.'

The lack of censure in his gaze as it roamed appreciatively over her exposed flesh made her cheeks heat. She tossed her hair over her shoulders, refusing to acknowledge the glow of contentment. So what if her many youthful transgressions didn't appear to bother him in the slightest? It was only because he was as big a reprobate as she was, and consequently unshockable.

'Sounds to me like you're definitely overdue for a visit to church, though,' he murmured. 'You need to atone for that sin and a whole lot more I happen to have firsthand knowledge of.'

'Not a chance.' She surrendered the sheet in favour of a mad dash to the bathroom—only to have him capture her in mid-flight. Her breath whooshed out as he scooped her up and her back hit his chest.

'FYI, honey,' he whispered into her hair, 'you'll have to cut down your two-hour morning shower. The service starts at eleven. And we don't want to be late.'

She struggled in earnest. 'Don't be ridiculous. I'm not going. I'd probably get struck by lightning.'

'God's a whole lot more forgiving than you think.' He nipped her ear lobe, laughing when she shuddered. 'If I've never been struck by lightning, I figure you're safe from divine retribution too.' The soft, seductive murmur of his breath turned her knees to jelly. 'Although, you may want to avoid going into the Lord's house the way God intended you.' He toyed with a nipple.

She slapped his hand away and escaped from his embrace, aroused now and more than a little disturbed by the invitation—and his insistence. 'You are kidding, right?'

He had to be. Surely? She didn't want to go to church. It would make her feel uncomfortable and hypocritical. Bringing back far too many memories of Sunday morning services at a succession of different boarding schools when she'd listened to the sermons with half an ear and refused to repent her many sins. And she definitely didn't want to go to church with Carter. There would be people he knew there. People he might introduce her to. People who might still be in touch with Marnie. But, worse than that, those same people might assume they were a couple. And they weren't.

'No, I'm not kidding,' he said, with strained patience, landing a playful slap on her butt when she stood rooted to the spot. 'Now put a fire under it. I'd hate to drag you there naked, and scandalise the minister. But I will if I have to.'

She grabbed the discarded sheet from the floor and wrapped it around her body, protecting herself from that far-too-possessive gaze, but not managing to do much for the shiver of unease.

'Carter, I am *not* going to church with you.'

His eyebrows winged up. 'Why not?'

'Because...' She wound the sheet tighter. 'Because people you know will be there.'

His mouth tilted in a puzzled smile. 'Uh-huh, so?'

Good grief, he actually was serious.

'So? So?' Her voice rose as irritation got the better of her. 'Meeting them would be…' *Wrong.*

'Would be what?' he asked over his shoulder, while selecting a suit from the wardrobe and tugging the trousers off the hanger.

'Pointless. Unnecessary,' she ground out, groping for the appropriate word. 'Misleading.'

His brows flattened into a frown as he zipped his trousers. 'Why don't you let me decide that?' he replied as if he hadn't just lost his mind. He shrugged on the suit jacket, then lifted her dress off the chair beside the bed and lobbed it to her—the same lemon-yellow shift dress that he'd peeled off her the night before. 'Put that on—it'll work.'

She caught the dress, and clasped it to her chest—starting to feel overwhelmed by that cast-iron will again, and not liking it one bit. 'Carter, you're not listening to me. There is no way I'm going to church with you.'

He approached her, looking impossibly debonair in the dark grey single-breasted suit. Placing warm palms on her shoulders, he massaged the tight muscles, digging into the knots of tension and making awareness skitter across her collarbone. 'I want you there—why are you worried about people I know meeting you? I'm not.'

You should be, she wanted to say, but she didn't, because it would make her sound cowardly and insecure. And she was neither of those things. Or she hadn't been until she'd fallen under Carter Price's spell again.

She gulped, refusing to give in to the flutter of panic—or the shimmer of arousal. And stepped out of reach of his magic hands.

Don't overreact. He's just a guy. He can't cast a spell on you unless you let him.

'Don't be silly—I'm not worried.' She was petrified and

she wasn't even sure why, but he definitely didn't need to know that.

'I guarantee they'll all be real polite,' he said lazily, but his eyes narrowed, his gaze sharpening. 'Southern manners mean they'll have to be.' He brushed a thumb across her cheek and sent her an easy smile. The panicked flutter intensified, as if she had a hummingbird trapped in her oesophagus. 'And anyhow, you don't have a choice.' His voice lowered in warning. 'Either you come peaceably or I'm going to cart you there over my shoulder.'

The teasing smile was still in place, but she could see the determined tilt of his chin and the muscle in his jaw flexing— and she couldn't be sure he was joking. Ordinarily she would have relished the fight, but right now her knees were too watery and the pulse of awareness in her belly too insistent to guarantee a win. So she went for the only option she had left—until she could think of another—grudging surrender. 'Fine, great, I'll go! But don't expect me to enjoy it.'

The teasing smile widened into a triumphant grin. 'This is the Riverside Christian Congregational Church, sugar. Attendance is about saving your immortal soul and making good business connections. And if you're a pillar of the community like me, you're not allowed to skip it or people will talk. But enjoyment is entirely optional.'

'Fabulous.' She marched to the bathroom, planning to indulge in her usual lengthy morning shower just to spite him— and hopefully postpone the inevitable. But before she had a chance to slam the door, she heard the wry comment from behind her. 'Make it quick. You've got ten minutes before I come in to get you.'

Blast the man, how did he read her so easily?

Ten minutes later she found out he wasn't joking about that either.

CHAPTER THIRTEEN

'ARE YOU GOING to sulk the whole day or can I expect a smile some time soon?'

Carter grinned at the surly expression Gina flicked his way from the passenger seat. He knew it was a cliché, but she looked cute when she was mad, especially with the wind blowing that sunshine-yellow dress against her figure as they drove down the river road.

'You know, you still haven't told me why you're so keen to drag me to church today.' She scowled at him. 'Apart from the obvious reason, of course.'

He shifted gear to take the bend and chuckled. 'Which is?'

'That you seem to get off on making me mad.'

She'd got that right, so he decided not to deny it. 'Hey? Is it my fault you look so damn sexy when you pout?'

She rolled her eyes. 'I'm going to be doing a lot more than pouting if this ordeal turns out as badly as I expect.'

He reached over the console to place a reassuring hand on her thigh—touched by the quiver of uncertainty in her voice.

He had to admit at first it had been a game getting her to hold his hand in public, getting her to cuddle up in bed each morning, hearing that sigh of surrender every time he increased the intimacy between them that bit more. But in the last week, he'd become addicted to pushing her boundaries, to seeing how far he could take it—and it didn't feel like a game any more. Because of that band that tightened around his heart now, every time the wary look flickered into her eyes when he got too close. For a woman who oozed sexual confidence, those moments of vulnerability intrigued and fascinated him and made him want to break down her barriers—to understand where her insecurities came from, and wipe them away.

He knew part of it had to do with her old man, whom she'd told him in a rare moment of candour had kicked her out as a teenager, but he couldn't quite shake the unpleasant thought that it also had something to do with him and what had happened between them a decade ago. Because every time he tried to talk about that, she shut up like a clam.

'Come on, sugar.' He patted her leg through the silk, the amusement gone. 'It won't be that bad, I swear.'

He caught her sceptical frown before returning his attention to the road.

'Why *do* you want me there?' she asked, again, putting him on the spot.

He didn't really have an answer, or certainly not one he wanted to admit to. How could he tell her that he wanted people to know they were together? That he'd gotten tired of the fiction that this was all just about sex? Without it seeming as if he was trying to back out of their deal?

He knew she'd be leaving soon and he was good with that. Ever since the failure of his marriage he'd made a point of not getting too attached to the women he dated.

But even if this wasn't permanent, he'd never liked subterfuge and he liked even less Gina's desire to keep their affair a secret. Why couldn't they enjoy each other's company in public as well as private? And while *he* knew that taking her to his family's church would make people think they were serious, she didn't know that, and he sure wasn't going to tell her. So what was she so damned scared of?

'No particular reason,' he lied smoothly. 'I just figured it would be cool to have you there, introduce you to some folks.' It was a non-answer and he could tell she knew it when he heard her scoff above the hot rush of wind.

'You know what drives me completely insane? The way you either answer a question with another question or give me an answer that means precisely nothing.'

He huffed out a chuckle. 'That's bull. I'm an open book.' He'd sure as hell been a lot more forthcoming about his past than she had. 'Go ahead and ask me anything you want.'

She swung round in the passenger seat and only then did it occur to him he might have given her too much rope. 'All right, then, answer me this: why did you despise your father?'

He mentally banged his head against the steering wheel. He hadn't seen that one coming. 'Why would you want to know that?'

'That doesn't happen to be another question you've just asked me, does it?'

Busted.

While he didn't much like getting caught on his own hook, he figured it would be smarter now not to give her the satisfaction of seeing him squirm.

Slowing the car to pull into the packed parking lot of the Riverside Church, he forced the words out on an indifferent monotone as he cruised into the only available slot at the end of the row. 'When I was fifteen, I caught my daddy making out with one of the help in my mama's parlour.'

'Making out? What exactly does that entail?'

He slung his arm over the wheel and stared at her, careful to keep his expression bland. 'He had his pants round his ankles, the girl was on her knees in front of him and his face looked like he was about to bust a blood vessel. Is that clear enough?'

He'd raised his voice, the old anger giving him away, but

instead of looking shocked or disgusted her eyes went dark with sympathy. 'Nasty,' she said. 'What did you do?'

'I told my mother and she went nuts.' He relaxed into the seat, the old anger dissolving in a pool of resignation. 'Not because of his *indiscretions*—she already knew about them—but because I'd had the bad manners to mention them.' He turned to Gina, the memory leaving a bitter taste. 'I knew they weren't madly in love with each other—I'd never seen them so much as kiss each other in public or in private. But until then I had no idea the marriage was such a dishonest sham. I promised myself if I ever got married it would be different. I would never cheat or lie to myself or my wife.' Damn, what a self-righteous hypocrite he'd been. 'Ironic, huh?'

Gina's pulse throbbed painfully in her neck. She hadn't expected his honesty and she didn't know how to make amends for the disillusionment that shadowed his eyes. 'I'm so sorry I made you break your promise.'

He shook his head and laughed, the deep rumble both genuinely amused and oddly comforting. 'Gina, sugar, no, you didn't.' He cupped her cheek. 'Meeting you eventually made me see I'd been kidding myself. My only regret now is that I didn't figure that out before I got into a marriage that was an even bigger lie than my parents'.'

She pulled his hand away from her face, knowing she couldn't have this conversation while he was touching her with such affection. But it was the first insight he'd given her into his marriage, and she couldn't stop herself from asking: 'How was it a lie?'

His gaze left hers and for a moment she felt sure he wouldn't answer, but then he shrugged. 'In a lot of ways.'

'What ways?'

The rueful grin returned. 'I believe you told me that night

that marrying a woman I had no knowledge of in the bedroom might end badly. Turns out you were right.'

'The *sex* was a problem?' Gina gasped, astonished, and unable to deny the sweet rush of vindication.

'Let's just say, she wasn't as enthusiastic about it as I was. Or you are.'

'That's not good,' she replied, stupidly pleased that the Virgin Queen of her imagination had been a little frigid after all.

'No, it sure isn't. It wasn't our biggest problem, but it felt big enough. Especially as I'd found out how good it could be…' He paused to clear his throat. 'With you.'

She should have stopped there, and let it go, this was all water way under the bridge now, but the sweet rush had turned to a torrent—and seeing the approval in his eyes only made it more intoxicating. 'What other problems did you have?'

'Eventually? Way too many to count.' The flush of colour hit his cheeks and the rush of vindication turned to one of sympathy. 'Before we were married she'd made me feel special,' he continued. 'She never challenged me, never contradicted me, never tried to tell me what to do like my daddy did. But then he died and I spent the night with you—and what we had didn't seem so special any more.' He gave his head a solemn shake. 'She said she'd forgiven me, that she still loved me, but she didn't trust me…' He sent her a wry look. 'And how could I blame her?' He shrugged. 'Whenever we argued, she always let me know I'd been the one to screw up our marriage before it had even started. Eventually, I began to wonder if I'd ever loved her—which only made me feel more guilty.'

Gina felt her throat close—choking on the knowledge he'd imparted so casually. 'You didn't love Missy?' she whispered, the shock twisting her stomach into knots.

He shook his head and her lungs seized—the sharp pain an echo of the agony she'd spent so long denying.

He banged his thumb against the steering wheel, his voice a tense monotone as he continued. 'Finally I stopped being such a gutless coward and asked for a divorce. Things got even uglier for a while. Marnie stopped talking to me and left Savannah for good.' He blew out a breath. 'But at least I finally figured out I sucked at being a husband.'

Gina stared at him, the brittle sunlight making her eyes water, and the knowledge that he'd suffered so much too making her heart hurt. 'I don't think that necessarily follows.'

'I don't see how you could draw any other conclusion,' he murmured, his head bent.

'Did you cheat on Missy while you were married?'

His head jerked up. He looked startled and annoyed at the accusation. 'Hell, no.'

'Then—while I know I'm hardly a disinterested party—I'd say you're being overly generous to your ex-wife.'

'How do you figure that?'

'If she couldn't trust you, why on earth did she agree to marry you?' she said, the knowledge that Missy had never understood him, and never appreciated him, making the pain lance through her. Why had she given up so easily? Let him go without a fight? 'And frankly, holding that one night over you like the Sword of Damocles for the rest of your marriage sounds pretty manipulative to me.' And not much like the actions of a woman in love. 'It takes two to make a marriage work and it doesn't sound as if she was doing her fair share.'

The chime of the church bell broke the pregnant silence in the car.

He raked his fingers through his hair, sweat slicking his brow. 'We better get in there before we melt.'

'Yes,' she said, grateful for the interruption—and the chance to get her emotions back under control.

'Thanks,' he said, helping her out of the car, and her heart leapt into her throat. 'You're right, Missy was pretty manipulative, and I guess I was so busy blaming myself, I never saw that before.'

He squeezed her hand as they walked towards the redbrick church building—which looked drab and utilitarian, unlike the brightly dressed congregation hurrying to get inside. As they slipped into the air-conditioned darkness and took seats in the back pew she tugged her hand out of his. But panic continued to claw at her throat and the sweat became clammy as it dried on her skin.

What the hell was she doing here? Letting herself revisit feelings that had nearly destroyed her once and she now knew had the potential to destroy her all over again? She'd assumed those wayward emotions couldn't trip her up a second time. That after what she'd endured and survived as a teenager, she was far too mature, far too resilient and self-reliant to make the same mistake again.

But the bubble of hope that had lodged under her breastbone told a very different story.

She needed to get away from him, get away from here, before she risked regressing into that wild, needy, insecure girl who had fallen hopelessly in love with Carter Price one warm summer night—and lived to regret it.

Way to go, Price. What made you shoot your mouth off like that?

It rattled him that he'd told Gina stuff he'd never told another soul. But what had rattled him a whole lot more was her response, and how it had finally lifted the weight he'd carried for so long over the failure of his marriage.

Luckily the pastor had been filled with the holy spirit this morning and the sermon had lasted nearly an hour, giving him time to settle. But as he bowed his head, reciting the Lord's Prayer from memory, he saw Gina fidgeting with the hymnal. He laid a hand over hers, but she stiffened and drew them away.

Frustration gripped. Why was she so tense and skittish?

After the service, he ushered her into the Fellowship Hall for the superb beverages and snacks the church ladies provided and the polite conversation that always followed—ignoring the glare that said clearer than words, 'I'd like to leave now.'

While the urge to show her off had been replaced during the never-ending sermon by the burning desire to take her back to his bed and show her a different kind of heaven, he wasn't going to indulge it.

She meant more to him than just a roll in the hay—and he was sick of pretending that great sex and her commission were all that existed between them. He'd told her about his marriage, and it meant a lot to know she didn't judge him, the way he'd always judged himself.

He didn't want her to go hightailing it back to New York. He wanted her to stay in Savannah, to see where this might lead. While he wasn't laying any bets on the long haul, one thing he'd learned from his hell of a marriage was that you had to be honest about your feelings—and, damn it, he had feelings for Gina. And he knew she had feelings for him too.

Why she refused to admit them, he had no idea, but he intended to find out. Because he was dammed if he was going to let her shut him out any longer.

CHAPTER FOURTEEN

'I NEED ANOTHER SHOWER.' Gina flung her purse on the bed and yanked the pins out of her hair. Agitation crawled over her skin to add to the clammy layer of sweat. Agitation and something that felt unpleasantly like fear.

They'd hardly spoken on the drive back but she'd sensed his frustration—his usually fluid, graceful movements jerky and tense as he drove home—and she knew his mood wasn't much better than hers. So she made a Herculean effort to keep a lid on her own temper.

She needed to leave, this afternoon. And she wanted to do it quickly and quietly and as painlessly as possible—which meant for once in her life she needed to avoid making a scene.

Kicking off her shoes, she headed towards the bathroom, but a hard hand gripped her upper arm and swung her round to face him.

'Don't you think it's about time you stopped sulking?' The surly, condescending tone was too much—even for Hercules. 'Everyone was real polite, just like I said they would be. And they liked you, just like I knew they would. So I don't know what's got you so riled up.'

She wrestled her arm free. 'Sulking? You think this is sulking? I'm not sulking, I'm so mad at you I could smack you, so I'd strongly advise you keep your hands off me.'

His eyes flared, a dark, dangerous, electric blue, and instead of taking the warning he grasped both her arms and dragged her to him until they were nose to nose. 'You want to smack me? Honey, I've been resisting the urge to put you over my knee since we walked into the house. So don't tempt me!'

The last thread on her control snapped and then detonated like a firecracker. She struggled against his grip as the fear and panic that had been building all week—every time he touched her as if he cared, every time he held her with too much tenderness, every time he looked at her as if she mattered to him—and had exploded earlier when he'd told her about his marriage, lashed out and took control of her tongue.

'How dare you pretend that I'm the one in the wrong here? You made me participate in that farce when you knew I didn't want to. This isn't a relationship. It's a fling. That's what we agreed and now you're trying to move the goalposts without my consent. I'm not your girlfriend, and I don't want to be.'

And if she could just make herself believe that, everything would be okay again.

'And I certainly didn't sign up for that grilling I got from the ladies at your church who obviously now think we're madly in love and you're about to declare your intentions.' She could feel her anger gaining force and velocity at the memory of the subtly probing interrogation she'd had to endure over iced tea and butter-pecan cookies. 'So I think it's probably best that we call it quits and I leave now.'

His fingers went slack, the stricken look shocking her into silence and making her realise how much she'd said. She brushed away the stupid tear that trickled down her cheek, hating herself for giving so much away.

'Damn, Gina. Where the hell did that come from?'

Inadequacy and panic writhed in her stomach like venomous snakes—she couldn't let him see, she couldn't let him know how easily he could hurt her.

'Nowhere.' She drew in an unsteady breath, and struggled

to regain her composure. If he saw a weakness he'd exploit it—and get even further under her guard. 'I'm fine. I simply feel this *fling* has reached its natural conclusion. And I'd like to leave.'

'Stop lying to me and to yourself,' he said, the dogged determination in his tone making the fear increase. 'This stopped being a fling days ago—for both of us. I'm not even sure it was *ever* just about the sex. Even ten years back, at Hillbrook. And you know it too, or you never would have come to The Standard to give me that dumb apology. What I wanna know is why you're too damn scared to admit it.'

She stiffened her spine, but couldn't look him in the eye. 'There is no why. I'm just not the sort of woman who makes those kinds of attachments. And I never have been.'

'Uh-huh.' He circled her arm, stroking the inside of her elbow with his thumb when a shiver ran through her. 'So how come you're shaking?'

She drew her arm out of his grasp, rubbed skin suddenly chilled despite the warm sunlight flooding through the window. 'Don't touch me,' she said, biting into her bottom lip to stop it trembling.

'Whatever it is, you can tell me.' He touched his fingers to her cheek but she jerked her head back.

'No, I can't. I don't want to.' But as soon as she'd said the words, she knew she'd given away too much.

'Is it because of your old man? Is it because he kicked you out when you were still a kid? I know how that goes—my daddy made me feel like dirt too. It makes it hard to trust people, to trust how you feel.'

'Don't psychoanalyse me.' Her whole body began to tremble but she forced herself to look him in the eye and keep the emotion, the need, on lockdown, the way she had learned to do with her father. The way she'd learned to do with him. 'You don't know anything about my relationship with my father.'

'Okay, then, why don't you tell me? Tell me why he kicked you out. What did you do that was so terrible?'

He was standing too close, looking at her in a way that threatened to crash through every last one of her defences. The panic and fear became so huge, the only way to save herself was to hit out. 'If you must know, I came back from college in the US pregnant with a married man's child.'

'What?' His face went blank with shock—but there was no doubting he'd made the connection, when he raked shaking fingers through his hair and murmured, 'Oh, hell, Gina. I'm sorry.'

The old misery, the cruel loneliness, the bitter agony of loss and rejection rose up her throat like bile. She swallowed, desperate to push it back down.

She couldn't bear his sympathy, or his guilt, not now, not ever, so she shut herself away in that place she'd found where she could always be safe, always remain invulnerable—and recited the details as if their baby had died inside someone else. 'My father insisted I get rid of it. I refused. So I ended up living in a bedsit in Bayswater, working nights in a pub—and discovering that being a grown-up is a lot harder than it looks.'

He cursed under his breath. 'Why didn't you contact me? Why didn't you let me know? I would have helped.'

'Why would I contact *you*?' She put all the bitterness she could into the question to maintain the charade—and bury the hurt deep. 'You went back to your fiancée. What was there to say? It was a one-night stand.' Even if she'd tried to delude herself it could have been so much more. 'And in the end I didn't need your help. Because, thankfully, I lost the baby.'

It wasn't a lie, not really, she *had* been thankful in the end—after all the tears and the soul-searching and the mind-numbing grief. Thankful that she would never get the chance to screw up motherhood, the way she'd managed to screw up everything else.

'I'd managed to pull my life together in the process and get clear of my father,' she added, when he didn't respond. 'So it was all good.'

'How could it be good?' The shock cleared from his eyes to be replaced by hurt and confusion—and temper. 'If I'd had any idea, I never would've gone through with the wedding. You should have told me. I had a right to know.'

'Maybe.'

'And why the hell didn't you tell me *now*? We've been sleeping together for over a week, living in each other's pockets, and you didn't think it was worth mentioning?'

'No, I didn't.'

'I don't get it,' he said, the anger edged with disbelief. 'How could I be so damn wrong about you? I thought we had something going here.'

'Well, you thought wrong.'

'I never would have guessed anyone could be so hot in the sack and yet so heartless out of it.'

She let the accusation wash over her, like all the others.

He can't hurt you, unless you let him.

'I suppose that's one of the many mysteries of the universe, isn't it, Lover Boy.' She scooped her purse up off the bed, slung it over her shoulder, and fisted her fingers on the strap so he wouldn't see them shaking. 'I'll catch a cab to the airport. If you could have my luggage sent on, I'd appreciate it. I'll email you when the website and blog are live.'

He didn't say anything as she walked away. But while the panic pushing against her chest began to ease as she ran through the mansion's hallways, the pain she'd spent ten years running away from turned into a living, breathing thing—as sharp and relentless as it had ever been as it consumed her.

CHAPTER FIFTEEN

'GINA, I NEED a favour.' Reese's furious whisper interrupted Gina's listless gaze out of the large mullioned window of the Manhattan city clerk's office.

'A favour, right.' She forced a smile, trying to get into the party spirit, which had eluded her ever since they'd arrived twenty minutes ago at the newly refurbished, and suitably ornate Manhattan Marriage Bureau in preparation for Cassie's wedding.

Reese threaded an arm through Gina's. 'Are you sure you're okay? You look exhausted?'

Gina sighed, wondering why on earth she'd bothered to spend half an hour plastering on foundation. 'I had the flu that's been going around,' she said, giving the stock excuse she'd prepared earlier, after a similar interrogation from both Marnie and Cassie when they'd all convened at Amber's Bridal two days ago, to bully Cassie into picking out a proper wedding gown. 'But I'm on the mend now.'

Or I will be, eventually.

What a fool she'd been, to think she could carry on an affair with Carter and not plummet back down the black hole that had claimed her once before. If she hadn't been feeling so fragile she'd have kicked her own backside.

Reese gave her arm a gentle squeeze. 'So that's why you disappeared off the radar and bailed on all the party plan-

ning.' She sent her a curious glance. 'You could have let me
know. I happen to be a champion pamperer. My chicken soup
is legendary.'

'Sorry, I didn't feel up to company,' Gina replied, deflect-
ing the sympathy she knew she didn't deserve. Lying to her
friends about Carter had been almost as unconscionable as
lying to herself.

'So what's the favour?' she asked, keen to steer them onto
a new, less debilitating topic.

Reese dipped her head towards the trio of guys collected
on the other side of the office's grand art deco antechamber—
who made a fascinating tableau as they awaited Cassie's arrival with Marnie.

Tuck, Cassie's husband-to-be, stood chatting with his
witness, Dylan Brookes. With his rangy athlete's build and
tousled blond hair, Tuck looked rugged and gorgeous in a perfectly tailored designer suit, the incessant tapping of his foot
on the marble floor the only sign of wedding jitters. Dylan,
on the other hand, looked more relaxed and debonair as he
kept Tuck's mind off his nerves.

Standing apart from the two close friends, Mason, Reese's
ex-husband and current fiancé—and the guy who had effectively stolen her away from Dylan on the eve of their wedding
earlier that summer—had his hands buried in the pockets of
his suit, the silk tie already tugged loose and listing to one side.

While Dylan was covering any awkwardness with his customary dignity, Mason looked agitated and a little surly. Gina
would hazard a guess the ex-marine would rather be charging
into a war zone under enemy fire than having to make polite
conversation with Reese's former fiancé while wearing a suit.

'I'm about to go rescue Mason, before he rips off his tie
altogether—but could you run interference with Dylan later—
once Tuck's all loved up with Cassie at the Tribeca.'

Oh, please, just kill me now.

Gina bit the tip of her tongue to stave off the inevitable
eye-roll. After her aborted two-week fling in Savannah she
wasn't sure she'd be able to flirt again in this lifetime. But how
could she mention that to Reese without dragging her friend
into her pity party? Which would be pointless in the extreme.
What could Reese say about it? Except maybe I told you so?

Carter and her had always been a mistake. Even without
the miserable secret of the miscarriage lying in wait to trip
them up, it never would have worked.

The cold, judgmental look when she'd told him the truth
was all the proof she needed that the two of them had never
been in line for a happy ever after.

The only thing she hadn't quite accounted for was how hor-
rendous the fallout would be after a measly two weeks with
him. And she laid the blame for that squarely at Carter's door.
The sex should have been enough for him. But he'd insisted
on wanting more, forcing her into an intimacy she couldn't
handle, and tricking her into loving him again.

'I can see how it's going to get a little awkward, once you
and Mason and Tuck and Cassie are paired off,' Gina ob-
served, trying to concentrate on the problem at hand instead
of the insoluble one in her past.

She watched Dylan give Tuck a hearty pat on the back—
the two men sharing a joke. 'But I think you may be worrying unnecessarily. Dylan appears to be way too smooth to
allow a minor social catastrophe like being jilted at the altar
to throw him off his stride.'

'I didn't jilt him,' Reese snapped. 'If you'll recall, he jilted
me.' She waved her arm, to dispel the subject. 'But that's beside the point. I don't want him to feel like a fifth wheel at
the TriBee. So I could use your super power. If you're suffi-
ciently recovered from the flu, that is?'

The flu—real or imaginary—wouldn't have stopped her
before, she thought miserably. Dylan Brookes, with his hand-

some face, immaculate manners and exceptional dress sense, was exactly the type of guy Gina would once have enjoyed zapping with her super power. But that was before her super power had met its kryptonite in Savannah. A kryptonite that had refused to stay buried.

Carter had attempted to contact her several times since her return home, but she'd deleted his emails and texts unread and erased his answerphone messages—and communicated exclusively with his PA about the commission. Her bags had arrived by special courier the day before with a note attached, addressed in his looping black scrawl, which she'd also thrown away unopened.

She didn't doubt that he had a lot to say to her on the subject of her heartlessness, but she had no desire to get into some long-distance slanging match about the choices she'd made ten years ago. It would only prolong the agony—and, although she despised herself for the weakness, she didn't think she was quite strong enough yet to cope with his contempt—even from a distance of eight hundred miles.

She shook off the depressing thought, and struggled to think of a way to deflect Reese gracefully. 'What about asking Marnie to run interference with your tempting ex? She's young, free and single—and she needs more practice than I do.' She tilted her head as if assessing Dylan's appearance—instead of measuring him against another man she couldn't seem to forget. 'And I bet he'd be her type.'

'You are kidding, right?' Reese did a double take. 'Dylan's exactly the opposite of her type. As you well know Marnie has a phobia of guys who command six-figure salaries and wear tuxes on a regular basis—something to do with the trauma of her debutante upbringing and having them thrown at her on a regular basis.'

Oh, yeah, there was that.

Reese gripped Gina's arm to propel her towards the guys

as Gina silently cursed Marnie and her Post-Traumatic Tux
Disorder. 'Come on, there's no need to give him the full Gina
today,' she continued, sailing across the marbled hallway in
full matchmaker mode. 'We don't want to blind him.'

The blushing bride arrived ten minutes later—in the nick of
time to save Gina from slow death by polite conversation.
Cassie's low-cut silk dress looked incredible. The silver thread
accenting the fabric shimmered in the afternoon light while
the snug bias-cut displayed a figure that Cassie had hidden
for far too long behind baggy T-shirts and jeans. But it was
the expression on Cassie's face as Tuck grasped her waist
and swung her around in a circle that had tears threatening
to ruin Gina's mascara.

'You look sensational, Cassiopeia!' Tuck announced as
his newly crowned Geek Goddess beamed with love and excitement.

The carefree laugh that floated across the antechamber
brought forth memories of a certain wicked grin and seductive gaze that had once turned Gina into a giggler too.

She gnawed on her bottom lip—the abject feeling of loss
warring with the foolish glow of nostalgia and starting to
give her a tension headache.

Thank goodness, she would never lay eyes on Carter Price
again or she'd be liable to turn into a complete basketcase.

But as the thought registered it was interrupted by Marnie's
choked whisper. 'What's my brother doing here?'

Gina's head snapped up, her startled gaze focusing on a tall
figure in a dark business suit weaving his way towards them
through the other bridal parties waiting in the antechamber.
Her mind steadfastly refused to acknowledge what her eyes
were seeing, but as his gaze found hers the heavy weight
pressing on her chest began to crush her ribcage.

'Who *is* that guy?' Tuck asked as he sent them all a quesioning look. 'He looks pretty mad about something and he's headed this way.'

'That's Carter, Marnie's brother,' Reese said, stating the obvious. 'Did you guys have a meeting?' She turned to Marnie, who shook her head in confusion. He didn't look pretty mad, Gina thought, her chest collapsing, he looked exceptionally mad—and his gaze was locked on her like an Exocet missile.

Cassie sent Gina a sympathetic look. 'I'm not sure it's Marnie he's here to see.'

Gina wrapped her arms around her churning stomach as questions bombarded her from all sides.

'Why is he staring at you, Gina?' Marnie sounded wounded and confused.

'Is something going on between you two, again?' Reese's voice rang out, urgent and concerned.

Gina shook her head but nothing would come out of her mouth. She could feel their worried looks but all she could see was Carter charging towards her and threatening to send her life into freefall again.

'Cassie? Do you know?' Reese's anxious enquiry buzzed in her head.

Before Cassie could reply, Carter marched through the gathered throng and grasped her arm. Yanking her towards him, he snarled, 'Why the hell didn't you answer my emails, or my phone messages, or my damn texts, or the letter I sent with your stuff?'

'Hey, buddy.' Dylan was the first of her shocked friends to come to the rescue—which in some small part of her brain Gina thought was remarkably gallant of him, given that she'd almost bored him to death with her sub-par flirting. 'Do you want to take your hands off the lady and ask her nicely?'

'Butt out, Wall Street,' Carter sneered back, not even sparing him a glance, his Southern manners apparently having gone the same way as his easy charm.

'The hell I will,' Dylan bristled, squaring up for a fight.

'Calm down.' Reese stepped in front of Dylan and touched Gina's arm. 'Gina, is everything okay?'

Gina managed a shell-shocked nod, all her focus on the pads of Carter's fingers digging into her arm, and the glitter of temper in those painfully familiar blue eyes.

What was he doing here? Had he come all this way to humiliate her in front of her friends? Surely she didn't deserve that? She tried to gather her outrage, her indignation, but she couldn't stop trembling.

'L-let go of me,' she stammered, disgusted by the chatter of teeth. To her surprise, his fingers released and he stepped back to thrust a hand through his hair.

Reese puffed out an exasperated breath. 'Now, can someone please tell me what the hell is going on?'

'We need to talk,' Carter said, the tone low as he bypassed Reese's request. 'I didn't plan to do it in public but I will if I have to.'

She tightened her arms, struggling to protect herself from the hard glare. 'No, we don't need to talk.'

She knew what he had to say and she didn't want to hear it. He'd rejected her twice already, once more might break her.

'Fine, you don't want to talk, you can listen.' The frustration in his voice snapped like the lash of a whip.

'Now wait a minute…' Dylan charged back into the fray.

'Who did you say this guy was, because he's starting to make me pretty damn mad too…' Tuck added, standing behind his friend.

'It's okay.' Gina lifted shaking palms to get her knights in shining Armani to back off.

For God's sake, pull yourself together and deal with this, before Cassie's special day degenerates into a complete fiasco.

'I can handle this,' she added, thinking no such thing as the tremor in her body refused to subside.

She could smell him, that unique combination of man and soap and tangy cologne—the memory making the emotion rush through already shaky limbs. She locked her knees in a desperate attempt to keep the trembling under control. 'What is it you wanted to say? I'm listening.'

To her astonishment the glitter of temper disappeared, to leave something she couldn't decipher. He stepped forward and took her arm again but this time his touch was gentle, tentative, the pad of his thumb pressing into the inside of her elbow.

'Let's start with I'm sorry.'

'Sorry? What for?' she asked, staggered.

He dropped his chin to his chest and let out a heavy sigh. 'Damn, this is tough.' He swung his head round, taking in her friends, who were watching with varying degrees of curiosity and astonishment on their faces—and, in Marnie's case, out-right shock. 'Especially with an audience,' he added, sucking in a breath as if preparing to face a firing squad.

His hand dropped from her arm. 'Sorry for everything, I guess. Sorry for getting you pregnant that night.'

'What?' Marnie's shocked yelp had him glancing over his shoulder, but he turned his attention back to Gina without acknowledging his sister.

'Sorry for walking away, and letting you think I blamed you for what we did together. Sorry for leaving you to deal with losing our baby alone.' His eyebrow lifted. 'Although, I don't consider myself entirely to blame for that one.'

'How could I tell you when—' she jumped in, but he pressed a fingertip to her lips, silencing her protest.

'Hey, don't. I get it. How could you tell me when I was too busy marrying the wrong woman?'

She looked away, not sure she could hear him say this now, when it was too late to make a difference. She chewed her lip, the metallic taste of blood doing nothing to stop the single tear slipping over her lid. He brushed it away with his thumb, then hooked a finger under her chin.

'You're such a faker, aren't you, sugar? You had me fooled there for a while, with your tough cookie act, but I figured it out.'

She raised her chin, blinking rapidly to stop any more stupid tears materialising. 'Figured out what exactly?'

Damn, she looked so forlorn and so determined not to show a single sign of weakness. How could he ever have doubted the existence of that brave, generous, honest heart behind the tough girl facade?

He'd screwed up. Not just ten years ago by not recognising how perfect she'd always been for him. But also a week ago, when he'd tried to bully her into admitting her feelings, without having the guts to admit his own. He just hoped to hell he wasn't too late to stop those screw-ups from destroying whatever chance they might have at a future.

But he had to tread gently now. She'd had her confidence battered over the years—not just by her old man, but by him too. He'd left her high and dry when she'd needed him the most, because he'd been too busy dealing with his own issues to appreciate what was right under his nose. The news of her miscarriage had been a shock—but once he'd got past the knee-jerk feeling of betrayal, the much bigger shock was how much it had hurt to know she had carried his child and he'd had no idea.

'You want to know my biggest regret, sugar?'

'Not particularly, but I'm sure you're going to tell me anyway.' She sniffed, still channelling the tough cookie act, even though the sheen of moisture in those large green eyes meant it was a total wash.

'My biggest regret is that while I was busy browbeating

you last week into staying in Savannah, I didn't take the time to tell you how I feel about you.'

Now for the tough part.

He gripped her hands and slid down onto one knee.

Her eyes widened in horror as she tugged her wrists, frantically trying to yank him back onto his feet. 'Carter? What the hell are you doing?' she snapped as she sent a panicked 'rescue-me' glance to her friends over his head.

He ignored that, as well as his sister's strangled gasp, the soft whisper of 'Someone pinch me, I think I've been transported into a chick flick,' from Reese, and the Texan growl of 'Who the hell *is* this guy?' from the man he'd recognised from his NFL days as the groom.

'Carter, please, get up, you're making a scene.'

His lips curved at the panicked plea, he was unable to ignore the irony of the situation. Who knew he'd finally get the better of Gina Carrington, not with temper or charm or hot and sweaty sex, but with a cheesy show of sentiment. If this worked out, he was so going to spend the rest of his natural life lavishing her with grand romantic gestures in public places to keep her in line.

'Damn straight I am,' he said, holding onto her wrists and swallowing down the big fat 'if' that had gotten stuck in his throat. 'I'm assuming the position here, because there's something I need to say to you. And this is the only way I know to prove to you I'm sincere.'

Her eyebrows had levitated to her hairline, but she'd stopped trying to free her hands, which he took as a positive sign.

'Right, here goes nothing.' He pressed his thumbs into her wrists and felt the butterfly flutter of her pulse. Even better, she wasn't totally immune.

'I love you, Gina Carrington.' She bucked but he held firm and kept going. 'I love your fire and your passion, your honesty, your integrity, your smart mouth and your bad attitude and that sexy dimple on your butt.'

She gasped and found her voice at last. 'I do not have a dimple on my—'

'I love the way your eyes go all squinty with temper when you're mad,' he interrupted, basking in that exact look. 'And I love the way they go all dazed and dewy when you come.'

'Oh, for Pete's sake!'

'I love the fact that you think you're such a tough cookie. And most of all I love that soft, giving, open heart that you try so hard to keep hidden—but you showed to me one incredible summer night a decade ago, and I've had several tempting glimpses of this summer in Savannah. I'm not a great bet for the long haul, I know that. But then neither are you, so I figure we're even there. And if you'd be willing to take a chance on me, I'm more than ready to take a chance on you.'

He lifted off his knees, cradled her cheeks, so desperate to hold her his body felt as if it were caught in a tractor beam. There was one more thing, though, that had to be said, and it was the hardest of all.

'Now, you can tell me you don't love me and I'll walk out that door and never contact you again.' He stroked her face, willing her to give him another chance. 'But don't lie, sugar. Because I'll know, and then I'll just have to get back on my knees and embarrass us both all over again.'

He could hear the hush of anticipation, not only from her friends but from the sizeable crowd in the hall who'd all been silenced by his declaration.

She swallowed audibly. 'Do you have any idea how much I want to kick your butt at this moment, Carter Price?'

The grin spread across his face—and his heart—because he could hear the hitch in that sultry purr, and knew he'd struck gold. 'You didn't just answer my question with another question, did you, sugar?'

A small laugh choked out through the tears tumbling down her cheeks. Then she flung her arms around his neck and whispered into his hair. 'I love you too, Rhett. But I'm still going to kick your butt the first chance I get.'

Spontaneous applause broke out around the hall as he covered her lips with his and sank into the long-awaited kiss.

When they were both forced to come up for air, he held her at arm's length and said with a smile that he was pretty sure reached both ears simultaneously, 'Frankly, my dear, I'd enjoy watching you try.'

After all the drama, Cassie and Tuck's wedding went off like a dream. The bride saying her vows in a sure, steady voice and then turning to smile at her friends once Tuck had said his.

Gina had to be grateful that Carter's warm palm anchored her hip to his side throughout the ceremony, or she would surely have floated off on a cloud of bliss. His insane declaration in front of half of Manhattan had terrified her at first, but as his words sank into her consciousness the strangest thing had happened—the panicked beat of her heart had slowed, the lead weight in her stomach had dissolved and all those barriers that she'd spent so many years erecting and maintaining had come tumbling down in one fell swoop.

She laid her head on Carter's shoulder in one of the limousines Reese had booked to transport them to Cassie's reception party, and listened to Carter chat easily to Dylan—the two of them having developed mutual amnesia about their earlier stand-off, like typical guys. Staring into space, she used the moment of calm to contemplate the difficult decisions in her future.

Carter had invited himself back to her place tonight and told her he'd organised a week's leave from the Mill, but the eight hundred miles that separated them were going to be the first obstacle they'd have to discuss.

But as the car cruised through the early evening traffic, and she watched the office workers flooding into the subway to begin the Labor Day weekend, she had a sudden yearning for the subtle pace and relaxed gentility of Savannah. While she'd once thrived on the manic energy of the City That Never Sleeps, it didn't seem quite so necessary any more, now she was embarking on a relationship that promised to generate enough energy to fuel a nuclear power plant.

Marnie sat on the other side of the limo, her unfocused gaze fixed on something out of the window, but when her eyes flicked to her brother and then back out of the window Gina knew the siblings' strained relationship was going to be a much bigger hurdle to overcome than her living arrangements.

The Tribeca Terrace was everything they had wanted in a surprise party venue. Reese had put her organisational skills to work on the ride over, ensuring an extra place setting for Carter appeared as if by magic amid the balloons, streamers and the enormous Just Hitched banner she'd already arranged to adorn their table.

Gina's thanks for her friend's thoughtfulness was greeted with a cocked eyebrow. 'Don't think I've forgotten your gross dereliction of shag and share duty. If he's not the Mystery Studmuffin, I'll eat my Jimmy Choos.' But then she added in a soft murmur that had Gina repairing her mascara again, 'I'm thrilled for you two. After all the heartache you've both been through, you deserve this chance.'

As the evening progressed Gina found her flirt gene shimmering happily back to life under Carter's heavily lidded gaze—the desire to race back to her apartment and tear his clothes off becoming increasingly imperative. But as they swayed together on the restaurant's small dance floor, the slow rub of his body against hers making her throat dry, she noticed Marnie pouring herself a hefty glass of Chardonnay while Dylan sat opposite her, engrossed in his smartphone.

Pulling Carter's head down by the ears, she whispered, 'You need to speak to your sister. Sort things out with her.'

He nuzzled her neck. 'I don't need Marnie's permission and neither do you.'

Gina sighed, forced to file 'fixing his relationship with his sister' into a folder marked 'works in progress'—Carter's response making it blatantly obvious that his relationship with his sister seemed to have arrested somewhere around Marnie's eighteenth birthday.

Her thoughts scattered completely when his hands drifted down to her butt: 'I suggest you save your freak out about Marnie for another time,' he murmured, giving her backside a proprietary squeeze. 'Because you've got something a lot bigger to handle tonight, sugar.'

The husky giggle, which was never far from the surface now, bubbled out as his hips brushed against hers—and the casual endearment settled around her like a golden fog.

She'd never considered herself a sweet person, but somehow Carter Price's good opinion had managed to shear off a lot of her sour edges and—while shedding that protective layer of sarcasm altogether would have to be another 'work in progress'—she couldn't wait to discover her inner Pollyanna.

Fisting her fingers into his hair, she dragged his mouth down to hers.

That said, she didn't intend to let true love turn her into a total sucker.

'Oh, don't you worry, Rhett.' She pressed provocatively against the rather prominent bulge in his suit pants. 'I think I've got the measure of you,' she purred, delighted when his heartfelt groan was followed by an exceptionally sinful kiss.

* * * * *

Marnie had forgotten about Dylan, who seemed to also be finishing off a drink—something dark in a glass, on the rocks. 'Tough day?'

'I lost my job this morning.'

'That does suck. I think I should buy you a drink.'

She could well afford to buy her own drinks, even without a job, and she didn't really need his company, either. Dylan Brookes wouldn't have been her first choice of drinking partners, but it did beat a total stranger, and he didn't seem in a hurry to leave, making her wonder if maybe he had a few woes to drown, as well.

'All right, then.'

'Another chardonnay? Or perhaps something stronger?'

She waved over a server. 'I'd like a shot of Patrón, two limes, with a Dos Equis back, please.' She turned to Dylan and shot him an innocent smile. 'And for you?'

Dylan shot her a smile that said there was *some* sign of life in there. 'Same.'

The server returned with their drinks, and Dylan lifted his shot glass in a toast.

She lifted her own glass and nodded. Then Dylan licked the salt off the rim of the glass and she nearly fell off her chair in shock.

Things were looking up.

Dear Reader,

I was so excited to be asked to be part of the first MODERN TEMPTED™ continuity—especially when I found out that I'd be lined up with Aimee Carson, Amy Andrews and Heidi Rice. We had so much fun creating the characters and the concept, and it was just an awesome experience working with such talented writers.

But the downside to working with such talented writers is that they're so darn *good*. Like utterly intimidatingly good. And my book would come last in the line-up. Talk about pressure! (Picture me hyperventilating into a bag of jelly beans when I read their fabulous books.)

In the end, though, I couldn't be more pleased with what we did. While I love Marnie and Dylan to pieces, I also love Gina and Carter, Cassie and Tuck, and Reese and Mason. Marnie and Dylan may be 'mine,' but I'm quite invested in the others, as well—very much like a doting auntie. I hope you come to love them as much as we do.

So big kisses to Aimee, Amy and Heidi—thanks for making this experience an amazing one. You ladies (and your books) rock!

And, as always, I'd love to hear from you, dear reader. You can find me on Facebook and Twitter or on my website at www.booksbykimberly.com.

Kimberly

THE WEDDING SEASON

Look out for Gina's story this month in *Maid of Dishonour* by Heidi Rice!

Don't miss Reese's and Cassie's stories, out last month!

It's a reunion to remember—with sizzling, scandalous, and *very* surprising consequences…

LAST GROOM
STANDING

BY
KIMBERLY LANG

First published in Great Britain 2013
by Mills & Boon, an imprint of Harlequin (UK) Limited,
Harlequin (UK) Limited, Eton House, 18-24 Paradise Road,
Richmond, Surrey TW9 1SR

© Kimberly Lang 2013

ISBN: 978 0 263 91067 4

Harlequin (UK) policy is to use papers that are natural, renewable and recyclable products and made from wood grown in sustainable forests. The logging and manufacturing processes conform to the legal environmental regulations of the country of origin.

Printed and bound in Spain
by Blackprint CPI, Barcelona

Kimberly Lang hid romance novels behind her textbooks in junior high, and even a master's program in English couldn't break her obsession with dashing heroes and happily ever after. A ballet dancer turned English teacher, Kimberly married an electrical engineer and turned her life into an ongoing episode of *When Dilbert Met Frasier*. She and her Darling Geek live in beautiful north Alabama with their one Amazing Child—who, unfortunately, shows an aptitude for sports.

Visit Kimberly at www.booksbykimberly.com for the latest news—and don't forget to say hi while you're there!

This and other titles by Kimberly Lang are available in eBook format—check out www.millsandboon.co.uk

To my aunt Lou Ann, who introduced hundreds of
children to the magic of books and the joy of reading.
I hope some of them are reading this now. ~Grin~

(And a quick shout-out to Jane—again—since your
dedication didn't make it into the last book!)

PROLOGUE

Ten years ago, Hillbrook University campus, upstate New York...

"She had s-sex with Carter."

Marnie Price stumbled over the word—sex wasn't something she was overly comfortable talking about, and ironically it was Gina's influence over the past year that had gotten her to the point where she could even talk about it at all.

She didn't know who was more in the wrong: Gina, who was supposedly her friend, or her brother, Carter, who had succumbed to Gina's wiles even though he was engaged to another woman. The betrayal cut deep for Marnie, and she couldn't quite make sense of it.

Lord, just when she thought she was beginning to figure things out... Everything she thought she knew was crumbling down around her, making the situation worse.

Reese stroked her hair, making soothing noises. Although technically her roommate and landlady, Reese was also the big sister she'd never had. At least Reese would understand. "I'm sure we're missing part of the story," she began.

Reese's willingness to let Marnie live with her so

her family would believe she was being properly looked after in the big, bad world was the only reason she'd been allowed to enroll at Hillbrook in the first place. And while Marnie would be forever grateful for that, Reese's attempted defense of Gina only drove the knife deeper. "It seems pretty straightforward to me. How could Gina *do* that? She seduced my brother, took advantage of him. Does she not think any man is off limits?"

"Carter's an adult, and he's equally responsible for his actions."

Marnie couldn't believe this was Carter's fault. They'd been raised with the same values, the same knowledge of right and wrong. Sex was for marriage, something saved solely for your future spouse, but Carter had still betrayed that fundamental belief—as well as his bride—making him a hypocrite of the worst sort.

Her heart constricted with pain for her best friend, who'd spent the past year planning the perfect wedding to start their perfect life together. Missy would be heartbroken.

She'd never been comfortable with Gina's overt sexuality, the way she treated sex like a recreational sport and men like disposable items, but there was something in her spirit and embrace of life that was attractive, too. It hadn't been enough to sway *her* morals, but then Gina had never tried to seduce her, either. The girl was a proud, self-proclaimed maneater.

Which, Marnie decided, was just another word for slut.

"No. Carter is a decent man." That much Marnie was sure of. Carter was a little overprotective, becoming even more so after Daddy passed five years ago, but he was everything a good man was supposed to be. He was even beginning to respect the fact Marnie wasn't a child anymore: just last week he'd suddenly agreed to let her go on the road trip with the others this summer.

"Carter was raised right, with honor and integrity and respect. He's a gentleman. Men can be weak sometimes when it comes to the flesh, and…and…" She struggled to find the right words, the right explanation for Carter's behavior. She couldn't find one at the moment, but she knew there had to be one somewhere. "Well, there's no way he would have done something like that unless Gina—"

Reese shook her head. "You can't just blame Gina. It takes two to tango."

She shrugged off Reese's embrace and stood. "You're *defending* her? Taking her side?"

"I'm not taking anyone's side, Marnie. Remember that Gina is your friend—"

"Some friend," she snapped. "A real friend would have left my brother alone. A real friend wouldn't hurt people I care about just so she can get her own thrills."

"I doubt Gina meant to hurt you with this."

"Then why tell me about it? Why do it in the first place? My friend? I don't need slutty friends who jump into bed with men they barely know."

Reese's cheeks took on a pink tint and she played with the square-shaped pendant on the necklace tucked under her shirt. She cleared her throat. "Marnie, remember how we talked about how you can be really judgmental sometimes…?"

"I'm sorry, Reese, but there's right and wrong in this world. Carter is in the wrong, too, but Gina has, once again, proved she's no better than a common *whore*!" She shouted the last word, well aware of how it would carry through the hall of Reese's beautiful house and straight up the stairs to Gina's room. "It's just more proof that Gina doesn't care about anyone except herself."

"Marnie..." Reese began.

Marnie waved her silent and stalked over to the glass of champagne she'd merely been toying with all night. In three long swallows, she drained it, then, ignoring Reese's shocked "Marnie!" reached for the bottle and refilled the glass.

"I think I've earned this," she said before she caught herself and sat the glass down instead. Her mother had never allowed alcohol into the house, and it wasn't until Marnie came to Hillbrook that she'd even tried it. Just more proof of how she'd changed thanks to her roommates—but maybe these changes weren't for the better.

She heard footsteps and turned to see Cassie returning.

"Gina says we'll talk tomorrow," Cassie said, as oblivious as ever. Usually, Marnie found the nerdy Australian's lack of understanding about social situations rather endearing, but tonight she was angry and lacked the patience.

"There's nothing more to talk about, Cas."

"I don't understand."

"Then let me explain this to you. I'm never speaking to Gina Carrington again."

"Why?"

"Because Gina is a selfish tramp who doesn't care who she hurts. I bet poor Missy and what this would do to her never even crossed Gina's mind."

Cassie nodded. "It's very unlikely since Gina doesn't know Missy."

Oh, my sweet God. "She knew Carter was engaged, though."

"As did Carter. I don't see why you're holding Gina responsible for Carter's decisions. He chose to be unfaithful, and having made that decision, the woman involved is irrelevant."

Marnie wanted to pull her hair out. "I can't believe you're taking her side, too. Wow, y'all are lousy friends."

"Marnie, we're trying to be good friends," Reese started carefully, "to both you *and* Gina—"

Cassie nodded. "Which is difficult when you're overreacting like this."

Reese put a hand on Cassie's shoulder. "Cas, let me handle this, okay?"

That was the last straw. "There's nothing to handle. Missy has been my friend—practically a sister—since we were little girls, and as her friend, she deserves my loyalty and support because *that's* what friends do. Real friends don't seduce your brother, and they don't defend and make excuses for the woman that did. If y'all don't see that, then I'm not sure I want you as my friends anymore."

Her voice broke on the last word, and she ran to her room before she burst into tears.

This wasn't how it was supposed to be. Marnie lay in her bed, staring at the ceiling as tears burned her eyes. *And it's all my fault.*

Everyone back in Savannah had tried to tell her this was a bad idea. Maybe they were right. Maybe she should have just gone to Simmons State and pledged Kappa like every other woman in her family. She'd only applied to Hillbrook to be polite—the recruiter who'd visited her school had been hard to ignore. She hadn't given it a second thought until the acceptance came—

along with an attractive scholarship that played to her
ego and made her feel like the school really wanted her.

Carter had protested, Mama had been heartbroken,
and her boyfriend horrified she'd even consider it. Coming here had been her first act of rebellion—ever.

And it had felt so good.

Even if she'd been scared to death.

But Reese and Gina and Cassie had supported her,
introduced her to a world beyond her carefully controlled Savannah circle, and encouraged her to come
out of her shell and experience so many new things.

Beautiful dark-haired Gina who talked of London
and Oxford and wasn't afraid of anything, always quick
with the perfect comeback delivered in her crisp British
accent. Nerdy Cassie who was almost as naive as she
was about the world, but driven by logic and science
instead of belief and Southern customs. And Reese,
who brought them all together in her house because she
thought it would be interesting to have such an eclectic
set of roommates—a far cry from her own Park Avenue background.

And it had gone well—Marnie had bragged to everyone back home, proud of both her grades and her
broadened horizons. Maybe she'd broadened them a
little too much.

It was so confusing. Life had been so much easier
to understand before she'd come here. And while the
others had laughed at her naiveté, she longed for that
innocence now.

Yeah, this is all my fault.

If she hadn't come to school here, she wouldn't have
met Gina and the others. Carter wouldn't have come
up to visit, and he'd have never fallen into Gina's web.
Missy was going to be hurt and it was all her fault.

Silent tears slid down her face. *Some friend I am.*

There was no way to repair the damage done here tonight, but there had to be a way to make this right for Missy.

As for Carter... She couldn't think about him right now. He'd been her hero—the perfect example of what a man should be—and the shattering of that image hurt more than she expected. He'd spit on everything they'd been raised to value and believe and yet he still had the nerve to leave town last week, fresh out of Gina's bed, it seemed, with an admonishment for *her* to behave.

The hypocrite.

Marnie could hear Gina moving around in the room next door and the low mutter of conversation from Cassie and Reese as they closed up the house and went to their own rooms.

She lay awake for a long time—exploring her options, figuring out what to do next, trying to make some kind of sense of it all in her head. Long after the house was quiet, she'd only come to one solid conclusion.

This wasn't where she was supposed to be.

She needed to go home.

CHAPTER ONE

MARNIE PRICE TOOK a deep breath to assess the situation and her options. This was not the time to react thoughtlessly. After a moment to think, she did what any rational, reasonable, adult woman would do in a situation like this.

She pulled the wine bottle from the ice bucket and filled her glass right up to the rim.

Despite the fact she'd had several already tonight, she remained frustratingly sober. It was a happy occasion—Cassie was married and bridges she'd thought burnt beyond repair were slowly being mended. She *should* be happy—and she *was*, by God, she really was.

Except, at the same time, she wasn't. She'd started the day by cleaning out her desk at work and ended it with finding out her friends had been lying to her for years *and* that years of estrangement had been all her fault. In the middle, she'd gone to a wedding and found out her brother was sleeping with Gina—*again*. Mercy, when losing your job wasn't the worst thing that had happened to you, the day officially sucked.

Hence the need for more wine. *Lots* more wine.

Her mother was probably spinning in her grave— ladies didn't overimbibe, much less in public—but this was New York City, not Savannah, and Marnie had intentionally given up the quest to be a "lady" years ago.

Old habits were hard to break, but she could drown the Southern guilt in another glass of Chardonnay.

The large table in the corner of the trendy Tribeca Terrace held the remains of Cassie and Tuck's small wedding reception, and Tuck had pulled Cassie to the dance floor a little while ago. It didn't take a genius IQ like Cassie's to see that they would be off to their wedding night very soon. Carter and Gina and Mason and Reese were also on the dance floor, doing that slow sway that said both couples would be leaving soon as well to a happy night themselves.

Marnie sighed into her glass. None of her friends had walked the easy path to happiness, but that was what made their stories so wonderful. The passion. Passion might be messy and difficult, but the proof it was worth it was right in front of her. And *that's* what she wanted. If she'd wanted a predictable and staid and unremarkable life, she'd have stayed in Savannah.

But the pairing off of the others had left her alone at the table with Dylan Brookes. Their party of eight had really been three parties of two and two parties of one, but that hadn't been too obvious or strange until everyone else coupled up. Being an extra wheel was awkward enough, but this situation took awkward to a new place.

Dylan had stood as Tuck's witness today, but it was just plain weird to have him around. Tuck was Dylan's best friend, but he was also Reese's cousin, and he'd met Cassie at what would have been Reese and Dylan's wedding—except that Reese had practically jilted Dylan at the altar in favor of Mason. It had been quite a mess. Reese and Dylan seemed okay with it now, but everyone else—including her—found the situation awkward at best.

Watching your ex-fiancée canoodle with the guy she threw you over for had to be uncomfortable, but if Dylan had a problem with that, he'd done a good job of hiding it.

He was currently typing something on his phone, and if he was feeling like an extra wheel, it didn't show.

Either he was a very good actor, or he simply didn't care. Marnie wasn't sure if she should envy him or pity him.

The music wasn't overly loud, but it was thankfully loud enough to not make the conversational silence at the table too noticeable. Not that she was in the mood for small talk, anyway. There was just way too much circling in her mind. She needed to process it all.

No one wanted to ruin Cassie's celebration, so conversations had been hushed and behind bathroom doors, everyone trying to bring her up to speed without involving the entire party or casting a pall over it. The result was information and emotional overload, *and* the beginnings of a massive headache.

By the time she finished this glass, she could head on home without anyone thinking it was odd. There was wine in her fridge, and drinking herself into oblivion seemed the best way to finish out this horrid day. Tomorrow would be soon enough to try to make sense of it all.

"I think I'm supposed to ask you to dance."

The comment caught her by surprise, as Dylan hadn't said much to her all night, choosing to talk to Tuck and oddly Carter mostly. "Excuse me?"

Dylan half pointed in the direction of the dance floor,

where Reese was making gestures over Mason's shoulder that did seem to translate into: "You two, dance."

The last thing she needed was a pity dance from him. "Thanks, but no."

"No, thank *you*."

Marnie had a brief flash of irritation at the relieved sigh in his voice as Dylan turned back to Reese and shrugged. Reese's lips pressed together in annoyance before she peeled herself off Mason and stalked over to the table.

"You need to dance, Marnie."

"Why?"

Reese seemed to think for a second. "Because it's bad luck for the bride and groom if the guests don't dance."

Reese should really know better than to try that. In three years at Simmons College, fourteen of her sorority sisters had walked down the aisle. There wasn't a wedding tradition or superstition she didn't know inside and out. "You made that up."

She shrugged. "Doesn't matter. *I* think it's bad luck."

"Well, *I* don't think Dylan really wants to dance," she countered. "And it's bad luck to dance with an unwilling partner."

She could tell Reese was trying to decide if that was an actual superstition or not. Finally, Reese cut her eyes in Dylan's direction. "But he will be willing if you just say yes. This is a celebration, and you two are sitting it out. I think that's a little rude, don't you?"

Reese knew right where to hit. The desire not to be rude was ingrained into her very soul and hard to ignore. Marnie weighed her options. Once Reese got an idea, it was nearly impossible to change her mind. She was a peacekeeper, a smoother-outer, the perfect hostess who wanted everyone to participate and have a good time. Reese had been born on the wrong side of the Mason-Dixon line; for a Yankee, she could channel a Southern matriarch with the best of them. Marnie could give in gracefully now or be politely and lovingly badgered to death.

"Fine." She took a long swallow from her glass and stood. Dylan, wearing a look that might have been boredom or annoyance—it was really hard to tell which—pushed to his feet, as well. *Talk about rude...*

"Excellent." Reese smiled as Mason pulled her back into his arms.

Marnie let Dylan lead her to the dance floor, his hand at the small of her back, and she caught at least one or two jealous looks being shot her way by other women. She totally understood why. Dylan Brookes was smart, successful and handsome, and the news he was back on the "eligible bachelor" list had brought a cheer to the lips of nearly every unmarried woman in the city looking to marry well.

Dylan looked every inch the Park Avenue aristocrat he was—which seemed a ridiculous contrast to the all-American frat-boy good looks of his best friend, Tuck. He radiated a suaveness, like he belonged in a tuxedo drinking dirty martinis at swanky events. Even tonight, with his dark hair slightly mussed, collar open and shirt-sleeves rolled up over tanned forearms, the adjective that sprang to mind was "debonair."

Her departed mother might be mollified now, as Dylan Brookes—the smart, rich, well-connected and respected attorney and philanthropist—was exactly the kind of man Miss Marnie Suellen Price, the only daughter of Marshall and Alma Price—God rest their souls—of Savannah, Georgia, was *supposed* to dance with.

And she hadn't danced with that kind of man—*intentionally*—in over five years.

She knew Dylan's type—she'd grown up surrounded by men just like him. Well-bred, well-read, and well-groomed, raised with every perk money could provide and trained to step right into their daddies' shoes and run the world. Bloodless, boring, and usually arrogant, but disguised under a thousand-dollar suit.

But she'd suck it up for one dance.

Dylan took her right hand in his, placed his other at her waist, and they moved gently to the music, both of them staring off into the distance.

God, this was worse than junior prom. A good foot of space separated their bodies. She bit her lip to hold back the snicker as the memory flooded back. Peter Stevenson, son of Savannah's mayor and the young man lucky enough to win the Price family seal of approval as a proper escort, had had sweaty palms. Looking back, it may have been the first time he'd ever actually laid hands on a girl. They'd kept that respectable distance between them all night—up to and including the chaste and proper good-night handshake on her front porch. And she'd been both satisfied and pleased, convinced it was proof Peter respected her.

Even now, she could still hear Gina's bark of laughter at the recounting of that story, and her sincere judgment of "How very pathetic." Even after everything that happened, Marnie had always been thankful to Gina for opening her naive eighteen-year-old eyes to the real world.

"What's so funny?" Dylan's question caused her to jump and brought her back to the present.

Her cotillion instructor would be horrified to know that she was neglecting the most basic rules of etiquette by ignoring her dance partner. But since she doubted Dylan would be happy to hear himself compared to her nervous seventeen-year-old prom date, she rapidly searched her mind for something appropriate to say.

She'd met Dylan a few times in social situations after he and Reese moved from coworkers to couple—their engagement party, that Thanksgiving she'd had lunch at Reese's parents' house—but she'd never really spent much time talking to him. She knew all about his career achievements, giving her a specific picture of Dylan, and she'd always been a little sad Reese had engaged herself to someone so dry, staid, and frankly unexciting. And if there was more to him—a hidden fire, exciting depths—Reese had never shared that information. Reese was just so private about things that there hadn't been much girl talk deconstructing their relationship during their infrequent lunches in the city.

So while she kind of knew Dylan, she couldn't say that she knew him *well*. And what she did know wasn't all that helpful at the moment.

The obvious seemed the safest conversational course. "Just thinking what an odd couple Cassie and Tuck are, but yet they're so happy together."

Dylan nodded. "You ladies did a good job with this party. I know they both appreciate it."

She grabbed the conversational rope gratefully. "Tuck…yes, and Cassie wouldn't care unless Tuck did. We just couldn't let her get married without *some* kind of celebration. It just seems wrong not to. It's one thing not to have the big white wedding, but just a run to the courthouse wasn't nearly enough."

Dylan nodded, and that topic was finished. *How long is this song?*

She laughed. "It just seems like I've been neck-deep in weddings since June…"

"I know the feeling. I'm rather tired of them myself." *Damn it. I shouldn't have brought that up.* "My apologies. That must be a sore topic."

Dylan shrugged. "Not really."

Her curiosity got the better of her manners. "Does it not bother you?"

"Does what bother me?"

"Being around Reese. Seeing her with someone else like that." Seeing Reese so openly cuddly with Mason made Marnie realize that she'd never really seen Reese act openly affectionate toward Dylan when they were engaged—nor vice versa. Reese and Dylan had made a good-looking *pair*, but it would be a stretch to call them a "couple" based on their behavior.

"I'm not a huge fan of witnessing large amounts of PDA from anyone, but beyond that, no."

Maybe that explained the lack of showy affection between them when they were together. "Well, you've been very understanding and decent about it."

His eyebrows went up. "There was another option?"

She tried to picture Dylan in a jealous rage or even a mopey lovelorn depression. Neither image worked. "I guess not."

"We're friends and I wish her well. I just hope she's not making the same mistake twice—"

It was rude to interrupt, but… "You think Reese and Mason are a mistake?"

"For her sake, I hope not. But the odds aren't good."

She rushed to defend Reese. "I'd say that after all they've been through, their odds are pretty damn good. They love each other—"

Dylan actually snorted.

"What? It's true."

"Yes, and love is probably the worst reason there is to get married."

That threw her off her game. "What other reason is there?"

"You're a romantic." His tone clearly said he saw that as a fault.

That wasn't entirely true. She had no starry-eyed misconceptions about the realities of relationships, but to just dismiss love outright? "For thinking love is a good reason to get married?"

"Love is ephemeral. Good marriages need a stronger foundation than that for a solid and successful partnership."

Ugh. She'd heard variations of that before. But even being taught that marriage was about creating a strong family foundation—usually with the wife playing the helpmate to her husband—love was still at least given lip service in the equation. "So you think that Mason and Reese won't have a solid and successful partnership? Simply because they're in *love*?"

"Would you marry someone just because he was good in bed?"

The bluntness of that question quite literally caused her to stumble. Dylan's hand tightened against her back as she regained her balance, and she wondered if Dylan had tried to shock her on purpose. No, Dylan wasn't the type. Gina might try to bait and shock, but Dylan... She couldn't really picture it. "Like love, it shouldn't be the *only* reason to get married, but it's a damn important one."

Dylan merely smiled at her response, and she could almost feel the metaphorical pat on the head. It had been a long time since anyone had patronized her like that, and she wondered what Reese might have said about her to make him think…

"Wait a second." She stopped the sway. "If love isn't the right reason to get married, are you saying that you never loved Reese?" Reese might be happy in love *now*, but she'd sworn to only marry for love and finding out that Dylan *hadn't* loved her at all would still hurt.

"Of course I loved her." What would normally be a passionate declaration in any decent romance novel sounded flat instead. Dylan could have been speaking about how much he loved pizza for all the emotion behind the statement. *Wow.* Reese had definitely dodged a bullet with this one.

"Well, Reese seems to be pretty good at avoiding mistakes these days."

An eyebrow arched up at her statement, but the music finally came to a stop, keeping Dylan from responding to her snark. Instead, he stepped back, and with a mocking bow, said, "Thanks for the dance, Marnie."

He walked over to Tuck and spoke quietly to his friend. A moment later, their whole party was tossing a shower of flower petals at Tuck and Cassie as they ran out the door and climbed into a black town car for their getaway.

She felt a hand on her elbow and turned to see Carter. Gina was hanging back a step behind him, seeming a little unsure. It brought back the weight of all that thinking she still had to do. *Damn.* If nothing else, she owed Dylan a debt of thanks for taking her mind off all that for even a few minutes.

"We're going to go, too," Carter said. "I'm sure we'll see you while I'm in town."

Marnie still wasn't quite used to the idea of that "we." It was going to take time to wrap her head around the fact that Carter and Gina were a couple. In the last ten years, her relationship with her brother had gone from good to really bad and finally landed in "strained" territory, and she wasn't entirely sure if his new relationship with Gina was going to improve that situation or not. But she and Gina seemed to be on the brink of repairing their damage, and she realized she very much wanted *that* to happen. She'd deal with Carter somehow. She'd have to. "Yeah. We'll do lunch or something."

Gina seemed uncharacteristically reticent to say anything, but Reese stepped in, purse over her shoulder, obviously ready to leave, as well. She wrapped her arms around their shoulders and pulled them in for a celebratory squeeze. "I think we did well today, ladies."

Gina nodded. "We did."

"And us?" Reese asked quietly, "Are we okay?"

While she'd asked the question generally, Marnie knew they were primarily waiting on her to answer. While she and Gina still had some baggage to unpack, Reese had to be feeling some weight, as well—after all, she'd known about Gina's pregnancy and miscarriage when it had happened and had kept that knowledge from Marnie all this time.

Yikes, something else to process. But Marnie returned Reese's squeeze and placed a hand on Gina's arm. "We will be."

Gina met her eyes directly and nodded, and that nod somehow helped clear through the noise. She felt her eyes burning. "I'll talk to y'all later."

"You're not going all the way home tonight, are you?" Reese asked.

The long train ride out to Brooklyn didn't hold much attraction now—wine waiting in the fridge or no. Thankfully, she had another option, and there were many stores between here and SoHo where she could pick up another bottle. "No, I'll probably stay at Sven's."

"We could drop you off on our way."

Gina's eyes widened. "Wait, there's a Sven?" she asked.

"Sven is gay and lets me crash at his place when I need to," she explained to Gina and then declined Reese's offer. The last thing she needed right now was more quality time with her friends. God only knew what *other* bombshells could drop. "I'm actually going to finish this wine and have a bit of a think. I'll grab a cab later."

Reese looked a little concerned, but nodded. There were general good-nights all around and Marnie pulled Gina aside. "One more thing... Please don't mention to Carter that I got laid off. I really don't want to deal with that right now."

"Gotcha."

The lack of hesitation warmed her. *Yeah, they were going to be okay.*

She waved off the other two couples and sank back into her chair with a sigh. Then she emptied the last of the Chardonnay into her glass.

"That's a waste of good wine."

She'd forgotten about Dylan, who seemed to also be finishing off a drink—something dark in a glass on the rocks.

"It's excellent wine and it's not a waste. I fully appreciate each and every delicious, mind-numbing drop." She backed up that statement by taking a large swallow.

"Tough day?"

Oh, so now they were going to do the small talk? "You could say that. I'm really happy for all of my friends, but..."

"Oh, God, you're not going to get all 'always a bridesmaid, never a bride,' are you?"

She nearly snorted the wine. "I actually wish that was the problem. It would be a lot simpler. Unfortunately, not all sorrows needing drowning stem from a love life or lack thereof."

Dylan's mouth *might* have quirked, but he didn't say anything. Was he waiting for an explanation? Was this actually a conversation now, making it rude for her not to provide one?

She didn't know what or how much Dylan knew about her past with Reese, Cassie and Gina, and she really didn't want to go into it. But she'd opened the door, and it would probably be polite to explain why she was pounding Chardonnay. Gee, was it good or bad that she had *another*, equally valid, reason to give? "I lost my job this morning."

"That does suck."

She bit back her surprise at his word choice. "I knew it was coming—budget problems, you know—but I really liked that job." Her glass and the bottle were now empty, and she debated having another before heading out.

"I think I should buy you a drink."

She didn't need the charity. She could well afford to buy her own drinks, even without a job—at least as long as the Price Paper Consortium continued to turn a profit. And she didn't really need his company, either, as it made far more sense to get hammered in private. At the same time, though, there was something pathetic about drinking alone. Dylan Brookes wouldn't have been her first choice of drinking partners, but it did beat a total stranger, and he didn't seem in a hurry to leave. Plus, he hadn't been abstaining tonight, either, and had to be working on a pretty good buzz himself, making her wonder if maybe he had a few woes to drown, as well.

It would be the polite thing to do. "All right, then."

"Another Chardonnay? Or perhaps something stronger?"

Either she was imagining things, or there was a challenge in his voice, and she was in the mood to call him on it. She waved over a server. "I'd like a shot of Patrón, two limes, with a Dos Equis back, please." She turned to Dylan and shot him an innocent smile. "And for you?"

Dylan shot her a smile that said there was *some* sign of life in there. Maybe he had layers. "Same."

As the server left, Marnie turned to Dylan. "I know—and now you know—why *I'm* drinking. What's *your* story? Woman troubles?"

"As you said, not all sorrows needing drowning necessarily stem from a love life or lack thereof."

Oh, she was now dying to ask if it was the love life or lack of.

"You're not the only one who can have a bad day," he continued. "Although since I didn't lose my job today, my day probably wasn't as bad as yours."

The server returned with their drinks, and Dylan lifted his shot glass in a toast. "To crappy days and the booze that gets us through them."

She lifted her own glass and nodded. Then Dylan licked the salt off the rim of the glass and she nearly fell off her chair in shock.

Things were looking up.

There was something very strange about watching perky blond cheerleader-looking Marnie Price throw back tequila shots like a barroom champ. Not that he could claim to know all that much about her, but Reese had always talked about her as some sweet little thing, and on the few occasions he'd been around her, Dylan hadn't seen anything to the contrary.

He'd been proven wrong tonight. Whatever she was drinking to forget, she was well on her way there. And honestly, he was happy to join her. It was a good way to end off a bitch of a week, and he was unexpectedly having a good time. He normally limited himself to no more than two drinks over the course of a public event, preferring to keep his mind clear and situations under control, but he'd found himself matching Marnie shot for shot and beer for beer all night.

Marnie might look like one of Botticelli's angels—all soft curves and rosy skin—but she had a wild streak under there. And while he couldn't say he knew her all that well, on the few occasions he had been in her company, Marnie had always been perfectly polite, but a bit distant and, in general, cool toward him. That had changed.

They'd covered everything from politics to Marnie's debutante ball, and she was both smart and funny as hell. While they had absolutely nothing in common beyond Reese, he was having a damn good time.

It was just what he needed, and he hadn't even known it.

When Reese had pulled him aside before she'd left and asked him to keep an eye on Marnie and make sure she got into a cab okay, he'd initially wanted to say no, not wanting to babysit for the evening. But he'd relented, and before he knew it, the bartenders were making the last call.

And while he'd consumed a ridiculous amount of alcohol, he didn't regret the choice, either.

And now Marnie was finishing up her monologue on the differences between Southern women and the rest of the world. "I'm just sayin', you do not want to tangle with Southern women. We can eat your heart from your chest and not even burp daintily afterward." She cut those big blue eyes at him in the most perfect flirt he'd ever seen. "And we'll make you *love* it. In fact, you'll *thank* us for it."

Marnie's accent had thickened throughout the evening, and the drawl was now so pronounced, her vowels were in the back of her throat and he could almost hear the Spanish moss hanging off her words. Maybe it was the booze, but that accent was almost hypnotic, honeyed and thick, sucking him in with each word and doing strange things to his insides. Seemed he had a hidden hot spot for Southern belles he'd never discovered until now.

"How on earth do you hide that accent every day, Miss Marnie?" he teased, mimicking her cadence.

"It's hard, but I've had lots of practice. Repression skills are taught right alongside the history of the War of Northern Aggression."

War had gained an extra syllable and, for laughs, he tried to repeat it back to her.

She frowned. "Don't mock me. I drink and drawl. It's a real problem." She sighed. "And since I feel a case of full-on magnolia mouth comin', I think that's my cue to go home. I'm hammered."

A little flash of disappointment cut through him. The flash sharply changed direction when Marnie licked her lips.

But that hadn't been a flirt, he realized, as Marnie laughed. "Yep. Lips are numb. I'm not even sure they're still attached."

That reminded him of the real purpose he was here with her. "I assure you they still are." He signaled for the bartender to close the tab. "Come on. I'll walk you out. We'll split a cab."

She shook her head. "That's okay, I'll walk."

"To Brooklyn? You *are* hammered."

Marnie laughed again. "No. I have keys to a friend's place, and he's away for Labor Day. It's only about five blocks from here. And, anyway, it's not exactly on your way back to your Park Avenue penthouse. Wouldn't want you to be seen slumming it in SoHo."

That was a slam, especially since he now knew she'd grown up a debutante. "I live on East Sixty-Fourth, thank you very much."

Marnie grinned. "Close enough."

There was no way he was letting Marnie walk anywhere alone—not this late and after that much tequila. "Then I'll walk you."

"That's very kind of you, but really not necessary."

"I just got an entire lecture on gentlemanly behavior from a Southern belle, so I'll err on the side of caution. I don't want my heart eaten from my chest." He offered his arm, and Marnie hesitated for a moment, looking up at him through her lashes before finally taking it.

"Why, thank you, sir. That's ever so kind of you," she drawled in a combination of Scarlett O'Hara and Blanche DuBois.

For someone who claimed to be hammered, Marnie was stable enough on her feet, and they walked the first block without incident. She took a deep breath of the night air and looked around. "I just love this area. I might have to look for a place here."

That caught him by surprise. Marnie didn't seem

like the right fit for this area. Brooklyn seemed better somehow. "You don't like Brooklyn?

"Oh, I like it there just fine, but I only moved to Park Slope because it was close to my job. Without that..." She shrugged. "I'm not attached to the area, and I've always wanted to live around here. Or maybe in the Village. Someplace really vibrant and in the middle of things."

"Looking for excitement in life?"

She grinned at him. "Always."

"No desire to go back to Savannah?"

He might have heard a tiny snort from Marnie. "None. I like being *from* Savannah, but I don't want to *be* there. Does that make sense?"

"Sure." He wasn't entirely sure it did, but he agreed nonetheless.

They walked quietly for another moment, but it wasn't an uncomfortable silence. Finally Marnie said, "Thanks for hanging out with me tonight. It was fun."

"It was, and you're welcome."

"I'm kinda sorry I didn't get a chance to know you better when you and Reese were...well, before. We could've been friends."

There was such a sigh in her voice that he wanted to laugh. Except that she seemed serious. "And we can't be now?"

"I think it might be awkward and uncomfortable— for everyone." She looked at her feet for a moment, then back up at him. "But anyway—and regardless of what you said earlier—I am sorry you and Reese didn't work out."

And so was he. Theirs hadn't been a great love match like Marnie sang praises of, but it had been stable. Secure. Solid. "Thanks. We made a great team. But Reese loves Mason."

"But you said love isn't a good reason to get married." He couldn't see it, but he knew she was rolling her eyes.

"I said it wasn't the *only* reason to get married, but it's especially a bad idea when one of the parties loves someone *else*. I think I knew all along that something wasn't quite right, but getting married seemed like the thing to do at the time, and you get to a point of no return pretty quickly. I was almost glad when Mason showed up and finally forced Reese's hand." That was true, too. If Reese really needed that kind of relationship to be happy, he wasn't the man to give it to her.

"So you're really okay about it?"

"Are you asking me if I'm over Reese?"

"Yeah, I guess I am."

He nearly laughed. That was something very few people had the nerve to ask to his face. "Reese and I were friends and we're still friends. But I'm not carrying a torch for her."

"That is a ridiculously reasonable and mature statement, all things considered."

He shrugged. "It's for the best. If you can't go into a marriage knowing absolutely sure it's the right choice, then you shouldn't do it. It won't end well."

Marnie laughed, but it was bitter sounding. "I actually agree with you on that."

"Really?"

She nodded. "I witnessed that in my brother's marriage. I encouraged them both to go through with it—and by 'encouraged,' I really mean 'browbeat'—and they were very unhappy until the day the divorce was final. It pretty much ruined my relationship with his wife, Missy, who I'd known most of my life and considered a dear friend, and it didn't help things between me and Carter, either."

He'd noticed the distance between Carter and Marnie. They'd barely spoken to each other all day, and the ride from the courthouse to the restaurant had been heavy from the tension hanging between them.

She patted his arm. "For both your sakes, I'm glad you figured it out before it was too late." Shaking her head, she smiled crookedly at him. "One could wish you two had figured that out *before* people bought non-returnable bridesmaids' dresses, though."

"I thought Reese picked dresses you all could wear again."

Marnie snorted. "That's a lie all brides tell themselves and their bridesmaids. I've been in more weddings than I can count and I've never worn a bridesmaid's dress twice."

"My apologies. I'll keep that in mind for next time."

"Next time? Jumping right back into the saddle, are you?"

"I wouldn't exactly call it jumping, but I do plan to get married at some point. Don't you?"

She shrugged one shoulder. "Maybe. One day. A very long time from now, though."

"Not such a romantic after all, then."

"Just picky. And not at all in any rush."

"Me, neither," he clarified, "but I think I'm getting to a point in my life where I'd like to have that stability."

"Stability?" Marnie laughed. "That's so romantic, I just might swoon."

Her heel caught in a grate and Marnie stumbled. He grabbed her arm to steady her as she regained her balance. "I didn't know you meant that literally."

"Don't sass me, mister."

Just to be safe, he offered her his arm and tucked her hand in.

Marnie shot him a look like she was sizing him up for something. Then she sighed. "While I swore I would never get involved in someone else's love life ever again, I will break that vow long enough to offer you one piece of advice."

He'd had plenty of advice, but he'd humor her. "And that would be?"

"When courting a lady, I'd avoid mentioning your philosophy about how marriage is more about a solid partnership than love and the importance of stability."

"And why is that?"

"Because it sounds ridiculously antiquated. Like a woman's value lies solely in her ability to be the perfect helpmate to her husband. You might as well just barter with her father for land and cattle, too."

How'd she get *there*? There was definitely bitterness under that statement. It seemed far safer, though, to just let it pass rather than open up a subject he had no idea how touchy she might be about it. He wasn't a therapist. He nodded. "Noted."

But Marnie was warming to her subject. "Women—I won't say all, but most—want some passion and excitement in a relationship. Something to get the heart pumping and the nerves sparking. A woman wants to be desired, not judged and rated on how successful a partnership it will make."

Partly just to goad her, he shook his head sadly. "Passion is highly overrated."

"Never."

"You do realize I run a foundation for victims of

domestic violence, right? I think many of them would trade passion and excitement for stability and peace."

"You're twisting the definition of passion. Just because it *can* go bad, that doesn't mean it *will*. Or that there's something inherently wrong with it."

He shrugged.

"Maybe you should spend less time at the foundation and more time finding a woman who makes your heart beat fast just to be near her."

Nope. "I thought you were only going to offer *one* piece of advice," he teased.

Marnie paused and turned to face him. Those blue eyes were laughing as she rose onto her tiptoes and grabbed his shoulders earnestly. "I believe you have layers, Dylan Brookes. Discover them. *Embrace* them. Find that passion and the woman who brings it out of you."

She was close, very close, her lips only inches from his, and her light citrus scent filled his nose. Something in the air around them shifted, and Marnie swallowed hard. Then she released his shoulders and stepped back.

Clearing her throat, she pointed to a nondescript door nearby. "That's my stop. Thanks for walking with me."

There was that strange feeling of disappointment again, only this time it held an edge he hadn't expected. "You're welcome, Marnie."

"Um…if you just go up to the end of the block, you shouldn't have any problem hailing a taxi."

The comfortable camaraderie had turned awkward and was only getting worse. "I'll be fine."

With a bright, but maybe slightly forced, smile, Marnie held out her hand. "Good night, Dylan."

He took hold of it, and like he'd done with any number of female friends, leaned in to kiss her cheek lightly.

He'd done the maneuver hundreds of times, but instead of landing on her cheek, somehow his lips landed on hers.

There was a brief moment of frozen shock, but Marnie didn't pull away. Instead, her mouth softened and she leaned in to him, tightening her grip on his hand. Her lips were smooth and warm and the kiss sent a bolt of fire straight through him.

That edge made total sense now. He'd been *wanting* to kiss her. Since forever, it seemed. And *that* feeling was more of a surprise than the kiss itself.

The world seemed to contract, until there was nothing else except the taste of Marnie and the feel of her body molded against his like she'd been custom-made only for him. That light scent of her perfume filled his lungs with each breath, and his hands tangled in the soft silk of her hair, holding her in place as his mouth devoured hers.

He heard Marnie's low moan, a nearly primal sound that reverberated through him, bringing every nerve in his body to life to beg for more of her touch, her taste. That response was new, as if Marnie was the first and last woman he'd ever get to touch. It put a sharp, almost desperate edge on the desire slicing through him, but it felt so good he only wanted more.

He didn't understand why or how Marnie could do this to him, but he didn't really care, either.

That kiss went on and on, until they were both gasping for air and his heart felt like it was pounding through his chest. His whole body felt hard and tight, and it took willpower he didn't know he had to break the kiss and set Marnie back on slightly unstable legs instead of pushing her up against the metal door and losing himself in her.

Marnie's eyes were wide and dark, her lips slightly swollen and moist. She gave herself a small shake and then blew out her breath. "Well."

What she meant by that, he had no idea, as his blood wasn't exactly circulating in the direction of his brain at the moment, and his mind was full of images and ideas that might scare Marnie if she knew.

"Um…" she began, only to stop and clear her throat. "I'm sure that Sven has a bottle of…um…" She paused again to swallow. "Something that probably needs drinking."

Her hand was shaking as she reached out to toy with the button of his shirt. His skin was hot; it should have scorched her just from proximity. Those big blue eyes met his, and what he saw there nearly brought him to his knees.

"Would you like to come up for a nightcap?"

CHAPTER TWO

MARNIE HAD NEARLY forgotten what it was like to wake up curled into the solid warmth of a sleeping man. Drowsy fingers stroked absently over her back, and Dylan's chest made a lovely pillow, his slow, deep breaths calming and hypnotic.

It was a nice way to start the day, except for the nagging feeling that this was wrong. Really, really *wrong*. Which was very confusing because it felt really good at the same time.

Of the million men in New York that she could have chosen for a drunken hookup, why had she picked Dylan?

Beyond the obvious, of course. The chest under her cheek was sculpted and tanned, the muscles defined without being bulky and bulging. *That* had been a pleasant surprise to find under Dylan's conservative gray suit. And that chest hadn't been the only surprise waiting for her...

The want had kicked up out of nowhere last night, slamming into her with an unexpected force that got completely out of hand. *Fast.* She could try to blame it on the tequila, but she doubted even tequila could explain the overwhelming feeling of *yes, now, please* that had taken over her body last night.

It made no sense. She wasn't attracted to men like Dylan, damn it. She craved artists, musicians, activists...interesting men who carried their hearts and their passions on their sleeves. *Not* disinterested, distant, society types. *Not* the Dylans of the world.

Just the thought caused her to feel the cage bars close in on her.

She wasn't sure how it had happened, what threw the switch. One minute she'd been lecturing Dylan on finding his passion, and while she hadn't quite meant for it to take the turn it did, the next thing she knew, he'd not only shown her he had it, but she'd been caught hard and unexpectedly by that very thing.

She'd been overwhelmed, to say the least.

Oh, she had a solid set of reasons to explain *how* she ended up here, but none of them erased that *wrong* feeling. Because one tiny fact outweighed them all:

Dylan was Reese's.

They're over. She's moved on. And as of last night, so has he.

That doesn't make this okay. You know that.

She'd made some questionable decisions in her life, but *this* was definitely a first simply because the repercussions were potentially huge.

She could tell herself that Reese and Dylan were over, but she still felt like she'd crossed a line.

Not that she knew *where* that line actually was...

Was there a proper waiting period? A statute of limitations? At what point did a friend's ex become fair game? And was it different when the ex was an ex-*fiancé*? Surely that was a bigger deal than just a random ex-boyfriend.

Some friend she was. A nasty feeling of déjà vu settled in her chest. *No.* This was not the same thing at all. Dylan and Reese were over.

But still… How was she going to face Reese? For that matter, how was she going to face Dylan?

She vaguely remembered saying that being friends might be awkward. That would be a piece of cake compared to this.

Oh, God. What if he started…*comparing.* Ugh. She felt something nasty coil in her stomach.

Dylan shifted underneath her. Somehow, he knew she was awake, as there were no surreptitious, try-not-to-wake-her moves. "Morning," he said, his voice gruff and husky from sleep.

Marnie peeked up at him and her breath caught. Suave, debonair Dylan was totally gone. His hair stuck up at crazy angles from sleep, and a dark shadow covered his jaw. There was something raw and yummy about him that sent sparks through her nervous system before she remembered that more sparks would just bring more wrongness to the situation.

Damn it.

She was going to have to get through this the best she could, regardless. She really could have used a few more minutes to think this through and formulate a plan before he woke up. *Pretend this isn't a big deal. Act normally.*

But she had no idea what normal should be. "Morning. I—"

She was saved by the phone. Somewhere, under the pile of clothing, she heard the vibration against the wood floor. A second later, the ringtone kicked in, and adrenaline rushed through her veins.

That was *Reese's* ringtone.

It was a slap in the face, a condemnation set to

Reese's favorite song, and guilt that had been tiptoe-ing across her mind landed on her conscience with a heavy thud.

She could ignore it, let it go to voicemail, but that just seemed *worse* somehow. It would be a cowardly admission of wrongdoing flavored with the attitude that it just didn't matter anyway.

She scrambled over the edge of the bed head first, ignoring the "oof" from Dylan as her foot landed on his stomach, and dug through the pile until she found her phone.

"*Reese!* Good *morning*! How *are* you!" She cringed at the over-perky sound of her voice.

There was a soft chuckle from the other end. "And good morning to you. You seem to be in a very good mood today."

Marnie struggled upright, pulling the sheet up to cover herself, and kept her back to Dylan. If she looked at him now, Reese would know somehow. "Why wouldn't I be?"

"I was expecting you to be a little hungover. You were certainly pounding the wine last night—"

"No. Nope. I feel fine."

"I was just a little worried, but I certainly under-stand the need. You had a lot land on you yesterday—"

She could hear Dylan moving around behind her. "And I appreciate it, but I'm good. So what's up?"

"Is everything okay? You sound funny."

A short hysterical laugh burst out before she could stop it. Clearing her throat, Marnie tried for a less insane-sounding level of perkiness. "I'm great. Just...um—"

"Wait... Did I interrupt something?"

Guilt slammed into her. "What? *No!* What could you possibly be interrupting?"

"Marnie…" Reese's voice dropped a notch. "Is there someone else there?"

Oh, God. "Of course not."

Disbelief and amusement crept into Reese's voice. "Did you go home with someone last night?"

Nausea rolled through her belly. She was such a bad liar, and she was about to be busted, big time. "N-no, I— I—"

"You *did.* Let me guess. That cute bartender?"

"No! No hooking up. What kind of girl do you think I am? I finished my wine and went straight to Sven's to crash. There's nobody here except me." She heard Dylan snort and without looking, waved her hand at him to shut up.

"Pity."

I should have let her call go to voicemail. "Reese, honey, if you're just wanting to chat, can I call you back—"

Reese turned serious. "I actually did have a reason for calling."

Oh. "Okay." She brushed her hair out of her face and tried to focus. "What's up?"

"I had the most brilliant idea late last night. I don't know why it didn't occur to me before."

Something about the way she said "brilliant" put Marnie on alert. "And?"

"*And* then I saw you talking to Dylan, and you seemed to be getting along okay—"

Marnie nearly choked. *Careful, now.* She tried for a nonchalant tone. "What does he have to do with anything?"

"I'm getting there. You need a job, right?"

"Yeah, and…?"

"As much as I'd love to ask you to come on board at

Second Chance, First Response, it's going to be a while before we're up and running."

"I know that—"

"Well, I happen to know that as of yesterday, Dylan still hadn't found anyone to replace me at the Foundation." Reese sounded almost smug.

Marnie stole a glance over her shoulder to where Dylan was leaning against the iron headboard like nothing was amiss at all. He raised an eyebrow at her. *Damn.* Now he knew they were talking about him. Unfortunately, she'd totally lost the thread of the conversation and had no idea what she should be saying next. "Oh, um..."

"I think you'd be perfect for the job. You've got experience with nonprofits and working with people trying to better their circumstances..."

Deliberately, she turned her back on Dylan. *Right. Job. Foundation. Focus.* "That certainly sounds interesting. Maybe we could get together and talk about it sometime—"

"Great. I'm so glad you're interested. Hang on, I'm going to get Dylan on this call."

"*What?* No, Reese—" But she was talking to dead air. Panicked, she grabbed Dylan's pants off the pile of clothes and threw them at him, even though he was seemingly unconcerned that her life had turned into a bad sitcom. "Get your phone."

"Why?"

"Just—" Before she could say more, Reese was back on the line, and she heard the ring on that end a second before Dylan's phone began to scream like a Klaxon in the silence. She coughed loudly and rudely into her phone to cover the noise as Dylan produced the phone and silenced the ringtone. She could still hear it vibrating, though, along with each ring on Reese's end.

"Marnie, are you okay?"

She moved off the bed and away. Sven's loft was totally open plan—basically a large studio—and unless she wanted to lock herself in the bathroom, where the echo would be both bad and obvious, the only thing she could do was try for distance. "Something caught in my throat."

Dylan held his phone in his hand, looking at her with a question on his face, and she tried to mime "let it go to voicemail" while still talking to Reese. Dylan obviously misunderstood, answering it before she could stop him.

"Hi, Reese."

Oh. My. God. Dylan's voice sounded caught in a loop—coming through the phone *and* bouncing off the walls of Sven's apartment back through her phone. Shooting him a dirty look, she got as far away as possible and plastered her back against the wall. The jolt of cold, rough brick against her back reminded her that she was stark naked. She crossed her arms as best she could over her chest and tried to look nonchalant about it.

"Morning, Dylan. I've got Marnie on the line, too."

Dylan's eyes met hers, then slid slowly and appreciatively down her body, causing shivers to dance over her skin. "Well, good morning, Marnie."

She could cheerfully strangle him, but Reese would probably hear the noise and wonder. "Hi, Dylan."

"Look," Reese began, "I won't beat around the bush. You wanted me to help find someone to take my place at the Foundation, and I think Marnie would be perfect. She's been working with the Refugee Center in Brooklyn for the last few years, so she has plenty of relevant experience. She's smart and sharp, and I know she'd do an amazing job."

The pride in Reese's voice squeezed Marnie's heart as the realization of what Reese was doing finally fully dawned. Reese had devoted herself to the Brookes Foundation and would not want just anyone taking her place. The fact she wanted Marnie to do it spoke volumes, and it only made Marnie feel worse about sleeping with Dylan.

Dylan cleared his throat. "It's certainly something to talk about. Marnie, why don't you send me your résumé—"

"I'll do that," she managed to squeeze out through a tight throat.

"Why don't we just all go to lunch?" Reese asked instead, and Marnie wanted to bang her head against the wall. "We can talk about the job and—"

"Sure," Dylan interrupted. "I'm just not sure what my schedule is like next week—"

"Which is why I thought we could do it today."

Horrified, Marnie squeaked, "Today?"

"Today?" Dylan sounded only slightly less horrified.

"Yes, today," Reese sighed. "I know you, Dylan, and I know your schedule. With the holiday Monday and everything else, it could be ages before there's a hole. If we meet today, get that part over with, Marnie could start officially interviewing and such as early as next week. You already kind of know her, and you know I wouldn't recommend her if I didn't know she would be awesome—"

Marnie tried to interrupt. "Reese, I've got—"

"Really? You're going to fight me over lunch? Jeez, I'll even buy. I don't know why you two are being so difficult when this is the perfect solution to everyone's problems. An hour, you guys, that's all I ask. Do you really have such pressing plans today that you can't spare an hour for lunch?"

Marnie couldn't figure out a way to say no, damn it. Reese knew full well that she didn't have plans today because Marnie had told her just yesterday that she didn't. She shot Dylan a pleading look, but he looked resigned to the inevitable. They were both being steamrolled, but it was impossible to fight because Reese did it with only the very best of intentions.

Reese took the silence for acquiescence. "Great. How about we meet at Vincent's, say eleven o'clock?"

Although she frantically scrambled to find one, she had no reason to say no. "Okay." Marnie tried to inject a little enthusiasm into her voice for Reese's sake.

"Fine." Dylan still sounded downright begrudging and Marnie wanted to throw something at him. She had to remind herself that Reese only had his best interests in mind, as well.

"Great. See you then. Bye!"

Marnie was left naked, leaning against a wall, holding a dead phone, staring down at the man she'd spent the night with—who, in addition to being the ex-fiancé of one of her dearest friends, was also going to interview her for a job in two hours.

This day was off to a very bad start.

And it was way too early to start drinking.

Dylan couldn't tell if Marnie was on the verge of tears, hysteria, or murder.

When she closed her eyes and banged her head gently against the wall, muttering something to herself he couldn't quite hear, he figured those three options were off the table.

Even so, Marnie was a tempting sight, blond hair rioting around flushed cheeks, all that creamy skin and those soft curves deliciously on display against the red brick walls of the apartment like a modern rendition of the *Birth of Venus*. As she continued to mutter, the possibility of her returning to bed for a proper wake-up seemed to be out of the question, as well, and he sent a stern memo to his body as he reached for his clothing.

Reese had lousy timing, that was for sure.

The movement brought Marnie's attention back to him—and her lack of clothing, it seemed, as she disappeared into the bathroom and returned with a towel wrapped around her. "Reese will kill me if I cancel the meeting," she said briskly. "You're going to have to do it."

"So Reese can kill me instead?"

"I simply cannot face her today. Not after…" Marnie's face, already pink, deepened to scarlet. "I just can't."

"Just tell her you're not interested in the job, and we don't have to have lunch. End of whatever problem you're having." He found his shirt, righted the sleeves and shrugged into it. "Not that I understand this problem…"

"Of course you don't." Marnie sounded miserable and angry. He'd been able to piece together that Reese had asked her if she'd gone home with someone, and while he'd heard her protestations that she wasn't "that kind of girl," this reaction still seemed extreme.

If she'd just calm down… "Then explain it to me."

"I owe Reese so much. If it weren't for her, I'd probably still be in Savannah, the perfect helpmate and wifelet to some banker or doctor, running the church bake sale and bazaar every year." Marnie began tidying up, talking more to herself than him now. "I owe her practically *everything* and now she's even helping me job hunt again, and how do I pay her back? By sleeping with her fiancé, of course."

Technically, they'd slept together before Reese decided to start headhunting, but it was a detail he didn't think Marnie would appreciate right now. There was one detail, however, that did require correcting. "*Ex*-fiancé," he reminded her. "And since she threw me over for Mason—"

All the color drained from Marnie's face so quickly, he was sure she was about to faint. "Oh, *God,* I'm a revenge lay? Reese hurt your feelings so you sleep with one of her friends to slap back? And I just helped you hurt her." She sat on the bed and ran her hands over her face. "I am a terrible, terrible person—"

"Whoa, there. You are *way* off base. First of all, I don't need or want revenge on Reese. That never even crossed my mind, and even if it had, it's a poor way to try to get back at someone. For God's sake, Reese and I are over—"

"Oh, like *that* matters. Do you honestly think she's not going to care that I slept with you?"

"I certainly hope not. I don't get a say-so in her sex life anymore, so I don't see where or why she'd get a say in mine."

Her head popped up. "But she does get a say in *mine.*"

"That's the most ridiculous thing I've ever heard."

"Reese is my friend," she said, looking at him like that explained everything. He shrugged and Marnie rolled her eyes. "It's just not done, okay? It's tacky. Some people are just off limits—exes, brothers, sometimes cousins…"

She was making a huge deal out of nothing. "That's rather juvenile."

"But that's the way it is. And I just can't face Reese today knowing I crossed that line last night."

This had just crossed the line into ridiculous. He wasn't going to get sucked into completely unnecessary drama. "And since I consider Reese my friend, as well, I'm not going to insult her unnecessarily by canceling." He looked her square in the eye. "It's just not done, you know?"

Marnie obviously didn't like having her words thrown back at her, and as she bit her lip hard enough to turn it white, he wondered what words she was keeping behind her teeth. Finally, she squared her shoulders. "Well, then, I guess we're having lunch with Reese."

"I guess we are."

"Fine." She sounded pained and her jaw was tight. "But let me be clear. I do *not* want Reese to know what happened last night."

"I see no reason why she should. It's not her business. As far as she's concerned, I put you in a cab just like she asked, and I have no idea how you spent the rest of your evening."

"Good. Wait..." Marnie's eyes narrowed. "What do you mean 'just like she asked'?"

Under that accusing stare, Dylan knew he'd stepped in it this time. He chose his words carefully. "Reese was concerned about you and asked me to hang out for a little while last night to make sure you got home okay."

Marnie rubbed her temples. "Oh, my God."

He found his watch on the nightstand but paused as Marnie moaned her misery. "What *now*?"

"That's why you stayed behind to drink with me. Because Reese asked you to babysit the drunk girl. And, *ugh*…" She made a face. "That's why you wanted to walk with me. I totally misread that—"

Here we go again. Marnie was just determined to overreact to every single thing he said. "Jeez, give me the benefit of the doubt that I'm not some pervert who was just out to take advantage of a situation. You may have morning-after regrets, but I'm not going to apologize for what happened between two consenting— albeit slightly intoxicated—adults."

Marnie was silent, eyes closed as she thought. When those baby blues found his again, she merely nodded. He wasn't sure if that meant she had regrets or didn't or what, but either way, she wasn't going to pretend she'd somehow been abused in this. That was good. "But I still don't want Reese to know."

"As I said, there's no reason she needs to."

"Excellent." Marnie looked around uncomfortably. "Well…um…you should probably go now. I've got to dash home and change…"

He wasn't exactly being kicked out, but it was close enough. And it bordered on farcical as Marnie followed him to the door, and still wearing nothing but a towel, shook his hand with a prim properness that belied the knowledge of what they'd done the night before.

There was a little coffee shop on the corner, and Dylan ducked inside gratefully. He'd barely been awake before Marnie's phone rang, and he'd been thrown right into the middle of a bad sitcom without even the benefit of coffee to help him make sense of it.

The aroma alone helped clear the cobwebs from his head, and the caffeine kicked in in the taxi. By the time it pulled to a stop in front of his building, Dylan was feeling marginally human. The doorman merely nodded as he made his walk of shame through the lobby to the elevator.

By the time he'd showered and let the hot water pound the stiffness from his muscles—Marnie's friend Sven desperately needed a new mattress—some of the morning made sense.

Based solely on what he knew about Marnie from Reese, he'd almost expected Marnie's morning-after regrets to come from some kind of old-fashioned moral objection. But he was still questioning all that he thought he knew about Marnie, especially since she wasn't at all the sweet innocent thing Reese had painted her to be. Reese's assessment of Marnie seemed to be several years out of date. She might look like an angel, but his skin was still burning with the memory of last night.

No, Marnie's regrets seemed to stem from a loyalty to Reese.

Loyalty to a friend was a good and noble thing, but Marnie was taking it a little far, in his opinion. He and Reese had been over months ago, and since Reese had so obviously moved on, it seemed ridiculous for Marnie to obsess on that part of his past.

Not that being roped by his ex-fiancée into interviewing the woman he'd slept with the night before for his ex-fiancée's job *wasn't* weird—he'd give Marnie that much—but honestly, he couldn't understand the extent of Marnie's freakout.

And honestly, he didn't want to. Drama and freak-outs were for people with nothing better to do with their time. It was one of the reasons he and Reese had gotten along so well, and if Marnie had a penchant for the dramatic, he wasn't sure she was quite as suited for the job as Reese claimed.

Maybe Reese didn't know. Maybe Marnie's dramatics were a new development. It's not like they were all *that* close. Which also added to the absurdity of Marnie's stress over Reese finding out they'd slept together.

Just another reason not to drink and pick up women in bars. The drama.

Dressed, shaved and feeling human, he went back down to the lobby and had the doorman hail another taxi. He'd humor Reese and do this, and then he'd figure out what, if anything, would happen next with Marnie—professionally at least. On a personal level, he had his answer.

It's was a good thing Marnie didn't really want the job anyway.

CHAPTER THREE

I REALLY, REALLY want that job.

Marnie dropped her keys and purse onto the coffee table and collapsed onto the couch. That knowledge had settled on her before their entrées had arrived and had only grown stronger in the subsequent hours.

While that had quite possibly been the absolute most uncomfortable interview she'd ever had, Marnie was absolutely sure about one thing: the job was perfect. Exactly what she wanted. The sad but true fact was that much of her experience from the Refugee Center would transfer easily to a battered women's organization like the Brookes Foundation. She knew people at every social service office, staffing agency and housing department in the Tri-State area, as well as every doctor, lawyer and therapist who'd work on a sliding payment scale.

Granted, her fund-raising experience wasn't nearly what it could be—or possibly should be—for the position, but Reese could coach her on that, and she could mine the memories of all that fund-raising her mother had done for various charities in Savannah.

I could do that job. I'd be awesome at that job.

Hell, it was practically the perfect job.

The only real problem was Dylan.

To give him credit where it was due, he hadn't said or done anything to hint at what happened last night. Even in her hypersensitive looking-for-every-possible-double-entendre state of awareness, no one would have been able to guess he'd seen her naked *just hours before*.

If anything, Dylan had been cool, aloof, nearly patronizing, as if the whole interview was simply his way of indulging a wild scheme of Reese's when he had better, more important places to be. It had set her teeth on edge, and she'd wanted to reach across the table and smack him more than once. It was the Dylan she knew before—and a completely different man than the one she'd spent last night with. She was having a hard time reconciling the two in her mind.

Obviously, Dylan needed large amounts of alcohol in order to become human. Or maybe she'd been drunker than she thought last night and *she* was the one who needed large amounts of alcohol to tolerate *him*.

And as if everything just wasn't quite awkward *enough* because of the nakedness thing and Reese sitting right there, she'd felt off her game, stumbling over simple answers about her education and experience, because she'd get distracted by something stupid—like when his hand had absently slid around his coffee cup like a caress and she'd flashed to the way his hands had stroked her last night.

Mercy, he had amazing hands, able to coax reactions from her in ways and with an intensity she hadn't known existed. If she left her mind unattended or unfocused for even a second, it went right back to last night and her skin would start to burn.

Even Reese had given her a couple of strange *get-it-together* looks, but, thankfully, hadn't pressed her for an explanation of her behavior.

Like there was a good way to say, *See, I had amazing sex with this guy last night and I'm sitting next to you wondering if he did that amazing thing with his tongue to you, too, or if he's making some kind of comparison between us and how I'm stacking up. Not that I want to know, but it's damn hard to remember facts from last year's performance review when my brain is far more occupied with a slo-mo replay of last night's activities.* Ugh.

Okay, maybe Dylan wasn't the problem. She was honest enough to say that the problem might just be *her* problem with Dylan.

She felt guilty, but at the same time she didn't regret actually sleeping with him. The only thing she *did* regret was that Dylan used to belong to Reese, which was rather like trying to get forgiveness for a sin only because it *was* a sin, not because she was actually repentant of the action itself.

Well, it wasn't the *only* thing she regretted. She hadn't realized it was possible to get drunk enough to intentionally sleep with Dylan. She'd readily admit it was a hormonal, chemistry thing, but the impossible-to-believe part was how her hormones had completely rebelled against everything she believed in.

She pulled a pillow over her face and groaned.

She'd come home from Hillbrook and enrolled in Simmons State with the sure knowledge it was exactly where she belonged and spent the next three years doing exactly as expected. She pledged Kappa and was named a Sigma Nu Sweetheart all three years. Honor society, charity work…she'd done all of it. And she'd been unhappy the whole time. But she'd kept on, figuring that eventually doing all the right things would click, and she *would* be happy. She'd graduated in time to go home to watch Carter and Missy's marriage start its death throes and take over Mama's position in the Women's Auxiliary after her funeral. And she *still* hadn't been happy. It had taken the sight of Richard Lee Mayton the Third on his knees with a rock the size of Georgia in his hand to realize she would never be happy in that life again.

Two weeks later, she'd been in New York, and she'd found herself and her happiness here, half a continent away from the life she'd been born and bred to have. And she wanted none of it. Including the men.

Just the sight of a suit was normally enough to shut her libido down. Good Lord, Dylan Brookes was everything she didn't want with a Yankee accent on top.

Yet, she'd wanted him. Badly enough to overlook a pile of reasons not to *and* conveniently forget—if only for a little while—that he was the ex of one of her dearest friends.

Which made the fact she really wanted this job a big problem.

If only Reese had come up with this "brilliant" idea earlier in the week, she wouldn't have let booze get the better of her libido and slept with him.

It certainly wasn't the ideal situation to preface what she was sure was the ideal job.

Pull it together.

So it wasn't the best start, but even the smartest people made stupid mistakes sometimes. It happened. She wasn't entirely sure how one moved on in cases like this—short of a convenient case of amnesia—but it *had* to be possible.

While Dylan was the head of the Brookes Foundation, from what she gathered today, he wasn't necessarily in the day-to-day business. The position answered ultimately to him, but it wasn't like he'd be around all the time. The man had a very busy law career to attend to, after all.

Reese had been able to juggle working for the man and sleeping with him at the same time...

Which wasn't the same thing at all, as she wasn't going to sleep with him again. It was a one-off, never to be repeated.

Pity.

No!

Marnie wanted to smack herself. This was insane.

Enough was enough. That was certainly enough replays of last night. It was also enough worrying about the job for today. Nothing more could happen until Tuesday at the earliest, when Reese could contact the other people at the Foundation and get the ball rolling for actual interviews.

Until then... Well, it *was* a holiday weekend. Surely there was *something* she could find to do to keep her mind off Dylan Brookes.

You mean the Brookes Foundation.

Exactly.

Then go find it.

The light on her machine was blinking. She pushed Play and regretted it the moment Carter's voice filled the silence. She hit Delete. That wasn't exactly what she'd meant when she'd wanted something to occupy her mind, but it did an effective job, as everything from yesterday landed on her in a big, heavy lump.

God, she'd been a sanctimonious, self-righteous little bitch, and while that Marnie felt like a long-outgrown sweater—tight, itchy, and out-of-style—she couldn't help but feel shame for what she'd done and the repercussions. She'd driven a wedge between her friends, expecting them to take sides, shifted blame...

And poor Gina… She'd suffered the most. If the roles were reversed, Marnie wasn't so sure she'd be willing to forgive Gina, so it was a little shaming to see Gina willing to move on and repair the damage—regardless of her relationship with Carter.

Her anger at Carter—which was always there, simmering—bubbled to the surface. Carter had been responsible for her losing her friendship with Missy, as well. When this thing between him and Gina went bad—which it was bound to, regardless of Carter's rather dramatic arrival and declarations yesterday—Marnie didn't want to lose Gina again in the aftermath.

Somehow, in less than twenty-four hours, her life had gone from somewhat normal to a death march through an emotional minefield.

Marnie went to the kitchen for wine. It was only three o'clock, but the wine felt deserved.

Tuck dodged past him easily, and the basketball arced up and into the basket. Dylan caught it as it came through, attempting a rebound, but the ball went wide and bounced against the wall of the small court at the gym.

Tuck laughed as he retrieved the ball. "Dude, you suck," he drawled. His accent was different from Marnie's, but like Marnie's, it was still strong, like it was harder to shake than other accents, regardless of how long the speaker had been out of the South.

"I was trying to take it easy on you. I assumed you'd be a bit tired after your wedding weekend. If you want your ass kicked…"

Tuck snorted. "Like that could ever happen." He tossed the ball to Dylan and headed over to the bench to grab a water bottle. Tuck's knee injury may have ended his professional football career, but he was still an athlete in excellent shape, while Dylan was beginning to feel the effects of too much time at a desk. Dylan could still hold his own on the court, but ass kicking of any sort was probably out of the question.

Dylan joined him on the bench for a water break. "So why aren't you with your bride today? Honeymoon over already?" Dylan had been surprised when Tuck had called earlier. Their games had become less frequent recently since Tuck had all but moved to Ithaca while Cassie finished her research for her PhD, but he'd only gotten married Friday. He figured they'd be holed up in a hotel for a few more days at least.

Tuck shrugged. "There's a lecture of some sort at NYU today that Cas wanted to attend."

"She's already ditching you in favor of *actual* stars?" Tuck might be famous, but Cassie was far more interested in the stars in the cosmos over the stars in *Cosmo*.

"I'm lucky I pried her away from her computer long enough to get married." He shrugged. "We'll do a proper honeymoon once she's done."

"A honeymoon in Antarctica... That sounds—" he paused "—horrible." Even Dylan knew of Cassie's research trip to Antarctica—although he didn't know exactly why she wanted to go there. And while Tuck fully supported Cassie's research aspirations, he was already grumbling over the necessary separation.

"I agree. I'm thinking more along the lines of Aruba. It's too freaking cold in Antarctica."

Dylan had always thought Tuck's dislike of cold weather and snow to be unique to him—or maybe just Texans in general—but Marnie had expressed similar opinions Friday night. Maybe it was a widespread Southern thing. *Why did Southerners move north, then?*

"But speaking of people who should be elsewhere," Tuck continued, "I figured you'd be in the Hamptons for the weekend."

He dribbled the ball absently between his legs. "I ended up having a lunch meeting on Saturday, and by the time that was done, I wasn't in the mood to drive."

"What kind of lawyer works on Labor Day weekend?"

"The very expensive kind." He ran a towel over his face and neck. Ass kicking or no, he'd worked up a sweat. "But it wasn't billable hours, unfortunately. It was Foundation stuff. Reese wants her friend Marnie to take over her old job, so we went to lunch."

Tuck looked at him sideways. "You had lunch with Reese?"

Dylan knew Tuck felt stuck in a bad place. Reese was his cousin, after all, and his loyalties were divided—however unnecessarily. "And Marnie, too," he added. "And it was just business." That wasn't entirely true, but his unprofessional thoughts hadn't involved Reese.

The lunch meeting had left him undecided on Marnie. Personally *and* professionally. He had to admit that her résumé was impressive, but Marnie hadn't presented herself all that well at the meeting. She'd seemed distracted and uncomfortable which, considering what happened the night before, was somewhat understandable. Even Reese had mentioned her behavior afterward, saying, "I think you make her uncomfortable for some reason."

Unfortunately, it didn't tell him if Marnie would present differently in a business setting, or if time would make it easier for her. He was at the Foundation quite a bit and she'd have to work with him, so if he was the problem, that was a problem.

But he could tell Marnie had a real passion for what she did—when she did manage to get her thoughts in order, she could be quite articulate and expressive about her enthusiasm for helping people. He'd definitely recommend her for an interview with the Director and staff, though, based on her résumé and Reese's recommendation.

But it left him in a quandary about Marnie herself. He was attracted to her—physically, for sure—but there was something else, as well. It was the "something else" that gave him pause, though. She didn't seem unstable, per se, but she certainly didn't sail on an even keel. Normally, that lack would be enough to send him in the other direction at top speed, but he'd found himself thinking about her over the weekend a little too often for comfort.

"Hel-lo?"

Dylan jumped as Tuck waved a hand in front of his face.

"Sorry. What were you saying?"

"I said you've really got to stop taking Reese's calls." There was exasperation in Tuck's voice, but something like concern underneath, as well.

"Why?"

"Because you've *got* to move on."

A lush, naked Marnie popped instantly to mind. That had to count as moving on, but considering Tuck's connections to two of Marnie's friends, it probably wasn't something he should bring up just now. He didn't want Tuck to feel *more* divided. "What makes you think I haven't?"

"Because Reese keeps calling you and you keep answering."

"So I should ignore her? That's a bit childish, don't you think?"

"She slept with another man just days before your wedding, and you're acting like it's no big deal. You just handed her off to Mason with a shrug. At the very least, you should be furious with her. But you're not. Hell, I seem angrier with her than you do."

He'd been angry at first, sure, but the anger had passed quickly. Feelings of betrayal had been fleeting, at best. His ego and his pride got a little dented, and the very public nature of everything had been a bit embarrassing, but he'd actually come out ahead. Women had flocked to console him, and Reese had caught the greater amount of flak for infidelity and flightiness. The fact that he and Reese were still friends had probably been the saving grace of the entire situation. It was damn hard for folks to get too worked up over something when the major players were so completely *not* making a big deal out of it. Thankfully, things had died down quickly, with the minimum of possible drama. He couldn't really ask for more than that.

"What did you want me to do, Tuck? Drag her to the altar by her hair? Challenge Mason to a duel?"

"Maybe. You could have put up *some* kind of a fight."

"She loves someone else."

"But—"

"Living life in the tabloid headlines has really warped your perspective. Real life isn't a soap opera, and normal people don't seek out that kind of drama."

"Especially you."

"What?"

"You don't do drama. You don't do conflict."

"I'm an attorney, for God's sake. I do conflict all day long."

"Not outside the office," Tuck countered.

"You say that like it's a bad thing. I think it shows good sense. Plus, it's good for my mental health and blood pressure."

"If your blood pressure drops any lower, you'll be dead."

Dylan wondered if it was too late to just go back to their game. "And your point is…?"

Tuck shrugged. "You're a shark. Act like one."

"Fine. I'll sue Reese for breach of contract."

"What?"

The look on Tuck's face was priceless and Dylan had to fight to keep a straight face. "That's what we sharks do."

"That's not what I meant at all." Tuck shook his head. "Boy, you do have ice water in your veins. You give sharks a bad reputation."

"Sharks *are* cold-blooded, you know."

"But they go after what they want."

"So do I. Just because it's not what *you* would want…"

Tuck nodded like he was coming to a hard-fought-for conclusion. "So *that's* why you paired up with Reese in the first place. No drama, no conflict…"

"Again, you say that like it's a bad thing."

"It is. It sounds boring."

Dylan shoved stuff into his gym bag in the hope Tuck would get the hint. When Tuck just kept sitting there, squirting water from a bottle into his mouth, Dylan gave up on the subtle hints. Unfortunately, he knew Tuck too well to hope he'd let the topic die. "I disagree."

"That's only because you're an emotionally detached control freak."

Oh, good Lord. "Since I know for a fact that you

lack the education or training to know what the hell you're talking about, I'd strongly advise you—as an attorney—not to practice psychotherapy without a license."

Tuck waved that warning away. "This is too easy to be considered psychotherapy. It's barely Psych 101." He raised an eyebrow. "Your parents still only speaking to each other in public?"

He nodded. "It's worked quite well for them the last four years. And it beats the hell out of the previous arrangement."

"You do know that's not normal, right?"

"Of course I do." No one would ever mistake his family for normal—not if they knew the truth, at least. Individually, both of his parents were nice enough people, and once upon a time, their romance had been written about in the society pages. But that had been a long, long time ago. The rest of the world thought his parents were *still* a perfectly lovely couple, but only because every employee who worked in his parents' house had signed a nondisclosure agreement, and the Brookes family paid well enough to buy loyalty. "But I also know that there's no way in hell I'm taking the chance of putting myself back into that kind of situation."

"Listen to yourself. You grew up in a household where your parents were constantly at war with each other." Tuck was warming to his subject and he leaned forward, forearms on his knees, as he spoke. "You now run a foundation for victims of domestic violence. Ergo, you seek domestic tranquility above all else—and at the *expense* of all else—when most people are actually able to achieve that without sacrificing love and happiness for the sake of stability."

Tuck had a point—or at least most of one—but Dylan really didn't want to deconstruct it. He knew what he wanted and he had his reasons for wanting it. There was no sense arguing the issue with someone deep in the throes of honeymooning bliss. "Now you're an expert on relationships? You've been married for three days to a woman you've known for three months."

He grinned. "When it's right, you know it." Tuck slapped his shoulder as he stood and grabbed his gym bag. "One day, you'll meet someone who lights a fire in you. It'll be anything but easy, but it'll be worth it. *That's* the girl you should marry. And you'll know because you'll definitely be willing to fight for her."

Hadn't Marnie said something similar? They were both wrong. Dylan grabbed his bag, as well, and followed Tuck to the glass doors of the court. "I could've taken Mason, you know," he muttered.

Tuck looked over his shoulder and grinned. "He'd have kicked your scrawny ass and then used it to wipe the floor. He's a marine, for God's sake, and you can't even get a basketball through a hoop anymore."

The trash talk was a nice flip back to normalcy from Tuck's unexpected foray into therapy. "*Former* marine," Dylan corrected.

"Which also means he probably knows a dozen ways to kill you without leaving a mark. What are you gonna do, lawyer boy?" Tuck shoved him good-naturedly. "Bury him in paperwork?"

He shoved back. "Hey, don't knock that idea. Death by a thousand papercuts is still death."

Tuck rolled his eyes. "A slow and boring death?"

"And painful. It's the most miserable kind of death there is. Quick and easy gains little satisfaction."

Tuck grinned. "*Now* you sound like a shark."

CHAPTER FOUR

THE SOUND OF Carter's ringtone blaring from the bottom of her purse was the *last* thing Marnie wanted to hear Thursday morning.

She was at a coffee shop three blocks from the Brookes Foundation's office and at least half an hour early for her interview, so she really had no reason *not* to answer. She'd been dodging his calls all week, but she would have to talk to him before he went back to Savannah.

If nothing else, it would take her mind off her interview for a little while. She didn't want to obsess and work herself into a nervous mess.

The truth was she'd never been able to shake that last thread of hope that things might get better with Carter. When she felt generous, she told herself that Carter had done the best he could—taking on both the responsibility of the family and the family business at a young age after Daddy died. It had been years before she realized how Carter had pulled the business back from the brink. His divorce had only made things more difficult for him. And them. She tried to convince herself that he meant well, that his attitude and actions stemmed from concern and were merely shaped by the nineteenth-century attitude of their upbringing.

It helped, but not nearly enough.

As always, she debated whether to answer. Then, with a sigh, she pushed the talk button before she could talk herself out of it.

Things would never be what they once were, but he was the only family she had left. She just didn't know if his relationship with Gina would strengthen or snap that last thread. Or would he ruin her renewed friendship with Gina instead?

She had to try. "Hey, Carter."

The words were barely out of her mouth before Carter jumped in without any preliminary pleasantries. "You lost your *job*?"

Ah, hell. The accusation in his voice rasped over already irritated nerves, and she fired back immediately. "You're *sleeping* with Gina?"

Carter seemed taken aback by her retort. "What does *that* have to do with anything?"

"Oh, I'm *sorry*," she said, injecting enough false sincerity into the words to ensure he got the point. "I thought we were playing the 'Things That Are None Of Your Sibling's Business' game. My bad."

"I think the fact you're now unemployed *is* my business."

Other brothers might call out of concern for their sister's feelings or self-esteem. This, however, was *her* brother, and she knew better. "How, exactly? You don't pay my bills."

"I would disagree with that statement."

Same fight, different day. "But, in reality, you don't, and you know it. I'm not a child. You may want to play big brother and call it an 'allowance,' but I *own* part of that business and the money is mine regardless."

"But I *run* the business and *make* the money—"

"Do you really want me to come stick my two cents in Price Paper to properly earn my money? Because I will." The threat had few teeth in reality, because she really didn't have the skill set or desire to involve herself, but Carter was a control freak as well as a workaholic who'd have to have any part of the business pried from his cold, dead hands. She knew it, he knew it and, more important, he knew she knew it.

There was a moment's silence, which meant he was conceding that round, however unwillingly. It was a small victory. Then, in a tone she hadn't heard in a long time, he asked, "Seriously, Marnie, what happened?"

The sincerity touched her. "Budget cuts. Last one hired and all that."

"I'm sorry. I know how much you liked that job."

"Thanks. How did you find out anyway? Gina wasn't supposed to tell you."

"I called your office to see if you wanted to go to lunch— Wait, *Gina* knew?"

Oops. Spurred by her need to make amends for old issues with Gina, she tried to defend her friend. "I asked Gina not to tell you because I didn't want that hanging over your reunion. I wanted to tell you myself." Carter made that noise that meant he was mollified for the moment. "And anyway, I already have a line on a new job and I'm interviewing today."

"That was fast."

There was a gruff, and possibly grudging, admiration in his voice. "I'm good at what I do, and unfortunately in today's society, there's always someone who needs that kind of help."

"When will you know?"

"I'm not sure, but I think they're wanting to move pretty quickly on this, so…"

"Good luck."

He sounded sincere, and it made something glow in her chest. "Thanks. But that means I'll have to take a rain check for lunch. Anyway, I'm sure you and Gina would like some time alone."

"That's kind of why I wanted to take you to lunch. To talk about Gina."

That sounded important. Almost ominous. "What about Gina?"

"I'm going to ask her to marry me."

She hadn't been prepared for *that*, and she nearly dropped the cup of coffee she was holding. Carter had been left so cynical after the divorce that even with every eligible woman in Savannah—and most of the surrounding states—lining up for him, he'd kept a distance from anything remotely serious. Carter was the last man on earth she'd expect to fall that hard or that quickly for anyone—much less Gina, who embodied the dictionary definition of "opposites attract." And while Gina might have once been a maneater, the one thing Marnie did know for sure was that Gina loved Carter—as strange as it might seem. She'd been so blown away by the revelations that she hadn't really thought about the possible long-term repercussions—much less thought that the repercussions would come this soon. "That's rather quick."

"Well, when you know it's right…"

Carter had dated Missy for at least two years before proposing. Things were moving at warp speeds. "And you're *sure* it's right?"

Carter got huffy. "I realize you and Gina had some problems, but I hoped you'd be happy for us nonetheless."

"And I *want* to be, but…really, Carter?" She was

breaking her vow not to get involved again, but this could end badly for Gina. And Carter, too. "She's not really your usual type."

"That's what I like about her." He sounded offended, but, for Gina's sake, she didn't care. It wouldn't be the first time.

"Well, be sure. You've put her through a lot already and…" She sighed. "Just don't hurt her, okay?"

"I won't." There was a wealth of emotion behind those two words that caught her off guard, but it eased her concerns. Of course, he hadn't proposed yet—and might still change his mind—so she'd have time to come to terms with this. And possibly even talk to Gina before Carter popped the question.

"Then congratulations. And tell Gina welcome to the family." *God help her.*

Carter muttered something and said goodbye, and Marnie had to assume she'd responded appropriately. She pondered her coffee as this new development rattled around her head.

Gina would be her sister-in-law. She hadn't seen that one coming, but maybe she should have. She gave herself a strong shake. *When* would she have been able to see that coming? She didn't even know it was a remote possibility until Friday, and she'd been a little preoccupied since then.

Gina was totally opposite from Missy, which was probably a good thing. Carter needed someone who'd stand up to him. She just wouldn't have expected Carter to admit that or fall for a woman who actually *would*.

This might be a train wreck in the making.

The world was just getting crazier by the minute.

But she had to shake it off. She'd needed a distraction, but not *that* much of one. She had an interview, and this time, she really had to bring her A-game. She'd worry about weddings and new sisters-in-law later.

Another wedding. *Ah, damn it.* This was getting ridiculous.

All three of her friends *and* her brother headed down the aisle. She really was beginning to feel like the eternal bridesmaid in the wedding season that would never end.

Marnie sat facing the Director and the senior staff across the Foundation's large conference table, while Dylan had intentionally seated himself further down the table, out of her direct line of vision. While he, technically, had the final say on who would replace Reese, he believed it was far more important that a candidate for the position be vetted by those she would be working directly with and for. This seating arrangement also allowed him to observe Marnie a bit more candidly.

She was a very qualified candidate, but he knew that already, and her résumé had already impressed Julia and the staff. She seemed far more collected today, less flighty, and while she shot the occasional glance his way, it seemed more as a way to include him in the conversation as opposed to the wary nervousness of Saturday's lunch with Reese.

Maybe it had just been the *unusualness* of Saturday that had thrown her.

Her well-cut suit was professional yet feminine, and her blond hair curled perfectly around her face. Knees together, spine straight and hands clasped in her lap—a posture she'd claimed Friday night to have mastered in endless cotillion classes—she leaned forward as she spoke, answering each question enthusiastically and thoroughly, her drawl present enough to be charming but muted enough to not be distracting.

It was almost disconcerting. He'd seen the bubbly, sparkly, social Marnie, the Marnie who could toss back enough tequila shots to fell a horse and still walk, a sultry-siren Marnie who occasionally haunted his dreams, and a Marnie who'd stuttered her way through lunch like a nervous schoolgirl. He hadn't expected to find *another* Marnie in there—regardless of the fact her résumé had claimed she existed.

He'd never met someone with so many personalities.

She was definitely a puzzle.

But she was killing this interview. Seemed she really did want the job after all, which was a bit of a surprise. And Julia looked ready to offer it to her.

"So, Marnie." It was the first time he'd spoken during the interview, and there seemed to be some surprise that he had now. "I'm curious as to why you want to come work for the Foundation."

She smiled. "This organization was one of Reese's favorite topics of conversation, and I've always been impressed by not only what the Foundation *does*, but also the way y'all work. And while I've never been a victim of domestic violence, I do know what it's like to feel trapped in a life you don't want but can't figure out how to escape." The smile dimmed a bit and her voice turned serious. "Any change is hard, but when we're talking about losing everything you have in the hope you'll find something better. It helps to have someone to not *only* say it's possible, but to offer that really basic, concrete support to make it happen. That's why I loved my work at the Refugee Center and why I want to work here."

It was a passionate, personal speech, and an effec-

tive one. If Marnie hadn't cinched the job before, she
had now. Julia shot him a look, seeking his okay, and
he nodded briefly. Then he stood. "I have a phone call
I need to make."

Marnie also stood and extended her hand. "It was
good to see you again, Dylan."

"And you, Marnie." As he took her hand, that rush
he'd felt last Friday night slammed back into him from
out of nowhere, catching him completely off guard. His
skin felt hot, and he realized that the feeling had only
been banked and held at bay by the situation, and her
touch had fanned it to life. It was very disturbing—and
not in the least part due to the fact it was happening in
front of four of his staff members.

Those blue eyes widened a fraction, her pupils dilating, and whatever it was, he knew she'd been hit by it,
too. Her grip loosened and he released her hand.

Julia was looking at him expectantly, but not oddly,
so maybe his reaction hadn't been outwardly noticeable. "Julia, once you all finish up, why don't you send
Marnie up to my office?"

Julia looked surprised but nodded and indicated for
Marnie to sit again. He quickly left the room.

How strange, he thought, as he went up the stairs
to his office.

The Brookes Partnership—the family firm whose
raison d'être was to make rich people richer—occupied the top four floors of the building, with space on
the lowest floor given to the Brookes Foundation and
the smaller, more broadly-focused Brookes Charitable
Trust. While this layout saved the Foundation and the
Trust the true cost of rent in Manhattan, more importantly, it had allowed his father, and now him, the ability to stay, quite literally, on top of everything.

He didn't really know what had possessed him to have Julia send Marnie upstairs after the interview, but he knew he needed to talk to her. He hadn't seen her since Saturday and all the awkwardness, and that had nagged at him—for a multitude of reasons. Whether it was unfinished business, or simple curiosity, or just some latent chivalry that said it was wrong to sleep with a woman and not even call, the simple fact was that Marnie was about to get this job, and they needed to be on the same page as they went forward.

He didn't like having things unsettled.

Yep. That was the problem.

It wasn't very long before his secretary was buzzing him to let him know Marnie had arrived.

She was hesitant but poised, as Karla showed her in, but the façade cracked a bit as the heavy wooden door shut behind her. For a split second, she looked cornered.

He motioned for her to sit in the chair facing his desk, and she nearly disappeared into the large wing chair. She struggled upright and balanced on the edge of the seat. "You wanted to see me?"

The innocent question struck deeper than she probably intended. Because he did just want to see her.

For some reason.

It would be nice if I could figure out what that reason was...

"How do you think your interview went?"

"I think it went well. It felt good, at least. Julia said she'd let me know something by early next week."

"Not to ruin the surprise, but it's a pretty safe bet that you're going to get the job."

A smile spread over her face, animating her features. "Oh, good." She paused as if she were waiting for him to say something else. "I'm very excited about this opportunity, and I'm looking forward to working with everyone."

He nodded, and Marnie paused again. Another second passed, then she said, "I don't mean to sound impertinent, but I'm not sure why you wanted to see me, so..."

"Why so formal, Marnie?"

An eyebrow went up. "You're behind a desk all boss-like, and it seems appropriate for an interview."

"The interview part is over. Like I said, I'm pretty sure Julia would have hired you on the spot if she could." He pushed his chair back and came around to the front of the desk to lean against it. "The Foundation is a rather *in*formal office, and the fact we—" He paused and Marnie flinched, making him rethink his word choice. "The fact we know each other already isn't a problem."

Marnie's lips turned white as she pressed them together, but she nodded.

He laughed. "You might as well spit out whatever you're holding back," he goaded her.

"Well, it is. A bit of a problem. For me, at least."

She seemed to be having difficulty, and though he should cut to the chase, he was rather enjoying watching her muddle through. She wasn't as rattled as she'd been Saturday at lunch, so it wasn't necessarily all him. "Why?"

"We have rather *intimate* knowledge of each other..." She cleared her throat as her cheeks turned slightly pink. "I don't normally have that kind of knowledge about my coworkers, much less my boss. And this situation is even worse."

"Because..."

She sighed and the words followed in a rush. "Because Reese is my friend and your ex-fiancée *and* the last person to hold the position I'm about to take and plus we…" She stopped. "Well, you know what happened."

"Understandable. In fact, that's actually why I asked to see you."

"Really?" He could see her looking for the catch in his words.

"Things were left rather unsettled Saturday morning, and I thought we could smooth that out before we moved forward."

Marnie's mouth twisted in annoyance. "Then *why* didn't you tell me that up front instead of making me stammer through all of that?"

He grinned at her.

Marnie rolled her eyes in response. "Oh, grow up." *This was kind of fun.* "So much for that 'being polite to the boss' thing, huh?"

Folding her hands in her lap, Marnie spoke primly. "Permission to speak openly to my soon-to-be boss?"

"Of course."

"It happened. Because of our personal relationships with Reese, it's a bit weird and awkward, and as I said, I'd rather she not know about it."

"And as *I* said, it's none of her business."

"Good."

"But while we're on the subject of Reese, there is one thing I want to make clear."

Marnie looked slightly ill. "And that is…?"

If nothing else, he could clear up one of her misconceptions. Out of all the things that had been said Saturday morning, there was oddly one that bothered him the most. "I want you to know that I originally agreed to stay while you finished your drink because Reese asked me to do her a favor. But everything that happened after you finished that last glass of wine had nothing to do with favors for anyone. I bought the rounds, if you remember."

She nodded. "Thank you for that. For clearing that up, I mean," she qualified, "not just the drinks." She blew out her breath. "So, with that cleared up, I think it's probably best that we just try to forget it happened—"

"Forget?" This was a first. He'd never had a woman ask him to forget her. But, then, Marnie wasn't just any woman.

"Well, at least pretend to forget," she corrected, "so that it doesn't get in the way of our professional relationship."

That made *some* sense, but he'd dated and planned a wedding to Reese when she'd held the job and it hadn't been a problem professionally. And he certainly didn't see himself marrying Marnie.

But it seemed Marnie wasn't quite done. "It really shouldn't have happened at all." She laughed, but it was forced. "I mean, really. Me and you? It beggars belief."

She didn't seem to be trying to insult him, but the insult was there, nonetheless. "And why is that?"

From the look on her face, Marnie realized she'd said too much. "Well, um… We're very different people, with little in common, and minus large amounts of alcohol probably would not have found each other attractive."

"I'm not sure which one of us that insults more."

She rolled her eyes. "Oh, please, we all know the mating call of the Southern blonde."

"And that would be…?"

"'Oh, my, God, y'all, I'm *so* drunk,'" she drawled before cutting her eyes at him. "I'm not blaming you or claiming you took some kind of advantage of the situation. I was fully participatory, and I think we both had a good time. But in the light of reality, it wasn't the best decision ever made and would best be forgotten."

"Hmm."

"'Hmm' what?" She scooted back a bit in the chair, increasing the distance between them.

"It's just interesting." A theory was coming together in his mind, but it needed testing…

"How? Things happen when people drink that wouldn't happen when they were sober. Thankfully, no one got hurt, so we can just stick this in the Bad Decisions file and go on with life—"

He was discovering how much he really didn't like being considered some kind of regret in Marnie's "Bad Decisions" file, and he didn't know which irked him worst: being in that file or the fact it bothered him that he was. It didn't make a lot of sense. "So you're going to blame it all on the booze?"

"Of course."

"That's convenient."

"Excuse me?"

"It's a convenient way to dodge responsibility for your actions."

"I'm not dodging anything."

"It sure sounds like it." He crossed his arms over his chest. "This job requires you to make decisions and I don't like employees to dodge the responsibilities and repercussions of making those decisions."

The sharp intake of breath told him he'd hit a nerve. Marnie's eyes narrowed and she pushed to her feet. "As a professional, I make decisions based solely on what's the right thing to do based on the options and facts presented, and I stand behind every one of my decisions, even if I turn out to be wrong. I may make the occasional bad decision in my personal life, but it has no bearing on my professional life, and even then, I live with the consequences of those decisions. That doesn't mean I can't regret them." Shifting her weight, she crossed her arms over her chest, mirroring his posture, and met his eyes evenly. "I don't know what you're getting all worked up over. You don't seem to think *any* of this is a problem, so what the hell does it matter to you how I justify my actions to myself?"

That was a damn fine question, and one he didn't have a fully satisfying explanation for. He pushed to his feet, but Marnie didn't back up this time. She merely lifted her chin so as not to break the stare.

He shouldn't have goaded her, and he definitely shouldn't have put himself in this position. Her crossed arms pushed her breasts together and up, and his height gave him a clear view straight down her cleavage.

The spark hit the tinder.

Marnie had just explained why this was a bad idea, and honestly, he agreed with her on the basic tenets of that argument. But somehow the message was getting lost between his brain and his belly.

It was unexplainable, uncontrollable, disconcerting... and very real.

When Marnie's breath hitched, he knew he wasn't alone in the realization.

She cleared her throat. "If we're done here, I should probably leave now."

That would be wise. "Yeah, you should."

She nodded, but didn't move. He could see her pulse pick up speed, fluttering the skin at the hollow of her throat. He should move, get the desk and some space between them, but his feet weren't receiving the message. The moment stretched out endlessly.

He didn't know who moved first, but Marnie was in his arms, her lips on his—hot, hungry and carnal.

Her hands gripped his hips, holding him against her, and he felt the tremor that rocked through her body. He backed up, bracing his hips against the desk and pulling Marnie into the vee of his legs.

It wasn't enough, so he reversed their positions, lifting her onto the desk and sliding the hem of her skirt up those sleek thighs so he could fit between. Marnie released her hold on him, bracing her arms on the desk as she leaned back to allow him access to her neck.

Her elbow hit the desk lamp, sending it clattering across the desk to hang drunkenly by its cord off the edge. Papers slid to the floor as he pushed them aside to lay her back. Marnie grabbed his tie to pull him down on top of her.

Bracing on one elbow, his other hand went to the buttons of her blouse, his elbow hitting the phone, knocking it off the hook, and Marnie's fingers moved to his belt.

It was the sound of the dial tone that cut through the fog.

Wrong time, wrong place. Staff just outside the door.

The rational thought was shut down when Marnie eased down his zipper and palmed him. He groaned, and what little concern he had left for civilized behavior melted away.

Marnie's buttons opened easily under his fingers, exposing a demure bra that belied the siren under his hands. He traced his tongue along the lace trim, hearing her gasp of pleasure and feeling the soft skin tighten. A twist of the clasp, and his mouth closed over her nipple, teasing it to a hard point as her hand came to his neck to hold him in place, tightening around the muscles until her nails bit into his skin.

The writhing and wriggling under him was driving him insane, but he was rewarded when Marnie's skirt finally gave way at the top of her thighs, rolling up to her hips and allowing for heated contact just where he needed it most. Marnie's groan as she arched against him sent a primal message, and he released her long enough to slide her panties down her legs. Marnie was wet and slick, her eyes rolling back in pleasure as he traced a finger over hot, trembling flesh. She bucked as he slid a finger inside, then began to shake as his thumb circled teasingly.

The small, rational-thinking part of his brain still working was shouting alarms, but that only fed the moment. The rashness and the risk of discovery only heightened the sensations, providing an air of danger that was exciting and fanned the fire.

Marnie, though, was the fuel, each muffled whimper and moan that fought to escape sliced into him, each tremor vibrating from her through him.

She arched as she climaxed, her back bowing up off the desk as one hand fought for purchase on the slick surface and the other clenched into a fist and pressed against her mouth to stifle the noise.

He was nearly shaking with need, his fingers feeling thick and clumsy as he fought his clothes and reached for her hips. Those big blue eyes were glazed with passion but focused as she wrapped her legs around his waist.

Then he just quit thinking.

The angry *buzz-buzz-buzz* of a phone left too long off the hook finally brought Marnie back to her senses.

Dylan lay atop her, shoulders heaving as he fought to catch his breath. Her breath wasn't much steadier.

It took a moment for everything to sink in, and when it did, she rather wished it hadn't.

I can't believe I just had sex on Dylan's desk. With Dylan. My future boss. What in the sweet hell is wrong with me? She'd never lost control of her hormones like that before. At least not while sober...

A bump and a muffled laugh filtered in from the outer office. She cursed under her breath. "Is that door locked?"

Dylan's head snapped up and he cursed, as well. "No."

His haste to get off her bordered on unseemly, but his urgency was contagious. Dear Lord, her skirt was hiked up to her waist, panties around one ankle, bra and blouse both wide open. *If someone walked in...*

Dylan was faster getting his clothes straightened, but his hair stuck up at funny angles all around his head and his skin was flushed. Dear heaven, she didn't even want to think what her hair and makeup looked like. She adjusted her clothes, but they were wrinkled beyond belief. How on earth was she going to walk out of here looking like...looking like... Well, looking like she'd been doing exactly what she *had* been doing.

"Embarrassing" wouldn't even begin to cover it.

She'd been able to chalk that other night up as alcohol-fueled and hormone-driven madness, but this was sober—if equally hormone-driven —madness. She couldn't begin to explain it because it defied any logic applied to it.

At the same time, little sparks were still dancing over her skin and her knees weren't quite steady. Dylan certainly had layers; she'd have never dreamed he was the kind of guy to have sex on his desk with the door unlocked.

But then, she wouldn't have said she was that kind of girl, either. It seemed she had a layer or two she hadn't peeled back before, as well.

Even as she thought it, Dylan was transforming back into the Dylan-who-wouldn't-have-sex-on-the-desk. Although his hair was still slightly mussed from where her fingers had threaded through it, the transformation was pretty much complete as he tightened the knot of his tie.

Except he had a smudge of lipstick across his cheek.

"Well, that was…" she trailed off, unsure of *what* it was.

"That wasn't why I asked you to come up here."

"I didn't figure it was." She dug her compact out of her purse. "It only makes things more complicated."

Dylan replaced the phone and lamp and bent to pick scattered papers up off the floor. "That it does."

The damage to her hair and makeup wasn't as bad as expected and easily fixed, even if her clothes were beyond hope. She passed Dylan the mirror. "You have lipstick on your cheek."

With an exasperated sigh, Dylan took the mirror, wiped his cheek and smoothed his hair. As he handed back the mirror, he said simply, "Maybe you're right."

"About what?"

"We should just forget about what happened."

"It's a little late for that, don't you think?"

"I like you, Marnie, and there's definitely chemistry there, but…" He didn't finish.

Honestly, he didn't need to. And she *agreed* with him, for goodness' sakes, so why was disappointment settling into her chest? "I was never very good at chemistry anyway."

Dylan merely nodded. Damn it, why did she feel like a wham-bam-thank-you-ma'am who just needed to grab her money off the nightstand on her way out? And why did *that* feeling bother her so much?

The tension was thick, and it felt so wrong on top of the lovely post-orgasm glow. She'd thought Saturday morning was the most awkward moment of her life. *This* was entirely new heights, and the tension only grew as they each busied themselves with clothes-fixing and desk-straightening. She wasn't sure how to make her exit.

When the phone on Dylan's desk beeped, she grabbed the distraction gratefully. "I'll let you get back to work." Grabbing her bag, she tried to hold it over the worst of the wrinkly parts of her blouse and skirt, and nearly tripped over her own feet in her haste to get to the door.

She nodded briefly to Dylan's secretary and focused on keeping her façade in place while waiting for the elevator. Thankfully, it was empty, and she leaned against the wall.

I am seven kinds of a fool.

She had a whole laundry list of reasons why *that* should not have happened.

But it had.

And, once again, she was regretting it for the wrong reasons.

CHAPTER FIVE

WHEN GINA WALKED into the coffee shop, Marnie could see the change in her. Oh, she looked as beautiful and put-together as always, but there was definitely something different now. It was that glow she'd come to recognize—and slightly envy—in both Reese and Cassie. Gina was in love and very happy.

She still couldn't quite wrap her head around the fact that it was *Carter* putting that smile on Gina's face, but okay.

The smile turned slightly uncertain when Gina spotted her, and Marnie instantly felt ashamed. This was her fault, and it had gone on far too long and done far more damage than she'd ever dreamed.

They'd taken steps this summer to repair that damage, and made a huge leap last Friday, but eight days later, Marnie was still a little nervous the damage was just too extensive.

But she'd had a week to think things over, and she knew one thing for sure: if they were ever going to actually get past this, she was going to have to quit pretending it was something it wasn't and take responsibility. Gina seemed willing to forgive, but it wasn't fair to accept that forgiveness without making amends the only way she could.

Marnie stood as Gina approached and wrapped her in a hug. At first Gina stiffened, worrying Marnie that she'd gone too far, but then she felt Gina's arms come around her shoulders to return it.

First big hurdle cleared. Marnie took a deep breath. "I'm really, really sorry. For everything."

"Me, too."

"No." She broke the embrace and pulled Gina into a chair. "The one thing I have realized over the years is what a self-righteous, sanctimonious little bitch I was back then."

"Don't be so hard—"

"It's true, so please let me say this and apologize properly. I know what I was like back then, but I'm not that Marnie anymore. I was shocked and hurt and mad at Carter and the world, and I took it out on you because you were the easier target. Then I made it all worse by driving a wedge between all of us because I was too immature to handle it properly."

Gina shook her head. "I think we all handled it poorly."

"If I could go back and change the way I reacted that night—"

"Neither of us would be who or what we are today without that night. I'm not that Gina anymore, either."

That was true. Everything changed that night, and she wouldn't be here *now* if she hadn't been an immature brat *then*. She nodded. "I'm also sorry about how I acted at Cassie's wedding."

"You had a lot dropped on you in a short amount of time. I think you handled it better than anyone expected. Not because we'd expect you to freak out or anything—" she quickly corrected.

"I know." She sighed. "Well, you were all certainly

correct not to tell me about the pregnancy ten years ago. I wouldn't have handled it well."

"That's understandable."

Now for the really hard part. She took a deep breath. "But I *am* sorry I wasn't there for you when you miscarried. I mean, I'm glad no one told me, because if I had known, I probably just would have made things worse. Please know it shames me to the bone to admit that."

"We were kids. We're not now."

"I know. But I'm here for you now, if you need to—"

Gina shook her head. "It was a long time ago."

"That doesn't undo the damage. And I know I can't make it up to you, but I want us to be friends again. Real friends. I didn't realize how much I'd missed you until I saw you again." Damn it, her eyes were burning. This was harder than she thought it would be. Gina reached over and squeezed her hand. And just like that, Marnie knew they really were okay. She'd been forgiven, even if she hadn't forgiven herself yet, and a weight she'd been carrying for so long that it seemed normal lifted off her shoulders.

Gina was just like that.

She looked at the hand squeezing hers, and felt her eyes widen. Gina noticed, and her mouth twisted.

"Carter proposed already?" *Wow.*

Gina nodded.

"That's my grandmother's engagement ring."

Worry creased Gina's forehead. "Is that all right?"

"Yes, of course." She swallowed and rushed to get the worry off Gina's face. "My Gran loved watching BBC shows. I'm sure it would thrill her to have her ring worn by a Brit." Missy had insisted on her own ring, one that was huge and flashy, but the old-fashioned setting suited Gina somehow.

Gina's smile was wistful as she examined the ring. "Carter brought it with him." The smile twisted. "Cocky little bastard."

"That he is." But it proved Carter was serious about Gina well beyond his assurances. But with Gina in New York until at least after Reese's wedding... Well, Carter would be racking up quite a few frequent flier miles if he wanted to see much of Gina *and* run the business.

"Carter told me that you didn't sound happy about it when he told you."

She had to pull herself together before she said something that accidentally hurt Gina's feelings. "No. That's not it at all. I was simply *surprised* when he said he was going to propose. There's a difference. Y'all are moving at warp speed and I'm still trying to catch up."

"So you're okay with this, then."

"Of course. If this is what makes you both happy, then I'm all for it. I've always wanted a sister."

"So you'll be a bridesmaid?"

"You bet. Have you set a date already?"

Gina laughed. "Things aren't moving *that* quickly. I need to catch my breath first."

"But you're *sure* you want to marry him?"

"Yes. After a nice *long* engagement."

Marnie bit her tongue, but she couldn't hold it back. "I'm sorry, but I have to ask. *Carter?* Really?"

Gina nodded. "Really."

"You're sure."

"Positive. So's he." A wistful smile tugged at her mouth. "Somehow, when he pulled out the ring I just knew. It was a surprise to me, too."

It sounded romantic, which was not something she could reconcile with Carter. "I'd ask why, but I'm not entirely sure I want to know. Does he not drive you insane?"

Gina's grin was wicked. "Definitely."

"I didn't mean like *that*. And please, no details. He's just so…" She searched for the right word. "Overbearing."

She shrugged. "You're his sister. I'm not. It's a different relationship."

"Don't I know it."

Gina seemed to be choosing her words carefully. "I really think that if you two spent more time together, you'd see he's not the person you think he is. He probably never was who you thought he was, either, you know?"

"I know. Another piece of clarity that comes with age and maturity. However, I do know enough about who he is—"

"I don't think you do."

"What?"

Gina sighed. "He's so proud of you."

Marnie's world skewed sideways. *"What?"*

"He is. I could tell, but he did admit it to me just the other day. You've accomplished so much so quickly and you did it almost entirely on your own, far away from home…"

That didn't really gel with reality. "He's never said that to me."

"I know. And, rest assured, I called him on it. I honestly don't think he knows how to tell you. Especially not the way things are between you now."

"He still treats me like a child."

"A fact I *have* brought to his attention. Look, I love your brother, but I'm not blind to his faults, either. I think if you two would just…talk, you'd both be happier. And we're going to be *family*. You know how much I want that."

"I do. God, I wish you weren't going to be moving away now."

"And I want you to promise you'll start coming back to Savannah more often."

Marnie didn't bother to hide her shock. "I was rather assuming you'd be coming to New York quite a bit. You've been to Savannah now. You know what it's like. Won't you miss the city?"

Gina shrugged. "It's a good thing my future sister-in-law lives here. I'll have a place to stay."

"Anytime you want."

The server brought more coffee, and it was much like old times again as they caught each other up on the last ten years of their lives. She told Gina about the job possibility at the Foundation, leaving out the fact that it was nearly a done deal so she didn't jinx it. And it would be hard to tell much more than she did without mentioning Dylan and she did *not* want to do that.

And that, of course, was the one thing Gina honed in on, however accidentally. "That's all great, but what about the love life. Are you seeing anyone?"

Marnie wanted to lie, but the now-interested look Gina wore told her that her face had already betrayed her. *A good reason why I don't play poker.* Gina leaned in. "There's *some*thing interesting to tell. So who is he?"

She wasn't really seeing Dylan, so leaving him out wasn't really lying, but she had slept with him twice in the last week, and that's probably what Gina was picking up on. "Just someone I met recently. It's very casual, nothing serious, though."

"I'm surprised."

Well, so am I, but for entirely different reasons.
"Why?"

"I never saw you as the 'casual' type."

"People change."

"Obviously."

"And I have you to thank for it—Reese and Cassie, too. A year with y'all, and I couldn't be that Marnie anymore."

"That's why you left Savannah?"

With Gina's obvious interest in brokering a truce between her and Carter, Marnie chose her words carefully. She didn't want to put Gina in the middle, but she had no doubt her words would get back to Carter. "Partly. It wasn't just any one thing. I just couldn't stay there. People expected me to be a specific person, and I knew that wasn't going to happen. But I couldn't become someone else in Savannah, either, so I had to leave."

"And now you're a Marnie who has flings with inappropriate men."

"Yeah. I guess I am. Are you surprised?"

"A little." Gina laughed. "Okay, a *lot*. Could it turn into something serious?"

She tried to picture it. "No."

After a moment of silence, Gina asked, "Just 'no'?"

"Just no. He's not the kind of guy I could get serious with."

"Why not?"

"Do I have to have a reason?"

"I guess not, but…surely you have one. Or two. *Good* ones, that is."

"Because…" She searched for a good reason, and was disappointed not to come up with any other than the reasons she couldn't say out loud. On paper, Dylan was a great catch. She didn't think Gina would understand why those same qualities would be such a problem for her. Especially since Carter had many of those same "great catch" qualifications. She tried to sound dismissive. "Because I don't want it to be."

Gina's eyebrows went up, but then she shrugged. "I guess that makes sense. I'm a little shocked, but good for you. Every girl deserves a fling."

Exactly. It was a fling. That's all it was, and that was no big deal. She could release a little of that confusion. "That's exactly what it is. It's been a crazy couple of months, and I need something easy and low key. Carter would be horrified, though, so..."

"Oh, I don't intend to share *that* knowledge with your brother. There are some things he just doesn't need to know about his little sister, and I wouldn't want to be the one to share those things, either. I, however, would *love* to hear details." She grinned.

Gina hadn't changed all that much. "I don't kiss and tell."

"Spoilsport."

Sunday afternoon was beautiful—sunny and warm with white puffy clouds floating in a blue sky—and Dylan was in his office going through piles of paperwork and an overflowing inbox. *Yes, this could definitely kill a man.*

Although it did give him a handy excuse to decline his mother's invitation to brunch, so that was a plus. If he went, his parents would feel like they had to dine together—not necessarily for his benefit, but more so that one of them would not feel like the other was overly influencing their only child. He'd sat through hundreds of meals just like it, and though it no longer would put a knot in his stomach like it did when he was a child, it would be stilted and awful and just the thought of it killed his appetite.

He knew a dozen good divorce attorneys who'd be happy to facilitate the proceedings—with the utmost discretion, of course—and end his parents' misery.

Or at least his. He had to be the only child on the planet who used to honestly wish his parents would divorce. He'd certainly like them better if they did.

Shaking his head, he signed off on the final plans for the Foundation's fund-raiser and then opened the email from Julia with the subject line "Marnie Price."

It was a standard offer letter—salary and benefits in line with the Foundation's employment package—and once he approved it, Marnie would be all but hired.

That would get Reese off his back, and he deleted the three unread emails from her that also had the "Marnie" subject line.

Marnie.

As much as he needed to focus on actual work, he was sitting at a desk that had had a half-naked Marnie writhing on it just a couple of days ago and that image made it very hard to concentrate on anything else.

Good Lord, he still couldn't quite believe he'd had sex, on his desk, behind an unlocked door in the middle of a workday. There was something about Marnie, though...

And that's what bothered him. That *something* about Marnie that made *him* act unpredictably and out of character. He didn't know what it was, but he was damn sure he didn't like it.

It was almost enough to make him not want to sign off on Marnie's offer letter. *Don't be ridiculous.* Marnie really was an excellent choice for the position, and it wasn't like whatever that *something* was could somehow waft up three floors through the building's duct-work and distract him on a daily basis.

He sent through the approval and decided he was done for the day.

Whatever it was about Marnie, it wouldn't last for-ever. That much he was sure of. Chemistry had a way of diminishing over time, and it was only those who confused chemistry for an actual solid relationship base and tried to build on it who got burned by it.

He glanced back at his desk one last time as he left. He couldn't deny the chemistry was attractive, possi-bly even addictive. It certainly gave him new perspec-tive on how people ended up in bad relationships and why they'd stay.

Maybe it even explained why instead of going home, he went to Brooklyn instead.

Marnie's place on a tree-lined street of Victorian row houses not far from Prospect Park was easy to find. The obviously family-friendly neighborhood seemed to suit her—certainly more so than SoHo would if she moved to be closer to her new job.

And what makes you think that? He was hardly an expert on Marnie Price. Hell, he'd come all the way out to Brooklyn without even considering that she might have something to do on a beautiful fall Sunday after-noon, and might not even be home.

This is why I don't like unpredictability.

With a sigh, he rang the bell.

A few seconds later, he heard footsteps, and then Marnie appeared in the window. Shock registered on her face before she schooled her features into a friendly, but slightly forced, smile, and opened the door.

"Dylan. What are you doing here?" She looked around and over his shoulder like she expected someone else to be with him. When she realized he was alone, confusion crinkled her forehead. "Seriously. What are you doing here?"

He didn't think it could be possible, but Marnie looked even more like a cheerleader today, with her hair pulled back in a loose ponytail, no makeup, and wearing an oversize Simmons College T-shirt and leggings. Her feet were bare with bright red toenails. It was a far cry from the chic sophisticate of Cassie's wedding or the conservative businesswoman he'd interviewed this week. It was definitely a far cry from the half-naked siren who'd been draped over his desk, but it was certainly working for him. He'd never been one for the cheerleader fantasy before, but as his skin began to tighten, he decided he might have to rethink that.

Marnie cleared her throat sharply and he realized he'd been staring at her, taking inventory. He held up the bottle of wine he'd bought on his way as part of his half-formed plan. "I got this for your friend Sven. We drank his, after all."

"You didn't have to do that." Marnie took the bottle and her eyebrows went up as she read the label. "*Really* not. Sven's wine normally comes in a box."

Maybe he should've paid more attention to his purchase. But it did provide insight into Marnie, as she obviously recognized the label. He'd seen her pound midlist Chardonnay and shoot tequila, but it seemed she had an appreciation for good wine, as well.

"It is very kind of you, though." She looked at the bottle one last time before tucking it into the crook of her arm. "But I have to ask…how do you know where I live?"

"I have your résumé. It's got your address on it."

"Oh, of course. Right." She took a deep breath. "Well, thanks—"

"We need to talk," he said at the same time.

Marnie looked distinctly uncomfortable. "Okay."

"First, the job is yours." He wanted to be very clear about that before they went any further. "I signed off on the offer letter this morning, and Julia will probably call you tomorrow."

She nodded.

"Whatever else happened between us has nothing to do with your job at all. I believe in keeping the personal away from the professional."

"So do I. You don't have to fear a sexual harassment lawsuit." She thought for a moment, then sighed, sounding resigned to something. "Would you like to come in, then, to finish this talk?"

He hadn't realized he'd been holding his breath until Marnie spoke. As he followed her in, that weird feeling in his stomach loosened, and he knew he'd made the right choice coming out today. He still wasn't sure exactly what had driven that decision, but at least he'd been correct to go with it.

Marnie's apartment was small, but open and airy, with a decent-sized living room that opened out onto a sunny terrace only slightly larger than a postage stamp. A book and coffee cup sat on the wrought iron table, indicating she'd been enjoying the sunshine before he'd arrived. Colorful art hung on the white walls above modern furniture with clean lines.

He'd been expecting chintz, big, overstuffed wing chairs, antiques... Another surprise from Marnie.

It was easy to tell Marnie came from money. He didn't know of many young singles working for non-profit organizations who could afford an apartment like this in this neighborhood. "Nice place."

"Thanks. It's not the Upper East Side, but I like it," she teased.

"Will you still be considering a move to Manhattan?"

Confusion crossed her face, then her mouth twisted. "Jeez, I babble when I'm drunk. I didn't remember telling you about that. But yes," she said, stopping in the middle of the room, "moving to SoHo or Tribeca is still on the possibilities list. Would you like something to drink?" She shifted topics quickly. "Coffee? Iced tea? Hell, we could even open this bottle as Sven certainly wouldn't appreciate it properly."

"Tea is fine."

Marnie disappeared around a corner, and Dylan stood in the middle of the room, feeling a little uncomfortable now. It was an unusual feeling, and not one he was accustomed to. And while he might be sure he'd made the right decision to come, he still didn't have a clear answer for himself as to *why* he was here. He needed to come up with one pretty quick, as Marnie was bound to assume there was a reasonable explanation for his appearance.

Maybe she wouldn't ask.

Framed photos on tables and shelves caught his attention, and he studied them as he ran through a list of possible reasons. From the pictures, Marnie was well-rounded and happy. Lots of friends. She was well traveled, too, as landmarks like the Arc de Triomphe and Diamond Head were recognizable backgrounds. There was a picture of an older couple—Marnie favored the woman, so he assumed those were her parents. If he remembered correctly from the other night, her father had died of an illness while she was still in high school and her mother had been killed in a car accident shortly after she'd graduated from college. Normally, those kinds of tragedies would bond siblings closer together, but Marnie and Carter bordered on estranged. He wondered how that would work out now that Gina and Carter were together.

On another shelf, there was a picture he recognized, as Reese had the exact same one at her place: a snapshot of a much younger Awesome Foursome, casual and smiling, taken at their shared house at Hillbrook ten years ago.

"Don't laugh," Marnie said as she returned. She carried a tray with two glasses of ice, a pitcher of tea with lemon slices floating in it, and a small plate of cookies. "I know my hair is ridiculous. It was a phase."

"We all have those photos," he said. As Marnie set the tray down on the coffee table and he got a good look at it, he ended up biting back a laugh. There was a doily under the cookies and crisply folded cloth napkins to the side of the tray. "I didn't mean for you to go to this much trouble."

She shrugged one shoulder as she sat on the opposite end of the sofa—facing him, but from a very respectable distance. "Old habits die hard. It's a little prissy, I know, but my mother would rise from her grave to haunt me if I just slapped cookies on a naked plate and served them to a guest." She laughed. "And since I have so many other unladylike habits, I'm kind of hoping that the occasional doily might help balance the scale and mitigate my guilt."

"That sounds…" he searched for the right word and when one didn't appear, settled on "reasonable."

"Oh, it's completely insane and I know it. *But*—" she looked him in the eye "—sometimes we do things just because we want to—but without really knowing *why* we want to—and the resultant guilt isn't always a rational response that can be dealt with in a practical, pragmatic manner."

That had been an unexpected twist of the conversation. He had to give her credit for acknowledging the elephant in the room, though, plus bonus points for doing so in such a tactful way. However... "Guilt is a waste of time. Especially when you have nothing to feel guilty for."

"Maybe guilt isn't the right word, then. How about a mild case of regret for possibly hasty and unwise choices?" She didn't give him a chance to respond before she sighed. "Dylan, I thought you said we were just going to forget it happened."

"That seems like the smart thing to do."

"Then why are you here?"

Damn it. He picked up his glass, stalling for time as he searched for the answer. He was a practical, pragmatic man, with a reputation for calm, dispassionate rationality. Yet he was here, with absolutely no good reason—other than he wanted to be. He settled for honesty. "I'm having a bit of trouble with the forgetting part."

"So you came here to..." Marnie's eyes narrowed suspiciously, then she sat up so straight it looked like she had a broomstick for a spine. "I can see where my previous behavior might lead you to believe differently, but you're mistaken if you think that means you can just show up here and expect me to—"

"Whoa, there. That's not what I meant."

Her posture relaxed slightly, but the suspicious look remained. "Then what did you mean?"

"Honestly, I'm not sure," he confessed. It wasn't like he could dig the hole he was in any deeper.

Marnie nodded. "Chemistry. I fully admit I feel it, too, and it's just as baffling to me."

"Well, that helps. I thought I was just losing my mind."

"You should have just said that up front."

"What?"

"It explains why you're here." His confusion must have shown on his face, because she laughed. "You like things controlled and orderly, and *this* is neither. It was great sex, just with the wrong person." This baldly pragmatic side of Marnie was yet another revelation. And a huge relief. Even if it was completely absurd in this situation. "I never understood how people could claim they were just swept away by the passion, even when they knew it wasn't a great idea. I do now." There was a dark undertone to her words he didn't quite understand—especially since she'd been so adamant about the need for passion. She rolled her eyes. "You know, we're adults and no one got hurt."

The words made perfect sense, but his body wasn't buying in. "I guess the question is what are we going to do about it now?"

"I like you, Dylan, so try not to take this the wrong way, but, you and me? We're not compatible *out* of bed. This can't go anywhere."

Once again, there was an insult in there, but since he happened to agree with her, the insult went both ways. Plus, it was ridiculous to be offended by the truth. "Very true."

"So we should just ride it out—" She winced and color crept up her neck. The visual that jumped to his mind at her words had him feeling warm, as well. She cleared her throat. "I mean, *wait* it out. Ignore it until it dies."

Marnie stood and her voice turned brisk and professional, which, considering the situation, took "baldly pragmatic" straight in to "absurd." "I'm *so* glad we took the opportunity to talk this over. It will be much easier going forward now, because I really am looking forward to doing y—*working* with you," she corrected, turning an even deeper shade of red.

He'd managed—admirably, he thought—to keep his libido in check, even as the conversation focused on how good the sex was, even if it was a bad idea. But Marnie's stumbling over her words spoke volumes about where *her* thoughts had gone and it had an instant effect on him.

He stood, as well. "All right, then."

"Right." Marnie's eyes flicked down to where his erection was reaching for her, tenting his pants. Almost absently, she moistened her lips, and he could practically feel her tongue touching him. "I'm *so* glad we had this talk."

"You said that already."

"I know." She swallowed hard, and he could see her nipples pressing against the soft cotton T-shirt as her fingers drummed her thigh. "You know what?"

His blood was thrumming in his ears. "What?"

"I think I'd rather ride it out."

The relief was immediate, followed quickly by a wave of lust so strong it caused his hands to shake. "Oh, thank God."

Marnie's grin was wicked as she reached for him.

CHAPTER SIX

DYLAN'S MOUTH WAS, quite possibly, the most amazing thing on God's green earth. His lips could be soft and demanding at the same time, his tongue wicked and promising. It was instantly intoxicating and addictive and her knees went weak.

Marnie wasn't sure what was possessing her, but she'd never been at so much of a loss to control herself. It was dangerous and scary in its strength, but she was happy to let it guide her, nonetheless.

Whatever it was, it was real and powerful, and more important, it was honest. And since they *were* both honest about it, she could abandon herself to it without regret or remorse.

Dylan's hands spanned her waist, anchoring her against him and sending a thrill over her skin. When his lips moved to her neck, her legs gave out completely, and Dylan caught her as she sagged, leaning her against the wall and holding her there with the weight of his body and caging her inside his arms.

Oh, *bliss.* The need to touch him had nearly overpowered her earlier, but she'd fought it back until he kissed her. Now, she gave in to that urge, indulging herself as she let her hands roam over his arms and shoulders, feeling the strength and virility most would be surprised to find under a clean-cut attorney's coat and tie.

He reminded her of an Olympic swimmer, his muscles long and lean and deceptively strong as he lifted her off her feet and supported her weight easily. Her legs hooked around his waist, and the groan that came from deep within his chest made her feel bold and powerful.

Her bedroom was right off the living room, and Dylan carried her to the bed and placed her gently on her back. He braced himself on his arms, hovering over her, and she could feel her back arching toward him like a filing to a magnet. Her hands went to the buttons of his shirt, wanting to see and feel, but she was clumsy and slow and glad when he pushed to his knees to take over.

Shrugging out of his shirt and tossing it to the floor, he lifted her to a sitting position and reached for the hem of her T-shirt. She lifted her arms, and the shirt was whisked over her head to land on the floor on top of his.

It was the middle of the afternoon, with sunlight streaming through the windows, and she was half-naked across her bed with the sexiest man in the city. There was a brief moment of feeling exposed and self-conscious, but then she caught Dylan's expression, and his slow, appreciative perusal chased the moment away.

She was burning, wanting more. She reached for his belt buckle, but Dylan stopped her hand. Confused, she looked up, and the wicked, sexy grin nearly did her in.

"This time, we go slow."

There was a promise in those words that caused her thighs to clench and her breath to catch. She hadn't had time to think or appreciate before. And while she didn't want to think too much, she did want to appreciate—more like revel, actually—in each and every moment.

Dylan, who always looked so suave and aloof, certainly didn't look so now: shirtless, his hair mussed from her fingers, eyes hooded and dark… He seemed almost predatory.

And she was happy to be his prey.

The frenetic rush was replaced by a driven, purposeful, and oh-so-thorough exploration of her skin. His mouth followed his hands over her collarbone, over her breasts, teasing nipples into hard points and wringing whimpers from her throat.

When his mouth came back to hers, she threaded her fingers through his hair to hold him there, letting his mouth devour hers.

It was an endless kiss, punctuated by small moans and the feel of skin on skin. Her skin felt hot but tingly, and she could feel Dylan's heart beating a rapid tempo against her chest.

Something in his response spurred her, and she tangled her legs in his, rolling them both over until she was on top, pressed against him from breast to ankle. Dylan groaned, sliding his hands down her back to her butt, slipping under the waistband of her leggings to knead the muscles while pressing her against the hard ridge behind his zipper.

She echoed his earlier movements, nipping at the hard muscles in his neck, letting her tongue dip into the hollow of his throat before sliding downward to map the ridges of his pecs. Dylan hissed as she flicked her tongue over his nipple, and his fingers gripped her harder.

Dylan inhaled sharply as she followed the thin line of hair to his navel, and his hands tangled in her hair as she worked the snap of his jeans. She felt powerful and sexy as she worked his jeans off, and the newfound boldness seemed right—and appreciated by Dylan.

Mercy, he was just gorgeous, and Marnie was now glad she'd left the blinds open and not hidden this sight in darkness. Long powerful legs, lean hips, and a torso that should be cast in bronze and preserved for the ages. She let herself take a long, appreciative wander with her hands and eyes, wondering if she was about to drool—but not really caring if she did.

When her eyes finally reached his, the heat there nearly scorched her. Then, with a sexy half grin, Dylan pulled her down onto the bed beside him.

After another kiss that curled her toes, Dylan leaned close to her ear. "My turn," he growled.

In a flash, her leggings were gone, and Dylan was moving slowly up her body, finding that sensitive place behind her knee, dropping a kiss on her inner thigh, nipping at her hipbone...

She went up in flames.

Oh, it was the best kind of torture—ongoing, complete, taking her right to the edge before ebbing back, leaving her gasping and wanting more. She grabbed the slats of the headboard, anchoring herself, as Dylan drove her further, higher, until nothing mattered except the pleasure.

And just when she thought she couldn't take any more, Dylan was kissing her again, sliding slow and deep inside her until their hips met. She reached for his shoulders and wrapped her legs around his hips, holding him tight as he started to move—slowly at first, then faster as the pressure began to build and their breath became ragged.

When everything exploded, she could only hold on

as the tremors nearly shook her apart, and she only vaguely heard Dylan's groan as he joined her there.

The room had grown dark, with only the last rays of sunshine providing any light. Marnie was draped over him, her breath ragged again, skin slick with sweat. She mumbled something against his neck.

He'd never been so physically drained and completely spent, but he managed to lift one hand enough to move her hair out of his face. "What?"

Her head shifted an inch to the left. "I don't think I can move."

"Then don't." She wasn't heavy, and she made an erotic blanket.

"But my leg is cramping."

He groaned as he mustered the energy to help roll her off, and she flopped onto her back with a contented sigh, one arm draped dramatically against her forehead as she stretched.

"You are certainly full of surprises, Dylan Brookes. That was…insane."

An hour ago, that would have caused him to reach for her again, but even though her words caused his blood to stir, he simply could not do anything about it. "You're pretty impressive yourself, Miss Price."

They lay there quietly as the shadows lengthened, and the depletion began to give way to drowsiness. But while the quiet had, at first, been comfortable, the continuing silence began to take on an air of uneasiness.

"Dylan?" The question was softly asked, but weighty.

He sighed. "Yes?"

"You certainly don't have to leave, but I'm not going to ask you to stay the night, either." She directed her words to the ceiling.

"I see." The onus was now on him. "What's your preference?"

"All things considered, I think it's wiser for you to go."

She'd dodged the question, but he had an answer nonetheless. "Do I need to leave now, or can I recuperate for a few more minutes?"

"Don't be like that."

He was exhausted and not in the mood for games. "Like what, Marnie?"

She rolled her head to the side to look at him. "You said yourself that you're looking to get married, and we both know that's not going to happen here."

"I don't recall asking you to marry me."

"Of course not. But if that is what you're after, you're not going to find the right woman waiting in my bed."

"Maybe I'm not looking at the moment. I just got *out* of a relationship. Maybe I want to be a free agent for a while."

"You're not my type, you know."

"Gee, thanks."

"But I know I'm not your type, either."

"Very true."

"At the same time...*damn*." It was an appreciative "damn"—stretched out to at least three syllables and containing the letter "y"—but then she shook her head. "Look, I'm just trying to do the right thing here. For both of us."

He scrubbed a hand over his face. "Marnie, after what we've just done together, I can't do word puzzles right now. Say it. Small words, simple sentences."

An eyebrow went up, and her mouth twisted. "Fine. I only want you for your body. That's all."

"Okay."

Her eyebrows pulled together in confusion. It was almost funny. "What do you mean, 'okay'?"

"I mean, I'm okay with that." Her confused expression only deepened. It was an unusual situation, but far from unheard of. And he found it very appealing. "I don't want you long-term any more than you want me. But as you said... *Damn.* That's enough for me right now."

He watched the play of emotions on her face as she processed his words. Finally, she shook her head. "You really are full of surprises."

"And I'm way too exhausted to get out of this bed right now."

"Then rest." Marnie patted him on the arm in a mock soothe. Then the corner of her mouth twitched. "If you're going to stay, you'll need your energy for later."

Julia called Monday with the job offer, just as Dylan had said she would. Reese took Marnie to dinner to celebrate. Dylan met her at her place later that night for another, more intimate and sweaty celebration.

On Tuesday, Marnie went shopping for new clothes more appropriate to her new position. Three different times she reached for her phone to call Dylan, and three times she put it away. It was tough, because she was craving Dylan like a drug.

You can't spend every free minute in Dylan's bed. Pity.

On Wednesday morning, she was officially employed again, getting the full tour of the offices, meeting the staff, and being brought up to speed.

It was a lot coming at her very quickly, but Marnie loved every minute of it. She'd only been unemployed a little over a week, but she'd missed working. She *needed* to work. It gave her a purpose and an identity.

She ate lunch at her new desk, filling out the endless forms of all new employees before turning her attention to prepping for the meeting she had with Julia in half an hour regarding the Foundation's big fund-raiser. It was only two weeks away, and it was going to be the majority of her focus until then.

She'd heard Reese talk about it in the past, and though she'd been a donor to the Brookes Foundation— a small one, but a donor nonetheless—she'd never attended it. Hell, she'd never attended *any* fund-raiser quite like this one. The Refugee Center had mostly relied on public and private grant money, and the few events they'd had were much smaller affairs.

Held in the Galaxy Ballroom of a midtown hotel, this fund-raiser was no less than a gala event—silent auctions of big-ticket items, open bar, hot buffet, live music... The guest list was a veritable Who's Who of New York, and they were guaranteed major press coverage.

She needed to find an appropriate dress. She added "ask Julia about dress code" to her list of notes for their meeting.

"You must be the new Reese."

She'd left her door open, but the voice still startled her. She spun her chair around to see a well-dressed woman of indeterminate age due to severe botoxing standing in her doorway. The woman looked vaguely familiar...

Dylan's mother.

Marnie shot to her feet and stepped around the desk. "I'm Marnie Price."

"Felicity Brookes." She extended a hand wearing

quite possibly the biggest sapphire Marnie had ever seen. Not that Marnie needed the name or the ring to know exactly the kind of woman she was. The air of money and upper-class privilege was obvious. Felicity Brookes was the Yankee version of her own mother: well-bred, well-married, pillar of the community.

"It's good to see you, Mrs. Brookes. You may not remember me, but I'm an old friend of Reese's. We met at the engagement party."

Mrs. Brookes's lips tightened briefly. *That's probably a sore topic, best avoided, and probably something she's well aware of anyway.*

"Of course, Marnie. Welcome to the Brookes Foundation."

"Thank you. I'm very happy to be here." *Okay, now what?* No one had said anything about Mrs. Brookes being a regular visitor to the office—or what to do if she did show up. She racked her brain for any scraps of information Reese might have dropped but came up empty. "Would you like to have a seat?" Marnie had to move a pile of file folders from the guest chair. "I'm sorry about the mess. It's my first day, and I'm still getting things organized in here. Could I get you a coffee? Some water?"

"No, thank you." Mrs. Brookes sat, so Marnie did the same. "Tell me, Marnie, what made you decide to apply for this position?"

There was no way to sidestep the landmine. "Reese loved working for the Foundation and talked about it constantly—I knew they did good work, important work, and they did it well. And since I enjoy important work done well, this seemed like an ideal situation for me."

"I assume you'll be focusing immediately on the fund-raiser."

Marnie couldn't tell if she was doing well in this interview or not. "Yes, ma'am. I'm familiarizing myself with it now. It's quite the event."

"It is, and it's very important that it's done well. It's our public image. I expect you to remember that."

Marnie automatically sat up straighter, feeling chastised. "Of course."

"May I be frank with you, Marnie?"

She swallowed. "Please do."

"I realize you came highly recommended by Reese, but in light of recent events, I've been forced to reevaluate my faith in Reese's judgment."

"I see." And she did. Clearly. Reese had embarrassed the Brookes family—particularly Mrs. Brookes—by choosing Mason over Dylan, and Mrs. Brookes wasn't happy about that. It was a good thing Reese had already planned to quit, or else she may have found herself fired by her former almost mother-in-law. As a friend of Reese's, she was tarred by that brush, and this was her warning she was already on thin ice. *Lovely. I've had this job less than eight hours and I'm already on the boss lady's hit list.*

"Excellent. I hope you are as good as everyone says you are."

Thankfully, Marnie was spared from having to come up with a response to that when Julia stuck her head around the door.

"We're all waiting on you, Marnie... Oh." Julia stopped, eyes widening. "Mrs. Brookes. How lovely to see you. I had no idea you were coming by today."

"I just came to meet the new addition to the team. But I won't keep her any longer." She stood and tucked her purse under her arm. "Julia, it was nice to see you, however briefly. I look forward to getting your update on the plans for the fund-raiser. Again, Marnie, welcome."

With that, she left, sending junior staff members scuttling from her path.

"Sorry I'm late for the meeting."

"Don't worry. You were a little busy."

"She hates me already."

Julia shrugged. "I think you're right. But don't worry about her. Dylan's really the one who makes all the decisions, so as long as you stay on his good side, you'll be fine."

Somehow, that wasn't any better.

He had a ton of work to do. And this morning, he'd had every intention of staying in his office and getting it all done. That intention was now a paving stone on the road to hell, thanks to one text from Marnie.

He'd left before his secretary—something that *never* happened—totally at the mercy of his libido.

Marnie was proving to be very dangerous. And one hell of a distraction.

The bad part, though, was that he really didn't mind.

She'd picked up food on the way—a pizza that had gotten cold when she'd all but tackled him as she came through the door—and they were picnicking on the coffee table.

Her blouse and skirt were on the floor of his bedroom, and she'd borrowed one of his T-shirts to put on while they ate. Her cheeks were still flushed pink.

She was even a distraction from food.

Marnie was bubbling over with excitement after her first day on the job, telling him things he already knew about the Foundation, but from a different perspective. She bounced from the office staff to what to wear to the fund-raiser without stopping for breath, and her passion about her new position pinged something in his memory. "Can I ask you something?"

She reached for her wine and settled back against the couch. "Sure."

"When you were asked at your interview about why you wanted this position, you said you knew what it was like to feel trapped and afraid to try to escape. What did you mean?"

Marnie sighed. "You couldn't ask an easy question, could you?"

He briefly worried he'd stumbled into something he shouldn't, but when she sat her glass on the coffee table, he assumed he was about to get an explanation.

"I didn't mean to sound so dramatic about it or imply that I'd experienced anything like what our clients have. It's not the same thing at all, and I know that." She snorted. "Break out the violins and cry the little debutante a river."

"Just because other people might not think it's a big deal, that doesn't mean you can't be affected by it."

She nodded. "I was raised in what you'd call a very conservative home. Politically, socially, religiously. There were very, very clear lines about life and the world and my place in it, and I never thought to question any of it. I was rock solid in my convictions. No gray areas. No questions. My life had a plan. I was supposed to go from my father's house, to the sorority house, to my husband's house. College was really just for finding a husband—preferably a doctor or a lawyer, because that has some real social clout, but anyone rich would do—then I'd have a few kids, join the Women's

Auxiliary…" She laughed. "Look at your face. Yes, that attitude still persists. The women's lib movement never quite took root in the Price family."

It sounded like Marnie had been raised in the fifties instead of Savannah. The contrast of the possibility with the reality in front of him was extreme. "I can't imagine you like that."

"Hard to believe, huh? I look back and just cringe. But something changed in me that year I spent at Hillbrook, even though I didn't know it. When I came home, my life didn't seem to fit right anymore. It took a while to figure out why, and when I finally did, I couldn't see a way out of it. My family and friends were a part of what I was trying to escape. I didn't have any money, and I wouldn't be able to access my trust until I turned twenty-five. I felt trapped, like I was in a cage, but I tried to make the best of it, hoping I'd eventually get that surety back."

"But you didn't."

"No. I finally swallowed my pride and reached out to Reese. She helped me find a job and get settled here, and I've never looked back."

That explained Marnie's extreme loyalty to Reese. "Is that the cause of the rift between you and Carter?" At her look, he added, "I talked to him some at Tuck's wedding, and I saw how you two *didn't* talk. It's easy to tell there's a problem there."

"Let's just say it didn't help." She shrugged again. "So, while it's not exactly an inspirational story of overcoming any real hardship, I do understand what it's like to want out of your life and not know how to actually do it."

"I won't lie to you and say folks should make movies about your trials, but it still took guts." He grinned at her. "And now I understand the doilies and your Southern guilt."

She nodded regally. "I may be a shocking disappointment to my mother, but I shall not shame her memory with poor hospitality and manners. I was raised better than that." She cut her eyes at him as she refilled her glass. "Speaking of mothers… I saw yours today."

Dylan tossed his piece of pizza back into the box. "And I just lost my appetite."

"Oh, don't be so melodramatic."

"You're going to tell me she *didn't* put a damper on your day?"

"It was a bit of a downer, especially for my first day at work…"

"And, see, you just made my point."

Marnie shook her head at him. "So what *is* the deal with your mother?"

She'd have to be a lot more specific. "What do you mean?"

"Don't dodge the question. You're the one who started this conversation."

"Then let's pick a new topic. Something more fun, like peace in the Middle East."

"Oh, no, no, no, you're not getting away with that. And anyway, if your mother is going to make random trips by my office, I think I should know what I'm up against."

"Make the Foundation look good, and my mother will be happy. And she doesn't normally stop by unannounced. It must be because you're new."

"That's kind of what she said. But then I got a warning not to screw up the fund-raiser. And, by the way, she's really not happy with Reese."

"It's kind of hard to blame her for that. She's still touchy on the subject."

Marnie bit back a laugh. "Fair enough." She met his eyes and swirled her wine in her glass. "So what's *your* deal with your mother?"

"She's crazy."

"No, seriously."

"I am serious. My father's just as bad."

Marnie shook her head. "They seem perfectly sane to me. I mean, your mom's a bit puckered up about Reese, but that's hardly a reason to question her sanity."

He sighed, debating what to say. But he had been the one to open the door to the confessional. He couldn't really complain that Marnie returned the favor. "You're right. My parents seem sane. They also seem like a happily married couple."

Marnie's eyes widened. "They're not?"

"My parents have not spoken to each other—unless in public—in over five years."

"That's...um..."

"That's an *improvement.* For the twentysomething years before that, they did nothing but fight—and I mean fight dirty. Yelling, throwing things..."

"Why don't they just get a divorce?"

"That's the million dollar question—and it has nothing to do with division of assets. My mother was a Caffery—which may not mean anything to you—but a Caffery-Brookes wedding made them both ridiculously rich and influential and it only grew from there. Neither one of them is willing to give up their position on the totem pole. So they present a harmonious, united front to the world."

"That is a little crazy. And since you know about my family, you know that's not a word I toss around lightly."

He tried to be nonchalant about it. "It works for them, though."

"But that had to suck for you. Growing up in a house that tense, I mean."

"They took over different floors in the house when I was about eight, so that helped. Then they sent me to boarding school, and that was a lot better." He saw the look of pity creeping onto her face. *That's* why he never talked about this. Not even to Reese—although she knew some of it—because he didn't want pity. "Don't."

"Don't what?"

"Feel sorry for me. I don't."

"I can't help it. That borders on child abuse."

"No one's family is perfect."

Her lips thinned out, but she nodded. "True." She took another sip of her wine. "It explains a lot, though."

He was getting to know Marnie pretty well. He didn't have to ask what, because she'd tell him soon enough. It took less than a minute.

"Your mother kept talking about the image of the Brookes Foundation and how important it was that it not be tarnished."

He nodded. "And that's why my parents seem normal in public. Reputations and images are what's important."

"It also explains all *your* emotional baggage about solid foundations for relationships and good partnerships for teamwork."

"That's not baggage. That's a solid life philosophy stemming from seeing the opposite in action."

"If your parents never loved each other—"

"I didn't say that. Quite the opposite, actually. It took a couple of years for the romance and chemistry to fizzle, but it was too late by then. They'd built their little mini-empire, and they weren't willing to give that up."

"But they're miserable. And they made you miserable. It's amazing they accomplished anything."

"My parents are actually pretty good partners—at least when it comes to the things they both deem important. They just had different expectations going into the marriage and when that didn't work out…"

"And that's why you look for that solid foundation instead of great passion."

"Exactly. I wouldn't put another person—much less a child—through that. My expectations are very reasonable."

Marnie stared into her wineglass. "Wow. Way to aim low."

He looked at her. "It beats the hell out of the alternative."

She shook her head. "Your parents are *not* the alternative. Your parents are an anomaly at best. I've seen the mirror image of your parents' marriage, and trust me, it's not real pretty, either."

"Oh, really?"

"Yes, really." She sat her wineglass down and crossed her arms. "My parents never loved each other. Their marriage was more a merger to create that 'good team' than anything else. They were never happy, but they were the perfect couple. My mother was the perfect wife and helpmate, hostessing the dinners, running the PTA and the Women's Auxiliary, raising the children. My father gave her everything she wanted. They were leaders in the community and the church, and they were *miserable*. My father started having affairs, and my mother accepted it even as she resented it. But they never fought and never considered divorce. My home was stable and peaceful and they made a hell of a team. But they didn't love each other and eventually they didn't like each other anymore, either. If I ever get married, I want a hell of a lot more than that. I prefer to aim high."

It was a passionate speech and a lofty goal. "It's a good way to miss and fail spectacularly."

"I'll take my chances."

"And I'll take mine."

Marnie shrugged and took a long drink of her wine.

It struck him a little late how very odd this conversation was considering what they were—or actually, *weren't*—to each other. The resulting silence was awkward and tense, and he didn't want awkward and tense.

But she wasn't getting up or getting dressed, so… "Maybe we should just declare that subject off-limits."

"Sounds very smart. I'm sure you'll find the woman who fits that bill one day, and I'll be happy for you when you do. I'm now going to recommit to my vow to stay out of other people's love lives." Just like that, her mood turned sunny, and she smiled as she passed her glass to him. "More, please." As he poured she laughed and added, "It's a good thing you're not my type."

"Amen to that."

And just like that, she let it drop.

It wasn't until later that night, after he'd put Marnie in a cab home and crawled into his bed alone that her words started to bother him.

CHAPTER SEVEN

MARNIE TOOK ONE look at the fourteen different types of cake to taste and wished she'd brought clothes to change into. The pencil skirt she'd worn to work today was classic and gorgeous and did wonders for both her figure and her confidence, but it did *not* have the extra space she was going to need for this.

Reese had gathered all four of her bridesmaids—including Amber, who Marnie didn't really know all that well, only having met her at dress fittings and such at her bridal salon. But since Amber was going to be marrying Reese's brother, Marnie wanted to get to know her better.

But she wasn't sure she wanted to eat fourteen different kinds of cake.

"Tell me again why we're doing this with you instead of Mason?" she asked Reese.

"Because Mason doesn't care and I need opinions," Reese replied. "Plus, it gives me the chance to hang out with you all."

Gina raised an eyebrow at the display. "I hope no one is on a diet."

"I'm glad none of us are diabetic," Cassie added.

Nearly openmouthed with surprise, Gina asked, "Did you just make a joke?"

Cassie's brow wrinkled. "Hyperglycemia is a very dangerous condition. Why would anyone joke about it?"

Marnie bit back a laugh. "You're right, sweetie. It's a very good thing none of us are diabetic."

"Okay," Reese said, handing out small notepads, "taste them and rank them and give me your top three when you're done. Let's not dawdle, ladies."

Marnie silently agreed with her. The quicker she got done here, the quicker she could get to Dylan's. Between starting her new job, Reese's wedding stuff and Dylan's work, she hadn't seen him since Saturday. It had been a beautiful day, probably one of the few left before winter arrived, so they'd gone to Central Park. It had been fun—not as fun as that evening, though, and if she'd known there would be a four-day lull, she might have been willing to skip the park. Or maybe she wouldn't have let Dylan leave quite so early that night.

Regardless, she'd been walking around in a constant, nearly desperate, state of arousal for four days.

How quickly can I get through fourteen freaking types of cake?

"I wonder if Reese wants these rankings in order of my personal preference or the assumed preferences of the guests?" Cassie asked.

It took Marnie a second to realize Cassie was speaking to her. "Um, both?"

"Well, how can I possibly assume preferences of Reese's guests without knowing who these guests might be?"

Gina bit her lip. "That's an excellent question, Cas. Why don't you go ask Reese?"

As Cassie went to do just that, Marnie shook her head at Gina, who looked completely unrepentant. "That was terrible of you to set her on Reese like that."

"But it will be amusing to watch."

It took less than a minute for Reese to get that glazed, confused look that Cassie's logic put on nearly everyone's face. She stifled a giggle.

It really was amazing how quickly and easily everyone had fallen back into the old, familiar roles of their youth. She picked up a fork and tried the lemon-tangerine cake before giving it an eight out of ten.

"How are you liking the new job?" Gina asked.

"I love it. I'm freakishly busy and the learning curve is killing me, but once we get past the fund-raiser next week, things will settle down and I'll get it figured out."

"Carter will be relieved to hear that. He worries."

It was still hard to reconcile Gina's view of Carter with her own. "And Reese has been a lifesaver. I've probably sent her ten emails a day and she's answered every one of them. It's really sweet of her to take time to help me while she's trying to plan a wedding."

"Well, I sincerely hope Reese goes through with *this* wedding," Gina said quietly. With a delicate shudder, she added, "You know, I still can't face a truffle."

The coffee-flavored cake was okay, but it didn't seem wedding-ish, so Marnie marked it low. "I take it you won't be having them at your wedding, then?"

Gina snorted. "I learned a lot of things from Reese's first wedding, and I'm sure I'll pick up some ideas at her next—and hopefully last—one. That said, I'm glad she ended up with Mason. She and Dylan just weren't a good match."

Silently, Marnie agreed with her, but she had different evidence to influence her opinion. She knew Reese and now she knew Dylan. That "great team" would have bored them both senseless eventually and made them both miserable.

"It's a pity, though," Gina continued.

"What is?"

"Dylan. It's such a waste. The man's yummy. He's got that whole James Bond debonair thing going for him that's really sexy."

Yes, yes, I know. Her thighs were getting twitchy just thinking about it. "You're engaged to my brother. Try not to drool over other men in front of me."

"I'm not drooling. I just know a pretty piece of man flesh when I see it. And it's a shame that all that gorgeousness is wasted on Dylan Brookes."

Marnie happened to agree with that, too, but she kept that opinion to herself. Gina was way too quick to pick up on the smallest hints in that direction. "I'll tell Carter you said so."

"I'm engaged, not dead. It's purely an observation." Gina took a bite of cake and made a face. "Who the hell makes coffee-flavored cake?"

Good. Let's talk about cake. Her relief was short-lived, unfortunately.

"You have to watch out for men like him, though. They can surprise you."

Marnie made a noise that she hoped was noncommittal enough.

"They seem all tightly wound and buttoned up, but under those suits…pure dynamite." Gina raised an eyebrow. "Maybe Reese has been withholding important information from us. I might ask her."

Marnie choked on the bite of coconut-with-mango-filling cake in her mouth. Gina handed her a glass of water. "Are you all right?"

"I'm fine," she managed to croak. "It just went down the wrong way." Everyone had a past, but she didn't like to even *think* about Dylan's and Reese's, much less get any solid details. She needed a new topic, fast. "Do you know where Mason is taking Reese for their honeymoon?"

"Not a clue." Gina marked something on her pad. "I think I'll skip the raspberry-filled one."

Marnie grabbed on to the subject gratefully. "Why the hell couldn't Reese have narrowed this down to a reasonable number before bringing us in? I'm not going to fit into my bridesmaid's dress."

Gina tapped Marnie's arm with the pen. "Speaking of withholding information, I'd still like to hear more about *your* friend."

"Gina, please. Not now."

"Why not? It's not like I know him." Her eyes widened. "Wait, *do* I know him?"

The lighter-than-air cake stuck in her throat like a rock. She wasn't choking this time, but adrenaline had tightened the muscles, making it impossible to swallow. Marnie just shook her head and made a point of obviously chewing.

Gina laid down her pen and paper, grabbed Marnie's elbow and pulled her out of the bakery to the sidewalk away from the glass windows full of fancy multitiered cakes.

Shock opened her throat enough to swallow. "Gina! What are you doing?"

"What is with you?"

"Nothing."

"Don't feed me that. Something is going on with you and I want to know what it is."

Gina was probably the one person she could tell. She was probably the only one who would understand, and she might even have some good advice. But still… "If I tell you something, will you swear not to tell anyone?"

Gina frowned. "I think we've proven that secrets are bad."

That was not what she needed to hear, even though it was true. "Gina, please."

"Okay, I promise."

She took a deep breath. "It's about Dylan."

Gina's eyebrows pulled together. "Reese's Dylan?"

That made her stomach roil. She'd jumped right past that part, convincing herself that it didn't matter. All that initial angst of sleeping with her friend's ex came rushing back. "He's *not* Reese's Dylan," she snapped.

"Jeez, no need to get so snippy about it."

"I'm sorry. It's just... See I'm... I mean, I've been..." She couldn't quite figure out how to say it. She settled for, "Let's just say that you're right about Dylan. And the dynamite."

Gina's eyes widened. She opened her mouth, but nothing came out. Gina closed her mouth, cleared her throat, and tried again. "You had sex with Dylan Brookes?"

Marnie nodded. It felt good to confess to someone.

"I did not see that one coming, pardon the pun."

"Neither did I."

"What did Reese say about it?"

"Reese doesn't know. Hence the whole swearing-you-to-secrecy thing."

"I don't think she'd care."

"But I'd rather not risk it. Especially this close to the wedding... If she *is* going to mind, I'd rather she find out after the wedding."

Gina shook her head like she was trying to clear it. "Okay, *when* did this happen?"

"It started the night of Cassie's wedding."

"Oh, then Reese has no reason to be bothered—wait.

It *started* after Cassie's wedding? As in *not* just one time?"

Marnie couldn't keep eye contact and examined her fingernails instead. "Not just one time. Many. Multiple. Ongoing."

Gina seemed to be having a hard time processing this relatively simple fact. "Dylan Brookes is the casual fling you were telling me about?"

"Yeah."

"Oh, my God. *Why* do we not know this already?"

"Could you lower your voice, please?" She glanced around, but the others were still inside. "I really don't want anyone to know."

"Then why tell me?"

"Because you won't think I'm some kind of slut. And you'll keep this news to yourself."

"I don't understand the secrecy."

"One, it's casual. Just physical. Two, it's temporary, so why get everyone worked up over something that's not going to last? Three, I work for the man, so that's just a little awkward, and four… It's weird. He's Reese's ex. She might not be okay with that."

Gina rolled her eyes. "One," she mocked, holding up a perfectly manicured finger. "If it were just casual and physical, you wouldn't have felt the need to tell me *or* defend Dylan's masculinity. Two, all things are temporary until they're made permanent, so unless there's an actual expiry date, you deal with what you have. Three, so what? If it were truly that awkward, you'd pick the one of the two you liked better. The fact you haven't says a lot. And finally, to four." Gina met her eyes seriously. "Reese really doesn't figure into this. Reese has moved on. To Mason, who she's quite happy with, if you haven't noticed."

"Yet, you, yourself, just called him 'Reese's Dylan'—"

"Simply as a way to distinguish him from every other Dylan in the world."

"But what if she doesn't feel that way? I know it would be strange if she did, but people can get weird about those kinds of things."

Gina waved a hand dismissively. "Reese gave up any right to feel proprietary about Dylan or weird about who he sleeps with the minute she picked Mason. Should she lose sight of that fact, I will remind her." Her voice dropped a notch, "Honestly, though, I bet she'd be thrilled."

She nearly snorted, but caught herself in time. "That's stretching it, don't you think?"

"Reese considers Dylan a friend, so she'd want him to move on. You're also her friend, and she'd want you to be happy. And you *know* Reese is far too realistic to believe that she has some kind of forever claim on the man. I tell you what, let's go ask her—"

Gina started to walk toward the door, and Marnie grabbed for her arm to pull her back. "God, no. Did you not hear the whole 'not before the wedding' part? Reese doesn't need to know this now, if ever. It could be over next week, and I would have upset Reese for no reason."

"What might upset Reese for no reason?"

Marnie spun around at the sound of Cassie's voice, but thankfully Reese was not with her. "Nothing."

"Marnie is having sex with Dylan Brookes and is worried it might upset Reese for some reason if she knew."

Oh, dear God. "Gina! You promised!"

Gina merely shrugged. "At the time, I thought it was going to be something important."

Now was not the time to argue the point. "Cassie, please just keep this to yourself."

"Cassie, tell her that Reese isn't going to be upset over this news."

Cassie looked confused. "I'm not sure I fully understand the problem."

"See," Gina said. "Even Cassie agrees it's not a problem."

"That's not what she means and you know it," Marnie snapped. "You know, this is a moot argument anyway. It's only a temporary thing."

Gina shook her head. "I'm starting to question that."

"Why?"

"Because you're awfully defensive," Gina said. "Is this really just a fling?"

"Of course it is. Me and Dylan? We have nothing in common beyond really, really good sex. It won't last. It couldn't."

"I wouldn't say that," Cassie interrupted in that matter-of-fact tone. "In reality, you and Dylan are quite a logical pairing."

Logical? "What the—"

"Oh, do tell," Gina interrupted with a smile on her face.

"Because Reese and Marnie are friends, they share certain personality traits and common interests. Those similarities could certainly extend to preferences in mates. Conversely," Cassie added earnestly, "those shared personality traits means that the same attributes Dylan found attractive in Reese would also attract him to Marnie."

She hated it when Cassie got logical. It was impossible to argue with her, even though she really wanted to. She didn't like the fact Cassie was making sense.

"In addition, Reese has, in a sense, already vetted Dylan as a satisfactory mate, as evidenced by her willingness to marry him. And Dylan, having lost his original choice, may see Marnie as a suitable substitute, particularly since they also share similar physical attributes."

Nausea rolled through her stomach. "Oh, God, that's just disturbing. I'm a Reese substitute."

"No, no, no," Gina interrupted, and Marnie caught the "Stop Talking" look she shot Cassie. "This is not about Reese. This is about you."

"*What?*"

"Cassie's mostly right." She held up a hand as Cassie started to smile. "*Except* about the substitution thing, because while you and Reese do have a lot in common, you are very different people. But if you ask me–"

"Which I didn't—"

"Actually, you *did*," Gina interrupted. "You wouldn't have said anything at all if you didn't want my opinion."

This was more than she could process at the moment. "Then let's just back up and forget I said any of it. Y'all are making my head hurt."

"If you like Dylan—which you obviously do, it's clear as day—you should explore it and see where it goes. But don't use Reese as an excuse to keep yourself at arm's length."

"You're way off track."

"Please." Gina tossed her hair over her shoulder and crossed her arms across her chest. "Do you honestly think it's not very clear to *us* what you're doing?"

"It's not clear to me," Cassie interrupted.

Gina turned to her. "Think, Cas. Use that big brain. When we used to talk about the kind of men we'd marry, what did Marnie *not* want?"

That was true, but that's why she didn't like him, and why it could only be a casual thing.

Cassie's brow wrinkled, then. "*Oh.* Dylan represents what Marnie rejected."

"Very good, Cas."

Cassie beamed. Marnie wanted to pull her hair out in fistfuls. Maybe she needed different friends. Ones who didn't know her back in the old days.

"What did Marnie used to call it? Umm…"

"The wifelet," Cassie supplied.

"Exactly. Dylan's the kind of man who needs a wifelet to host the parties and make him look good while he rules the world. You like him, that scares you, and so you're coming up with all kinds of excuses."

Her head was about to explode. She knew it. "That's enou—"

"What is going on?"

They jumped and turned. Reese and Amber stood in the bakery door wearing matching frowns. But neither of them looked shocked or surprised, so most likely, they hadn't overheard the conversation.

"Why are you all out here? You're supposed to be helping me pick a cake."

"Marnie doesn't want you to know," Cassie said, and Marnie died a little inside.

Gina elbowed Cassie and then smiled at Reese. "Because it's a surprise. Um…" She looked at Marnie for help, but Marnie was still reeling and had nothing to offer. "Um…for the rehearsal dinner," she finally said.

Reese teared up. "Aw, you guys are so sweet."

Marnie managed a weak smile in return.

"But can you please come finish with the tasting? I need decisions." Reese and Amber went back inside with Cassie in their wake, leaving Marnie and Gina alone.

"Give it a think, okay?"

Like she had a choice. "I'm still going to kill you, but not until after the wedding."

Gina patted her on the back. "We'll see."

Marnie tried all nine remaining cakes, feigning sincere interest for Reese's benefit, but Gina and Cassie's words were banging around in her head and they all tasted like wet sawdust to her. She needed to get out of here and clear her mind. She randomly picked three to recommend to Reese, grabbed the bridesmaid's dress Amber pushed in her direction, and claimed a headache as her reason for a hasty exit.

A text came in before she was halfway down the block.

"Let me know if you want to talk more—G"

Unfortunately, Gina had said more than enough.

Marnie should really have been here by now. She said she had a wedding thing with Reese and the others right after work, but that it wouldn't take long. He'd showered, shaved, ordered dinner, and opened the wine and still nothing. As the clock ticked past seven, Dylan still hadn't heard from her.

She'd sent him several explicit texts today, more than enough to keep him on a low boil, and since she claimed to be feeling similarly, he couldn't understand why she was so late.

He wasn't worried yet, but there was concern.

Then the doorman called. "Mr. Brookes? This is

rather unusual, I know, but your friend Miss Price is here."

How was that unusual? She'd been here enough that they normally just waved her through now. "Then send her up."

"That's the thing, Mr. Brookes. She's not actually in the building. A taxi dropped her off about twenty minutes ago, but she's been sitting outside since then. We're not sure what to do. And it's about to start to rain."

What the hell? "I'm on my way down."

He dialed as he walked to the elevator. Marnie answered on the second ring. "Everything okay?"

"Fine. Things just ran a little late, and I'm kinda tired. I'm heading on home."

This was beyond strange. A complete turnaround. "Did something happen?"

"No. I've got a headache and all that cake has made me a little ill, so I think I just need to crash tonight. Rain check?"

The elevator doors opened into the lobby, and as he stepped out, he could see Marnie through the windows. She sat on the bench just beyond the awning, a garment bag draped across her lap. She had the phone to her ear and a hand over her face. He went and sat beside her.

Marnie looked over and did a double take before rolling her eyes and disconnecting the call.

"You might want to get a better app for your phone," he said, trying to lighten the mood. "There are faster, more direct routes to Brooklyn."

"You're funny."

"Not as funny as you, obviously. Want to tell me why you're sitting out here?"

"I'm trying to think."

"Is everything okay?"

"Of course," she said brightly, but then she seemed to realize that she wouldn't be on a bench outside his building if that were true. "Gina said something and it kind of messed with my head."

From what he knew about Gina, she was very blunt and very capable of doing exactly that. "What did she say?"

"It doesn't really matter. It's just…" She trailed off and shook her head.

He leaned forward and braced his forearms on his thighs. "Tell you what…why don't you come up, have a drink and think about it there. You don't have to talk about it, but you need to come inside. You're starting to worry the doormen by sitting out here."

His point was even further made by the raindrops that began to fall.

Marnie didn't seem to notice the raindrops. Whatever Gina had said to her had really spun her. She sighed and toyed with the zipper on the garment bag. He recognized the gold and silver logo on the bag from earlier this summer as Amber's bridal shop, and he'd bet it was her bridesmaid's dress for Reese's wedding.

The rain began to fall in earnest. "Come on. We need to go inside."

She hesitated.

"Your bridesmaid's dress will be ruined if you stay out here."

That, as much as it irritated him, finally seemed to motivate Marnie. She stood and allowed him to lead her into the building and into the elevator. She stayed quiet on the ride up, but she gave herself a strong physical shake as the doors opened again.

She draped the dress across a chair and gratefully accepted the glass he offered. Easing onto the couch, she kicked off her shoes and curled her legs under her. "Sorry. Let me drink this, and I'll be back to normal."

"Finished thinking already?"

"Yeah."

"That was quick." Especially considering how upset she'd been outside.

"Sometimes Gina is…" She sighed. "It's complicated."

Even he'd picked up on that. And while Marnie was claiming to be okay now, he had a sneaking suspicion it was a show for his benefit. "What *is* the deal between you and Gina?"

Marnie looked at him like he was slow. "She's engaged to my brother."

"No, I mean from before. Reese said there was a big fight, but she never went into details."

"It's a good thing she didn't or I probably wouldn't be sitting here right now." Her mouth twisted. "I don't come out looking too good in that story."

Which might also explain why Gina had the ability to mess with her head. "You all seem okay now, so it couldn't have been all that hard to clear up."

Marnie snorted. "You have *no* idea."

He waited.

"Fine. It was right at the end of the spring semester, freshman year. Right before Reese transferred out of Hillbrook and married Mason—but we didn't know any of that was coming. Carter came up to see me, and he and Gina slept together."

"Oh." That explained a little of Marnie's rant about certain categories of people being "off-limits."

"That's just the beginning. Carter was engaged to one of my best friends, Missy, *and* we had been raised to save ourselves for marriage. It was a double whammy.

I, of course, blamed Gina. I just couldn't see how Carter could have done that, so it had to be all her fault. I threw the biggest fit and said some really terrible things." Marnie sighed. "By the time the dust settled, Gina had just packed up and left, I was mad at Cassie and Reese because they *weren't* mad at Gina, and it drove a wedge between all of us."

Honestly, that sounded like teenage girl stuff, hardly worth a decade of angst, but then, he'd never been a teenage girl. And it had bothered Reese—not so much the Carter-Gina thing, but the way it had divided them.

"It took a while for Reese and I to start to talk again, and even longer for me and Cassie. Gina, though…even though I knew she was talking to Reese and Cassie, I just refused to forgive her. Then I refused to forgive myself. Until I got to the estate for the wedding, I hadn't seen Gina since that night."

She looked at him when she said that, but Marnie wasn't actually talking to him now. Her focus had turned inward.

"Gina, Reese, Cassie… They changed my life. I came from Savannah this sheltered, self-righteous brat, and a year with them completely changed my world-view. The fallout shifted it even more so. I'm a different person now—and I like who I am—but I wouldn't be who I am now if I hadn't thrown my friends under the bus then. That's the part that's hardest to swallow."

He leaned over to refill her glass. "I think they've forgiven you, if that helps."

"Yeah, but it gets worse. Carter and Missy still got married, but they were miserable—not just because of what Carter had done, but it certainly didn't help. When their marriage imploded, I felt partly responsible because I'd nagged them to go through with it. Carter was my hero, and what part of that wasn't destroyed by finding out he had feet of clay continued to erode because I held him responsible for the destruction of my friendships with Reese and Gina and Cassie and ultimately Missy, too. I barely speak to my brother anymore. I didn't know he and Gina had even seen each other again until he showed up at Cassie's wedding."

"No wonder you looked so shocked."

Marnie snorted. "Would you believe there's even *more* to that story? At Cassie's wedding, I also found out that Gina had gotten pregnant from that little fling with Carter. She miscarried, and Reese and Cassie kept that knowledge from me. Which was the right thing to do, but do you know how horrible it is to find out you were such a rotten person that no one would tell you a friend had gone through something terrible because you would have only made it worse?"

And she'd lost her job that day, as well. "No wonder you were pounding the Chardonnay that night."

"Exactly. So, to say that my relationship with Gina is complicated is a bit of an understatement. But the thing is, all the bad stuff that happened to her was really good for me. It totally changed my life, made me more accepting and sure of myself, made me less judgmental and self-righteous. It wasn't fun, but it was good for me in the long run. Gina, though, got the short end of that stick. I can't change what happened or make it up to her, but I am trying to fix things now so that we can be friends again." Marnie laughed bitterly and took another sip of wine. "I bet now you're sorry you asked."

"I think you're being too hard on yourself for mistakes you made when you were young and stupid. Quit beating yourself up."

"Easier said than done." She rubbed a hand over her

face. "Wow, I just put a real bummer on the evening, didn't I? That wasn't what you signed up for."

He hadn't. But he didn't mind, either. "How is that related to whatever she said that spun your head today?"

"It means that it's not so easy for me to ignore what Gina says. Because she might just be right again and I can't see it."

"Then what *did* she say?"

Marnie thought hard, her forehead furrowed. "I'm afraid she may have told me the truth."

In retrospect, he really should have pressed Marnie harder for an explanation to that slightly ominous statement and not let her change the subject. But Marnie was his own special kind of Kryptonite, and the coulda-shoulda-wouldas of rational thought crumbled under her ability to distract him like a dog catching sight of a squirrel.

When they finally did circle back to it, two hours later as Marnie slipped back into her skirt, she laughed. "It's just stuff with Carter. Gina's in the mending-fences groove and wants to see me and Carter kiss and make up, too. There's a lot of work there to be done, and she gave me some marching orders I didn't quite like."

It rolled easily off her tongue, but the more he thought about it, the less honest it seemed. At the same time, though, he really didn't have the right to press her for more. It wasn't his business.

Even after several days, he couldn't shake the feeling that something wasn't right, but he had zero evidence to back it up. He couldn't justify looking for the evidence, either, because everything with Marnie seemed perfectly fine.

It had been a brief blip on an otherwise clear screen,

an anomaly that could—and should—be forgotten. But it bugged him. He felt like he should revisit the subject, but why?

Marnie padded back into the bedroom, dressed now. She never spent the night here—nor he at her place. He rolled to his side. "How are things with Carter?"

She looked at him oddly. "About the same. Why?"

"So no improvements in the fences." At her blank look, he added, "I thought Gina had you and Carter—"

"Oh, *that*. I needed to think about what Gina said for a couple of days before I could decide what I wanted to do."

"And have you decided now?"

"Yeah." She smiled. "I think I have. I just want to get through the fund-raiser tomorrow night and then I'll tackle it."

"That's great, Marnie."

"Yeah. I'm pretty excited about it. Nervous, too."

"If it's what you want, I know it will work out exactly how you want it to. You're practically a force of nature, Marnie Price."

"Thanks." She leaned over and kissed him. "You don't need to walk me out. I'll see you tomorrow night."

"It'll be late, so bring a bag and plan to stay."

She looked at him sideways. "Okay."

He'd expected a bit of a protest, and was strangely pleased that it didn't happen.

CHAPTER EIGHT

MARNIE DIDN'T BELIEVE in Fate, but she did believe that sometimes bad things turned out to be good in the long run. Sometimes the suffering was worth it in the end because you could learn and grow from the experience.

Case in point: she'd lost a job she loved, only to turn around and land a job she loved even more. And she was good at it, too; even this gala, which was new to her, seemed to be awakening bits of dormant Southern DNA and bringing out her inner hostess.

The hotel staff ran with competent efficiency, leaving little for her to do on the organizational side. Instead, she felt almost like a guest herself, with meeting and mingling with the donors and VIPs the largest—but certainly not most onerous—requirement of the evening.

And while she seemed to be good at the mingle, oddly enough, she was enjoying it, as well.

Loss turned to gain. Suffering leading to happiness. Things working out the way they should. It was a revelatory time for her.

Personally and professionally.

An hour into the event, the band started to play, and Marnie took the chance to run to the ladies' and freshen up. It was silly, but Dylan had arrived a little while ago, and she hadn't had a chance to speak to him yet.

Dylan. A happy flutter landed in her stomach. It had taken a couple of days for Gina's words to stop panicking her and start making sense. What she'd realized had scared her at first, but now it was a sweet secret she kept close.

But not for too much longer, she hoped.

If Carter, of all people, could love and appreciate Gina for what she was, then there was hope for every man. Even Dylan. And that knowledge had finally freed her from her fear and made Gina's words ring true.

She was falling for Dylan Brookes. Oh, it was beyond insane, but it was true, nonetheless. And, tonight, when she was back at Dylan's, she was going to tell him so.

Suffering to happiness. Things working out the way they should. She didn't know where they would go, but she was willing to travel down that road and see, at least. He'd asked her to plan to stay the night. That was new. And it felt big. She didn't feel like she was going too far out on the ledge alone.

After checking her lipstick one last time, she went back to the ballroom.

The Galaxy Ballroom was semi-famous for its theme—which it explored through mosaic tiles on the floors and murals on the walls. While it provided otherworldly and unusual atmosphere to black-tie events like this, Marnie also knew that many a *Star Trek* party had been held on the site, as well.

At the bar, she ran into Tuck. She didn't recall seeing his name on the guest list, but then she hadn't been looking for it, either. Confused, she automatically looked for Reese. "What are you doing here?"

He looked at her oddly. "I'm a donor, darlin'. Dylan makes me come every year."

Marnie wanted to smack herself. She automatically

thought of Tuck as Reese's cousin, forgetting he was Dylan's best friend, as well. Of *course* he'd be a donor to Dylan's family's foundation. "Is Cassie with you?"

"She went to check out the murals while I got drinks."

They were interrupted by a short, balding man who recognized Tuck and the conversation immediately turned into a discussion of football. "Tell you what, why don't I take that drink to Cassie and let you two talk?"

Happy to make such an easy escape, she went to the biggest mural, and sure enough, Cassie stood in front of it, studying it intently. It was beautifully done by an artist whose name she couldn't remember but was considered important. It covered the wall from floor to ceiling, drawing the viewer in like a visitor to the galaxy.

Suddenly nostalgic, Marnie wrapped an arm around Cassie's shoulders. Like she'd done hundreds of times all those years ago at Hillbrook, she said, "Tell me about the stars, Cassie."

Cassie sighed. "They're wrong."

"What?"

"They're all wrong. There is no place on earth from where this particular configuration of stars would be observable."

Marnie bit back a laugh and searched for something familiar, but it had been a long time since Cassie had taught her the constellations. "But isn't that Pegasus over there?"

"Not unless Pegasus is also half lion. And upside down."

"But it's pretty, don't you think?"

"It would be prettier if it were correct. How hard would it have been to bring in a consultant from the Planetarium or the NYU astrophysics department to provide direction?" Cassie shook her head sadly. "This is more harmful than good."

"It's art, honey."

"Then it's bad art."

Only Cassie would take offense on behalf of astronomy everywhere. "Here, Tuck got you a drink. And may I say *you* certainly look lovely tonight." Cassie was still learning girly ways, but she *was* learning. Her dress was feminine and fit well, and while her hair was pulled back, at least it was in a jeweled barrette instead of that horrid floral scrunchie. It was hard to tell in this light, but she might have even been wearing lip gloss. Marnie just wanted to squeeze her. She settled for, "I'm so glad you came."

With a final grimace at the offending mural, Cassie turned to her. "I should tell you that I'm under instructions tonight from Gina to subtly observe your behavior around and regarding Dylan for any indications that you two are progressing in your relationship."

Marnie felt her eyebrows go up.

"I am also supposed to occasionally make mention of how handsome Dylan is and what an attractive and happy couple you would make."

"Really?" She might kill Gina after all.

Cassie nodded earnestly.

"Then why are you telling me?"

"Because I don't know how to do any of that. And I don't want to."

Cassie's logic could sometimes be refreshing. "I don't blame you at all."

"But what am I going to tell Gina?"

"That I was here in a professional capacity and kept quite busy. Therefore, you were unable to make any observations and have no data to report."

Relief flooded Cassie's face. Shame on Gina for putting her in that position to satisfy her own nosiness. "Don't worry about Gina. I'll handle her."

A dreamy haze clouded Cassie's eyes at that moment, and Marnie did not have to look behind her to know that Tuck had escaped his fan and found his wife. It was the same look Cassie *always* wore when she saw or spoke of Tuck. It was sweet. Reese and Gina had variations of that look for Mason and Carter.

For the first time, she was a little jealous of them.

Tuck snugged Cassie up against his side and gave her a firm kiss that left Cassie swaying slightly.

Okay, so I'm more than a little jealous.

"Where's Dylan?"

Her eyes snapped to Tuck. "I'm not sure. I assume he's somewhere around." There were over three hundred people in the ballroom.

"I thought for sure you'd know."

Her stomach fluttered a little. Had Dylan told Tuck? And if so, what had he said? "W-why on earth would *I* know? I'm not his secretary."

Tuck winked at her, then grinned at Cassie. "And that, sweetheart, is what you'd call 'observable phenomena.'"

Her stomach sank. *"Cassie."*

"I needed his assistance," Cassie said by way of explanation. "But don't worry, I only told him that you two were having sex. I didn't theorize any further."

She could feel her cheeks burning. Cassie's detached clinicalism could be as bad as Gina's bluntness.

Tuck seemed to be enjoying her discomfort. "I knew Dylan was seeing someone, I just didn't know who."

"Why didn't you ask him?" Cassie said.

"Because we're not girls," he answered.

Marnie didn't know how to process that tidbit in light of her own new feelings, and she didn't have time before Tuck turned back to her.

"I never dreamed the woman in question was you, though. No wonder Gina has Cassie on reconnaissance."

She had to step carefully here. While Tuck may have dismissed Cassie's question with the "we're not girls" response, he was still Dylan's best friend. "Gina is merely overreacting. Dylan and I are just friends."

"The kind with benefits," Cassie added.

"That was implied, Cas, but yes." She turned back to Tuck. "I'm sorry you were dragged into this—"

"Marnie," Cassie interrupted, "if you're Dylan's current sexual partner, why is he with another woman?"

Marnie turned her head so fast, her neck spasmed. Sure enough, there was a tall, beautiful and *very* buxom blonde resting her hand on Dylan's arm in a rather proprietary manner. Dylan was talking to his parents and the woman was hanging rapturously on every word. "I have to assume they know each other."

Cassie looked at Tuck expectantly.

He cleared his throat. "That's Analise Wilson. They dated before he and Reese got together."

Irrational jealousy clawed her stomach. *You don't know what that's about. And it's not really your business anyway.*

Except that it sure felt like it was. "Oh."

"I'm sure it's nothing," Tuck added. "They were over a long time ago."

"That doesn't look like nothing to me," Cassie grumbled.

"I appreciate the loyalty, Cas, but it's fine." Dylan didn't know how she felt about him or that she wanted to change the nature of their relationship. It made per-

fect sense that he'd be looking for another woman at the
same time. She was not going to overreact like some
kind of jealous shrew from a made-for-TV movie. "Remember that Dylan and I are just friends."

Cassie looked like she was going to argue.

"Tuck, can you explain it to her? It's about time for
the silent auction, and I need to go. I'll talk to you later."

As the Foundation's director, Julia handled the an-
nouncements, and all Marnie had to do was stand there,
smile, and hand out the occasional item. Dylan, his family, and Analise Wilson were seated directly in front of
the podium—with Analise almost in Dylan's lap.

Not jealous. I'm not.

Then Dylan caught her eye and rolled his.

She bit back a laugh.

A few minutes later, one of the junior staff brought
her an envelope. "Mr. Brookes—Mr. Dylan Brookes,"
she clarified since his father was here, as well, "asked
me to give you this."

Inside, there was a key and a note: *If you beat me
home, let yourself in. I'll meet you later.*

Marnie pocketed both quickly, but she smiled to herself. *Analise who?*

Dylan walked Analise into the lobby of her building
while his parents waited in the limo. It had been a long
night—successful, but long—but he was hit by a burst
of renewed energy at the thought it was almost over.

"It's so good to see you again, Dylan. I had a wonderful time." Analise looked up at him through her lashes,
but it was a calculated flirt, not a natural one.

"It was good to see you again, as well," he lied.
Analise Wilson had to be the most boring woman on
the planet. She was kind and charming and well-bred,

but dull. Really dull. Mind-numbingly dull. He found it very hard to believe they'd once been a couple. What on earth had they talked about?

Analise had attached herself to him like a barnacle the moment he'd walked in the door, much to the delight of his mother, who'd done all but propose to the woman on his behalf. She was probably in the limo planning their wedding right now. "Well, good—"

Analise interrupted him. "Maybe we could go to dinner sometime soon. Get caught up on each other's lives?"

Put on the spot like that, what was he supposed to say? Lie and say "sure"? Be rude and tell the truth? He wished he could call Marnie. She'd have the perfect, polite Southern phrase to get him out of this without committing him to anything or hurting Analise's feelings. "Things are a little busy for me right now, so I can't make plans, but I'm sure we'll see each other soon." Her face fell and he felt like a jerk. "I've really got to get my parents home." *I certainly don't want to leave them alone in a confined space for very long.* "Good night, Analise."

The icy tension that waited for him in the car wasn't much better than the disappointment he'd just left behind in the lobby. It was a feeling he was accustomed to, though, and one he associated with home. His father was reading something on his phone and his mother was gazing out the window like she'd never seen the Upper West Side before. They sat as far apart as space allowed, each pretending the other wasn't there. Once he took his seat, though, and the car started to move, they both turned their attention to him.

"It was lovely to see Analise again," his mother said. "She's such a beautiful girl."

"Tonight went well," his father said a second later.

Since his mother spoke first, he responded to her first. "Analise did look very lovely tonight." Then he turned to his father. "It did. Definitely a success."

"I had lunch with her mother just last week, and Delores was telling me all about her time in Paris. Did Analise tell you about the shoot at Versailles?"

He'd spent several hours in the woman's company tonight, yet he had no idea what his mother was talking about. He was only vaguely aware that Analise had been in Paris for the last year, but had no idea what she'd done there besides shop. What the hell had they talked about all evening? His brain must have checked out from the boredom. "No, she didn't."

"Did you have a chance to speak with Tom Daniels?" his father asked. "His firm is looking to expand their overseas investments."

"I did. We're going to set up a meeting for next week sometime."

"Well, you must ask her about it when you see her again."

He swiveled his head back toward his mother. "I doubt I'll have the chance, Mother. I'm not interested in getting involved with Analise again."

"But you two made such a nice couple, and the Wilsons are a very good family."

"Take him to play golf, but let him win."

"You should ask your father if the Wilsons still own that house upstate. It would be—"

The absurdity of the situation struck him hard— especially since he was so accustomed to having two separate conversations at the same time that it hadn't struck him as absurd immediately. "Why don't you ask him, Mother? He's sitting right beside you."

Both his parents looked at him in shock. His mother recovered first, shaking her head and pursing her lips. "Dylan..." she admonished.

"Normal people speak *to* other people who are in the room. Or else they get a divorce and not pull other people—like, say, their children—into their sick little power games."

His father frowned. "This isn't some kind of game, Dylan."

"You're right. It's not." Marnie had called it child abuse. He hadn't felt abused, though, until right now. "It is, however, a very sick and twisted way to live." He had a flash of his future: twenty years from now, he might not be talking to *his* wife, either, and not see it as odd in the least. "This has gone on long enough. Way too long, actually, and I'm done."

"What do you mean by that?"

"What are you talking about?"

He'd *just* told them, and yet neither one of them had so much as glanced in the direction of the other. And they didn't think that was unusual in the least. They'd been ignoring each other for so long, they may have actually lost the ability to even physically *see* the other unless they were in public. "I'm not going to humor or enable you in this. Talk to each other or don't. I don't really care at this point, because I'm not going to play anymore. Continue on as you will, but I think I'll only talk to the two of you when you're in public and pretending to be normal from now on. I value my sanity too much to keep this up. It's insane."

"We are adults, Dylan."

"Then act like it. But this? It ends tonight." He pushed the intercom button and told the driver to pull over. He had the door open before the car even came to a complete stop. "Good night to you both."

He was only about four blocks from home, and would have been home in only a few minutes anyway, but he'd rather walk it in twice the time than spend even another few minutes in that charade. The cool night air helped cool his temper—at both his parents and himself. Getting out like that wasn't the most mature thing he'd ever done, but it still felt good. And the looks on his parents' faces were priceless.

It was amazing he was even remotely sane and stable after so many years of that insanity. And his parents had convinced themselves long ago that this wasn't only acceptable but normal. And by shoving Analise at him, they were only setting him up for the same life.

He didn't want his parents' marriage—cold and angry and separate in order to keep peace, living like contentious roommates. But they hadn't always been like that, so there was no safety in letting heart and hormones lead the way, either. Where was the line? The safety zone?

He just wanted stability and a smidgeon of happiness to go with it. Was that too much to ask? He'd built his career on conscientiously keeping people's fortunes out of risky situations where they had a lot to lose, and he sure as hell wasn't going to flip that for his personal life.

Maybe he was just destined to live a bachelor forever. At least he'd never end up like his parents. It wasn't all that bad of a proposition.

As the elevator ascended, he realized the fatalistic ridiculousness of *that* idea. Maybe he needed therapy. Serious therapy. Maybe some shrink might be able to make heads or tails out of this because he sure couldn't.

One lamp burned in the foyer as he opened the door,

and he saw Marnie's purse and the spare key on the table beside it. Faint strains of music and muted light spilled out of his bedroom door into the hall. He could almost smell the scent of citrusy perfume in the air.

He'd forgotten that Marnie would be here.

His anger and frustration began to lift. *That's* what he needed more than therapy. There was no stress or pressure with her. It was simple. Easy. A mini-vacation from his life. Someone who accepted the crazy and didn't dwell on it. Someone who didn't really demand or want much of anything from him.

He loosened his tie and took a deep breath as he walked toward the bedroom, so glad and ready to forget everything else.

Marnie sat on the bed, draped deliciously across the pillows. The sequins and beading of her dress caught the light, and her creamy skin glowed against the black of her dress and the deep blue of the bedding.

It was simply incredible. *She* was simply incredible. Breathtaking.

Marnie handed him a glass of champagne as he approached.

"What are we celebrating?"

Moving over to make room for him, she said, "A successful fund-raiser, of course."

He clinked his glass against hers. "You should celebrate. You did an amazing job."

She shrugged. "I can't take much—if any—credit for the event itself, but as far as my assignment to schmooze and mingle, I think it went well."

"I heard nothing but compliments."

That put a smile on her face. "Oh, good. I like compliments."

He dropped his forehead to hers, breathed in her

scent, and let his hand slide over the bare skin of her shoulder to trace her collarbone. "You look amazing tonight."

He kissed her temple, her cheek, and the soft spot where her shoulder met her neck. She shivered slightly, and gooseflesh rose under his lips.

"That wasn't the compliment I was fishing for, but thank you." She fiddled with the lapel of his jacket, straightening it. "You look pretty amazing yourself. Very dashing and James Bond-ish."

He removed the tie and tossed it onto the nightstand. Shrugging out of his coat, he tossed it aside, too, and released the shirt studs from their holes. "It's not very comfortable, you know, but the ladies seem to like it," he teased.

"Very true. A tux is catnip to the ladies. You certainly had the interest of several wannabe Bond girls."

He cut his eyes to her and saw her lips twitching in amusement. "Don't remind me."

"Analise Wilson is a lovely woman." Marnie's tone was serious, but she ruined it with a smirk. "And your mother seems particularly enamored of her."

Analise and his mother topped the list of things he really didn't want to discuss any more tonight. He sighed. He could feel his earlier frustration returning. "Honestly, can we find another topic of conversation?"

"Poor thing." She patted his thigh in mock sympathy. "It must be so difficult to be a successful, attractive bachelor. It's very *Pride and Prejudice*."

"Very what?"

Marnie shook her head sadly. "Tsk, tsk. And here I thought you had a good education. The opening line in *Pride and Prejudice* is, 'It is a truth universally acknowledged, that a single man in possession of a good fortune must be in want of a wife.'"

Good Lord. "'In want' does not mean '*I* want.'"

An eyebrow went up. "Oh, really? Just a few weeks ago you were saying you *did* want to get married."

Yeah, and end up like my parents. "I've decided I was wrong." His cufflinks joined the pile.

"Oh." Marnie stared into her champagne flute.

"What 'oh'?"

"I'm just surprised to hear that. It's a bit of an attitude change."

"Well, none of the women in my current crop of acquaintances meet my needs, so I'm giving up the search. I'd rather die alone." He drained his glass and reached for the bottle to refill them both. Feeling a little bad for putting a damper on their evening by letting those black thoughts loose, he clinked his glass against hers again. "Here's to us, Marnie, and things that are simple and uncomplicated and easy."

Marnie nodded, but didn't drink. She had a strange look on her face.

"Marnie? Are you okay?"

She nodded, but the look didn't change. "Yeah."

"What's wrong?"

Blinking, Marnie focused on his face. Then she cleared her throat. "We have to talk."

That didn't bode well. His good mood deflated again. "Okay."

"Wow, this is awkward." She took a deep breath and blew it out, her cheeks puffing. "Really awkward."

"Then you're just going to have to say it."

"Yeah, I guess I am." She met his eyes evenly. "This is our last night, Dylan. I've met someone else."

* * *

The lie came out easily. Much easier than expected. It nearly killed her to say it, but what the hell else was she going to do? Dylan's casual attitude was stomping on her heart, making it very clear that these newfound feelings of hers were very one-sided and that he would not welcome the news.

Dylan pulled back, shock written across his face. *"What?"*

"I've met someone else."

"Are you kidding me?"

Pride was a bitch. Injured pride was worse. "No."

He rolled off the bed. "Who? And *when*, for God's sake?"

She tried to keep her voice even. "I've actually known him for a while. I thought we were just friends, but I realized recently that my feelings for him have changed. I want…more from him." That was actually the truth. "I can't have something 'simple and uncomplicated' with you and something more from him at the same time. I have to make a choice."

"And you're choosing him."

She couldn't quite meet his eyes, afraid he might see through the lie. "Yeah."

"Then what the hell are you doing in my bed right now?"

Something nasty coiled in her stomach as the repercussions of her lie tangled around her. That was a very fair question, and she didn't have a good answer because she'd been making it up on the fly. Now she was stuck in the lie and it didn't make her look like a very nice person at all. *Damn it all straight to hell.* She hadn't planned for *this* to happen. In the rush of her new feelings, she'd conveniently forgotten to question whether

Dylan might return them or what she'd do if he didn't. "I thought we'd have one last night together, but..." The look of disgust that rolled over Dylan's face matched the feeling in her stomach as she fought to keep her face neutral. Now she sounded like a slut. "But I realize now that I can't go through with it."

"Why didn't you tell me about this guy?"

Her eyes were burning. Thank God the lights in here were too dim for Dylan to see. "I just did, Dylan."

He raked a hand through his hair and cursed. He didn't say anything, just stared at a place just beyond her shoulder, and she didn't know what to say or do next. The silence stretched out and Marnie felt physically ill.

Dylan finally spoke. "So this is it, then."

Pain slashed through her chest, and she realized she'd been hoping for... What? What did she think was going to happen? That Dylan would drop to his knees and beg her to stay? That he'd suddenly admit that he had feelings for her, too, beyond just an easy, comfortable time? She scooted to the edge of the bed and swung her feet to the floor. "Yeah. I guess it is."

Her overnight bag and shoes were at the foot of the bed, and she had to pass Dylan to get to them. She inhaled as she passed, breathing in his scent one last time.

She stepped into her shoes and shouldered her bag, steeling herself to face him. "It's been great, Dylan. Really. I mean that. And I sincerely hope you find someone wonderful very soon who will make you very happy."

Dylan's face was a combination of shock and anger, and as much as she wanted to kiss him goodbye, she held herself back. "Bye."

She kept her pace even and unrushed as she walked away. As she picked up her purse and saw Dylan's key lying next to it, her heart cracked a little more at the reminder of how excited she'd been just a short while ago. *Fool.* Her eyes started to burn again, and this time she could feel the tears about to fall. Picking up the pace, she made it to the elevator before they did.

She'd walked into this relationship with the expectation it would be casual. She'd never considered it would be something else. She shouldn't be so hurt that it wasn't going to be.

She'd been right to try to keep her distance from Dylan—but for the wrong reasons.

She was ten kinds of a fool, and she had no one to blame but herself.

Damn it all to hell.

CHAPTER NINE

WORKING FOR THE Brookes Foundation while trying to get over Dylan Brookes was going to kill her. Or drive her to drink. Possibly both.

After a miserable weekend, putting on a happy face as she walked around a business named for the source of her misery, with pictures of her misery on the walls, and listening to people talk in glowing terms about the man making her miserable was just insult to injury and salt in the wound.

Maybe I should have thought this through a little more. The minute she realized that Dylan was going to be an attraction, she should have pulled her résumé from consideration here.

That's the problem with wanting it all, the proof you can't have your cake and eat it, too. Even in the best case scenario, you'd have lots of cake but many inches on the waistline.

But the job was going to be her consolation prize. At least she didn't have to see him at work and the job didn't require her to interact with him. But knowing he was somewhere in the building had her holding her breath every time the elevator doors opened.

She just had to hope that it would pass. And pass soon. It should. It *had* to.

They'd only been together about a month, so it wasn't like she was *really* in love with him. She had just started *falling* in love with him. She just needed to catch herself, get her feet back under her and go on.

Why, then, did it feel like she'd already gone *splat*?

She frowned at her computer, dreading the work that needed to be done. The press had covered the fundraiser extensively, and part of this morning's assignment was to review that press for both the archives and possible future opportunities to follow up with.

There were plenty of pictures, of course, of Dylan and his parents, and Dylan looked magically delicious in each one. She'd resigned herself over the weekend to the facts of the situation, how difficult it might be, but seeing him at the event and knowing how happy *she'd* been at that moment... The pain was more raw than she'd expected.

This was a special kind of torture.

And it didn't help that Analise was in many of the pictures, thanks to her near-surgical attachment to Dylan all evening.

She wasn't jealous of Analise. She really, really wasn't. Analise wasn't the "other woman." Dylan didn't want Analise—that much was clear—but when and if Dylan did decide to get serious with a woman, it would be with someone like her.

The very cruel irony was that Marnie *was* someone like Analise. Her background wasn't that different from Analise's. She'd been raised to *be* Analise, only she'd rejected it.

This was the first time she'd ever questioned that choice, and she hated the fact that she wanted Dylan enough to have the regret.

And while she'd hoped there was a happy medium

there, it didn't matter. Dylan hadn't changed his mind about her.

She wasn't what he wanted or needed. Now she just had to accept that.

It was easier said than done. She gave herself a shake and tried to focus on what she was doing. A few minutes later, the intercom buzzed.

"Marnie, your brother is here to see you."

Oh, damn. She hadn't even known he was back in town, and Carter was the *last* thing she needed today. She couldn't send him away, though, so she girded herself for the inevitable. He'd be going back to Savannah for good after Reese's wedding, so she really had no excuse to keep avoiding him.

And she was already miserable, so it wasn't like he could ruin her day or anything.

"Hi, Carter."

He closed the door behind him. "Nice office."

"It's certainly a step up from my old cubicle." She motioned for him to have a seat.

Carter looked distinctly uncomfortable. Of course, their conversations were usually stilted and awkward, and she wasn't feeling her best, either. "I'm back in town."

"So I see."

He leaned back in the chair, arms and legs crossed in a position reminiscent of Daddy. "I seem to be spending a lot of time in New York, but none of it with you."

"I understand. You've got Gina now, and that's where your focus needs to be. My feelings aren't hurt."

"But you're my sister."

She shook her head. "I'm not an obligation, Carter."

"I never said you were. It's not an obligation if you want to spend time with the person, sibling or not. But the way you've been avoiding me and my calls, I'm starting to think you find it an onerous obligation for *you*."

"I've been a little busy recently—new job, weddings... I've barely had time to catch my breath."

"So it's not intentional avoidance." His eyebrow cocked up as he spoke, and an amused challenge crept into his voice."

"Maybe a little."

"Well—" he reached into his pocket and pulled out a roll of papers that he then smoothed out on her blotter "—avoiding me or not, I still need your signatures on these."

Carter was constantly needing her signature on things for the business—and it often irked him no end—but this didn't look familiar at all. She scanned the first paragraphs, then looked up at him. "What is this?"

"Exactly what it looks like. I've removed myself from all of your accounts. Your money—dividends, trust, all of it—now goes directly to you. No more channeling through me."

Wow. This battle was so old, she'd all but given up. Daddy's will had Carter as a signatory on her accounts until she turned thirty-five, and she'd just resigned herself to that fact. For Carter to let that go... Gina was exercising a lot of influence over him these days. She'd won the war without even firing a new shot. She kept reading, looking for the catch. "This is unexpected."

"You're plenty able to handle your own affairs."

Marnie nearly swallowed her tongue in shock. "Are you feeling all right?"

"You never come home anymore and I barely see you when I come up here. The only way I've been able to keep in contact with you at all is by controlling your money. I know it's wrong, but I was willing to take what I could get."

Much more of this and Marnie would fall off her chair. "Thank you for admitting that."

He cleared his throat. "I hope Gina might be a big enough incentive for you to come visit more often. She'll miss you. And I'd like to see more of you, too."

And the hits just keep coming. "Maybe we could work something out."

"I hope so." She could tell this was very hard for Carter, but the words were still sincere.

"I'm really proud of you."

Her head reeled, leaving her dizzy and confused. "Excuse me?"

"I'm proud of you, Marnie. Impressed, too. You've made a brand-new life for yourself—without help from anyone and far away from home. And you've been successful with it. Impressed is the very least I can say about it."

Really? "You could have told me that before."

"In a way, I thought you knew." He smirked. "And if you'd taken my calls recently, you'd know it already."

Her eyes were still burning, but that brought a smile to her face. "If I'd known you weren't going to yell at me about something, I might have taken your calls."

"I tell you what, take my calls from now on, and I promise not to yell at you anymore."

"That's a deal." This was a much-needed high point in an otherwise horrible week. Carter stood as she came out from behind her desk. Then, because it felt right for the first time in nearly ten years, she wrapped her arms around him in a hug. A surprised second later, Carter hugged her back.

"Can I take you to lunch?" he asked carefully.

"I'd like that. Just let me get my purse." Also for the first time in longer than she could remember, she didn't feel all tense and cautious and angry around Carter. She was learning to accept her own past and forgive; she owed Carter the same courtesy. After all, she wouldn't be who she was today, either, if Carter hadn't done the things he'd done, and the wisdom of age brought with it the understanding that he hadn't intentionally tried to hurt her. There was a lot she needed to just let go of if she wanted happiness in her future. "What are you hungry for?"

"You pick." He followed her through the offices and into the elevators. His eyes narrowed and looked at her closely. "Is something else bothering you, Marnie? You still have that *look*… It usually means you're upset with me, but I'm not sure what I did now."

Mercy. She was so miserable-looking that even her brother noticed. "It's not you this time. I've just got a little problem I don't quite know how to solve."

"Can I help?"

The offer, made so quickly and without hesitation, warmed her. "Thanks, but no. I need to figure it out on my own." They exited through the lobby, right past the large portrait of Dylan that made her heart lurch a little each time.

"If you change your mind or think of something I can do, let me know— But not because I think you need my help," he quickly clarified. "I know you can handle it. You've succeeded at everything you've ever put your mind to, and always on your terms."

The pride and support, *especially* coming from Carter, buoyed her. And she really needed it right now.

But it was all she could do to keep the smile on her face.

* * *

Once was bad luck. Twice meant there was something wrong with him. Twice in less than four months probably meant he needed therapy to find out what it was about him that made women choose another man over him.

Oh, there were probably plenty of women who *would* choose him—he had money, fell within the common accepted standards of good looks, was generally considered a nice guy—and there were probably even a few out there who would choose him over someone else.

That knowledge was just enough to keep him from developing a full-blown complex of some sort, but it was cold comfort in the harsh light of day.

At least Marnie hadn't strung him along. It was over and done with as quickly as it had begun, the bandage ripped off quick instead of bit by painful bit. Why was it, then, that the day after his *fiancée* had chosen another man over him, he'd been absolutely fine, but Marnie was still haunting him painfully almost a week later?

It shouldn't be like this, because it wasn't *supposed* to be like this.

He and Marnie had agreed to just kill time until someone else came along. He could wish that Marnie's someone else hadn't come along quite so quickly, but all things considered, it was probably for the best.

He'd been getting too used to her, because it was just so *easy*. There were no games, no unreasonable expectations, no pressure. It had been the perfect relationship, and against all the earlier expectations, he'd been beginning to believe it meant something more. And he'd been unwilling to see it end because he wanted to see where it could go.

Unfortunately, that knowledge had come a little too late for him to tell her *before* she found someone else.

But he'd nearly told her so—even after she'd told him there was a someone else. His pride, thankfully, had held his tongue and not made the situation worse than it had to be.

If nothing else, Marnie still worked for him. Anything he might have said Friday night would have made the professional situation awkward and unsustainable.

As it was now, all he had to do was let time do its thing.

He sighed as he went back to work. Here was solid proof that maybe this was for the best. He was way far behind on a dozen different things, and while he couldn't blame Marnie for it, she was certainly the cause. He'd been letting things slide, leaving the office at normal times instead of staying late to work, turning his phone off over the weekend.

She was a distraction, an excuse to neglect anything less interesting—and everything was less interesting than Marnie.

Yep, definitely for the best.

Maybe you could get Marnie to give you another chance.

She'd made her choice.

But you didn't even try to change her mind. You just let her go. You didn't even put up a fight.

I shouldn't have given up so easily.

Damn it, he *wasn't* going to give up so easily. He knew Marnie cared about him; they were friends as well as lovers. He just needed to convince her that her feelings for him could be stronger than those feelings she had for the other guy.

He wasn't going to let her go without a fight.

It would be totally out of character, but then he hadn't really been himself since the moment Marnie kissed him for the first time.

She'd wanted him to find his passion. And now he had.

It was Marnie.

It was impossible not to love The Plaza. Sitting in one of their suites overlooking Fifth Avenue with her best friends, drinking champagne and nibbling on appetizers had to be one step away from heaven on earth. Reese bounced from phone to computer, obsessing over last-minute details, despite their instructions to sit and relax. Gina stood behind Cassie, curling iron in hand, adding soft waves to Cassie's hair over her protestations. Amber, who had arrived about fifteen minutes ago with Reese's wedding dress, was carefully arranging the yards of fabric and eyeing them critically for even the tiniest wrinkle. This was girlfriend time, as the men would meet them at the restaurant, and Marnie was determined to enjoy it. She kept a small smile on her face while she sipped at her champagne.

It was difficult, though, because while she was happy, having fun with her friends, and excited for Reese, there was a little dark spot on her heart that she just couldn't ignore. It put a damper on things, but she tried to hide it as best she could for the sake of her friends.

They had another half hour before they had to be at the rehearsal dinner, and while she would go and do her very best to be the perfect bridesmaid and guest and have a good time, she was headed out as soon as dessert was served.

Gina kept giving her odd looks and trying to get her

alone, so Marnie was staying as close to Reese as possible—and definitely in a crowd when Reese wasn't around—to prevent that from happening. Gina wanted to talk about Dylan, and Marnie didn't know how much longer she could keep Gina and her questions at bay.

Because even after a week of moping and thinking, she didn't have any good answers for those questions. The truth sounded just too pitiful—and she didn't want pity—and somehow Gina was always able to tell when she was lying. Avoidance was her best option right now.

And anyway, she was trying to keep the stuff that hurt out of her mind before it really put a damper on her enjoyment of Reese's wedding. Talking about it would only reopen wounds that were scarcely closed as it was.

Reese dropped next to her on the couch, eyes on her phone. "What do you think of Andrew?"

"Who?"

"One of the groomsmen. Tall, blond hair, wide shoulders…"

Reese could have been describing any of Mason's groomsmen and most of his friends, as every last one of them seemed to be current or former Marines with the physique to prove it. As a group, they looked much like a swimsuit calendar come to life. "He's okay, I guess. Why?"

"Mason says he's asking for intel on you, so I thought I'd rearrange the seating chart and put you two together at the reception."

"No," Gina snapped, brandishing the curling iron like a weapon in Reese's direction. "You are not messing with the seating charts again."

Marnie grabbed the excuse. "Gina's right. Those things have caused enough drama and we shouldn't mess with them at the eleventh hour."

"It's not that big of a deal, and you never know, you two might really hit it off. Then the four of us could do couples' dates."

Marnie drained her glass in one big gulp.

"Maybe Marnie doesn't want to be set up with her own hunky Marine," Gina said sweetly in spite of the killing look Marnie sent her way.

"I can't imagine a woman who *wouldn't*." Amber laughed, joining them in the sitting area, seemingly satisfied with the condition of Reese's dress. "I mean, have you *seen* those guys? Talk about a few good men… *Whew.* I keep hoping that if we put on the right kind of music tonight, they might secretly turn out to be a group of male strippers."

Reese snorted. "And you claim to be in love with my brother."

"I am. That doesn't mean I've lost my ability to appreciate good man candy when I see it."

Pouring herself another glass of champagne, Reese winked at her. "So what do you think, Marnie? Feeling patriotic? I'm sure Andrew would love to show you a little 'uncommon valor.'"

She shook her head. "I'm an army of one. Thanks, though."

Reese gave her an odd look and opened her mouth like she was going to say something else, but Amber saved Marnie without even realizing it. "It's almost time, ladies."

That threw Reese back into a flurry, as she found her shoes and looked for lipstick all the while encouraging the rest of them to move quicker, too. Ten minutes later, she was herding them out the door.

It was only a few short blocks from the hotel to the

Italian restaurant, and while there was a definite nip in the air, they elected to walk it.

"I think my necklace is caught in my hair," Cassie said. "Can you help?"

Marnie stopped and moved Cassie's hair aside. It was a minor tangle, easily fixed, but Reese and Amber were a full half-block ahead by the time she finished. Gina, however, was leaned against the stone wall, waiting.

She looked at Cassie accusingly. "You did that on purpose."

Cassie shrugged and Gina grinned. "You're avoiding us."

"I've been busy."

"I just want to see how things are with Dylan. Cassie's reports from the gala were inconclusive at best."

"I couldn't get much data. I can't report data I don't have," Cassie protested.

"I know exactly what you're after. But I don't want to talk about it." She started after the others.

"Wait," Gina caught her arm. "What's going on? Did something happen?"

"I told you not to get too worked up over me and Dylan." A lump formed in her throat, making it hard to talk. "It turned out to be just as temporary as I said it would be."

"Oh, *no.*" Cassie's face was the picture of sympathy and exactly what she didn't want—or need right now.

Gina was a bit more blunt. "What the hell? You two broke up?"

"We weren't really together to begin with, so you can't really say we broke up. But, no, we're not seeing each other anymore."

"It wasn't that Analise cow Cassie told me about,

was it?" Gina's eyes were narrowed to angry slits, indignant on her behalf.

"No." She started walking again.

Cassie and Gina trotted to catch up. "Then what?" Gina asked.

"If you must know, *I* broke it off."

Gina grabbed her arm again. "Okay, you need to stop for a second. These shoes were not made to run in. Back up and tell me what happened."

Marnie sighed. She had zero chance of getting out of this, so it might be best to get it over with quickly. "Dylan and I need different things right now, so it—"

Cassie shook her head. "Even I'm not going to believe that."

"But it's true."

"Because...?" Gina prompted.

She swallowed hard. "We were supposed to be just a casual thing. It didn't stay casual, and it is, unfortunately, a one-sided development."

Cassie leaned into Gina. "What does she mean by that?" she whispered.

Gina kept her eyes on Marnie as she answered Cassie. "It means she's in love with Dylan."

There again was that *splat* feeling that came from falling alone. "But Dylan's not in love with me." She held up a hand as Gina started to argue. "He was pretty clear. He's enjoying being single, liking the casual, easy, relationship."

"But that doesn't mean..."

"Gina, he said that the right girl for him did not exist in the current crop of women in his acquaintance and that he'd rather die alone. I don't think it's possible to misinterpret that."

"That's a pretty stupid thing to say."

"I'm just glad he said it before I…" she couldn't finish it.

"Before *you* said anything," Gina supplied.

"Exactly."

"Ah, honey, I'm sorry." Gina pulled her into a hug. She felt Cassie patting her back.

"I can't cry right now. My mascara will run. And I don't want anything to ruin Reese's party."

Gina carefully ran a finger under her eyes to repair the damage. "I wonder if Reese knows Dylan is an idiot."

"I wonder if Reese knows *I'm* an idiot."

"You, honey, are in love. You get a pass. Dylan doesn't have an excuse, because if he *wasn't* an idiot, he'd be in love with you."

"It's not altogether unsurprising, considering Dylan's family situation and his aversion to drama or conflict of any sort."

That came from Cassie, causing both Marnie and Gina to look at her in surprise. "Cas, what are you talking about?"

"Dylan avoids drama at all costs. He intentionally remains emotionally detached because he doesn't like conflict in his personal life. I mean, look at how he walked away from the Reese situation completely unscathed. I think it has something to do with his parents."

Marnie couldn't quite get her jaw closed, so it fell to Gina to ask, "And you know this how?"

"Tuck, of course. He says that's why Dylan didn't put up a fight when Reese chose Mason. He doesn't do conflict, so he doesn't overly attach himself to anyone for that very reason."

And I told him there was someone else. Her lie was coming back to bite her in the butt.

Gina patted her arm. "See, honey, it's not you. It's Dylan. He's emotionally stunted and therefore unable to see how fabulous a person you are. And if he's not willing to put up a fight, he really is an idiot. And he's certainly not worth your tears. He doesn't deserve you."

CHAPTER TEN

As ALWAYS, REESE threw one hell of a party. The food was delicious, the drinks flowed generously, and Marnie was among friends. All things considered, she really should be having a much better time. The déjà vu was killing her. Was she destined to be miserable at all of her friends' weddings?

She kept a smile plastered on her face and concentrated on her conversational companions. Andrew, it seemed, did have a bit of an interest, and he'd parked himself next to her at the table, and if nothing else, it was flattery her ego desperately needed. Andrew was good company—funny and charming and sweet, if not particularly smart—but Marnie's patience with the evening as a whole was wearing thin.

The temptation to shotgun a whole bottle of Chardonnay was strong, but she wasn't going to go down that path again. Hell, that was what had put her in this misery in the first place, so she was carefully nursing her first glass.

It wasn't a large event, just the wedding party, their dates, the families and some out-of-town guests—maybe fifty people total.

Even Carter seemed to be aware that she wasn't quite into the spirit of things, and though he gave her some funny looks, he didn't press her for information. She assumed Gina had told him at least part of the situation, but she didn't want Carter to get all big brother or say something rude about Dylan. Hell, Tuck was at the table, and insulting his best friend wouldn't be conducive to polite dinner conversation.

But Gina and Tuck and Andrew kept the conversation going, and she was able to participate at an acceptable and appropriate level. She was quite thankful for that. It kept her from getting *too* broody or self-pitying.

Andrew was telling her immediate group about the heat in Afghanistan, so the buzz that went around the room barely registered. The near-silence that fell in its wake *did* register, however, as did the fact Tuck cursed and pushed to his feet.

She followed everyone else's gaze to the door.

Dylan. Striding in like he owned the place, a determined look on his face.

Damn.

Reese jumped to her feet in surprise, which caused Mason to jump to *his* feet, irritation stamped on his face, and then his entire platoon did the same.

Oh, my God.

Marnie started to slink down in her chair.

"Oh, no, you don't," Gina hissed in her ear, hauling her back up by the arm.

"Dylan, what are you doing here?" Reese asked.

Since only Gina, Cassie and Tuck—and probably Carter, too, based on his look—understood that Dylan wasn't here because of Reese, the stunned reactions of most of the party guests were understandable.

"Pardon the interruption and congratulations to you both," Dylan said, eyes scanning the room. Marnie felt his eyes land on her, but she couldn't quite bring herself to look at him directly yet. "But I'm here to talk to Marnie." He crossed the room to stand in front of her.

"This isn't a good time," she said quietly, well aware that every eye in the room was on them.

Dylan frowned, then tilted his head toward Andrew. "Is that him?"

"Him who?"

"Your someone else. Is this him?"

Damn it, damn it, damn it. Her lie really *was* about to bite her in the butt. She looked up, ready to try to explain and froze. She'd never seen Dylan look like this.

"What's he talking about?" she heard Gina ask.

"Can someone explain to me what the hell is going on?" That was Reese's voice.

"No. That's not him," she said quietly.

"Marnie?" Reese again.

"You shouldn't be here, Dylan."

Everyone seemed to be talking all at once, but Marnie couldn't really make sense of the words. And she couldn't stop staring at Dylan.

Andrew stepped forward. "Is he a problem, Marnie?"

Cassie tugged on Andrew's arm. "You should sit down now."

"Hel-*lo*," Reese said, the frustration evident. "Would you like to tell me why you're causing a scene at my rehearsal dinner?"

Gina motioned her closer. "They've been seeing each other."

Reese's eyebrows knitted together. "What?" A second later, she seemed to get Gina's meaning. "*Oh.* I did not know that. *Why* did I not know that?"

"Because it's not your business," Dylan snapped.

Mason obviously took offense to Dylan's tone. "You crashed our party, so it's now our business."

Amber stepped in. Quietly, but firmly, she said, "Okay, I think this needs to go to the hallway now."

"Who is he, then, Marnie?" Dylan asked.

"What makes you think she's seeing someone else?" Gina butted in.

It felt like she'd been standing there with Dylan staring her down forever. "Because I told him that."

Reese's eyes widened. "And you came storming down here to pick a fight with a marine?"

"I'm so sorry, Reese," Marnie whispered. "I had no idea he'd do this."

"Neither did I," she replied. "Wow. I'm impressed. And feeling a little disappointed, too."

Dylan flicked his eyes her way. "Don't take it personally."

"I'm not." Reese sounded like she was reassuring him, but Marnie was having a very hard time understanding everything when her brain felt both foggy and on speed at the same time. Reese patted Dylan on the shoulder. "I'm happy for you both. Now, could you please take this to the hallway like Amber said?"

Marnie was so shocked to hear the easy acceptance of the entire situation that she didn't put up much resistance as Amber hustled them to the hallway and closed the dining room doors behind them.

The hallway seemed very quiet and still after everything that transpired. She was burning with embarrassment and shame, but at the same time her heart had kicked up a beat just seeing him again, like that movie moment when the hero comes in to sweep the heroine off her feet. Instead, he'd been jealous and nursing some dented pride. And while the jealousy was heartening, it didn't change the fact that Dylan didn't want her for more.

Dylan looked both angry and uncomfortable, which echoed her mood nicely. Only she was also humiliated beyond belief, as well, so the anger grew stronger than the uncomfortability. "All right, you have my attention. What do you want, Dylan?"

"Major Attitude in there is obviously not the one I'm looking for. Who is he, Marnie?"

"It doesn't matter."

"It does."

She took a deep breath. "Why? We were just a fling. And now it's over."

That had not gone as planned. In retrospect, his plan was inherently flawed, and what had just happened was one of the better possible scenarios.

If he needed more proof that Marnie was dangerous to his higher brain functions, the fact he'd just crashed a party—where several of his and Reese's mutual friends were bound to be—and made a fool of himself, should have made that *very* clear.

If he were smart, he'd take this lesson and walk away instead of trying to put himself back into the very situation that had led to this and had a high probability of leading to more craziness on his part.

He was dumber than dirt, it seemed, and a fool to boot.

Now that he was here, though, he should try to salvage it. He could be honest up-front and quit the little games. *Or* he could try not to make a bigger fool of himself than he already had. He started at the easiest—and currently the most frustrating—question. "Who's the other guy, Marnie?"

Her hands clenched into fists of frustration—or possibly anger. "What difference does it make?" she gritted out.

"I think I should at least get to know who you're throwing me over for."

"Dylan, we weren't an actual couple. I can't 'throw you over for someone' when we weren't actually together to begin with. It was just sex, and now we're done. Why is that so hard to accept?"

"Pardon me for being blindsided by this."

"Did you expect something different?

Yes. Not at first, but... He wasn't sure how to best answer that.

Marnie sighed. "I'll be honest with you."

"Please do."

She took a deep breath. "There's no one else."

He hadn't been prepared for that. "Then why say there was?"

"I thought it would be easier that way. I wanted out of our arrangement and it seemed less complicated and on the path of least resistance. I guess I was wrong."

The blow landed hard. He'd thought Marnie choosing another man over him was bad, but... This was even worse. He was very glad he hadn't made a bigger fool of himself by declaring all kinds of romantic feelings for her.

Well, he'd wanted answers and now he had them. He didn't *like* them, but he had them.

Marnie wasn't making eye contact and her face was scarlet from either embarrassment or anger. Possibly both. Restaurant employees were giving them strange looks and a wide path as they walked by.

He should be feeling a bit of shame and embarrassment, too. He knew half the people in that room tonight, so everyone he knew would know the whole gory story by tomorrow.

Honestly, he was too angry to care.

This was why he didn't do drama. Drama fed on itself, making people act like idiots instead of adults.

Marnie sighed. "I'm sorry I hurt you with a lie. I was trying to save face and salvage my own pride."

"Why?"

"Because you want to die alone."

He felt his jaw drop a little. "What?"

"You told me that based on the current crop of women available to you, you'd rather die alone."

Had he really said that? "My apologies. I was frustrated and angry at my parents. I shouldn't have said it, and I certainly didn't mean it."

"Thank you for that."

He nodded, not sure what else to say. A cute little furrow appeared between her eyebrows, a sure sign Marnie seemed to be thinking about something. He waited, holding his breath.

Finally, she looked at him. "Why did you come tonight, Dylan? What did you possibly hope to accomplish?"

He had nothing to lose at this point. Honesty was all he had left. "Obviously, I came to see you. To tell you… to ask you to give us—me—another shot. I couldn't let you walk away with putting up a fight."

Dylan was willing to fight for her. And not just figuratively, it seemed, as he'd been ready to take on Andrew.

Dylan didn't like drama. He didn't like conflict. He'd walked away from women before without looking back or putting up a single word in protest.

Tonight, he'd done all of that. Publically. Dramatically. He'd taken a huge risk, embarrassed them both…

For her.

Her heart began to beat again, and a bubble of hope expanded in her chest.

"You have layers I never expected, Dylan Brookes."

"You told me to find my passion. The girl who would make my heart beat faster just being near her." He grabbed her hand and held it to his chest, so she could feel the heavy thump of his heart. "I found her."

Marnie expected to feel the cage close in around her, but there was nothing but excitement and joy and anticipation of what might come next. She didn't know what to say and wasn't sure she could get the words past the lump in her throat anyway. She launched herself at him instead and found herself pulled close against him.

"Oh, thank God," she heard him mutter.

She pulled him closer, and the restaurant staff burst into applause and cheers. A second later, a cheer went up from inside the dining room as well. She expected embarrassment to follow quickly behind, but, amazingly, she didn't. She was too happy to care if Reese's entire rehearsal dinner guest list had been listening.

She pulled back far enough to meet his eyes. "I'm so sorry. I'm ten kinds of a fool—"

He squeezed her. "Join the club."

"No. I really am." She wiggled until he lowered her feet to the ground, and cradled his face in her hands. "I lied about there being someone else, because there's *not* anyone else. I lied because I'm falling for you and you said you didn't want things to change and—"

He put a finger over her lips to stop the words. "I lied, too."

"What? When?"

"When I said passion was overrated. That love wasn't enough. That I didn't want excitement, only stability. That was a lie. I wanted more passion in my life, but I didn't want to admit it."

Marnie smiled. "I just need you."

He dropped his forehead to hers. "I think I'm falling in love with you, Marnie Price."

It wasn't the most passionate of declarations and until recently, she'd have dismissed it outright. But she knew how difficult that would be for him to realize, much less admit, and suddenly she felt like he'd shouted it from the stage at Madison Square Garden. "I'll be honest and say that I *know* I'm falling in love with you, Dylan Brookes. It doesn't make a lot of sense, but I don't care." She twined her fingers in his. "*This* makes sense and I'm sure everything else will fall into place, too."

He squeezed her hand and ran his other hand over her hair and the curve of her jaw. The simple rawness of the motion clawed at her heart. "Come home with me? See if we can't start finding where all those pieces fit?"

She nodded, and raised up onto her tiptoes to kiss him again. Then she remembered and let loose a string of very unladylike words.

Dylan's eyebrows went up in surprise and concern filled his eyes. "What?"

"I'm supposed to stay at the Plaza with the others. Quality girl-time tonight and an early start at the spa in the morning before the wedding." She rolled her eyes. "Reese's weddings are really starting to annoy me."

"How about I get a room at the Plaza tonight, and instead of sleeping with your girlfriends you just come there when you're ready for bed? You'll still be able to get up plenty early in the morning."

"That sounds like a good compromise." She glanced

at her watch. "You know…it's still kinda early, and they'll probably be in there for at least another hour or so. Why don't I start in your room and then just go visit once the others get back?"

"I like the way you think."

"I'm just full of surprises, you know. Can I borrow your phone so I don't have to go back in there?"

He handed it over. "I know. And that's one of the things I love about you."

She paused in her typing to grin at him. "Hopefully, you'll find more."

"I'm sure I will."

EPILOGUE

REESE LOOKED BEAUTIFUL in her wedding gown, but more importantly, she looked radiant with happiness. She was also remarkably calm, Marnie thought, which just underscored the fact she was making the right decision in marrying Mason.

More importantly to Marnie, though, was the fact she'd decided *not* to marry Dylan back in June. Not only for their sakes, but hers, as well.

She was running on very little sleep; after bringing the others up to speed on the momentous change that happened after she left, she and Dylan had stayed up late, mostly talking.

But not *just* talking.

It was a scary jump to make, but having made it, she was completely sure it was the right choice.

Funny how that knowledge gave her that same calm Reese had. And it was also probably responsible for the goofy grin the others kept teasing her about but she couldn't seem to wipe off her face.

She did not care. She was happy.

For once, all of them were ready early, and they had another twenty minutes to kill here in the bridal ready room before the wedding started.

There was a loud pop as Gina opened the champagne.

She poured five glasses and then asked, "Where's Amber? We need to toast the bride."

"She went to find Parker for something," Reese answered. "But that's okay, 'cause I'd like the four of us to have a toast first." She lifted her glass. "It's been a long, strange trip, but the Awesome Foursome are back."

"Hear, hear," Gina said, and they drank.

"Oh, wait," Cassie said, digging into her bag. "I brought popcorn." She produced it proudly and opened the bag.

"We really are back," Marnie said, and reached for a handful.

"And better than ever," Cassie added.

Marnie lifted her glass again. "To Reese and Mason."

Gina lifted hers. "To Cassie and Tuck."

"To Gina and Carter," Reese added.

"And to Marnie and Dylan, of course" Cassie said. "We've now got another wedding to plan."

Marnie choked. This newfound knowledge didn't mean she was quite ready to go *there*. "Let's not jump the gun, okay?"

Cassie shrugged. "It's only logical."

Gina and Reese laughed as Marnie tossed popcorn at Cassie.

It had been a long, strange, *tough* road, but they were definitely back.

This time, Reese didn't have to make Dylan ask her to dance. When the music started, Dylan extended a hand and held hers as they walked to the dance floor, and this time, he pulled her close against him.

She smoothed a hand over his shoulder. "Thanks for coming today. You didn't have to."

"Hey, I know what happens when you go solo at wedding receptions. I couldn't risk you finding a grooms-man you liked better."

Marnie smacked his arm. "Hey, now. That's rather a rude thing to say. I'm not that kind of girl."

Dylan raised an eyebrow at her.

"Okay, so I was sort of that kind of girl. You are an exception to many rules."

"I kinda like that idea."

"Whoa, look at you, stepping out of your comfort zone."

"You bring out all kinds of new things in me, Mar-nie. Like…" With a wicked smile, Dylan leaned close to her ear, and his whispered words made her thankful for the low lighting of the reception that hid her hot face.

"That's mean, Dylan Brookes. We can't leave until after they cut the cake."

She was beginning to quake with desire, but Dylan just shrugged. "I'm not in any rush," he said way too casually.

"Well, hell, I am now." She rose up on her tiptoes and nibbled at his earlobe. Then she whispered her own ideas into his ear. She felt him harden against her, felt his pulse kick up a notch.

"You know," he said, "I wasn't even officially in-vited to this damn wedding, so I'm under no obliga-tion to stay."

"And you said passion was overrated."

"I told you I lied."

* * * * *

THE WEDDING SEASON
continued this month with Gina's story in
Maid of Dishonour by Heidi Rice

Special Offers

Every month we put together collections and longer reads written by your favourite authors.

Here are some of next month's highlights— and don't miss our fabulous discount online!

On sale 1st November   **On sale 1st November**   **On sale 18th October**

Save 20%
on all Special Releases

Come home this Christmas to Fiona Harper

From the author of *Kiss Me Under the Mistletoe* comes a Christmas tale of family and fun. Two sisters are ready to swap their Christmases—the busy super-mum, Juliet, getting the chance to escape it all on an exotic Christmas getaway, whilst her glamorous work-obsessed sister, Gemma, is plunged headfirst into the family Christmas she always thought she'd hate.

Wrap up warm this winter with Sarah Morgan...

Sleigh Bells in the Snow

Kayla Green loves business and hates Christmas.

So when Jackson O'Neil invites her to Snow Crystal Resort to discuss their business proposal... the last thing she's expecting is to stay for Christmas dinner. As the snowflakes continue to fall, will the woman who doesn't believe in the magic of Christmas finally fall under its spell...?

4th October

www.millsandboon.co.uk/sarahmorgan